KT-160-147

J.T. ELLISON

LIE TO ME

mira

If you purchased this book without a cover you should be aware
that this book is stolen property. It was reported as "unsold and
destroyed" to the publisher, and neither the author nor the
publisher has received any payment for this "stripped book."

mira

Recycling programs
for this product may
not exist in your area.

ISBN-13: 978-0-7783-3095-0 (International Edition)

ISBN-13: 978-0-7783-1364-9 (Library Hardcover Edition)

Lie to Me

Copyright © 2017 by J.T. Ellison

All rights reserved. Except for use in any review, the reproduction or utilization of this
work in whole or in part in any form by any electronic, mechanical or other means, now
known or hereinafter invented, including xerography, photocopying and recording, or in
any information storage or retrieval system, is forbidden without the written permission
of the publisher, MIRA Books, 225 Duncan Mill Road, Don Mills, Ontario M3B 3K9,
Canada.

This is a work of fiction. Names, characters, places and incidents are either the
product of the author's imagination or are used fictitiously, and any resemblance to
actual persons, living or dead, business establishments, events or locales is entirely
coincidental.

® and TM are trademarks of Harlequin Enterprises Limited or its corporate affiliates.
Trademarks indicated with ® are registered in the United States Patent and Trademark
Office, the Canadian Intellectual Property Office and in other countries.

For questions and comments about the quality of this book, please contact us at
CustomerService@Harlequin.com.

www.BookClubbish.com

Printed in U.S.A.

For Amy, who believed

And as always, for Randy

LIE TO ME

IN WHICH INTRODUCTIONS ARE MADE

You aren't going to like me very much. Oh, maybe in your weaker moments, you'll feel sorry for me, and use those feelings of warmth and compassion and insightful understanding to excuse my actions. You'll say to yourself, "Poor little girl. She couldn't help herself." Or, "Can you blame her? After all she's been through?" Perhaps you'll even think, "She was born to this. It is not her fault."

Of course it's my fault. I chose this path. Yes, I feel as if I have no choice, that I'm driven to do it, that there are voices in my head that push me to the dark side.

But I also know right from wrong. I know good from evil. I may be compelled to ruin the lives in front of me, but I could walk away if I wanted.

Couldn't I?

Never mind that. Back to you.

Truly, deep down, you are going to despise me. I am the rot that lives in the floorboards of your house. I am the spider that

scuttles away when you shine a light in my corner, ever watching, ever waiting. I am the shard of glass that slits the skin of your
bare foot. I am all the bad things that happen to you.

I steal things.

I kill things.

I leave a trail of destruction in my wake that is a sight to behold, wave after wave of hate that will overwhelm you until you
sink to the bottom of my miserable little ocean, and once you've
drowned I will feed on your flesh and turn your bones to dust.

You're mine now. You are powerless against me. So don't
bother fighting it.

I hope you enjoy the show.

WE FIND A BODY

The body was in the woods off a meandering state road that led into a busy, charming, historical downtown. It was completely obscured from view, deeply hidden, under several pine boughs and a thick layer of nature's detritus. Synthetic clothing was melted to the flesh, making it difficult to tell race or gender at a glance. Closer inspection would show hair that was long and a curious shade: not blond, not red, possibly chemically treated. The left hand held evidence of rings, a wedding set, and the body would eventually be determined as female.

The shroud of melt and bough had not stopped the forever daisy-chain progression of decay. Instar maggots and adult flies delighted in their found treat. A genus party started soon after. Diptera and coleoptera were evident three days in, paving the way for the coming colonization of Calliphoridae. Though the body was burned beyond ready recognition, the insects didn't seem to mind; it was simply a barbecue feast to them.

Outside of this natural progression, the body lay undisturbed for two days. Birds of prey flew in long, lazy circles overhead. Cars drove past less than fifty yards away, drivers unknowing, uncaring, that one of their own lay rotting nearby.

Three Days Gone, a severe thunderstorm knocked free several of the funereal branches, allowing the body to be exposed, pelted by hail breaking through the leafy canopy. The heavy rains saturated the ground and the body sank deeper into the muck, where it canted on its side.

Four Days Gone, the body was ravaged by a starving coyote, forty-two razor teeth shredding everything available.

Five Days Gone, the body disarticulated, the fire and the heat and the wet and the insects and the coyote and the natural progression of things breaking it down quickly and without thought to the effects this would have on the loved ones. The idea of a nonintact body was sometimes more than people could take.

Six Days Gone, they found her.

ETHAN

"Chaos is a name for any order that produces confusion in our minds."

—George Santayana

SOMETHING'S MISSING

Franklin, Tennessee
Now

Ethan found the note ten minutes after he rolled out of bed that Tuesday, the Tuesday that would change everything. He came downstairs, yawning, scratching his chest, to…nothing. Empty space, devoid of wife.

Sutton always began her morning at the kitchen table with a bowl of cereal, a piece of fruit, and a cup of tea. She read the paper, scoffing at the innumerable typos—the paper was going under; paying for decent copyediting was the least of their worries. A bowl full of cereal, a glass of milk, and a spoon would be laid out for him, the sports page folded neatly by his seat. Always. Always.

But this morning, there was no evidence Sutton had been in the kitchen. No newspaper, no bowl. No wife.

He called for her. There was no response. He searched through the house. Her bag was in her office, her cell phone, her laptop. Her license was stashed in her small wallet, all her credit cards present and accounted for, a twenty folded in half shoved behind them.

She must have gone for a run.

He felt a spark of pleasure at the thought. Sutton, once, had been a health nut. She'd run or walked or done yoga every day, something physical, something to keep her body moving and in shape. And what a shape—when he'd met her, the woman was a knockout, willowy and lithe, strong legs and delicate ankles, tendons tight and gleaming like a Thoroughbred. A body she sculpted to match his own, to fit with him.

Ethan Montclair couldn't have a dog for a wife, no. He needed someone he could trot out at cocktail parties who looked smashing in a little black dress. And not only looked good, but sounded good. He needed a partner on all levels—physical and intellectual. Maybe it was shallow of him, but he was a good-looking man, drew a lot of attention, and not only did he want his wife to be stunning, he wanted her to be smart, too. And Sutton fit the bill.

He knew they made a powerful, attractive couple. Looks and brains and success, so much success. That was their thing.

After Dashiell, she'd bounced back into shape like the champion racehorse she was; though later, when their world collapsed, she'd become tired and bloated and swollen with medications and depression, and she no longer took any interest in being beautiful and fit.

That she'd decided to start running again gave him hope. So much hope.

Spirits lifted, he went back to the sunny, happy kitchen and got his own bowl, his own cereal. Made a pot of tea, whistling. Went for the stevia—no sugar for the health-conscious Montclairs, no, never.

That was when he saw it. Small. White. Lined. Torn from a spiral-bound notebook, a Clairefontaine, Sutton's favorite for the smooth, lovely paper.

This…thing…was incongruous with the rest of their spotless kitchen. Sutton was above all things a pathological neatnik. She'd never just leave something lying about.

All the happiness fled. He knew. He'd been all wrong. She hadn't gone running.

He picked up the note.

Dear Ethan,
I'm sorry to do this to you, but I need some time away. I've been unhappy, you know that. This shouldn't come as a big surprise. Forgive me for being a coward. Forgive me, for so many things.
Don't look for me.
S

She was gone.

He felt something squeezing in his chest, a pain of sorts, and realized that his heart had just broken. He'd always thought that a stupid, silly term, but now he knew. It could happen, it was happening. He was being torn in two, torn to shreds. No wonder there were rites warning against this—*what therefore God hath joined together, let not man put asunder.*

God was ripping him apart in punishment, and he deserved it. He deserved it all.

He didn't cry. There were no tears left for either of them to shed.

He put the note down carefully, as if it were a bomb that might go off with the wrong touch. Went to their bedroom. Nothing seemed out of place. Her brush, her makeup case, her toothbrush, all lined up carefully on the marble. Her suitcase was in the closet.

He went back downstairs to her office, at the back of the house. Double-checked.

Her laptop was on her desk.

Her cell phone was in the charger.

Her purse was on the floor next to her chair.

Her wallet inside, the smiling DMV photo that made her look like a model.

Like a zombie, he moved back to the kitchen. He opened the refrigerator and got out the milk. Poured cereal in the bowl. Dropped the stevia into his tea. Sat at the empty table, stared at the spot where his wife's head should have been.

What was he supposed to do now? Where could she be? He ran through the possibilities, the places she loved, rejecting one after another. Surely he was wrong in his thinking. Surely she'd simply run away, to one of her friends. That's where she'd gone. Should he give her some time and space, like she asked?

She left without her things, Ethan. Sutton's lifelines are her laptop and phone. They are her office, her world.

A dawning realization. Sutton hadn't shaken the depression, not completely. She was still prone to fits of melancholy. She might have done something stupid, crazy. She'd tried once before, after... Oh, God. Her words. Perhaps she was telling him exactly what she'd done.

I'm a coward. Forgive me. Don't look for me.

He threw the bowl of cereal across the room.

"Bloody fucking hell. You selfish, heartless bitch."

DID SHE, OR DIDN'T SHE?

Don't look for me.

Those were the last words she'd used to him.

And so he didn't. Not right away, at least. He sat and wrapped his mind around the situation. Then he searched through everything of hers he could find, looking for something, anything, that might give answers.

Nothing. It was like she'd gone to take a shower and disappeared through the water into another land.

He went into deep, irreversible denial. *She is fine*, he told himself. *She's taking a break.* The self-talk worked. His morbid thoughts fled. He knew, deep in his heart, Sutton would never be that selfish.

He gave her three hours to come back, three long, quiet as the bone hours, and then, when the idea that she might actually be in some sort of trouble started to eat at him, began calling round. Of course he did. He wasn't a total asshole, despite what most people thought. It was the success—people automatically assumed because he was a man and he didn't like to give interviews and held people at arm's length at signings and he kept himself off social media and focused on his work, he was a dick. Maybe he was.

He called her friends—there weren't many, but the ones she had were close, bosom buddies, BFFs.

Rachel hadn't seen her and was brusque, late for work. Out of character for her; a yoga teacher, she was generally the most calm and friendly of Sutton's friends.

Ellen, the head of library sciences at Vanderbilt University, didn't answer her mobile; he left an innocuous "Hey, call me," message.

Filly—Phyllis, really, but she hated to be called by her given name—answered her landline on the first ring, no doubt assuming it was Sutton calling. Even at Ethan's voice, her greeting was cheery and excited. When Ethan asked if she'd seen Sutton, she seemed genuinely concerned, but claimed they hadn't talked for a few days because Sutton had been so busy. He couldn't help it, Filly's concern was so genuine and helpful he immediately suspected she knew something, but when pressed, she reassured him Sutton was probably just out for a run and told him to call her when Sutton showed up, then got off the phone with a lame excuse about her baby crying. *Way to twist the knife, Filly.*

Ivy was out of town on business, or he'd have called her first. Ivy was friends with them both. She was Sutton's closest friend and confidante, a true part of their lives. Had been for three years now. He glanced at his watch, hesitated for a minute, then sent a text. A self-employed stockbroker, she was good about keeping her phone on her. She'd get back when she was able, she always did.

He sat at the table, head in his hands. Jumped a mile when the phone rang. He didn't bother looking at the caller ID, answered with a breathless, "Sutton?"

"It's Siobhan. What's wrong?"

Oh, bloody retching hell. Sutton's mother was the last person he wanted to involve in this. To put it mildly, Siobhan and Sutton weren't close, and Sutton would be furious with him if she knew he'd spoken to her at all.

Deflect, and get her off the phone.

"Good morning, Siobhan. How are you?"

"Has something happened to Sutton?"

"No, no. Everything is fine."

"Let me guess. She stormed off and won't return your calls."

"Something like that. Have you heard from her?"

"I haven't seen or spoken to my daughter in weeks. By the way, thank you for the cruise. The Adriatic was amazing. You should take her sometime."

The sudden urge to confess, to shake this venal woman from her self-absorbed life, was overwhelming, and the words spilled from his mouth.

"She's gone, Siobhan. She left a note and walked out on me. I'm worried about her. She didn't take her things—her phone, her computer, her wallet are all here." As if that would explain it all.

And it did, enough at least that his mother-in-law reacted. "I'm on my way over," she said, and hung up on him.

Oh, bollocks. All he needed was Siobhan wandering the house looking for clues. Looking in the corners, at the dust and secrets.

You're an idiot, Ethan. Whyever did you tell her? That desperate, are we?

He poured himself a fresh cup of tea, looked around. Fuck cleaning up. So the place wasn't pristine. Who cared? Siobhan would find a flaw, a fault, no matter what. They could scour the place top to bottom, have it *Architectural Digest* photo-shoot ready, and she'd still want to move a vase or find a small part of the counter with a smear.

Siobhan Healy—*Shiv-awn*, for the uninitiated, which she delighted in sharing, loudly—took pride in being different. Her friends, and some of her enemies, Sutton included, called her Shiv for short. She was Sutton's opposite in every way. Looks: small and dark, Black Irish with her ebony hair liberally streaked with gray, and cobalt eyes, face pinched and mean. Temperament: brash and extroverted; Siobhan adored attention, good or bad. Speech: lowbrow; though she didn't have an accent, she claimed she was from a Dublin slum and never hesitated to share the story of her continually upward journey.

She'd come to the United States and married a succession of men, each wealthier than the last. She was on husband four now, a meek-mannered man named Alan, who liked to make jokes, corny jokes—*hey, we should go into business together, call ourselves... Ethan Alan. Ha, ha, ha, ha, get it? Ethan Alan*—when he drank too much.

Ethan wasn't sure how this woman could have created her daughter, often wondered about their storied past, but Siobhan and Sutton both refused to ever talk about her childhood, or the one-night stand sperm donor who was her father. He wasn't, as Sutton said, one of the husbands. He was anonymous. Never around. Sutton had never met him.

Ethan found that wretchedly sad. His own parents had been kind, generous people, though he hadn't understood them well, nor they him. They were both gone now. They'd died quietly and unobtrusively four months apart when he was twenty-two. He'd been quite upset, but not devastated. They'd sent him off to Mount St. Mary's as a boarder when he was a wee lad, and he'd only seen them at breaks. Ethan had always been bookish; it was the school he attended that shaped his personality: cocky and wildly creative. It was a fine way to grow up, but Ethan wanted something different for his life. He'd always dreamed of a close-knit, exuberant household for his own family one day. Children running in the backyard, dogs playing and barking, a knockout wife, madly in love. Safe and stable.

The American Dream. That's one reason he'd moved to America, after all.

Safe and stable. He'd tried. Lord knew, he'd tried.

A text dinged. Ivy.

I haven't seen her or talked to her since I left on my trip. We chatted Thursday and she seemed fine. Do I need to come home? Do you need help?

Ivy, always the one willing to lend a hand, pitch in, make their lives easier.

He texted back. No, I'm sure she's just gone off to upset us all.

Ivy sent back an emoji that he took to mean "eye roll." He didn't understand emojis. Or text abbreviations. *LOL. BRB.* For God's sake, when had it become so difficult to actually use words anymore?

The doorbell sounded, impatient, as if it were being stabbed repeatedly with a thick finger—which of course it was. He opened the door for his mother-in-law, who sailed through like the *Queen Mary*, then turned on him. "So what did you do to upset my daughter now?"

Her dyed black hair was shoved under a dingy Nashville Sounds baseball cap; she was unkempt and smelled like stale liquor. She and the mister must have been hitting the bottle hard the night before. They liked to party, liked to hang out at their country club with other well-soused individuals, eating good food and drinking good wine and lamenting their fates. Such a lovely couple.

"I didn't do anything. I woke up this morning and she was gone. She left me a note."

"Show me."

Biting back the response he wanted to give, he instead led her into the kitchen and handed her the paper. She read it three times, lips moving as she did, and he wondered again how this dull, crass woman had created the glorious Titan he'd married.

Though during Sutton's bad times, the breakdowns, he saw bits of Siobhan in her.

Siobhan set the note down and crossed her arms on her chest.

"Where do you think she's gone?" Her voice was curiously dispassionate, missing its usual aggression toward him.

He shook his head. "I was hoping you'd have an idea. I've called her girlfriends. They say they haven't heard from her."

"Did you tell them about the note?"

"I mentioned it to Filly and Ivy. I got the sense Filly might know something but wasn't willing to say."

She waved a hand. "Filly has always loved Sutton's drama, and is hoping it will rub off on her. She's a sad little woman living through everyone around her. She doesn't know anything, or she'd already be here, glorying." Siobhan played with the edge of the paper, sat down at the table.

"Sutton's been in bad shape since the baby," Ethan offered, almost unwilling to open that door. But he needed help, damn it.

Siobhan nodded, surprisingly grave. "Can you blame her?"

"Of course not. But I kept hoping... Siobhan, is there something else I should know? Did she tell you she was leaving me? You don't seem terribly surprised by this."

She gave a windy sigh that smelled suspiciously like dirty martinis. "Sit down."

Ethan wasn't used to taking orders in his own house, especially from a woman he wasn't fond of, but he perched on a stool and set his hands on his knees. Siobhan watched him for a moment.

"When we spoke last, a few months ago, Sutton told me she was very unhappy. It wasn't like her to confide in me. You know we don't always see eye to eye about her choices."

"If you mean how you suggested she leave me last year after Dashiell...I know. She told me all about it."

"Do you blame me, Ethan?" That strange, dispassionate tone again. Almost as if they were confidants here, not enemies. "You treated her badly. You handled things poorly. She was in bad shape and you were too busy with your little fling to notice."

His little fling. His stomach clenched. No one could know the truth there. It would destroy them all, Sutton especially.

"I made a mistake. I came clean, I apologized. We were getting things back on track. We'd talked about... We talked about moving, maybe, getting away from all the bad memories. Starting over."

"Moving? Where?"

"Back to London."

"I see. And Sutton was happy to do that?"

"We hadn't made any concrete decisions. We were talking. Planning. The future... Bloody hell, Siobhan, at least she was talking to me again. You have no idea what the past year has been like, not really, for either one of us. It's been torture. Oh, yes, we've put on a brave front. But once the door closed and the people disappeared, once the funeral was over and the neighborhood stopped tiptoeing around, we were left alone to try and muddle through. It was hell."

"I can imagine," she said, and she sounded almost like she cared. He knew she didn't, not really. She was in it for the money. Siobhan and Sutton had a weird, twisted relationship, more like catty girlfriends who despised one another than mother and daughter. But despite all his advice, Sutton refused to cut her out completely. Ethan would never understand.

"I don't care what Sutton told you, or didn't. She's been on edge lately, secretive. Something has definitely been going on with her. Do you know what she's been planning?"

Sutton's mother suddenly looked gray and old. "No. But her note doesn't sound like someone who's gone gaily off to do the Lord's work. Why don't you call the police? If you have nothing to hide..."

"Give me a break, Siobhan. I didn't hurt her. It's not like she's a missing person, either. She left a note, after all. Besides, they won't even take a missing persons report for seventy-two hours on an adult."

"How do you know if you haven't talked to them?"

"I do research my work, Siobhan."

"For your books. Yes, of course."

Oh, the disdain in her tone. Ethan tried not to place his very large hands around his mother-in-law's neck. Siobhan had never understood the creative gene that he and Sutton shared. Sutton said Siobhan wanted her only child to find a rich man to marry, one who would allow her to play tennis at the club and host fabulous backyard garden parties. His temperament was optional. What were a few black eyes and broken ribs in the face of never-ending wealth and comfort?

They'd never told Siobhan how much Ethan was worth, how much he made on his novels. It was none of her business.

The uncomfortable silence grew between them. Finally, Siobhan stood.

"I'm sure she's simply run off. She is always very dramatic when she gets upset."

"And if she isn't being dramatic?"

"You're worried. I understand. You asked my advice, and here it is: Sutton's been unhappy, and she probably doesn't want to be found. But if you're not content with that answer, call the police. Let them look for her."

"You don't seem very upset by the news that your daughter is missing. Or that she could have been harmed somehow."

"Because I don't think she's missing. I think my daughter finally left you. Something she should have done long ago."

"Thanks a lot, Siobhan."

"You're welcome. Now, my check? It was due today. If Sutton's not here, perhaps you should see to it."

And there it was. She didn't give a flying fuck about Sutton, just wanted to get the money she wrenched out of them. That's why she'd called, and then come over. Not to help. To take her cut.

Sutton generally handled the quarterly allowance she stubbornly insisted on paying her mother. It was a sore spot between them; having Siobhan standing with her greasy paw out all the time nearly sent him over the edge.

"You must be joking."

"I'm leaving town this evening. We have a trip to Canada. I'd like to deposit it before I go. And who knows when Sutton will resurface."

"You are a seriously cold woman, Siobhan."

"You have no idea."

Ethan went to his office, pulled out the checkbook. He filled in the check, dated it, and stormed back to the kitchen.

"Here." *If only I could lace it with rat poison and watch you die, you miserable, uncaring witch.*

"Thank you. Keep me apprised if she shows up, will you?"

"Why would I? You've made it quite clear you don't care about Sutton, or about me. All you care about is your precious money."

"I care more than you realize, Ethan. But you're her husband. You do what you think is right."

"I will. Trust me."

As the door closed on her, she turned. "Ethan? Even after all these years, I don't think you know my daughter at all."

THERE ARE CRACKS
IN EVERY MARRIAGE

Ethan shut the door on Siobhan, proud of himself for not slamming it. He went into his office and poured a crystal lowball half-full of Scotch. He had a nice mirrored bar cart set up in the corner; it felt very Fitzgerald to him, and he'd always taken pride in it.

Now it looked like failure. He'd been drinking too much this year. Understandable, of course, but he'd been using it as a barrier against Sutton.

It was early to get pissed, he knew this, but he downed the Scotch and poured another. If it was good enough for Fitzgerald and Hemingway, it was good enough for him.

He sat at his desk, glanced at the picture of the three of them placed discreetly in the corner, between the drooping spider plant and the phone. He'd never had the heart to put it away. He liked the photo. They were all happy. Smiling. They'd been at the beach, noses sunburned, the baby wearing a silly sun hat, a breeze blowing Sutton's gorgeous red hair around. Toothy smiles and hugs and goodwill. Their lives, captured, a moment in time that could never be re-created.

He reached out and touched the silver gilt frame, then drew his fingers back as if burned.

He'd thought having a baby would fix things.

It was a stupid thought. Barmy. He should have been committed for thinking a baby would make things perfect again. But at the time, he hadn't thought it through. He'd been driven by his own emotions.

Yes, that was it. His emotions had led him astray. Men weren't supposed to have such deep feelings. It was the artist in him. He wanted things from this life—a career writing, a wife to love him, a home to call his own. Heirs were simply part of things, a fact unstated and understood.

Still, the baby. He didn't think the concept was terribly complex. Sutton was a woman. All women wanted babies. Right? She said she didn't, that her life was perfect the way it was, and really, how would they write with a tyke underfoot, but more than once, he'd caught her looking after women with prams with such bald yearning on her face that he expected she'd start hinting it was time. And she'd told Ivy that she loved kids; he'd heard them in the kitchen one day, gossiping over the teapot.

But she never did hint, and every time he broached the subject, Sutton always told him no.

Maybe it was selfish of him, maybe it was wrong. But he'd wanted a baby. He'd wanted to change things between them. He'd wanted Sutton to look at him with wonder in her eyes again. Because he knew, without a shadow of a doubt, that Sutton used to love him.

He just wasn't sure when she'd stopped.

He shook himself like a wet dog, the old images of their once-happy life shedding onto the floor. He didn't know what to do, so he got up and paced through the house. Went from room to room, replaying memories, seeing shadows of his wife in all the right places—the couch, her feet tucked up under her legs like a cat; her office, head bent over the keyboard in that odd way that made her chin look pointed like an elf's; the bedroom, where she lay willing and open, ready for him to come into her and make her scream.

Their life had always been amazing. Sutton used to make him feel sexy, witty, smart. Every word he wrote was meant to impress her, everything he did was a subtle bit of bragging. *Look at me, wife. Look at all that I am for you.*

He tried harder for her than anyone he'd ever been with. Gaining a smile, a laugh, made him happy to his core.

He didn't know when things went south. Didn't know when she'd stopped loving him, when she gave up on their marriage. It was well before Dashiell, that he knew. Was it when they'd renovated the behemoth? Weren't renovations a major driver in divorce cases, like Facebook and affairs? He thought he'd read that somewhere.

Or was it when the words he wrote for her dried up, and he stopped working entirely? Before he got desperate. Before he made the greatest mistake of his life.

No, he thought it was maybe before all of that when his warm and sexy wife had grown cold. Frigid. Unwilling. Distant.

The laughs had become few and far between. She'd looked at him with a mix of derision and bemusement, as if she'd woken up one morning married, and to a stranger, to boot.

He'd asked her, one very drunken night, why she'd stopped loving him. She'd laughed, harshly. "I love you more now than the day we met. That's the problem." And she wouldn't say anything more.

And here they were. Five years later, parents of a dead baby, their ruined marriage strewed on the rocks, mistakes piled like a stack of ancient newspapers against the door.

He was responsible for Dashiell's death. For Sutton's madness. For the missed deadline, the stalking, the canceled book contract. Ethan knew this, knew it to his bones.

He'd made so many mistakes, there was no recovering from them all.

There was just one problem.

He loved Sutton to his core. He'd never loved a woman as much as he loved her. He would do anything for her. Anything.

He had to decide whether Sutton was simply hiding from him for a few days, or if she'd left for good. Problem was, if she didn't show up by this evening, he was going to have to bring the police in to search for her, because everyone would be suspicious of him if he didn't, and the subsequent investigation was going to rip apart their very carefully cultivated lives, and who knew what sort of roaches would scurry out of the woodwork?

If she was hiding out for a few days, all well and good. If she'd actually run, he would have to go after her. For her to disappear permanently and thoroughly would have taken planning.

Either way, Sutton was a very cunning woman. He simply had to think like her, and he'd find the path to her again.

And then it hit him.

The bank account. He hadn't checked the bank account.

BEAUTY AND THE BEAST

Then

Ethan's agent nudged him. "There is a woman watching you from across the room."

Ethan glanced over, didn't see anyone of note. Then again, he was lubed up, like a lock drenched in oil. He'd already had a few cocktails, and had plans for a few more before he passed out in his soft king bed upstairs. He liked the rooms in the hotel; they were clean and spacious and pleasant, not at all threatening, unlike some of the aggressively modern places his publisher put him up at, thinking the extravagant price tag was a justifiable expense to keep their cash cow happy.

All he wanted from the evening was a solid drunk and a good night's sleep. He didn't have to fly back to Nashville until late in the afternoon. He could sleep in, have some room service delivered, take a long, hot shower, and grab the car to the airport with plenty of time to spare. He had nothing else on his calendar, and he was glad for it. The week in New York had damn near killed him. Breakfasts and lunches and dinners, a few women taken back to that soft king bed, endless talking and applauding and schmoozing.

He needed a break from his life.

You wanted this, jackass. Be careful what you wish for.

"Ethan. Did you hear me? There's a woman over there who's practically drooling."

"Bill, I have no time for more women. You know that."

A hearty laugh and a punch on the arm. Sometimes he wondered if Bill was humoring him, being kind because he was making them both so much money. He thought they were friends; Bill knew almost everything there was to know about Ethan. Almost everything. But sometimes he wondered. Ethan had made Bill rich. Very, very rich. It wasn't out of the realm of possibility that the man loathed him and was simply in it for the house in the Hamptons he would soon be able to buy with his 15 percent.

Bill leered at him. "If you're not interested, maybe you could throw an old dog a bone."

"You're married."

"I'm married, I ain't dead. I can look. Pretty please? Her dress is cut so deep in the front I won't even have to stand on my tippy toes to look down it."

Ethan glanced down at the much smaller man, shrugged. "Fine. Let me get a beer and we'll wander over so you can gander at the lass."

There were two lines at the bar. It was moving quickly. Maybe he'd have a Scotch instead of a beer. He started looking at the bottles lined up behind the bartenders, saw a Macallan 18. Nice. That would do.

He felt a hand on his arm. Glanced to his right. A woman stood next to him. Not the one from across the room. This one was tall, with long strawberry blond hair pulled back in a severe ponytail, and seemed endlessly fascinated with his arm. It wasn't like she was touching him to get his attention, it was almost as if she was caressing him. It was a strange touch, wildly erotic, and the rest of the room bled away in an instant.

Was she drunk? She didn't seem drunk. She seemed...hungry. And not in the *let me take you to dinner* way.

He smiled down at her. "I have another, if you're wondering."

She jerked back as if burned. Her face turned a becoming shade of red. She had freckles across her nose. Clean skin devoid of makeup. She didn't need any. But no mask? In this mess? Interesting.

"Can I help you with something?" he asked.

She started to move away, still watching him.

"Wait." *What are you doing, you fool? Chick's crazy, just another groupie. Let her go, stick with the plan.*

The stranger halted, a deer in the headlights. Her eyes showed deep embarrassment and something else, something intriguing and attractive.

Her voice was soft, and he felt something stir deep inside when she spoke.

"I'm so sorry. I don't know what came over me. I promise you I don't go around touching strange men." She turned on her heel and started away.

He stopped her, grabbed her hand. "Wait. Don't run off. I don't even know your name. I'm Ethan."

She froze, glanced down at his hand, so large over hers. "I know. Ethan Montclair. I'm a fan of your work."

He heard it so often it had become rote, but from this woman's lips, it felt different. Like a prayer. A promise.

"Who are you with?"

"I'm sorry?" She finally met his eyes, and he had his first good look at her. What he saw was entrancing. She was pretty, wholesome, Irish descent, probably, with that reddish hair and the blue eyes. Her sleek black dress showed off a great figure, hourglass but lithe. She looked fresh, innocent. Girl next door, the kind you grow up crushing on, your best friend's older sister. And then you become old enough to bed her legally, and the tables turn. This one, though, still had the suburban stink all over her. *Intern*, he thought.

"I meant, what house are you with?"

"Oh. None."

"What are you doing here, then?"

"I..." The way she dropped her eyes when she was embarrassed, like a courtier looking up at him from her lashes, was maddening, in all the best ways. She took a deep breath. "Okay. We're at the same house. You're light-years ahead of me, though."

A small zing. "You're not an intern?"

"I'm a writer."

"Do you have a name?"

The blush deepened. "Sutton. Sutton Healy."

Irish all the way, though she wasn't accented. Second generation, then, but he'd bet a pound her family was recent. He knew the name, but he wasn't about to give her the satisfaction of that knowledge. He was enjoying her discomfiture. Most women he met went all sycophant on him within moments. This one was truly tongue-tied, and eyeing him like he was a juicy steak. He thought it was cute. Check that, he thought it was hot.

"Can I buy you a drink, Sutton Healy?"

"From the open bar? Sure."

She'd touched his arm again then, slower this time, and he'd known. He was going to take her upstairs, and they were going to spend the night together, and he was going to get to know Sutton Healy biblically, and he was going to enjoy every minute of it.

He heard Bill's voice behind him, a harsh whisper overlaid with laughter. "Sucker." Ethan flipped him off behind his back.

Sutton Healy wanted Macallan, too, so he ordered doubles. They wandered off to a corner of the ballroom. He turned her to face the room so his back was to the crowd. They managed to stay that way, uninterrupted, for half an hour. He may have run his hand through his hair a few times. He was a little fuzzy on that, but it usually drove women crazy.

Two drinks later, he admitted he'd heard of her work.

"Historical romance, right?"

"Did your agent slip you a note with that information?"

"I read."

"You read historical romance? You have to be kidding me."

"It's very soothing. Besides, I like seeing how women think heroes should act. Gives me guidelines. I need all the chivalry schooling I can get, especially now, with the sensitivity training they make us do. It can get very confusing, where the lines are supposed to be drawn. If we acted toward eighteen-year-old virgins the way your heroes do, we'd be jailed. Can you imagine the juice the press would get out of it?"

"You, Ethan Montclair, are full of crap."

"Maybe I am. Maybe I'm drunk." Yes, he had run his hand through his hair then, knowing the thick waves would stand up a bit, mussed, as his mother used to say. He'd given Sutton Healy a slow, lazy smile. "Or maybe it's the way you're affecting me. Speaking of crossing lines, you want to get out of here?"

He worried for a moment he'd shifted gears too quickly, sounded too wanting, but she hadn't hesitated. "God, yes. I can't stand these parties. Can we go now?"

He remembered every one of the fifty steps it had taken to get to the elevator, anticipation buzzing in his veins. He had a hand on the small of her back—gentle, proprietary—could feel the smooth column of muscle where her spine met her finely shaped rump. He waited until the doors slid closed to kiss her. Her mouth was sweet and smoky from the Scotch, and when she threw her arms around his neck and pulled him deeper into the kiss, he felt his heart begin to race. It was more than the usual turn-on, too. There was something about this woman that was absolutely intoxicating. He had a feeling he would remember this trip to New York for a long time to come.

They had rooms on the same floor, the conference block. He motioned toward his door, but she shook her head. "I need ten minutes. Give me your key."

He swiped the small plastic card, opened his door, and handed her the key card. "Don't disappoint me."

She grinned, eyes a wee bit unfocused. "Never."

She scooted off down the hall. He paced. He brushed his teeth. He debated pouring another drink from the minibar, decided he was pretty well pissed and would ride the buzz a while longer.

And true to her word, she returned eight minutes later. He couldn't remember the last time he was so happy to see anyone.

Inside the room, she rubbed up against him like a cat. He quickly discovered she'd taken off her knickers, and he was so turned on by the juxtaposition of naughty and nice he barely got her to the bed before he was inside her.

At four in the morning, sated, sitting naked in the rumpled sheets with an array of strawberries and chocolates and champagne he'd managed to have delivered from a very grumpy front desk overnight manager, watching his dress shirt fall off her pale, freckled shoulder, he decided that he loved her.

DISCOVERIES
ARE MADE

Now

He left the Scotch in his office, grabbed the semiwarm cup of tea from the kitchen counter, went to Sutton's lair on the other side of the house, and booted up the desktop. The banking was always done on her computer. She had the tax files, so it made sense that the financial info was in the same place. Sutton had never shown an interest in the money Ethan brought to the marriage—she paid her mother out of her earnings, as he insisted—but was diligent about making sure the quarterlies and annual taxes were paid.

His family money. Most of it was gone now anyway, eaten up by the price of the house and subsequent renovations. They should have gotten a mortgage, it was insanity to pay $1.4 million in cash, but Sutton wanted to be free of debt, so Ethan had signed on the line and handed over his nest egg.

At the time, money gone wasn't a big deal. It was simply expected that he could continue earning; his highly anticipated third novel was due to release the following June. But, despite his best efforts, the trials of the past year had been too much for even his prodigious mind to handle; he couldn't make it happen—the ending was elusive, the words juvenile and trite. Without any sign of a book the publisher had gotten antsy and the contract had fallen through. Bill tried everything he could to stall them, but, apologetically, the publisher had asked for—demanded—the very substantial million-dollar advance back. The brilliant book with the plot that ruined his marriage was officially canceled; Ethan was publicly humiliated in the industry trades and on social media. How does a man recover from such an embarrassment?

But far worse, far worse indeed: Ethan was now reliant on Sutton's income to support them. Even knowing a royalty check would be coming, they had to reassess their expenditures.

It made him feel like less of a man, less of a husband, less of a writer, but even those indignities hadn't broken him free of the writer's block.

Ethan simply hadn't been able to write a word since Dashiell died. Every time he laid hands on his keyboard, it all felt so fruitless. Pointless. The words drowned in the accusations, in the horrors and sobbing and cries. He'd helped create a life, and helped take it away. The child had depended on them for love and nurturing, and they'd nurtured him right into the grave. How could they forgive each other? How could they move on, move past? Worse, how could words—insignificant, paltry words—heal such a wound?

But dead baby or not, they had to eat. And Ethan wasn't the type to get a job. Family money had lasted him this long, the small but flush trust fund to which he'd added the impressive advance of his debut novel, but once his parents bit it, there was an estate issue, and some of the money was tied up in a trust, and some went to pay off the accumulated debts, and the rest he'd sunk in the house, so he had all he was getting, at least for now.

And it wasn't enough to make the monthly nut.

So Sutton became the breadwinner. Sutton was the one bringing in the money.

It had gone to Sutton's lovely little head, the one who couldn't be bothered with all his money, but took a sort of sinful pride in hers. She'd callously talked about investments and 401(k)s over breakfast, ways to save for the future, how they would have to be careful from here on out.

No *thank you for supporting us all these years, Ethan.* No *I am so grateful you wiped out your family money to buy us this house, Ethan.* No *don't worry, sweetheart, you'll find your words again. I promise,* either.

They were alone now. No nanny. No baby. Just the two of them, knocking around in the grand old Victorian, the incessant tap, tap, tapping away from her end of the house, at all hours of the day and night, Sutton pouring her heart and soul onto the page while Ethan suffered through his drought alone.

She could work. She could talk about finances. Why couldn't she talk to him?

They hadn't had a real conversation in months.

Bitch.

Stop that, Ethan. My God.

He felt odd sitting at her desk. There was a half-full teacup with a scum around the edge, notepads and notebooks and pens—her favored fountain pen, a simple Pilot Metropolitan. He ran a finger along the edge of the pen. It was white, pearly, and he imagined it still held a hint of warmth from her touch. Ethan preferred the Blackwing 602 pencil—sturdy, reliable, never running out of ink or exploding onto unsuspecting fingers. Sutton had laughed at how persnickety he was.

You're dithering.

He didn't want to see the bank accounts, because knowing it was all hers made him feel...less.

"Man up, you bloody fool," he said, and opened the bank's website.

They had two accounts, one for day-to-day expenses and one for the investments.

Neither seemed disturbed. The last entries on the daily account were for Publix, $124.76, and a $25 charge to Starbucks, both dated Thursday of last week. Groceries, and she'd refilled her card. Ethan much preferred the grocery delivery service, but Sutton liked going to the store. He used to tease her that she only went to show off the baby. Of course, that wasn't the case anymore. They'd taken to using the service lately, so Ethan was a bit surprised by the fact that she'd gone to the store directly, but hey, there was nothing sinister about it.

The Starbucks card, though, that was a regular expense. Ethan knew she refilled the card religiously once a week. He saw the entry with a pang of... Was it happiness, sadness? He didn't even know. Sutton always loved walking to the square, loved the crowded Starbucks with its skinny building and long wooden tables. She went there every day, either with Ellen and Rachel after yoga, or with Filly, when they could push the strollers, their ponytails bouncing, or with Ivy, when she was in town and didn't have early-morning meetings, but every day, she was there. It was her favorite part about their house's location in downtown Franklin—how everything that mattered to her was within walking distance.

Who buys groceries, refills their Starbucks card, then decides to run away? It made no sense.

He scrolled back through the records. As far as he could see, the day-to-day account had no unusual charges for the past several days, and the last substantial withdrawal was one he'd made that past Friday. Sutton used a debit card for everything, hated carrying cash. Ethan was the opposite; he loved the tangible feel of money.

Part of him was relieved, and part of him was frightened. She hadn't fled with cash in her pocket.

Call the police. You need to call the police. Something is wrong. The note, it could have been written under duress.

The other side of his mind said, *Just...assemble all the facts first.*

He switched to the investment account. This one was much more complicated, with multiple subaccounts, separate ones for tax and investments, the latter loaded with high-performing stocks, puts and lets and shorts. There was even one account with a separate money manager who essentially did day-trading on a variety of stocks and bonds for their well-managed portfolio. He thought it a waste, thought they should use Ivy, but Sutton had put her foot down. Money and friendship never, ever mix.

He kept scrolling. He was surprised by the balance of the managed account, much more than he'd expected.

It took him an hour to find the pattern of withdrawals, because she varied the time of the visits and the amount, and made cryptic notes in the withdrawal slips. But when all was said and done, there was at least $50,000 unaccounted for.

It wasn't a huge sum. Truly, he could probably explain it away as incidentals, money Sutton had spent on clothes, or things for the house.

But something in him said, *No, mate, this is it, this is something.*

He printed out the spreadsheet he'd built with all the withdrawals and their corresponding dates in it, then shut off the computer. He was barely out of the office when the phone rang.

He glanced at the caller ID. Ivy.

He grabbed the phone, ignoring his fumbling desperation. Depressed the Talk button and practically shouted, "Have you heard from her?"

Ivy's voice was smoky and low. He could hear a din in the background. She was at a conference, somewhere in Texas. Sutton had been invited—Sutton was always invited; Ivy thought the different locales good for research—but Ethan knew she'd declined this trip, saying she wasn't in the mood to travel. She hadn't been in the mood for much of anything lately.

"Ethan? I can hardly hear you."

"I said, do you know where she is?"

"No, I don't. There's been no word, and her accounts are turned off. You still haven't heard from her? Where could she have gone?"

"What do you mean, her accounts are turned off?"

"It looks like she committed social media suicide."

"I thought she'd done that ages ago."

"Oh. Maybe she did, I don't keep up with Facebook like I should. Where could she be?"

"I don't know, but I've been searching our bank accounts, and there's some money missing. The note she left… Ivy, I don't know if she's run away or if she's hurt herself."

An intake of breath. "Have you called the police?"

"No. They won't do anything, you know that. Not so soon."

"Ethan, you need to talk to them."

"Don't take this the wrong way, but do you think I need to speak with a lawyer first? I assure you, I haven't done anything wrong. There's nothing to protect myself from. But the moment I call them, you know how this is going to look."

To her credit, Ivy didn't slam down the phone. Her voice got mean and tight. "Swear to me right now, Ethan Montclair, that you have not done something to my best friend."

"My God, Ivy, of course I didn't. I love Sutton. I'd never hurt her. I'm scared, okay? And embarrassed. I know how the world thinks. The minute I call them…"

She sighed. "They will look at you. The husband is—"

"Always the first person the police look at. I know. But I'm not worried about that. I haven't done anything wrong. I swear. I was only thinking, just in case, a sounding board wouldn't be a horrible idea."

"The police may see things differently. Didn't you guys have dinner a few months ago with Joel Robinson?"

"He's not just a lawyer, Ivy, he's a well-known criminal defense attorney. Wouldn't hiring Joel look bad? I was thinking just a regular guy."

"What, you thought you'd talk to the man who drew up the contracts on your house? Look, you're a British national, even though you have dual citizenship. You're a public figure. Your wife is missing. No matter what, when you involve the police, they are going to take apart your lives. If you're going to talk to anyone, Robinson is the best choice. Trust me."

"Okay. I'll call him. I promise. It's only…"

More noise, the fever pitch growing louder, then a sudden silence. Ivy's voice echoed. "Sorry, it's madness here. I'm coming home right now."

"I don't know if there's anything you can do to help, Ivy. I don't need—"

"Stop it. Of course you need help. You two always need help. I'll be there as soon as I can. Hang tight, okay?"

The relief he felt was palpable. Lately, Ivy was always better at handling Sutton than he was. His eyes closed and he said, "Okay. Travel safely. And, Ivy? Thank you."

A TWIST OF
THE KNIFE

Hanging up with Ivy, Ethan felt partially vindicated. Sutton *was* hiding something from him. He'd known that from the beginning. She wasn't the kind of girl to reveal herself on the first date—well, not in a *this is my past, warts and all* sort of way. She wasn't one for looking back.

Especially because of Sutton's awful relationship with her mother, Ethan had always believed there was something about his wife's past she was keeping private, keeping secret. Truth be told, he found it rather alluring, for the first few years, anyway. He'd asked once or twice what she was holding back, but she'd go ice-cold and would stop speaking to him. When he left it alone, she warmed up. Live in the now, and his ice princess would positively melt, and their lives would be spectacularly peaceful again.

He glanced over his shoulder. He almost expected her to be there, watching him. This was all a test, just to see how far he'd go to invade her privacy again, and Sutton would be livid that he'd been in her things.

Again. Because they'd been through this once before.

He used to—*used to*—check her internet history, trying to understand the mercurial woman he'd married. It was fascinating, her focus, and terrifying, all at the same time. Two years ago, for two weeks straight, she'd done nothing more than delve deep into something called borderline personality disorder. For a while, he'd thought she was researching for a character, but, curious, he started reading the same websites, and everything he saw startled him. She was researching herself. Looking for ways to handle the disease.

God, it explained so much. The narcissism, the coldness, the inappropriate affect when bad things happened to good people. She seemed so compassionless to him, lacking some sort of inner core that he'd never experienced in another person. Sometimes it turned him on, but other times, it scared him to the bone.

He'd known then he should confront her, get her to a psychiatrist, get her on medication. But the mind of a writer is a curious place. It can see the smallest fragment of reality and spin it into a world heretofore unknown.

So instead of sitting down with his wife and asking what he could do to help, he'd made an epic, life-changing mistake.

He'd taken the kernel of the idea, married it to the research, and built himself a character.

Strike one, buddy.

And of course, that character came alive for him in ways no one could ever imagine, considering the model was only an arm's length away. The story unfolded in front of him, and he was helpless to stop it. Once the woman in his brain came to life, it was as if he were on a train, barreling toward the station.

If only he'd known he was actually on a steep descent into the depths of the earth.

He'd pitched the idea to Bill, a story about a sociopathic young mother struggling to be normal, and Bill had sold the idea to Ethan's publisher the next day, for a gigantic wad of cash.

He had asked them to be very careful when they publicly discussed the sale, wanting to be sure no one let slip the subject of the book. Of course, some intern blew it, entranced with the description, and posted the blurb of what the book was about from his proposal in the actual announcement. And Sutton had seen it.

He thought he'd known coldness from her before. Now he was face-to-face with an Antarctic glacier. His own fault, too. That breach started them down the long path, unraveled their relationship quickly and neatly. The things that followed—the affair, the death of the baby, the book cancellation, now Sutton's disappearance—were all because he'd decided to be an arse and profit on her back.

Oddly, they never discussed what they both knew—he'd been spying on her, and had taken her work for his own. Her work on herself. She mentioned casually she'd changed her passwords, citing a hack of her email, but they both knew she was furious. So angry she couldn't even confront him. An anger so righteous and pure he deserved to be divorced.

And instead, she'd gotten pregnant.

Why hadn't he just told her the truth then? Would honesty have stopped the progression of their disastrous world?

Ethan, you are responsible for this.

Back from his remembrances, sitting at her desk, he really, really didn't want to snoop. After all that happened, it made him terribly uncomfortable. He knew better. But under the guise of *the police might be called, I need to do my homework*, he started opening drawers.

Top drawer: ink, Post-it notes, Clairefontaine notebooks, all pristinely kept.

Second drawer: stapler, scissors, checkbooks, and deposit slips.

Third drawer: her current files.

And one from the past.

The folder was labeled—Brother P-touch labeled; Sutton was nothing if not organized—*Baby.*

The pain seized his heart and he gasped aloud. The baby was always in the back of his mind. A whisper on his lips. But seeing the file, he knew what was inside, and he lifted it carefully, as if it were a bomb that might explode and shatter all the windows. He couldn't help himself. As he pulled it from the drawer, something hard and white slipped out and landed on the floor, and he fumbled the file, and all the contents spilled out onto the white oak planks.

Doctor's files, an ultrasound, and a pregnancy test.

God, she'd kept the pregnancy test. The pregnancy he'd forced on her after he'd broken her trust.

Sutton was right in her silent reproaches. He was a reprehensible creature. Who did that to their wife? To the one they loved more than life itself?

What the fuck did the word *love* mean, anyway?

AND THEN THEY
WERE THREE

Then

Sutton was green.

They sat together at the kitchen table, and Ethan watched his wife over the rim of his teacup. She was truly green around the gills.

"Are you okay? You don't look so good."

She gave him a panicked look, made a horrible noise in her throat, then bolted from the table. He was right behind her. She made it to the half bath in the foyer, started retching the second she was above the toilet. He caught her hair, held it back, crooned, and rubbed her back.

After a while, she collapsed in a heap next to the toilet. He handed her a cold, wet washcloth. She wiped her face and turned those huge eyes on him.

"You must have had something bad at the event last night. I hate those catered parties. You never know how long the food's been sitting out. Those bacon-wrapped scallops—"

"Ethan."

"—I never saw anyone change the tray. I'm going to call and complain, they shouldn't be allowed—"

"Ethan!"

"What? What?"

"I don't think it was the food."

"What else could it be?"

There was a long pause, searching looks, then dawning comprehension. A spark of joy built in his chest. "Oh my God, Sutton. Are you…?"

"Pregnant," she said, the word dripping with contempt and hate.

"Pregnant!" he cried, dropping to his knees, gathering her in his arms. She was stiff as a board, didn't move. "My darling, this is brilliant news. Brilliant! We have to call the doctor, we need to decide which room to use as the nursery, we—"

"Stop. Just stop. There will be no baby."

Ethan froze. Her tone was so coolly detached now he almost didn't recognize her. If he could see into her head, he'd realize his beloved, crouched on the bathroom floor, a string of vomit in her tangled hair, was slowly plotting the demise of their child.

"What do you mean, no baby? Of course there will be. You're healthy, this will go wonderfully. How far along are you?"

He didn't say he'd suspected all along because the trash can hadn't filled with the usual monthly accoutrements. He didn't tell her he'd noticed her breasts were a touch fuller, the nipples gone the color of wine. He couldn't, because if he did, it would be clear to Sutton he'd been paying attention to her cycle, and if she knew that, she might realize more about her "surprise" pregnancy, and right now, all he cared about was getting her mind wrapped around a little one.

"A baby, Sutton. We made a baby."

She stood up. "I don't want to have a baby. I have absolutely no interest in having a baby. I can't do this. I can't."

"So…what? You're going to do what?"

"I'm going to have an abortion."

Ethan reared back as if slapped. "Over my dead body."

There was something in her eyes when she looked at him. He should have taken a moment and tried to understand what she was telegraphing in her gaze, but he was panicking. It couldn't happen. She couldn't get rid of their child. He had to find a way to convince her this was meant to be, that a baby would be everything to them.

Purged, she headed to the kitchen, and he followed, pleading, demanding.

"You can't. I forbid it."

"It's my body, Ethan. I'm the one who has to deal with this. You don't get to tell me what to do."

"It's *our* child. Ours. You can't just make a decision like this without my input."

"The law says I can, Ethan." She took up her teacup. Wrinkled her perfect nose and dumped it into the sink. Pulled out a bottle of Diet Sprite, the only soda she'd allow herself, and poured a glass. Took a sip and turned green again.

"Ugh." He saw her glance at him, sideways, under her lashes, measuring, and knew the discussion was still ongoing. Thank God.

"Come here." Ethan led her to the table, got her seated gently in the chair, knelt in front of her so they were face-to-face. "Darling. My sweet brave girl. I know you're scared. I know you don't think you want this. But a baby... Sutton, we have so much to give a child. We have freedom and money and a beautiful home. We were born to be parents."

"You might have been. Me? No. I'm not interested in diapers and sleepless nights and car pools and the PTA. I just can't figure out how this happened. I'm religious about my pills."

He looked away, bit his lip. *Do not tell her, Ethan. Don't make that mistake.* His knees were beginning to burn. He stood and pulled a chair close, pulled her limp hand into his.

"Sutton. I want this child. I want us to have a family. Like you said, you're religious about your pills. Sometimes, things happen, and you know I believe everything happens for a reason."

"How will I write? How will you write?"

"We'll get a nanny. We'll hire a night nurse. Anything you want."

Sutton hadn't moved. "What's the point of having a child if you aren't the one raising it?"

"Sweetheart, would you rather I suggest you give up your work to raise a child? It's very 1950s, but if you want me to act the caveman…"

"I think you should give up your work."

Ethan didn't move.

"Seriously, Ethan. If you want a baby so badly, then you give up your work, and take care of it."

"I'd be willing to do that if you truly want me to."

"A baby means more to you than your books? Than your mark on the world? You're leaving something concrete behind, Ethan, we both are. Children aren't the same—it's a genetic lottery. It could be smart, it could have birth defects. You never know. And we aren't at all equipped if this child isn't absolutely 100 percent perfect, in every way. I don't want to be saddled with a child. You can't take the risk of a child ending your career. It's better for us to just take care of things, and never think about this again."

"You don't mean that," he whispered. "Please, Sutton. I know you don't. I know you want this, too, deep inside. I know it. And I swear, I will handle everything. If you truly want nothing to do with raising our child, I will do it all. I am more than will-ing to abandon my art for this. For us, and our family."

She sat quietly, watching him, the red hair floating around her face. "God, you actually mean that, don't you?"

"I do. I swear it."

She said nothing, stared over his shoulder. There was a bird feeder outside the window; he could hear the birds, dancing around the edges of the feeder, grabbing a bite, fluttering off, then rushing back. Wings beat the air. His heart stood still.

"I'll think about it," she said, finally, and he realized he'd been holding his breath. He gathered her into a hug, and she let him.

THE FRIENDS COME A-CALLING

Now

Ethan went through the rest of Sutton's things quickly. There was nothing unusual about anything, outside the fact that the lifelines she clung to like air were here, and she was not.

He saw nothing that stood out on her computer. Her Dropbox was password protected so he couldn't open her current work in progress—he knew she was working on some sort of big set piece fantasy novel, lots of bursting seams and knights with hard-ons—but she'd always been totally paranoid when it came to her work; she hid it from everyone until it was finished and in the hands of her agent.

The agent.

Stupid, Ethan.

He opened her contacts, pulled up the name—Jessamin Fleming—picked up the phone, and dialed the number. Jessamin's assistant answered perkily.

"Ms. Fleming's office."

"This is Ethan Montclair. I need to speak with Jessamin straightaway. It's an emergency."

"Oh! Yes, sir, of course. Hold, please."

A moment later, Jessamin herself came on the line. She was a big woman, tall and shapely, with a voice like a truck driver after a lifetime three-pack-a-day habit. He liked her.

"Ethan? What's wrong? Did something happen to Sutton? Ally said it was an emergency."

"Have you spoken to her, Jess?"

"Not since last week. Why? What's wrong?"

"She's gone. She left me a note, said not to look for her."

Silence. Dead, empty, cold silence. Then, coolly, "Well, Ethan. This sounds like something between you and Sutton."

Shit. "Please, Jess. If you know anything, tell me. I'm very worried about her. She left everything behind, her laptop, her phone, her purse. She's been upset, sad, and I'm worried she might have tried to hurt herself."

"Or she's left you."

"Without her things? I mean, yes, I'm a right bastard, but without her things, there's no way. Something's wrong, I can feel it."

"New things can be bought. Perhaps she truly doesn't want you to look for her, Ethan."

The doorbell rang, and Ethan started moving toward the foyer. "Jess. You know her as well as anyone. Did she tell you she was leaving me? Because if she is, that's fine. I'll be devastated, yes, but I won't fight her. I'm truly worried about her. If I know she's left purposefully, then I can stop pacing the house, freaking out."

"She didn't say anything to me, Ethan. If you're so worried, perhaps you should call the police."

"That's my next step."

"Well, then. Keep me posted."

"You don't even sound concerned, Jess."

"I am concerned, Ethan. But Sutton is her own woman, always has been. And since Dashiell…"

"Yes. I know. Thank you, Jess."

Thanks for absolutely nothing, you loathsome old bitch.

He pocketed the phone and swung open the door, was faced

with a trio of women. Filly, Ellen, and Rachel. He couldn't help but think, *Fair is foul, and foul is fair: Hover through the fog and filthy air.* These three brought chaos and destruction in their wake, and he could smell it coming off them like brimstone.

"Ladies."

"Have you heard from her yet, Ethan?" Filly had both her babies, the one born alongside Dashiell, only a few days apart, and the accidental second baby, still a newborn, conceived the first time she and her husband had sex after the gynecologist cleared them. Of course Filly had waited the proscribed six weeks. She was not a rule breaker. Not like Sutton... And never mind that it might cause him pain to see the perfectly wrapped cherubs in their ridiculously expensive running stroller.

"No, I haven't." He noticed the little yellow-haired girl from across the street playing on the sidewalk in front of her house. She stopped and stared at him, then burst into tears and rushed into her garage. Jesus, was the whole world convinced he'd done something wrong? Or was he just being paranoid?

Focus, Ethan.

He stepped aside and let them in. Ellen was all darting eyes and pinched mouth, as if she expected Sutton's body to be hanging and twisting in midair from the upstairs banister. Filly entered as if this were her castle, her domain, bumped the stroller over the threshold, marched straight through the foyer, and veered off toward the kitchen. Rachel, though, locked eyes on Ethan and didn't break the gaze. Was she just stoned, or was she trying to discern something? Probably reading his aura or predicting his demise from the numbers of hairs standing up at the crown of his head or some such nuttiness. He blinked first, and she followed him into the kitchen.

They formed up, half circled him, a scrum prepared to take him down. Filly had been nominated as spokesperson for the group. She was standing slightly in front of the other two, aggressive, even for her. She cleared her throat importantly.

"We've talked it over, and we think you should go to the police."

All three women nodded. The elder baby woke, gurgled, and cooed.

He leaned against the counter. "What would you like me to tell them? My wife left me a note and said she didn't want me to look for her, then disappeared. There's $50,000 cash missing from our accounts, by the way. She's done a runner."

Ellen—cool, logical Ellen, her hair in a simple ponytail, crisp and clean—spoke at last. "She hasn't been happy. It's possible she'd leave. But to not tell us? I don't know that I buy all of this."

"Meaning what?" Ethan asked.

She waved a hand. "You expect us to believe she up and left, without a word to any of us, without her things? You say she left a note. Now you tell us she took money, too? It just doesn't feel right to me. Sutton would confide in us if she decided to do this." A deep breath, a glance to her friends. "Did you hurt her, Ethan? Now is the time to come clean."

"Hurt her?" As he said it, he realized all three women were shivering. Rachel was downright shaking. A dawning realization. They were afraid of him. That's why they'd come in hard and fast together—this was more than a confrontation. They were protecting each other.

"I didn't do anything to Sutton, and I believe it's time for you to leave."

His sharp tone woke the infant, who wailed to life like the squawk of a siren. Filly shot Ethan a nasty glance, reached for her bundle of joy.

"I'm serious. You lot, leave, right now. I can't believe you've come over here to accuse me. I didn't hurt Sutton. I'm worried sick about her."

Rachel, her voice quivering but her pointed chin inching up, said, "Sutton is a gentle soul. She's been badly bruised by everything that's happened the past year. And you've been fighting lately, she told me as much."

"All couples fight, Rachel. Ours are no worse than anyone else. You fight with Susannah all the time."

"That's different. We have a sacred space for conflict, we have rules—"

"Oh, for God's sake. I didn't hurt her. If anything, I'm more worried she went off and hurt herself."

Three uneasy stares. He shouldn't have said that. It just came out.

Ellen was the first to speak. "Are you saying she was suicidal?"

Ethan pinched the bridge of his nose. "No. She isn't. I'm saying I've thought about every possibility this morning. She left me. That's what I know for sure. But Rachel is right. Sutton has had a very hard time since the baby… No, I don't think she'd do that." He was rambling. *Shut up, Ethan.* "I think she wants some drama, is all."

Wrong thing to say, take two.

Filly clutched the crying baby closer. "You are a coldhearted bastard, Ethan Montclair. How could you say such a thing? Your wife is missing!"

"That's it. I want you all to leave." When they didn't move, he shouted, "Now!" at them, which had the effect of throwing a rock into a flock of pigeons.

"This isn't over, Ethan. Now that we know… Either you call the police, or we will." Ellen threw in the last bit over her shoulder, and five seconds later the door slammed behind them. The finality of it shocked him.

Bloody hell. Women.

He paced the house for a few minutes, gathering himself, planning. He had to do something here, had to make a decision. Had she left him, as the note and $50,000 missing from their accounts indicated? Was she up for a bit of drama to punish him for his lack of attention lately? Or was it possible that she had hurt herself, and the money was for something else? Misdirection?

A moment of actual sanity hit him. Sutton's friends thought he'd hurt her. The police would, too. It was time to talk to the lawyer.

BURN ALL THE LAWYERS

Joel Robinson's office was three blocks away. Ethan decided to walk. If the lawyer wasn't there, he'd leave a note. He simply had to move, to get out of the house. Get away from Sutton's shade, lingering about like a malevolent ghost.

Robinson was short, round, red-nosed, a cheerful Santa Claus with white hair and a long beard. He worked out of the third story of a lovely Victorian on Fifth Avenue that had been converted to individual offices a decade hence. He had no secretary, opting to manage all of his clients in a state of utter secrecy. While they'd been social acquaintances for several years, Ethan never thought he'd grace the man's professional door. Yet here he was.

Thankfully, said door was unlocked, and Robinson himself was inside. What luck.

Ethan rapped his knuckles on the door frame.

"Joel? Am I interrupting?"

"Ethan. Hello. Just prepping for a case, court later this week. What's up? You ready to schedule that drink?"

"I was hoping I could buy you lunch. I need to run something by you."

Robinson cocked his head to the side. "Sorry, no can do today. Client coming in shortly. Why don't we shoot for tomorrow?"

In his hesitation, something must have shown on Ethan's face, because Robinson waved a hand and said, "But I have fifteen minutes now. Tell me your troubles."

Ethan gave a humorless laugh. "It seems my wife has left me. Here's the note."

Robinson read it, brow furrowed, then handed it back. "That's too bad. I always thought the two of you were thick as thieves. Don't worry yourself too much. With any luck, she'll see the error of her ways and come home soon."

"Here's the issue, Joel. She's left without her things. No wallet, no phone, no laptop. Fifty thousand is missing from our accounts. On the surface, this all looks standard, I know. But I have a bad feeling. Something's wrong. She's been very depressed and upset since our baby…since Dashiell died. My head says she left. My heart is concerned that she's done something stupid."

Robinson tapped his fingers on the desk, rhythmic, endless, processing.

"Suicide makes no sense. Why take money? If you're planning to off yourself, why the cash?"

"Exactly. I agree. Problem is, none of her friends know where she is, and get this, they think I had something to do with her disappearance. They came by to confront me. I could tell by the way they were acting, they're scared of me. They said if I didn't call the police they'd do it for me. I don't—"

A hairy white brow rose, and Robinson held up his hands. "Stop. I don't want to know."

"I didn't—"

"Seriously. Stop. Right now."

"No. Listen to me. I didn't hurt my wife. But I think it's time to call the police. Get out in front of this. Just in case."

Robinson was shaking his head, eyes closed. "You're screwed if you do. They will tear your lives apart."

"I can't sit around and do nothing. I'm worried about her."

"Sit down."

Ethan hesitated for two seconds, then sat.

"Here's how this is going to go. If you call the police, they will immediately consider you a suspect. Every word you utter will be parsed. Say they find her living it up in Rio, all fine and dandy. But say something *has* happened to her. God forbid, I know, but if someone has harmed her—"

"God, no. Don't even say it."

Robinson sighed. "It's a terrible thought, I know. But no matter the circumstance, you are going to be turned inside out. They will investigate you until warrants are coming out your ass, and if they find nothing, you'll be convicted in the media regardless. You know how they love to spin things. Once word gets out on this, you can't turn back. Have you tried looking for her?"

"Not really. I mean, I've been giving her space. She asked me not to look for her. I'm honoring that request." He sounded prim, like a schoolmarm, and Robinson shook his head again.

"Come on, Ethan. Think. That's a guilty man's answer. The media will spin your hesitation into the story. They'll claim you've been buying time, making sure your tracks are covered."

"What would you have me do then? Lie? Say I've been combing the town looking for her? If she left, that makes me look like an abusive asshole."

"Lose-lose, dude. Sorry."

"Great. So now what? I go home and wait for her to show up? What if something has happened? They find her dead, and I *haven't* reported her missing? Then I *do* look guilty. You know I have to call them. If I don't, her friends will. I don't have a choice."

"I want to be there."

Ethan felt a surge of panic. "I was worried you'd say that. If

I show up with you by my side, isn't that going to look even worse?"

"If anything, it will help. I know everyone on the force down here. If I'm there, no one's going to try and jam you up without cause. They will interrogate the living shit out of you, though, so it's better if I'm there in case they start off into territory that could get dicey for you later on. I'll just sit quietly in the corner unless something goes awry. I promise. But you want me there."

"All right. When do we call?"

Robinson glanced at his watch. "I need to get going. Give me two hours. I'll meet you at the house at five."

"Thank you, Joel."

Robinson stood, shuffling papers into his briefcase. "No thanks needed. I'm just trying to watch your back. Now, for God's sake, go out and look for her."

THE TANGLED WEBS
WE WEAVE

Ethan took his time going home. He knew he needed to search for Sutton, but he had no idea where to look. Where would she go if she was trying to hide from him? Franklin was a small town. She had no real ties outside of it, no family in California or anything so convenient.

He stopped in the Starbucks, looked around, as if Sutton would be sitting at the table in her favorite corner, writing away. *She can't write here anyway, mate, her laptop's at the house.* A pang in his heart. He sometimes walked up to meet her, days when he couldn't do his own work. Just a quick *hello, popping in for a cuppa, how are you getting on?* Though it wasn't exceptional interest in her work that drove him to seek her out, and she knew it. He didn't like being far from her for very long. Three hours was enough to make him jittery. Three days felt like a lifetime. Leaving was an effective punishment; she knew how hard he found their separations.

Nothing at the Starbucks, so he moved on. Walked down the street to the Coffee House at Second and Bridge, his preferred haunt, ordered himself gluten-free crepes and a cup of tea. He ate in the back room, the plate balanced on his knee, the squashy leather chair he was in almost too comfortable. It felt terrible to him, eating and drinking tea as if nothing was wrong in the world, as if Sutton was simply off at yoga, or working.

Keep up your strength, mate. You need to keep things in hand.

He kept the refrain on a loop as he walked home. *Keep it together, keep it together, keep it together.*

What if someone *had* harmed her? His stomach heaved at the thought.

Inside the too-empty house, he puttered from room to room. Imagining. If she wouldn't be coming home, was he obligated to keep the heavy orange silk curtains he didn't like? Then admonishing himself: *Don't be daft, man, she's coming back.*

He'd felt this same way when Dashiell died. He'd known his son wouldn't ever be found giggling in his crib again, and yet he'd circle the house and find himself staring into the nursery as if he could conjure the child from thin air.

Ghosts. He was surrounded by ghosts. Of those he'd wronged, and those he'd disappointed, and those he'd failed.

The doorbell rang. He ran to the foyer and pulled open the door with teeth bared, only to see Ivy on the step, suitcase and briefcase in hand, an UberBLACK Suburban driving away.

A calm came over him. He took his first real breath all day.

"Thank God. Sanity arrives. You got here fast."

"I was able to get an earlier flight."

He took her suitcase, ushered her inside, and shut the door gently behind her. "Why didn't you go home first? It's not like it's far."

"I could tell how worried you were. Are. I'll go home once we have a handle on what's happening."

"You're a good friend, Ivy."

A good friend, and a handsome woman. He didn't want to notice, but he was a man, after all. It was hard not to. Since she'd moved to Franklin, and she and Sutton had become bosom buddies, he'd been treated to Ivy in every stage of dress. She didn't try to hide her real self from them.

Today she was all done up, and the effect was pleasing. Short black skirt, long bare legs, those nude pumps Duchess Kate wore all the time. She'd cut her hair since he saw her last—what was it, two weeks ago, when they'd had dinner at Grays? It was blonder, a fashionable long bob with the back slightly shorter, asymmetrically driving toward the front. He purposely skipped over her torso, did not see the button undone nor the black lace spilling out of the crack in her blouse, no he did not.

"Nice do."

She touched the back of her hair self-consciously. "Thank you. Still no word?"

"No. The weird sisters were by, though."

"I wish you wouldn't call them that. They're my friends, too, you know."

"But you're the only one who can remotely understand the reference. Outside of Sutton, of course."

"I know, you're the intellectual giant among us. I'd think Ellen would get it, at least. She *is* a librarian—"

"Ellen's an ignorant shrew, and you know it."

That brought out a rare smile. "Still." Ivy helped herself to a glass and pulled a bottle of water from the fridge. "Talk to me, Ethan. What do you really think is happening here?"

"Honestly? I don't know. Maybe she's paying me back for everything by making me sick with worry. I expect her to come waltzing in the door any minute and yell, *'Surprise!'*"

"Sarcasm doesn't become you."

"I'm only half kidding. What I don't get is the missing money."

Ivy didn't bat a perfectly groomed eyelash. "I agree, that is odd. How much, and from where?"

"Our investment account. Fifty thousand. Withdrawn over six months." He handed over the spreadsheet, felt a small spark of pride. Ivy understood money. It was in her blood. She'd appreciate his effort, at least.

She perused the paper, biting on her lower left lip. A bad habit she had; it made her seem young, breakable. It was the only dent he'd ever seen in her armor. Not that he'd been paying attention.

"This could be for anything."

"It could. But it's not. I think she's fled."

Ivy set the paper down on the marble. Took a sip of her water. "Why would she run away from you, Ethan? Sutton has been through hell, yes, but so have you. I can't imagine her just up and leaving without a word. She's stronger than that."

"She left word. She left a note."

"Oh, that's right."

She read it with the same concentration she'd given the spreadsheet, carefully, fully, allowing the words to sink in.

Another little lip gnaw.

"Well, Ethan, what do you want to do?"

"I want to find her and strangle her for making me worry like this, that's what."

"I'm not sure that's the most productive angle. The police might take offense were they to hear you talking in those terms, too."

He ran both hands through his hair, shook his head. "It's just…what the hell is she thinking? If she wanted out, why not be up front about it? Why steal fifty grand and sneak away in the night? It doesn't seem like her. Something's not right about all of this. I'm no longer feeling comfortable with *she decided to leave* as an answer."

"Then it *is* time to call the police. Let them make the decision for you. Don't you think?"

"I went to see Joel Robinson. He wants to be here when I talk to them."

"That's good. At least you'll be protected. Don't worry. We'll get to the bottom of this. I promise."

He looked at his Breitling, a relic passed down from his grand-father. Took a deep breath. "Joel said he'd be here at five. It's 4:40 p.m. now. Here goes nothing."

He reached for the phone and dialed 9-1-1, trying like hell to keep his mind focused on his missing wife, not thinking about the last time he was forced to do this.

SIDS, OR NOT TO SIDS

Then

The baby wasn't breathing. He was cold and blue, and Sutton was standing over the crib with a look of shock on her face. Her voice was high and reedy, bordering on complete hysteria. She was slapping at her head.

"Do something! For God's sake, Ethan, do something!"

What was he supposed to do? The baby was clearly dead. He'd seen enough dead things to know. The numbness spread through him, burning and cauterizing as it went. *This is your son, not some…thing in a backyard, on the side of the road, or in a coffin. This is your son. Feel something.*

Shock, you're in shock.

Sutton had gone over the edge, was keening. She started to reach into the crib to pick up the baby—*Dashiell, his name is Dashiell*—but Ethan grabbed her arm. "Stop. Call 9-1-1. Don't touch him."

She lost all affect, the hysteria fleeing. Her calm was eerie, unsettling. It was as if his touch had switched off a light inside her; one flick of the switch and the wife he knew was gone. Her voice was hollow, girlish. "He's my baby. I want to pick him up. I want to hold him."

"Sutton, we need the police to see that you didn't do anything to him."

She turned, eyes wide, and slapped him, hard across the cheek. The fire returned to her eyes. "How dare you? How *dare* you? I didn't hurt him, you know I didn't. I'd never hurt him. How could you possibly insinuate that I killed our baby? You bastard!"

He grabbed her by the arms, squeezed hard, as if he could keep the demons from spilling out. "Sutton, listen to me. They'll look at you. They always look at the mother. And now that you know... Calm down. Please, darling, just calm down."

She ripped herself from his grip and rushed out of the room. He heard her crying, cursing, begging, the words running together, a wailing crescendo: *No, no, no, no, no.*

He stared once more at the still body of their tiny son. *Oh, Sutton. What have you done?*

He had to call the police.

Time passed in a blur. Strangers came. Neighbors lined the streets. Rain started, chasing all but the nosiest inside to watch through their windows.

Ten hours—a lifetime—later, they carried Dashiell's body from the house. When the door closed behind them, it felt so empty. He didn't know how to feel. Sutton had been given a sedative and was passed out cold in their bed. He wanted a sedative. Why did he have to be the brave one, the together one, the strong one? Because he was a man? He'd lost his son, too. And probably more. His marriage, his wife. His life, so strategically built.

He opened a bottle of Scotch, poured half a glass, drank it down without breathing. The liquor burned, and he swallowed hard to keep it down.

Two drinks later, he'd finally admitted to himself this could have been his fault. He shouldn't have told her. It was a stupid thing to do. But the guilt of it was weighing on him. Holding the secret inside, letting it eat at him, tear away at him, had become a permanent Charybdis churning in his soul.

Sutton loved Dashiell. Carried him with her everywhere. He'd outgrown the withy basket she kept by her desk and spent his out-of-arms time in a car seat stationed within five feet of her at all times. Ethan had finally won the battle to let the tyke sleep in his crib in his nursery instead of in their bed. It had been hard for Sutton, even harder for him. It was impossible to sleep well knowing Sutton was getting up to check on the baby every hour.

He'd told her because he knew she'd gotten used to it. To being a mother. To having a child. To being a family.

He knew she loved Dashiell.

But when he admitted what he'd done, it was like something inside her snapped.

THE STRANGE CASE OF THE MISSING WIFE

Now

Dialing 9-1-1 felt holy, prophetic. He'd only done it once before, the night they'd found the baby dead, and the whole event replayed itself in minute splashes of memory. Pick up the phone *the police arrived* depress the buttons *they looked right through you, as if they knew you were responsible* it rang, once, twice, three times *there will have to be an autopsy, I'm sorry.*

"Nine-one-one, what is your emergency?"

My baby is dead.

Ivy was staring at him. He cleared his throat. "My wife is missing."

A slight exhalation from the operator, as if she were relieved it wasn't a real emergency.

"Is your address 460 Third Avenue South, Franklin?"

"Yes, that's it."

"What's your name, sir?"

"Ethan. Ethan Montclair."

"What's your wife's name, sir?"

"Sutton Montclair."

"How old is she?"

"Thirty-eight. No, thirty-seven. Oh, her birthday…"

"Height, weight, hair color?"

"Five-eleven, strawberry blonde, maybe 140, 150? I don't know exactly. She hasn't been working out. She's very pretty."

"When did you see her last?"

"Monday night."

"Yesterday?"

"Yes, that's right."

"Is there any reason to assume she's in danger, sir? Has she been receiving strange phone calls or threats?"

"Um, not that I know of. There was a reporter who was hassling her—she's a writer, we're both writers. But it wasn't physical."

"And why do you think she's missing?"

"She left a note, told me not to look for her. Normally I'd respect her wishes. But I, we, lost our baby recently. It's not probable, but she could have tried to hurt herself."

A pause, then a kinder, gentler operator emerged. "I see. I understand. The police will be there shortly, sir."

"Thank you. Thank you very much."

He hung up. Ivy raised a brow. "They're sending someone."

"Good. Now, let's see if we can get into her computer while we're waiting."

Ethan followed Ivy to Sutton's office. "Do you know her password?"

"I can guess."

"I couldn't."

Ivy gave him another strange, appraising look.

"Why does everyone suddenly seem to know my wife better than I do? First her mother, then the weird sisters, now you. What the bloody hell is going on around here?"

"God, you talked to Siobhan? Sutton won't like that one bit."

"She came for her allowance. It was poorly timed."

Ivy sat at Sutton's desk, opened the laptop, touched the track-pad. The screen saver disappeared and the password page came up.

Ivy stared at it for a moment, caught her lip in her teeth, then typed in a few letters and hit Return. The password dock shimmied but didn't let them in. She tried again. Same result.

"Do it too many times and you'll just lock us out. Doesn't she keep it written down somewhere?"

Ivy tapped her finger on the return key. "Of course she does. It's in her notebook, on the last page. I don't see it here on her desk."

"I didn't know that. She keeps the old ones in the closet, in chronological order. Maybe it's in one of them." He pulled open the doors and went rummaging. It only took a moment to find the most recent notebook—Sutton's organizational system put the local library's Dewey decimal system to shame.

He flipped it open to the last page. Sure enough, there was the list, written in pencil.

He swallowed hard when he saw Sutton's master password. He leaned over Ivy's shoulder and typed it in. When he hit Return, the black screen fragmented away, and they were faced with Sutton's home page.

"Open sesame. What was it?"

"The password? 'I love Ethan Montclair.'" His voice broke, and pain bloomed in his chest, bright and hard. Would these be the last words he heard from his wife?

"How perfectly adorable."

"Email first," Ethan said gruffly.

Ivy hovered over the mail icon, clicked it. Ethan gestured, and Ivy stood, let him take over the chair.

The first five messages were all from this morning, from the weird sisters, from Jess. All asking if Sutton was all right. All after Ethan being in touch to see what they knew.

Then there was an array of the kinds of email Ethan himself received—used to receive—editors and publicists and marketing folk, all with terribly good news or don't-worry-about-it news. Sutton had received a starred review from *Publishers Weekly* for her latest book that was due out in a month. Nice that she hadn't mentioned that to him. A familiar seething anger started inside him, made up of equal parts jealousy, pride, and his own unique brand of self-loathing. His wife, the writer, was getting serious accolades for her bodice rippers, while Ethan, the author whose work actually mattered, whose literary contributions would be *remembered*, sat on his hands unable to write a fucking word.

And then there were the nasty-grams. His animus melted in the face of them. He hadn't realized; she hadn't told him. They were still coming in, no longer hundreds a day as they were in the beginning, but still too many. He counted twenty over the past week alone. She had them all saved to a folder, a filter labeling them. Hate mail from her previously loyal readers. He opened her sent folder. Nothing since Thursday. A chill paraded down his spine.

"You find anything?"

He hadn't realized Ivy had disappeared, but she now held her sweating glass of water. He knew she'd left it in the kitchen.

"Nothing of use. I haven't gotten into her files yet, I've only looked at the email. Could she have a different account?"

The doorbell rang.

"Better go get that," Ivy said. "It will be the police. I'll keep looking here for a minute, see if she left anything unfinished in her files. And I've only ever gotten mail from her from this account. But, Ethan, anything's possible."

"Ivy, you don't think…"

"What?"

He shook his head. "Never mind. You keep looking."

THE POLICE ARRIVE

Two officers stood on the front porch, appraising the house. Ethan knew the effect it had on people—the wide, graceful wraparound screamed Southern luxury. The double doors with their lion's head knockers, the dormer windows, the tower. The whole house was special, each piece lovingly crafted, and it showed.

He'd always taken pride in it, though it was Sutton who'd made it a home.

One cop was a young woman in uniform. The second was an older, grizzled man in his fifties wearing a rumpled blue suit. The woman spoke first. "Sir? I'm Officer Graham, and this is Sergeant Moreno. We understand you've reported your wife missing?"

"Yes, I—"

A voice from the street called, "Hold up!"

Joel Robinson was motoring up the sidewalk as fast as his short legs could carry him. The white picket fence—for God's sake, they even had a white picket fence—had a kissing gate, and Robinson fiddled with the latch for a moment, then barreled through, smiling, hand outstretched. "Roy, you old dog. How are things? How's Beverly?"

Moreno shook hands with Robinson.

"Bev's fine."

"Still making that tuna noodle casserole for the church ladies?"

"She'll never stop."

"Give her my best, will you? I've missed the last few weeks, getting ready for a trial, you know how it is."

"I do. Why are you here?"

Robinson stepped past the cops and took up position at Ethan's side. "Ethan's a friend. I thought I'd stop by and see if there's been any news on Sutton. Has there?"

Ethan shook his head mutely.

"Well, then, let's go inside and have a chat. Terrible thing. Terrible thing."

And he hustled everyone inside. Ethan was starting to get an idea of why Joel Robinson was so respected as a criminal defense attorney.

Inside, Moreno introduced Graham. Robinson was all smiles again. "I know your daddy, he's a good man. Fair, and not unwilling to admit it when he's wrong. You tell him his pal from the other side of the fence says hello, will you?"

"I will. He's spoken of you to me before. He says the same thing about you."

"Good to know, good to know. All righty, then, let's get down to business, shall we? We've got ourselves a gorgeous redhead to find."

GLORY DAYS

Then

"Oh, Ethan. I love it! It's absolutely perfect."

They were standing on a sidewalk in the quaint downtown community of Franklin, Tennessee. The house was Victorian, ruined, and needed a ton of work. All he could see were dollar signs, but Sutton was bouncing around like a puppy on crack, begging to call the Realtor and look inside, and he couldn't say no to her. He never said no to her. It wouldn't kill them to look. Looking wasn't buying.

Half an hour later, the Realtor gave them the key. "Take a walk around the place, see what you think. It's not the turnkey you were hoping for, but the bones are there. She could be a real stunner with a little work and TLC."

And the commission would be twice what the Realtor would get from the other houses she'd shown them, but Ethan bit back those words and followed his lovely wife into the run-down beast.

The Realtor was right, it did have good bones. The house had been abandoned; the previous owner ran into bad times and couldn't make the payments, and the bank had foreclosed on this monstrosity. The floors were blond teak but scraped and scratched; the owners must have had a large dog. The front porch needed a complete overhaul; he could see a large crack in one of the plaster Doric columns.

Sutton came tearing around the corner from what he assumed was the kitchen. She had a smudge of filth on her cheek and was smiling wider than he'd seen since the first time he'd taken her to bed. Her eyes danced with happiness.

"Oh, Ethan," she breathed, and he knew, without a doubt, the cause was already lost. They'd be putting in an offer this afternoon. This was their new home.

Would he have allowed her to fall in love with the old wreck had he known where the house would lead them? The agony they'd experience behind these very walls?

Bloody well not. The house would bring them nothing but pain and sorrow. He didn't care if they were supposed to learn and grow from their experiences, this place was damned, and he'd known it that day when he'd allowed her to fall in love, allowed her to deviate so wholly from their plan. They'd had a plan, and if they'd just stuck to it, none of this would have happened, none of it.

They didn't need five bedrooms and three fireplaces and an albatross of a house that would require an entire renovation inside and out to make it livable. They didn't need anything but each other, a bed, a bottle of champagne, and their laptops.

He started to tell her so. He did. Something told him, as lovely as the house could be, they were making a mistake. But the words wouldn't pass his tongue, and then Sutton was there, pressed against him, lush lips against his, her excitement coming through in passion and fire and promises of things to come, a future of love and happiness, and the next thing he knew, he was dizzily writing a check for fifty thousand more than asking, cash, to assure they wouldn't get into a bidding war.

He wanted to say no, but he didn't know what was to come.

So he walked out onto the falling-down porch and signaled

to the Realtor, whose face lit up like a candle from within when she saw the rectangle of paper in his hand, mirroring his wife's delighted visage.

They moved in a few weeks later, having painted the living room a soft dove gray and installed a sofa bed. They were planning to do most of the renovations themselves, but had found a local carpenter-cum-handyman who was going to do the detail work.

Days of scraping and painting and gutting bathrooms ensued. When they weren't working on the house, they were working on their books, individual islands of words, adrift in the chaos around them. Their breaks consisted of runs to Home Depot and Porter Paints. They lived on takeout until the appliances arrived: the massive Sub-Zero they had to knock down part of a wall to fit in, the double convection oven that just barely slid into the wall space Ethan had designed, the Bosch dishwasher that made no noise when it was running. And then it was time to pick the counters, and Sutton fell in love with that bloody gorgeous marble, and the fighting began.

It was a stupid thing to fight over, a large slab of marble. But fight they did, and the house must have fed off the negative energy, because suddenly everything started going wrong. The paint peeled in the living room, they found asbestos in the attic that the inspectors had missed, a family of mice took up residence in the bedroom, partying and carrying on at all hours of the night. The crack in the damn Doric column gave way, and the porch crashed to the yard below, ruining $500 of plants and shrubs they'd put in the day before.

There were tears and arguments and cold shoulders, and when Ethan began to worry they wouldn't find their way back, he gave in on the marble. Like a hurricane's passing, life suddenly calmed. The fights ended. The house came together. They moved the furniture in from the storage unit, and then they were happy. So happy. Sitting together at the kitchen table over their cereal bowls, that big bloody slab of marble glowing gently under the soft white lights, their days were finally unencumbered by the specter of renovation.

Words, all they wanted was words. The two of them, heads bent over laptops, making, creating, in their perfect, customized new home.

How was he to know where things were headed?

It was all his fault. It really was.

He'd gone on a trip. Speaking to a library association. The hotel was small and intimate, the bar cozy. He'd gotten drunk. He only fucked her once, but when he missed his usual goodnight check-in, Sutton had known immediately, and when he got home, they'd had the row to end all rows. The house—the goddamn house, that goddamn marble—took her side.

No matter what they did, no matter how they tried, they couldn't get her blood out.

TELL ME YOUR SECRETS

Now

Ethan sat at the counter in the kitchen, elbows parked in defeat on the wide slab of Carrara marble. The female police officer stood opposite him, notebook out, pen poised above the paper, a quizzical smile on her face.

"Mr. Montclair? Are you all right?"

"I'm sorry, Officer. Yes, of course. You were saying?"

"When was the last time you saw your wife?"

He traced a gray vein in the white. That damn marble. He could never escape the unhappiness it reminded him of. He hadn't wanted it, knew it was going to be ruined within a week, stained with wine or etched by the endless amounts of lemon juice Sutton poured into her water. He lost the battle, as he had so many others.

If forced, he'd grudgingly admit it had kept up surprisingly well, with only one real stain. Mulberry red, near the Sub-Zero. Sutton told their friends it was from the skins of blueberries left overnight.

They'd been at it for two hours now. Joel had said nothing,

just sat in the corner owlishly watching the proceedings, coughing every once in a while, which Ethan took to mean *stop talking, fool*. After the first round of questions, Sergeant Moreno asked to see Sutton's computer, and Ivy showed him where Sutton's office was while Officer Graham grilled Ethan. She was looking at him sideways already, he could tell. Everything he said was being measured and weighed. Joel had warned him this was how things were going to go. They always looked at the husband. Everything he said sounded weak, insincere. He realized the interview was going badly. Very badly.

"Sir? Mr. Montclair? I know we've been over it once before, sir, but let's run through it again. You never know what you might have forgotten or omitted, even accidentally."

He glanced at Robinson, who inclined his head in a brief *go ahead* nod.

"I'm sorry. I saw Sutton Monday night, before she went to bed. Before we went to bed."

"Did you go to bed together or separately?"

"Separately, but at the same time."

Graham looked up from her notebook. Apparently he hadn't mentioned this the first time around. "You don't share a bedroom?"

"We've been having some issues lately."

"Right. You mentioned that." The notebook lowered. The cop was young, thin, flat-chested in her patrol uniform. White-blond hair, practically colorless, cut in a pixie, eyebrows the palest shade of blond he'd ever seen. Looking closer, he wondered if it was natural. It looked natural. Striking, as Sutton would say. Her name tag read H. Graham, the silver rectangle perched over the pocket of her uniform, which lay nearly flat against her ribs. Bigger breasts would have made the pocket rise away from her... *Jesus, Ethan. Stop already. Just look at her face. Meet her eyes. They'll think you have something to hide if you keep looking away, or that you're a creep if you keep staring at her tits.*

He shouldn't have noticed the officer's breasts. That was wrong of him. Especially because his wife was missing, and H. Graham looked like a towheaded child, fresh out of the Academy.

Moreno came back into the kitchen, silently watching.

"So nothing in the past few weeks to indicate she could be in any sort of danger? You believe she left of her own accord?" Officer Graham asked, but it was more than a question. An indictment.

Focus. "I thought so at first. Like I said, we had a fight Monday afternoon. Nothing important, the usual, just sniping. I know how it sounds, but it's not what you think. I haven't hurt my wife. If I had, I wouldn't have called you." He laughed, a hearty *ho-ho.* Graham took an involuntary step back, and Robinson closed his eyes.

Brilliant, well done. Could you sound any guiltier? Stow the fucking charm already.

Ethan held up his hands. "I'm sorry. This isn't funny. I'm embarrassed. She's left before. Things are a bit…rocky right now."

"And the note? Where did you find it again?"

"It was left on the counter, where I wouldn't miss it. When I read it, I knew something was wrong. If it's real, I wanted to respect her wishes, which is why I've waited until now to call you. But things have been so strange lately… I got worried. I called her friends and her mother to see if they knew anything, but no one did."

Officer H. Graham picked up the note and read it aloud. She'd already done this once. Every word felt like an accusation. She set it gently on the marble. "Not exactly benign, this note. It feels very final. You say she's left before. She was clear in her note that she didn't want you to look for her. This seems rather straightforward. So why call us? What really has you worried?"

He took a deep breath. He knew exactly how this was going to sound. "She's never left a note before."

"Okay."

He heard the inquiry in her tone. "It's not just that. Like I said, she left her phone, her keys, her purse, all her clothes. Her laptop is still in her office. She hasn't used her email—she lives on email. Nothing on her social media accounts. She left the note, and then she disappeared. Yes, she's left before, but only for a few days, and she goes to stay with friends, or gets a hotel room, and lets me know that's where she's going to be. And she always comes back. Always. She's never disappeared without her things. She's a writer. She's working on a book."

"A book about what?"

"Novels. She writes novels. Very good ones." He paused. "I do, as well. We're both in the industry. She had a spot of bother recently, with a reviewer. It was embarrassing for her, for me. The publisher was upset, and canceled her contract. Maybe she ran off to lick her wounds, but without her things…" He trailed off. He was babbling and the more he spoke, the more words that came from his mouth, the guiltier he sounded.

He realized he *was* genuinely upset for Sutton. Despite how the day had gone, with everyone attacking him, Sutton had been going through hell for a while. He had been concerned about her for many months, concerned about her mental state after what happened to Dashiell, after what happened with the reviewer. *Sincerity, Ethan. You need to actually* sound *concerned.*

He did manage to look H. Graham in the eye then. "Listen, we can keep talking and go over it a thousand times, but none of it will change the fact that no one's heard from her since she left. Her agent, her mother, her friends. She's very good at keeping people up-to-date. She's been in touch with no one, and now we're all worried."

The older cop was more direct. "No sign of anyone breaking into your house? Neighbors didn't report anything odd? Strangers hanging around?"

"No. Nothing. Not that I've noticed."

"What was the—" Graham glanced at her notes "—*spot of bother* with the reviewer?"

"It was just a fuss. An online thing. Sutton received a bad review. She'd had a terrible day, she responded, and the whole thing blew up."

"Blew up, how?"

He hesitated.

"If it's online, I'll be able to find it. Why don't you just tell me now and save us both some time? Was she in danger?"

"No, she wasn't in danger, just embarrassed. People can be cruel. She took pride in her work, and when she responded, she was very...blunt. Told the reviewer to shove it. It seems innocuous, ill-mannered, yes, but in the scheme of all that happens online, it wasn't such a horrible thing to say. But a blogger picked up on it and wouldn't let it lie. He started hassling her."

"You mentioned this in your 9-1-1 call. What sort of blogger, and what sort of hassling?"

"Have you ever heard of a website named Stellar Reads?" She shook her head.

"No?" He knew he sounded incredulous. Who couldn't have heard of Stellar Reads? Apparently Officer H. Graham, who was staring at him with a raised brow.

"I don't spend a lot of time online, sir."

"Right. Well, it's a site where people can rate books, leave reviews. When Sutton popped off, the blogger wrote an essay about it, posted a one-star review. Instead of just staying out of it, Sutton responded, tried to justify the choice—something writers aren't smart to do. It always backfires. And it did here, too. The blogger called out all of his friends and they attacked the hell out of Sutton. Really nasty stuff, tore her work apart, gave her hundreds of one-star reviews even though they hadn't read her books. Some of her loyal readers got into it and they were attacked, as well. Put Sutton through the wringer, claims of authors behaving badly, all of that.

"Anyway, there was a reporter from one of the trades who wanted to interview her. Sutton took the call, told the reporter she hadn't been involved and all of it was a smear designed to make her look bad. Saying my account has been hacked, no one ever believes that. They just think you're trying to cover your arse.

"Sutton tried to calm the whole situation by posting on her Facebook fan page explaining that she had never been in touch with the reviewer, hadn't left the comments, that someone had impersonated her. She explained about losing our son, and you'd be amazed at the things people said. Horrible, appalling stuff. We closed the account and tried to walk away. Thank heavens, someone else came along and did something stupid, became the flavor of the week, and the fervor died down. But after everything that happened… She couldn't handle it, had a bit of a collapse. It broke something in her."

He paused. "It was out of character, actually. Her reaction, I mean. Sutton usually took reviews of her work with a grain of salt. Believe the bad, you have to believe the good, and all that. For some reason, this one upset her tremendously. Hit her at the wrong time, I guess. Most of it's been taken offline now. Stellar Reads even sent apologies."

Enough, you don't need to tell them everything. This is irrelevant.

"Has the situation been resolved?"

He shook his head. "Sutton has at least twenty new hate emails this week alone. So, no, I'd say it hasn't been."

"We'd like to take the computer with us, let our forensic technicians go over it. Are you okay with that?"

Robinson cleared his throat. "I would think, if you want my client to hand over information related to his wife's disappearance, a warrant would be in order."

Ethan wanted to climb inside the bloody marble and disappear. Now he was Robinson's client? *Fuck. Fuck, fuck, fuck.*

"Coming, right after we leave here. Unless Mr. Montclair—"

Ethan had to get this back under control. "You don't need a warrant. Feel free to look at anything in the house you want.

I've done nothing wrong. You're welcome to take the computer with you."

He tried to block a vision of his wife, his very private wife, her face drawn in shock, allowing him to let the police walk away with her computer.

You've given me no recourse, wife.

"Ethan," Robinson warned, but Ethan held up a hand to stop him.

"Seriously. Look at the computer. Then you'll see. I have absolutely nothing to hide."

WHAT'S REALLY
GOING ON HERE?

The female cop nodded. "Okay. This is very helpful information. I'm going to need names and dates. But before we do all of that, would you categorize your relationship with your wife as volatile, Mr. Montclair?"

"Never. We just didn't always see eye to eye."

The cop glanced at the older one, who nodded slightly. "We have a number of domestic calls to this address."

Ethan took a deep breath. "I know how that looks. Sutton and I fight. We argue. We're very passionate people. Sometimes we argue on the porch, or in the backyard, and neighbors take it the wrong way."

"So your wife hasn't called the police? It's only been the neighbors?"

"Yes. No one will admit who made the calls, but you'll see in every incident, no charges are filed. There is no evidence of abuse, no physical altercations. Just some nosy neighbors who don't like to mind their own business. It's been hard on us, since the baby..."

Graham looked around the kitchen. "Where is the baby, sir?"

Beams of light pouring in the kitchen, the small crystal Sutton had hung in the window above the farmhouse sink catching the sun, suddenly spinning, shooting fractured light through the room. It looked so homey, so normal, except for the albino cop standing across from him.

He took in a breath. The cop's head had cocked to the side, like a spaniel. Now she was really paying attention.

"You don't know? I just assumed, but no, you're so young, so new, I suppose you wouldn't know. Our son, Dashiell, died. SIDS. Sudden Infant Death Syndrome. He wasn't even six months old. It was headline news for a few weeks, raising awareness for the condition, all that. Sutton didn't handle it well." Ethan's voice cracked. "Neither of us did."

"I'm sorry for your loss. When did he pass away?"

"Last year. It was in April. Tax day, April 15. We went to check on him, and he wasn't breathing."

He choked a little on the last word, suddenly having difficulty catching breath himself. God, he'd wanted that baby. When she fell pregnant, he was ecstatic. After all he'd done to help her get pregnant, after all their arguments, his cajoling, begging, her final agreement to have the child, to lose him in an unexplained death sometimes felt like punishment.

He knew Sutton had grown to love Dashiell. He'd seen the joy on her face when she didn't think he was looking. And now he was gone. His perfect son had been taken from him. And his wife was missing.

Your wife is missing, your wife is missing.

"So she disappeared on the anniversary of your son's death?" Moreno asked.

It hadn't hit him, the significance. He'd been too caught up in his own unique brand of self-flagellating mourning to realize, and too worried about where she might be to look at the calendar. He hated to think back to that day. There was no such thing as an anniversary with grief this new, this raw. It was a daily, visceral, animal thing that ate at him constantly. He didn't think in terms of dates, or months since, years since. There was just Before, Dashiell, After.

"Yes, that's right. The anniversary."

H. Graham looked to the older officer, then closed her notebook and stuffed it into her back pocket, like a professional golfer. "We'll put together a report, sir, be on the lookout, check everything we can. But I think it's safe to say your wife isn't in any danger. I bet she comes home anytime now. People deal with grief in different ways. Sounds to me like things were just too much for her. An anniversary like this, it's difficult. Add in complications from work? Sounds like she's been having a really rough go of it."

He felt relief. They believed him. They didn't think he was involved.

Ivy came into the kitchen, so quietly they didn't hear her until she said, "Ethan, you need to tell them everything."

Ethan saw the cops both start slightly.

"Ma'am?" Graham asked.

"We are very concerned Sutton may have harmed herself. She has been having a hard time lately," Ivy said.

"Mr. Montclair mentioned things have been tenuous with her."

"*Tenuous.* That's a good term. She's been on edge, upset, angry, and crying."

Ethan shot Ivy a glance. *Whose side are you on here?*

"What's had her upset, ma'am?"

"What hasn't? I mean really, can you blame her? First her baby, then her career? Anyone would be laid low. Sutton is a brilliant artist. She's sensitive."

Ethan stepped closer to Ivy, put his hand on her shoulder. "Ivy and Sutton are very close. She's been helping me search for Sutton."

Officer Graham looked at him again, this time with wariness

on her lovely face. He dropped his hand, in case it looked bad. He wouldn't want her to think there was anything untoward happening with Ivy.

"Was she suicidal? Being treated with medication?"

"Not now. No. Other than the incident with her publisher, she's been fine." A lame word, *fine*. What did it really mean?

"If she's fine, recovered from these two blows, as Ms. Brookes calls them, why do you think she harmed herself? Why now? Why not right after the baby died, or when she lost her contract?"

He took a deep breath. "It's confusing for me, too. Sutton went off the rails after Dashiell died. Not that I blamed her. She was very distraught."

"And how were you after this unfortunate incident, Mr. Montclair? Did you cope well with your son's death?"

The police officer had pretty eyes, hazel, changeable. They'd softened when she'd heard about Dashiell's death. She wore the barest hint of pink lipstick. He wondered what she was like in the sack. She seemed like she might be a wild one. The sweet ones usually were; she had that look.

"I coped," he said, cringing a bit at how sharp he sounded. "It was difficult, of course. You shouldn't have to bury a child. Not only did I lose Dashiell, I lost Sutton, as well. After the baby… died, she went to a very dark place. We feared for her life. Then this fuss with the reviewer happened. We had to have her committed. Please keep that between us. She is very ashamed of her breakdown. Very upset. It's been a difficult time. But she'd managed to pull herself back from the brink. She was getting better."

Ivy shifted next to him. "I think we're all simply concerned she wasn't bouncing back the way we thought. She could hide her despair very well when she needed to."

The young cop tapped her finger against her gun strap. *Tap, tap, tap.* It was the sergeant who said, "Mr. Montclair, please be straight with us. Do you think your wife is taking a break from the marriage, or are you reporting her missing because you're afraid she may have harmed herself?"

Ethan heaved out a sigh. "Officers, let me be very clear. I don't know. I don't know anything anymore."

He cracked then, finally. The tears began. "I can't lose her, Officers. Not after losing Dashiell, too. Please, help me find my wife."

H. Graham held out a hand as if to touch him, to comfort him, but stopped, realizing it made her look unprofessional.

Robinson came to life in the corner. "I think this should cover it. What do you say, Roy? Should we mount a search? Might put everyone's minds at ease."

Moreno looked from Ethan to Robinson and back again. "We'll look into this and get back to you. No sense wasting resources if the lady doesn't want to be found."

"Fair enough, fair enough."

Hands were shaken, cards exchanged. They took Sutton's laptop and datebook. Glanced around a few more times while they stood on the porch.

When the door shut on the cops, Robinson turned to Ethan. "You idiot. I told you. You're completely screwed."

THE INVESTIGATION
BEGINS

"Tell me, Holly. Do you believe him?"

Sergeant Roy Moreno was head of the homicide unit, and Holly Graham's current superior officer, about six times removed, seeing as she was a simple patrol officer, and he was in charge of homicide. He was her superior, in all ways. Moreno knew a lot about this town, about investigations, and lucky for her, had shown an interest in her from the beginning. Not in the creepy way some of her fellow cops had, but a sincere interest in her as a person and an investigator. It was her dad's doing, probably. Derek Graham was a well-respected district attorney, but who cared? Holly was getting a chance to work with the old horse directly, and that was going to be nothing but good for her career.

The old horse in question was currently sucking on a toothpick, staring out of the windshield of the patrol car. The laptop between them glowed. They were parked in the lot of the five-star Mexican joint down the street from the Montclairs' lovely home, having rolled away just as a news truck came sharking around the corner. She watched the truck pull to a stop at the curb. Heading to the Montclairs' gorgeous Victorian mansion, perhaps? The media in Nashville were very good at ferreting out drama, and the missing wife of a major author was bound to pique their curiosity.

"Should we do something about that?"

She glanced over at Moreno. Not only an old warhorse, a veteran of the force, he was a genuinely good man. She was lucky to have him riding with her to do some investigative training. His son was on the force, too, a few years ahead of Holly.

"Montclair's a big boy. Let him handle them. I asked you a question."

"He's very believable. But I also think he knows a lot more than he's saying. Something wasn't right in that house. Did you see the bloodstain on the counter near the refrigerator?"

"I did."

"It's in the kitchen, so anything could have happened, from a nosebleed to a knife cut. It was such a small amount, and it was old, it had been there for a while. Who knows? We'll have to pull the incident reports, look at the details on the domestics. But add in a deceased child, the wife's supposed history of mental illness, the husband being a minor celebrity, a recent online kerfuffle, and the fact that he hired one of the best criminal defense attorneys in the state before he called us? There are so many angles we can take it's not funny."

"Robinson being there made me sit up and take notice, too. Makes him look guilty as sin."

"I don't know, Sarge. This day and age, people are always thinking three steps ahead. And like Robinson said, he's a friend of the Montclairs."

"You're right. So. What do you suggest we do?"

"First, we put Sutton Montclair in the missing persons database, let the MP detectives see what they can find on her. Check her passport, bank accounts, tear apart their lives a little bit. I want to find out more about the online situation with the reviewer. Stalkers have hurt people before."

Moreno looked over at her. "You think she was telling the truth that her account was hacked?"

"No idea. But it's worth a look. Might explain where she went, or if she was in danger, where she's been taken."

"What's your gut say? Do you think she's missing, or that she's being held against her will somewhere, or she got sick of the pretty boy and her pretty life and hoofed it?"

"Too early to make a proper assessment, sir. Like I said, something doesn't jibe. I'd like to know more, about them both, before I make any decisions about what might or might not have happened."

"It's probably just a domestic gone wrong. She's tired of the fighting and takes off. Might even have a piece on the side who helped. It's been known to happen."

Holly tapped her pen against her teeth. "I don't know, Sarge. Not to play devil's advocate, but if she'd really left him, why would he talk to a lawyer and bring us in? He knows we'll be digging into everything. He knows any investigation on our part will draw attention. Is he doing it for personal gain, wanting his fifteen minutes in the spotlight? Did he hurt her, but he's clever and wants to look innocent? I don't know, but toward the end I got the sense that he was truly distraught and feared for her life.

"Sutton Montclair may not want to be found, she may have wandered off, may have hurt herself, or she may have been kidnapped. We don't have all the pieces of the puzzle, but I don't think he killed her, either. It felt like he really was worried for her."

"But?"

"He didn't tell us everything. I think we should keep looking at him, hard. Find out what he's holding back. The friend seemed pretty concerned. If he'd kept the friends out of the loop, I'd lean more toward he hurt her, but that he was worried enough to call in someone who was close to his wife tells me there's something here. I can't help coming back to the idea that if he did something and didn't want to get caught, why would he put himself under such scrutiny? I mean, I know it's the way psychopaths operate, for the thrill of it all, but he didn't strike me as a psychopath. Only a man looking for answers."

Moreno took the toothpick out of his mouth, wrapped it in a napkin, and stashed it inside his empty Starbucks cup. Stared out the windshield some more. Holly knew he was a thinker; she'd grown accustomed to his silences while they worked.

Finally, he said, "I like how you think, Graham. I like that you're not jumping to conclusions because of what he's told you, or because Robinson was there. So we're going to play this a bit unorthodoxly. You've had excellent training, and you have a background in this, with your dad's work with the DA's office. We all know what your trajectory holds. You're only a few steps from plainclothes, and every uniform wants their chance to play detective, so this is your go at it. I want you to run the case as it moves forward. I think you made a connection with Montclair, and it might pay off later in this investigation."

Holly couldn't believe what she was hearing. Yes, she was going to be a detective, everyone expected it, and she wanted it, bad. It just wasn't supposed to happen for another year. But if Moreno wanted to bump her up the line, she wasn't going to quibble.

"Of course, sir. I'm happy to."

"We'll give it a few days. See what shakes out. Sound like something you can handle?"

"It is, sir. Not to look a gift horse in the mouth, but why me?"

Moreno smiled at her, his eyes crinkling with good humor. "When you're a full-fledged detective, you'll figure it out soon enough, Officer Graham. I'll tell you this, when a suspect makes a connection with an officer, we don't ignore it. Now, get to work. I want everything you can find on the Montclairs by morning."

READ ALL ABOUT IT

It happened like a lightning strike, fast and furious and devastating. Somehow, the whole world knew Sutton Montclair was missing.

The reporters started calling and knocking and ringing the doorbell and peering over the backyard fence about twenty minutes after the police and Robinson and Ivy left.

Ivy had reassured Ethan as she walked out the door. "It's going to be okay. We'll find her. I'll talk to the girls, dig around, see if anyone's talked to her. They might be more willing to open up to me instead of you." He hadn't seen her since. Robinson hadn't called. He'd been so alone, just him and the bottle, and the intrepid media seizing the meaty story in their carnivorous jaws.

The fucking reporters, who were much more interested in the news of Sutton Montclair going missing than the police were, wouldn't leave him alone. He didn't want to answer the phone—what if Sutton called?—but he had no choice.

So he drank, and shouted *no comment* into the phone. Every time it rang, he answered with a breathless, "Sutton?" Every time, it was a stranger. New voices, same requests.

"Mr. Montclair? This is Tiffany Hock from NewsChannel 5. We understand your wife has been reported missing, and we've been trying to reach you, we'd really like to speak with you—"

He didn't even bother saying no comment, just hung up. Moments later, the phone rang again. He eyed it like it might poison him. Lifted the receiver. It was a man this time.

"Ethan Montclair? Tim Mappes, *New York Times*. I understand your wife, Sutton Montclair, is missing. Would you like to give me a comment?"

Click.

The doorbell rang. He could hear someone calling his name, a strange woman's voice. "Mr. Montclair? Mr. Montclair? Will you come talk to us?"

Holy Christ, he was under siege.

You knew this would happen, didn't you, Sutton? You knew the whole world would want to find you. Well played, wife.

Finally, exhausted, drunk, but unable to sleep, he turned off the ringer, took one of Sutton's Xanax, and passed out cold for a few hours.

Ethan woke to a blinding headache. The front of the house was dark. He'd passed out on the couch.

Smart move, idiot.

He groaned as he sat up, perched on the edge of the couch with his feet on the floor and his head in his hands until the worst waves of nausea passed. Managed to make it to the kitchen and put on some tea. Popped three Advil, drank a bottle of water. The kettle took forever to boil. When it started whistling, pain rippled through his head.

He needed…something. Help. Support. Getting pissed and passing out wasn't going to solve things. The media wasn't simply going to walk away because he told them to. There was a story here, and everyone knew it.

The phone was sitting quietly on the counter, innocuous. He picked it up, ignoring the wave of burning bile that forced its way into his throat, and turned the ringer back on. It started to ring immediately. This number he recognized, and wasn't entirely unwanted.

"Hullo, Bill."

"*Hullo?* That's all you have? Where the fucking hell have you been? I've been trying to call you for two hours!"

"Asleep. Drunk. Like most normal people."

"It's been half a day, Ethan. You're not a normal person, and you're definitely not in a normal situation. The *New York Times* is printing a story about Sutton being missing. Since you've been ignoring me, I have a flight to Nashville first thing in the morning. We have to coordinate a plan, figure out how we present this—"

"Would you calm down? It's *my* wife who's missing."

"And I'm your agent. You should have called me the minute you realized this was turning into a story. I could have helped. You really don't have any idea where she is?"

Shafts of light cruised across the kitchen, first there, then gone, then back again, fading. The beams from the news trucks as they shuffled positions out on the street. The on-again, off-again light reminded him of the past few months with Sutton. If only he could count on the clouds parting. He managed a sip of tea.

"For Christ's sake, Bill, if I knew where she was I wouldn't have called the police to start looking for her."

"You called the police?"

Ethan hadn't known a man could shriek, but Bill had just offered a full-fledged shout that would make a pterodactyl proud.

"And a lawyer."

Bill started moaning into the phone.

"Listen to me. Sutton left a very ominous note. I am worried sick. I'm worried she may have hurt herself. She asked for time, but now…something's not right. She left everything behind, and…it feels wrong. She's been gone too long. I had to involve the authorities. I needed help. So get off my back."

"Bullshit. She's just trying to hurt you. She could be holed up with some lover, laughing up her sleeve while the police make a case against you. We gotta get out in front of this. Right now."

Ethan rolled his eyes. "Bill, you read too many novels. There is nothing to get out in front of. I've done nothing wrong, and neither has Sutton. It's been a bad time for us both. She's had a lot to deal with, and I'm praying all she's done is take off for a few days, like her note said."

"There's your quote. I'll call the *Times*, say that exactly."

"No story. Seriously. You have to quash it. I can't face the scrutiny."

"It's too late. And it sells books, buddy."

"You didn't just say that to me. Go away, Bill. Make sure the story isn't run. Don't come down. I'll call if I have news."

He hung up. The phone rang immediately. He debated for a moment, then turned off the ringer again. Drank some more tea. Foraged in the refrigerator, found some prosciutto-and-mozzarella wraps. He needed fuel. The idea of eating was repugnant, especially with the constant visions of Sutton lying dead and broken in a ditch that inundated him, but he'd do her no good drunk and empty.

Ethan ate. He looked out the window. The media were still lined up, camera lights on, beautiful young reporters fluffing their hair and straightening their ties. The local evening news was about to start.

He debated for a few moments: Turn it on? See what Sutton had wrought?

Then: *Dashiell.*

The thought of his dead son, of the things the reporters would be saying, made him want to crawl right out of his skin. Bolts of panic shuddered through his body. He was stuck in the house; he knew the moment he tried to step foot outdoors, the media would pounce on him. Stuck, trapped in this moment in time, unable to walk away, unable to function. He simply didn't know what to do.

He watched the scrum of reporters on his front step. He decided to stay away from the TV, decided against any internet reading. He was afraid what he might see there. Himself cast as the villain. Sutton, his beautiful Sutton, dragged across the coals again. The baby, resurrected and killed, all over again.

He couldn't take this. He couldn't stand it anymore.

So he poured a drink. And then another. He walked around the house for some exercise, looked at pictures of Dashiell, and for one long, odd moment, stood in Sutton's closet and smelled her scent and masturbated.

What else was a trapped man supposed to do? It's not like he could open his laptop and write, could he? Could he? Yet a little voice said, *You're a selfish man, Ethan Montclair. Might as well take advantage.*

How in the name of God it happened, he didn't know, but when he opened the manuscript that had lain dormant for the past two months, the words just started to flow.

THE FIRST BREAK

The call came very late that evening, while Ethan Montclair sat in his lonely house, contemplating whether he should go searching for his wife or continue to allow the inertia and ennui to consume him. Get lost in a bottle, or possibly stumble across his dead wife's body?

An easy, unsurprising decision. He'd poured a drink and continued to type.

Officer Holly Graham, though, had already gone to bed. When her cell phone rang, she fumbled with the phone—who wouldn't, that late? When she finally got it to her ear, there was silence. She feared the caller had hung up. They hadn't.

"Officer...Graham, is it?"

The voice was female, deeper than normal, but feminine. Graham glanced quickly at the caller ID—private. That could be anything from a blocked number to a pay phone.

"Yes. Who is this?"

"You need to look closer at Ethan Montclair."

"Who is this?" Graham had asked again.

"A concerned friend. Sutton Montclair is my friend. I'm afraid, we're afraid, Ethan's hurt Sutton."

The voice was clear and confident, though Officer Graham

could hear a waver in the very last words, as if the caller were scared.

Graham did everything by the book.

"Ma'am, I'd appreciate it if we could make this official. Can you meet me at the station, give a statement?"

"No. I won't help if you make this official."

"How did you get this number?"

"Look closer at Ethan. He's not what he seems. The baby… It's not what it seems."

"You'll have to give me more to go on, ma'am. What am I supposed to be looking at?"

The voice, now a vicious hiss: "Everything."

IN WHICH WE RECEIVE A CLUE

The intensity of the voice sent Holly's heartbeat ticking up a notch. She called Sergeant Moreno directly, as he'd instructed.

"Sorry to call so late, sir. Can someone dump the LUDs on my cell phone? My personal phone, not my work phone. I just got an anonymous call about Ethan Montclair. Said to look closer at him, and at the baby's death."

"How'd they get your personal cell phone number?"

"I don't know. It doesn't matter."

"It does, but we'll worry about it later. I'll have a trace run, see if we can nail it down." He yawned. "Damn, it's late. But I'm awake. Might as well take the time now to update me. Where are you on the case?"

"Everything Montclair told us is checking out. Sutton was committed to Vanderbilt on an emergency psychiatric hold six months ago. I called the doctor, but they won't talk to me without a warrant in hand, so all we have is the court filing. It checks out, everything Ethan said shows up there—suicidal ideation, psychosis. He's telling the truth about her breakdown.

"The baby's death was ruled SIDS, the autopsy showed no

signs of trauma. Baby was well nourished and taken care of, no signs of neglect, nothing to indicate he was purposefully suffocated or given something that stopped his heart. It really looks like a terrible tragedy, and not one of their making. There are about 3,500 idiopathic SIDS deaths in the country every year. It seems Dashiell Montclair is a statistic."

"That's a shame."

"It is. Very sad."

"What else?"

"Multiple domestic calls. We've been out to the house four times in the past year. Mrs. Montclair declined to press charges, so there was nothing we could do."

"He was abusing her?"

"That's the odd thing. All four times, she swears she didn't make the call. That yes, they were fighting, and yes, it was bad, but she hadn't called the police."

"Nine-one-one have the records?"

"The calls came from her cell phone."

"Sounds like buyer's regret to me. Pretty typical."

"Yeah. There's not a lot to go on here, that's for sure. Clearly there were problems, clearly she's bailed. The question is, did she leave of her own volition, or did he help her along?"

"How do you propose to answer that?"

"Time, sir. It's going to take more time for me to sort through it all."

"Get some sleep. Hit it fresh in the morning. That's an order."

"Yes, sir." They hung up. But she couldn't sleep. She lay in her comfortable bed, thinking about the photos she'd seen at the Montclairs'. They seemed so happy. So settled and content. The three of them, beautiful and glossy. And then tragedy struck, the baby died, and their whole world collapsed. Anyone's marriage would fall apart under those circumstances. Anyone's.

So why did she feel like she was missing something?

VOICES, I HEAR VOICES

Me again. How're you getting along? Me, I'm a bit annoyed.

I have to ask, was that bad of me, the call? Should I not have turned the screws on Ethan so soon? It's only been a day, and the cops are heading in the right direction, yes, but they're so sloooow.

I want to see him twist.

I want to see him hurt.

I want to see him bleed.

And I want it to happen now.

Lest you think I'm some sort of mustache-twirling villain, let me assure you, Ethan deserves every moment of torture he's receiving. He is a bad man. A tin man. A man without honor, without a soul, without a heart.

Forgive me. Or don't. But I really don't think people are taking this seriously enough. My friends are such a disappointment. I mean really, one confrontation, that's all? That's the best they can do? I teed them up and made sure they had all the ammunition they needed, and not one of them has had the guts to come forth and point the finger.

I have to move things along.

I wasn't planning on doing this quite so soon, but now I don't know that I have any choice.

I'll give the cops another day to put it together. But time is running out.

Tick tock. Tick tock.

ANOTHER DAWN IS DAWNING

Six in the morning, the sun's weak light radiated through the windows. Holly rubbed her eyes, stretched, felt a pleasant series of pops down her spine. She'd been up too late, hunched over the computer after trying and failing to sleep. The call ate at her. The hissing voice, the animosity. Someone truly hated Ethan Montclair.

She knew the couple better now. There was so much information online about the Montclairs. They were—had been—literary darlings for several years. The death of their child and the subsequent fall from grace had been documented in alarming detail. It made Holly uncomfortable. People did so love a tragedy.

She was trying to pin her mind on the something she was missing, the something that wasn't quite right about the house on Third Avenue and the stories of the people within. Her scattered dreams had been infused with horror scenes: women, covered in blood, screaming; children walking through walls, beckoning to her to follow.

She shoved a pod into the coffeemaker, stood watch as the

dark liquid purled in the cup. Took it and a granola bar into her small study, booted up her laptop.

She lived in the house she'd grown up in. The study was an annex off her bedroom, still filled with the detritus of her teenage years. Her parents had taken a maintenance-free condo in downtown Franklin a few years earlier, leaving the house to Holly and her sisters. Holly was the only one who wanted to stay in town. She wanted to be a part of the community. To change lives. To protect people. Her sisters got the hell out of Dodge the first chance they had, running to New York and LA, respectively, both pursuing acting careers, one on the screen, one on the stage, but Holly stayed. She was that kind of girl. The kind with staying power.

She was stuck, so she took a lesson from her dad's playbook. Drank her coffee, cleared her mind, and started over.

The first step was a global search for Sutton Montclair. The results came immediately, by the thousands. These were public people. There were as many articles online about the "incident," as Ethan Montclair had referred to it, as there were reviews and stories about the baby's death. There were a number of stories about Ethan Montclair and his stratospheric rise to the top of the literary world, and the subsequent disappointment of his canceled novel. The rise and fall of ages, the push and pull of celebrity; it was a fickle beast.

Holly chose to focus on Sutton's fall from grace.

She pulled out her notes from the night before. In a nutshell, Sutton Montclair, historical fiction author, had received a one-star review on a popular review site and had gone ballistic. It started simply, asking for the review to be changed, arguing that the review had no merit, and then, when the reviewer went public, saying she felt like she was being threatened, that she didn't feel safe and was scared, it all devolved. The attacks moved on to Montclair herself, who was disparaged in the most horrible ways. Her books were loaded up with one-star reviews, and she was forced to abandon all of her social media accounts. A trade magazine had done a huge piece on the situation, ascribing her actions to the phenomenon they called "Authors Behaving Badly."

There was a single quote in the piece from Sutton Montclair, taken from the blog on her website. A paragraph of denial.

This entire incident is a sham. My accounts have been hacked. Nothing you've seen with my name on it in the past forty-eight hours came from me. I know that sounds like an excuse in the aftermath of bad publicity, but I assure you, I would never, and have never, threatened a reviewer for not liking my books. I fully encourage open and honest reviews, and have never tried to censor anyone's opinion of my work, nor will I ever do so.

People hadn't bought it. There were nearly five thousand comments, where the battle had raged on for weeks.

Holly clicked further. Found a magazine article that mocked Sutton Montclair as a lunatic who stalked her reviewer. The article claimed the reviewer had been forced to take out an order of protection against the author.

Bingo. Finally, something to go on. Something Ethan Montclair hadn't mentioned.

Holly switched to her law enforcement database and began the search for the order of protection. It had been taken out in Kentucky, by a woman named Rosemary George. Holly found the order with ease on the first try. Reading it, she wondered again about Sutton Montclair's state of mind following the death of her son.

According to Rosemary George, Sutton had come to her house, knocked on the door, then fled, leaving a bag of canine excrement—that's how the order parsed it, canine excrement—aflame on the porch. She then proceeded to call the complainant at her place of business, demanding that she take down the offending review. When George hung up, Sutton had called

George's boss and claimed the woman was using the computers in the office for personal activities during business hours, which got George in all sorts of trouble. George consequently went online and told the world Sutton Montclair was insane and had threatened her livelihood, which started the brouhaha up all over again.

It was petty, stupid, tit for tat, and it got them both into trouble. The reviewer lost her job, and Montclair lost her publishing contract. According to the trades, Sutton delivered a day late and the publisher terminated the contract, which was atypical, but in this situation, Holly assumed it was an easy out.

Sutton hadn't shown in court to defend herself against the stalking charge, the order of protection had been put into place, and life continued on.

The stories had petered out in the past couple of months. Ethan Montclair was truthful there. He'd said things were calmed down, back on track.

But now Sutton Montclair was gone.

Holly sat back in the chair. To her, this was looking more and more like an unsettled young woman who'd been pushed over the edge. It was a shame, but there wasn't a crime here. She didn't think Ethan Montclair had hurt his wife, either, even if there was something else at play.

The phone rang. Moreno's name on the caller ID, no preamble when she greeted him.

"Missing Persons will be sending you a report shortly. They've found nothing. Sutton Montclair hasn't used her credit cards or passport. I'm afraid things aren't pointing in a good direction for her."

"Good morning, sir."

"Right. Morning. Talk to the husband again. We may mount a search, but a lot will depend on what he says. Maybe he'll crack."

"Roger that. I'll head there shortly, see if his story has changed at all. Has he done any media?"

"Not a lick. He's been holed up in the house since we left him yesterday. There's enough media to sink a ship out there, but he's not having any of it."

"Weird. You'd think he'd want to make a plea for her safe return, all that."

"You'd think. People react strangely. Anything you have pointing to the husband?"

"Honestly? No. It looks like Sutton Montclair was relatively unstable. And I get it. First her kid dies, then her career implodes. She's fighting with the husband. By all accounts, she's a complete head case, falling apart, total self-destruction. People have offed themselves for much less."

"Very true. I hear a *but* coming."

"But…"

Moreno laughed. "You're okay, Graham. I take it the call from last night is bugging you?"

"Yes, it is. It was so vehement. So completely convinced that Ethan hurt Sutton."

"You're right to be concerned. It was a burner phone. It will take more resources than we have to trace its origins. It could have been bought anywhere. Have you talked to her friends?"

"We have a coffee date late this morning. At the Starbucks they all hang out at, on the square."

"My advice? Bump it up. Get with them now, get with them individually. See if you recognize a voice."

"All right. I'll do that. The online situation is really the most interesting. The blogger who did the majority of the stories on Sutton, his name is Wilde, Colin Wilde. He spends his time doing Page Six–esque reports on authors and publishers. Silly stuff, faux-scandals. I didn't realize writers were such divas. His readership is rather large, considering, so he has enough of a platform to make trouble for people."

"Could he have something to do with this? Maybe he's try-ing to create his own news event?"

"It's possible, though violence seems to be a big leap. He strikes me as a creep but not one who has the guts to actually do any-thing, if you know what I mean."

"Keep on him."

"I read through Sutton's responses to the online accusations, and she doesn't seem hysterical to me. She seems rather cold, actually. Practical, I guess that's the word I'm looking for. Her verbiage is very precise."

"Could a PR flack have prepared it for her?"

"Sure, I guess so. I need to find this Wilde character. So far, there's no information on his whereabouts outside of a PO box. I was going to start digging into him this morning. And now you're up to speed."

"Keep me in the loop. And, Graham? Good job. If this gets any bigger, I'll partner you up with one of my detectives, give you some more brainpower."

She hung up half-flushed, happy for the praise, hoping she'd made a good impression, and grateful she might get a chance to work with someone who would assure she didn't leave any stones unturned.

She grabbed her notebook and dialed the first number on her list, Ivy Brookes. Ivy answered on the first ring.

"Officer Graham? Did you find her?"

"We haven't yet, ma'am. I know we're scheduled to talk later in the morning, but could I come by now? I have a few ques-tions I'd like to clear up."

"Sure, it will be good to talk. You know how it is with a bunch of women, you'll never get what you need. But can you give me an hour? The markets are about to open and I need to make a few calls before things get heated up."

"Sounds good. I'll see you soon."

She hung up and called the next. Phyllis Woodson. Ethan had called her Filly. Phyllis was more than happy to accommodate.

"Oh, yes, please. Come over right away."

Holly got the sense Phyllis needed to unburden herself. She promised to be there in thirty minutes. Maybe this would all break open and things would resolve themselves today.

Two of the four was a good start. It was nearly seven now. She'd reassess after the chats.

She shot the coffee, put her gun on her hip and a fresh notebook in her pocket, and headed to the car.

LIFE AS WE KNOW IT HAS ENDED

Drunk on words, on accomplishment, on the very idea of communicating the thoughts that had been logjammed in his head lo these many months, Ethan stumbled to the kitchen, made tea, and flipped on the television. A mistake. Sutton's face stared out at him from the screen. The crawler below said *Have You Seen This Woman?*

He turned up the volume. He counted back, trying to ascertain what day it was. Thursday? No, it was only Wednesday.

"Local writer Sutton Montclair is missing, and the Franklin police aren't speculating as to the reason for her disappearance, but people inside the investigation say the husband, Ethan Montclair, is a serious suspect—"

He flipped it off. He didn't need to see what people were saying, he could practically feel it coming from all sides. Everyone thought he'd done something to his wife.

Even he had to admit it all looked very bad.

He ignored the euphoria rattling inside him as he prepared a quick breakfast. He was famished; cereal wouldn't do. Frozen oatmeal, with some added nuts and seeds and raisins, orange juice, tea. He scarfed it all down, purposely ignoring the fact that his appetite had returned along with his words.

The words.

They were good. He knew this. He was his own worst critic—most writers are—but these words were transcendental. Intense and lyrical and stunning. Bill would be thrilled. The publisher would be thrilled. Sutton...

And that quickly, the pleasure fled. Sutton wouldn't be thrilled, because there was no way for him to let Sutton know.

The oatmeal felt like a lump of rock in his stomach.

Shake it off, his mind said.

You're a horrible person, his wife's shade replied.

The phone rang. The morning's round of media speculation was gearing up. He could see them moving around outside, hear the shouting and calls.

A text appeared on his phone. Robinson.

I see you're still inundated. Let me know if you need anything. You may want to think about making a statement. It might make them back off.

A chance to set things right. A chance to create some space. He wrote back almost greedily.

I'll do anything. Tell me what to say, I'll say it.

I'll be there in three minutes. Back door.

Of course it backfired. Of course it did. Ethan was terrible on camera, for all the wrong reasons.

Robinson was a family guy. He wanted Ethan to play the family angle. Which meant mentioning Dashiell. He wanted Ethan to talk about the marriage, how happy they were, how far they'd come since their son's death.

Ethan balked. Refused. All he wanted was to plead for Sutton's safe return. They argued for ten minutes, and then Ethan
quite effectively ended the discourse by marching to the front
door. He swung it open and waited for the frenzy to begin.

Holly saw the news alert pop up on her phone. She opened
the news app, watched the presser with astonishment. Ethan
Montclair looked like he'd been on a three-day bender. His
hair was sticking up; he was unshaven. His eyes held a glint,
and the lights from the multiple cameras facing him caught it
full-on. The result was a visage that was slightly demonic and
definitely unkempt. The very expensive front door hung half-
closed behind him. Joel Robinson was standing in the shadows, frowning.

She turned up the volume.

"Thank you for your attention to the disappearance of my wife,
Sutton Montclair. We are unsure at this time of her whereabouts,
and are very anxious to have her home. Sutton, honey, if you're
watching this, please call me. I'm worried sick for you. And you
lot—" he pointed to the journalists gathered, hanging on to his
every word "—instead of lounging around here, harassing me,
why don't you use your resources to look for my wife? Please, do
the right thing. Help me bring her home. That is all."

And the door shut.

There was a moment of collective silence, then Holly watched
the whole scene devolve. She could hear the cacophony of voices
through the microphone.

The reporter turned to the camera with a wide smile plastered
on. "There you have it, classic Ethan Montclair, telling off the
press. This is definitely going to feed the flames."

Inside the house on Third Avenue, Ethan clutched his head
in his hands. He was ashamed of himself. All he had to do was
keep himself together for five minutes, and instead, as had been

known to happen when he was put in front of a camera and microphone, he'd turned into a full-on raging dickhead. It was one of the major reasons his publishers rarely sent him on publicity jaunts; Ethan was a snob. He had a tendency toward priggishness that caused people to think him an asshole. And he did not like to be challenged.

Robinson was on the phone, scrambling to clean up the mess, giving a more cogent statement to someone. Finally, he hung up. "Well. That was flamboyant. Certainly going to get them off your back."

"Stow it, Joel. I'm tired."

"If you'd just listen…"

"I said stow it."

A sigh. "Listen, buddy. I'm on your side. But you have to work the media. Massage them. They are your ally here. You turn them against you and the court of public opinion becomes a disaster in the making."

"I have to do no such thing. They are as happy to let me drown as they would be to throw me a rope, because the drowning will make the ratings go higher."

Robinson's pants were a shade too big. He kept hitching them up over his hips.

"Remember that text, when you claimed you'd say anything I wanted?"

"I'm a rebel."

"No, Ethan, you're rapidly making yourself look like a suspect in your wife's disappearance. Get it together. Either you start doing things my way, or I'm out."

"Fine, then. Brilliant. Leave. I can handle this alone."

A flash of hurt, then Robinson nodded. "As you wish, friend. Good luck."

The back door closed quietly, and Ethan was alone again.

Shit.

FRANCOPHILES
IN FRANKLIN

Phyllis Woodson: tall, lanky, long-faced, slightly bucked teeth. Horsey. When she told Holly to call her Filly, she couldn't help but think the nickname fit. There was a baby attached to her like a barnacle in an oversize sling, another, slightly older, playing on a multicolored rubber pad. The husband was going to be working late—he was always working late—and dinner was already bubbling gently in the Crock-Pot. The house itself would have been modest in another neighborhood, but in downtown Franklin, it was a million-dollar cottage, done up in creams and sea green, impeccably decorated. Holly resisted the urge to make sure there was no mud on her boots when she came through the door.

They were at the kitchen table, a glass wheel somehow devoid of sticky handprints, sipping organic chamomile tea from Royal Doulton china.

Her father's voice in her head: *Remember, Holly, appearance is everything.*

"Mrs. Woodson—"

"Oh, Filly, please."

"Yes, ma'am. Filly. I've hit a dead end searching for Sutton. I can't seem to find anything that explains her actions. And there's no sign of her at all. So tell me. Is there anything we need to know about Ethan Montclair, and their marriage? Anything at all?"

A genteel sip, a clink of china. "Sutton is my best friend. We were pregnant together, did you know? Dashiell and *mon petit Henri* were only a few weeks apart." She said the name with an impeccable French accent: *moan pa-teet Ohn-ree.*

"Is your husband French?"

"Oh, no. I'm a Francophile. I've always been fascinated with France—the country, the language, the food, the wine. Sutton and I have been talking about going. Though I suppose that's never going to happen now." A small sob escaped her lips. "What has he done to her?"

"He, who?"

"Ethan, of course."

"Why do you think he did something to her?"

"It's the only logical explanation. Sutton isn't the type to run away. She's strong. One of the strongest women I've ever known. Smart. Cunning, even. Loyal and intense. If there was ever a person who wouldn't run in the face of adversity, it's Sutton."

"From what I've heard about her, she was broken. The death of her son, the problems with her publisher, the reviewer—"

"It's not true. I mean, yes, she was devastated when Dashiell died. Anyone would be. But she'd come out of it. The thing with her publisher, the reporter, the reviewer? It's been completely blown out of proportion."

"I've read the reports, the articles—"

"It was a stunt. I'm convinced."

"What?"

"She was writing a book. A new book. About how modern society is collapsing. In her spare time, that is. She was stuck in a contract she couldn't get out of, writing a book she hated and didn't want to do. Her publishing house had been bought, her longtime editor was canned, and they gave her some kid barely out of school who had no clout. Her old editor got in touch, told Sutton privately she'd take her on at the new house if she could get out of the contract.

"And Sutton was game. She told me she'd rather go up in flames than write the book they'd contracted for. She wanted to switch gears. Wanted to write something much more serious, postmodern. Like her husband does. The reviewer is a jerk, and the blogger, well, everyone knows not to believe anything that appears there. It's a parody of sorts."

"A parody."

"Yes. If you ask me, it seems things just…got out of hand."

Lips then pursed, she sat back and let Holly put together the pieces.

"So you're saying this whole thing was staged? She planned it all? That she attacked the reviewer for giving her a bad review, which was supposed to get her out of the contract, and things fell apart from there?"

"It's the only explanation. I mean, it went much further than anyone could anticipate, absolutely. That blogger, Wilde, he stuck his nose in and the whole thing blew up. The publisher was going to let her go quietly into that good night, she was out of her noncompete, and everything was moving along perfectly. Of course, when Ethan found out, he was beyond furious. I think he just didn't want the competition—Sutton is the better writer, and we all know it."

"Furious enough to hurt his wife?"

Filly's eyes were a watery blue. "You don't know Ethan Montclair very well, Officer Graham. So let me make this very clear. He has a temper. They fought, all the time. Screaming, plate-smashing fights. I've never seen anything like it. She was scared to death of him, of what he'd do to her when he was in a black rage. She wanted a divorce. She wanted out. She just didn't know how. If I'm going to make a guess at what happened? She finally told him she wanted an official split, and he killed her."

"All right. What about abuse?"

Silence.

"Mrs. Woodson? Were you aware of any physical or emotional abuse going on in the house?"

"What do you think? I've already told you how they fight."

"But arguing isn't hitting. Did he hit her?"

"I don't know. And that's the truth. I never saw any black eyes or bruises, but that doesn't mean anything. She was scared of him. That I do know."

"Can anyone corroborate your story, Mrs. Woodson?"

Filly stood and started clearing the tea things. "I don't know who else she confided in. Like I said, she was *my* best friend." Her tone was mulish, as if she'd been caught lying.

"Your best friend, who you were planning to go to Paris with?"

"France in general. It was a dream for both of us."

"Had you made any plans?"

"Nothing concrete. Nothing official. We were only daydreaming. It's not like we could abandon the boys and the babies, and run off."

"Is it possible Mrs. Montclair was doing more than daydreaming?"

"Anything is possible, Officer."

"That's good to know. Is there anything else?"

"She didn't get along with her mother. Not at all. Siobhan Healy is her name, and that is a seriously vile woman. None of us can stand her. She's so…gauche. Crass. Obsessed with money, and she's a drinker, too. She and Sutton couldn't be more opposite."

"Does her mother live nearby?"

"Yes. She's out by Leiper's Fork. I'm sure Ethan has the number. He doesn't like her, either. No one does."

"Great. Thank you. You've been very helpful."

Woodson showed her out. As the door was closing behind her, she heard the baby begin to squall. She turned and caught the handle before it closed, tucked her head back inside.

"One last thing, Mrs. Woodson. About their baby. Any chance something else went on there?"

Phyllis Woodson's long face creased, her mouth shrinking into a thin, sharp line. "Absolutely not. Dashiell was an angel, and they both loved him dearly."

STOP THE MADNESS

Then

They're fighting again.

They are easily heard: their voices, vicious and stressed, carry so well. They are taking it out on each other. They are punishing one another.

You were supposed to be watching him.

You weren't supposed to come home falling-down pissed.

How could you think I am responsible? You're the one who tricked me, remember?

I love you.

I hate you.

Their words seep into my bones. How has it come to this? How has the hate between them grown to this level?

We sip tea and look at each other, listening. Do they not know we can hear them? Do they not care? It's understandable to a point, their loss, so great, so unimaginable. No one should have to bury a child. No one should bear that burden.

And yet…people do. All the time. Children die, incrementally, all the time, whether their hearts stop or their babysitter decides to teach them the birds and the bees or their parents do drugs and beat them. They all die, little pieces falling off them as they age. Some go in the ground; others, the ones who are still breathing, are stripped of their inner joy.

It is inevitable. It is life. Even if they make it out of their adolescence, especially then, the sparks that flame them into individuality are extinguished.

Is it better to be a walking corpse, a shroud of who you could be, or leave this world before the disappointment of your lack of potential emerges?

Philosophy. Such a devious monster.

But the yelling, the yelling.

We sip more tea and look wide-eyed at each other.

Should we do something? Should we call someone?

If we do, the police will come, and it will be embarrassing for them both.

But she will be safe.

We must keep her safe.

We make the call. Wait, and watch, as the cruiser pulls up. The officer marches to the door, knocks three times. Another car slides around the corner.

The screaming stops.

We smile.

It's hard, keeping up this facade for everyone. You know I like the fighting, don't you? You're putting it together, I know you are.

SHE WHO KNEW
HER BEST

Now

Holly left the Woodson home with a spark in her stomach. She'd known there was more going on. She needed corroboration about the fighting, and the fear, and the next stop was Ivy Brookes. The woman who was by all appearances the Montclairs' *real* best friend.

She decided to let the conversation move organically, like it had with Phyllis Woodson.

In comparison to the sumptuous Woodson home, Ivy Brookes's condo was spartan, practically empty. Not at all homey or welcoming. It almost looked like a sterile hotel room. It was also diagonally down the street from the Montclairs as the crow flies, though the entrance was on Fourth Avenue.

Brookes waved her in, saw her taking in the living room. "I know, isn't it awful? I travel so much I've never seen the need to decorate. Coffee?"

"Water is fine, thanks."

Ivy handed over a bottle of Fiji water, took a thick white mug half-full of murky brown liquid for herself, and gestured to the sterile couch. Holly took a seat.

"So, Officer Graham. What can I help you with?"

"I'm going to cut to the chase, Ms. Brookes. What do you think has happened to Sutton Montclair?"

"Honestly? As much as I hate to say this, I think it all got to be too much for her and she probably took her own life. I expect you'll find her body in a hotel room somewhere. She was on the knife's edge lately."

"How so?"

She sipped the coffee, her look faraway, as if she were remembering something awful. "Seriously? The woman lost her baby, her career, and was precariously close to losing her husband, all in a short year time frame. Things weren't going according to plan."

"How did you and Sutton meet?"

Ivy's face broke into a smile. "She bought me a coffee. It was pouring rain, one of those drenching downpours. I dashed from the parking lot into Starbucks, but when I got in there, realized I'd left my wallet in my car. I plopped down at a table to wait for the rain to let up, and I happened to sit next to her. She asked me what was wrong, bought me a latte, and we started to chat. I was surprised when she said she was thirty-five. She looked so much younger than that. I thought she was my age. For a while, at least. Then all hell broke loose and her world fell apart. Not that you can blame her."

"Phyllis Woodson seems to think Sutton is exceptionally strong and self-reliant."

Ivy scoffed. "A hamster would seem strong and self-reliant to Filly. I've never met someone so utterly without a backbone."

"Wow. You're actually friends?"

Ivy shut her eyes and touched a hand to her mouth. When she spoke again, her tone was apologetic. "I know, that came out terribly. Yes, we're all friends. You know how it is with a group of women. Not everyone loves everyone else to the nth degree.

We all tolerate Filly because Sutton seems to have a real connection to her. Filly isn't the sharpest tool in the shed. I never really understood why Sutton let her hang around. That's not true. It was the baby.

"But once Dashiell died, they really had nothing in common anymore. The rest of us don't have small kids—though Rachel and Susannah are trying to get pregnant, but they wouldn't tell Sutton that. Why hurt her? Ellen's kids are older, in college. Filly was the one with the step-by-step instructions. That woman is a walking *What to Expect When You're Expecting* encyclopedia." She gave a delicate little shudder. "The things they'd talk about, put you right off your coffee. Sorry. You have children?"

"No. Talk to me about the baby for a minute."

Ivy closed her eyes again, as if remembering. "He was such a cute kid. Of course they blamed each other. The finding was SIDS, but what is that, really? The baby stopped breathing, for some unknown reason. They found him on his stomach, that I do know."

"*They* found him? They were together?"

"No. Sutton…Sutton found him. Ethan, well, he blamed her. She wasn't supposed to put the baby down on his stomach."

"He was old enough to roll over, right?"

"I guess. I don't really know the milestones. No, Sutton put him down, and a few hours later he was dead. Ethan will never not blame her. Even if it was an accident."

"You don't think it was intentional, do you?"

Ivy's eyes were clear chips of ice blue. "Did Ethan tell you the story? About how they got pregnant?"

"No. Did they have difficulties?"

"You could say that. Sutton didn't want to have children. Ever. She wasn't the mother type."

"It was an accident?"

"I guess you could call it that. Ethan switched out her birth control pills. He didn't tell her until after she had the baby. And she hated him for it."

"Seriously?"

"Yes. She felt raped. Completely violated. You know, in the beginning, she wanted to abort, but I talked her out of it."

"Why?"

Ivy sighed. "She didn't want to be a mother. Didn't want to have a child. Everyone supported her in that, except for me. I was the only one who thought she should keep the baby. Everyone else wanted her to get rid of it. But I knew that would put a fork in their marriage, once and for all. They belong together, Ethan and Sutton. They complete each other. They just don't always know it."

"So they fought?"

"Oh, yeah. They fought. You're the police, did you not see the list of domestic calls in the past year?"

"I did. Sutton never pressed charges."

"Of course she didn't. She never would. She and Ethan are explosive."

"She also claimed she never made the calls."

"Well, how's that possible? How else would the police find out they were arguing?"

"I'm inclined to agree. Abused women often regret their calls for help, especially if their aggressor is still nearby."

"Very true. Back to the baby. In the end, Sutton waited too long, and then the choice was made for her. I don't know that she ever truly bonded with Dashiell, though. Ethan, on the other hand, was overjoyed. He loved that child."

"And she didn't?"

"No, she did, don't get me wrong. But you have to wonder, sometimes, if she was in a self-destructive mode, whether she wasn't as careful as she could have been. I mean, everyone knows not to put babies on their stomachs. And she was drunk when she came home that night. Ethan told me, after."

Holly chose to ignore that last statement for the time being. "Sutton was often self-destructive?"

"At times. That's why I'm so worried about her."

"So for the record, you don't think Ethan had anything to do with Sutton's disappearance?"

Brookes chewed on her lower lip. "I don't know if I'd phrase it that way. Sutton may have gone off to punish him, but if she did, it's because Ethan drove her to it. His standards were impossible to keep up with. And he's not been writing, which makes him utterly insufferable. He may not have pulled the trigger, but if she's dead, he's certainly responsible."

"So he *was* abusive."

"You didn't hear that from me." She looked at her watch, jumped up. "Goodness, I am so sorry, but I have another appointment. Please excuse me. And if there's anything else I can do, don't hesitate to get in touch. I am worried sick about her. I really hope she's just holed up somewhere, making us all sweat."

"Thanks for your time."

Holly went to her car, reviewed her notes, adding a bit here and there as she recalled something. Two women, two somewhat disparate views of who Sutton Montclair really was.

Her voice mail was blinking. A message from Ellen Jones. Holly hit Play.

"Officer Graham, I will be home in about an hour. Please feel free to stop by."

Holly looked at the car's clock. *Good timing, Mrs. Jones.*

AN UNEXPECTED SURPRISE

Then

"I have a secret," Ethan said.

"Oh?" Sutton poured the wine into the large glasses she favored, the ones without stems, so the bowl sat directly on the table. He didn't like them—the stem served a purpose, to keep fingers off the bowl, so the heat wouldn't interfere with the wine's opening process—but she thought they were fun and had consigned all the traditional Waterford stemware to the attic. At least she'd let him keep the lowballs.

"Out with it, then. What's this big secret?"

He took a mouthful of the Brunello. He'd opened it especially; had decanted it for an hour. This taste was like heaven. Rich, spicy, bold. *Be bold, Ethan. Be very bold.*

"It's ancient history, really. You'll have a laugh when I tell you."

She was making stir-fry, with chicken, and the wooden spoon hovered over the wok. He saw a shadow cross her eyes.

"If you've had an affair, I don't want to hear about it. Truly, Ethan, I don't. After the last time...it nearly broke me."

"Sutton, no, it's nothing like that. I swore to you I would never be unfaithful again, and I've been true to my word. Never mind. Forget it. I was being silly. I'll set the table, and we can have dinner. It looks delicious."

She set the wooden spoon in its pewter holder. Crossed her arms on her chest.

Shit. This wasn't how he wanted her tonight, defenses up. He wanted them to have a nice, normal evening. Dinner, a lovely wine, maybe a little adult playtime before the baby had to nurse again.

He stepped to her, massaging the back of her neck. Nuzzled for a moment. She let him. She'd been so much more physical since the baby, the whole pregnancy, really. She liked being touched, and not only during sex. It was as if the old Sutton was back, the woman he knew in the beginning, ravenous for the touch of his skin on hers.

She smelled like milk and baby and honeysuckle, a weird combination that managed to be both off-putting and erotic at the same time.

"Taste the wine. Tell me what it reminds you of."

She shut her eyes, sniffed, took a sip.

"The dinner at the vineyard in Montalcino. The wine tasted like liquid gold. When I told the owner he laughed at me."

"He didn't laugh at you, he was delighted, and wanted to change the name of the wine to Sutton's. I've bought a case. That's my secret. I thought you'd like it for special occasions."

She opened her eyes. The warmth in them was hard to miss. They shone with pleasure, her beautiful eyes, luminous and wide, the gray blue of late-summer evenings, thickly rimmed in lashes women would pay money for.

"What a lovely surprise. This is a special occasion, I take it? The outing of your secret?"

Good, she was back to playful mode. He kissed her, lingering and slow, until he felt the muscles unclench in her back and she leaned into him, soft and wanting, and gave him a regretful look when he pulled away.

"There's more, I'm afraid. I used the monthly deposit into Dashiell's bank account to buy the wine. I hope you're not angry."

"That you're drinking away your son's future? That the poor child will have nothing left to live on when we pass, much less go to college? You're forgiven." She took another sip, comically smacked her lips. "Actually, I heartily approve of your fiscal ir-responsibility."

Goodness, she *was* in a good mood.

"I think you have another secret," she said. "You can tell me. I swear I won't be upset. I think it's high time you told me any-way, don't you? I mean, I already know."

Could she possibly be serious? "About Dashiell?"

"You have a secret about Dashiell? Let me guess. You're not his real father. No, that's not it. I'm not his real mother." Her eyes began to dance, and she stepped back, a wide smile on her face. "No, silly. I heard you typing. You've started a new book, haven't you?" She snapped his leg with the dish towel. "That's why you bought the fabulous wine. I can't believe you've been holding out on me. What's it about? Please tell me."

Ethan turned away, busied himself with the wine. *Shit. Shit, shit, shit. Lie. Lie, right the fuck now.*

But Sutton had already caught on. So perceptive, his wife.

"You haven't started a book."

"No."

"Then what did you mean earlier? You have a secret about Dashiell? Did you drop him or something?" She sighed, huge and gusty, the wine sweet on her breath. "I've told you a thou-sand times, you need to pick him up with both hands, not try to hoist him out of the crib like a football—"

"Darling, please. Stop. I didn't drop the boy. He's fine. Let it go, okay? Let's just drink the wine and have dinner."

But that wasn't going to happen; he could see the anger simmering in her eyes. It all turned on a dime with them. It always did.

"Tell me what you've done to him."

He didn't answer. She gave dinner a stir.

"I'll give you one more chance. Talk."

Oh, he was so royally, completely screwed. But the weight of it was dragging him down. It was time to be out with it. She'd hate him, but she'd forgive him, eventually.

"It's a funny thing, actually. When we're old, you'll look back on this moment and laugh and laugh."

Silence.

He took a sip for courage. "Before you got pregnant, I switched your birth control pills out with sugar pills."

More silence. Then she took a step toward him, her face aflame. "What? What did you just say?"

He held up his wineglass, smiling. "I knew you needed a little nudge toward getting pregnant. I knew you had doubts. I figured if it happened, great. And it did. Look what we made." He gestured toward the baby. Dashiell was parked in his seat on the dining room table in his carrier, deeply asleep, a small mobile of butterflies hanging above him, barely disturbed by his breath. "He's perfect!"

Sutton's face went blank with shock.

"I wanted a child so badly, and I knew you did, as well. Deep down, you did. And it's been so good for us. He's been so good for us. Our marriage has never been stronger. You love him so much, and so do I. He's made everything right between us."

He was babbling now. She'd turned inward, wasn't present anymore, not in this room, though her body was standing next to the stove, methodically stirring the contents of the wok.

He'd seen it happen when she was thinking hard about a book idea, assumed his face did the same thing when he came up with a line and turned it over and over in his brain. He stepped closer to force her mind back to him, to the present. To the truth.

"Darling, forgive me. I promised myself I'd never mention it, but clearly, that wasn't the right thing to do. You have a right to know what I did. It was wrong. So wrong. But look at our son."

The words were low, broken. "You bastard."

"Please, please forgive me, Sutton. Because I want us to try again. I want to have another child."

He tried to take her in his arms again, but she turned and fled, splashing him with vegetables and hot oil as she rushed away, into the garage. She slapped the button as she went out, and the door began to rise. The house door slammed, her car turned over. She peeled out of the garage and was gone before he'd made it to the door.

She didn't come back for several hours. When she did, she was drunk.

And the next day, Dashiell was dead.

A VIDEO IS WORTH A THOUSAND WORDS

Before she went to Jones's place, Holly checked her email in the car, looking for the missing persons report Sergeant Moreno had promised. It was there, black and white: no signs of bank account use, Montclair's passport and license unflagged at any port of call, email untouched, social media dark. Sutton Montclair had simply disappeared.

The lack of activity wasn't good news. All they had to go on now were witness statements, which were already contradictory, and the internet, which was a cesspool of possibilities.

She glanced through the rest of her email, saw one from an address she didn't recognize. It was halfway down the page. The subject line was KENTUCKY.

Thinking about the random call she'd received, she clicked it open. A video began to play.

Holly watched as a woman, who she immediately identified as Sutton Montclair, appeared on a small porch. She was wearing a trench coat and sunglasses, carrying a small brown bag. She placed the bag squarely on the mat, bent down. A few seconds later, a small fire began, tiny flames shooting up. She waited a second to make sure the bag was well aflame, flipped the bird toward the front door, then rang the doorbell and scurried out of the frame.

The video ended with someone from the house opening the door.

Holly sat back and shook her head. What the heck was this?

She played it back a few times, looking for a date stamp, any identifying information. The video looked like it had been shot from a home security camera. But who had sent it? The email address was a jumble of letters and numbers; how it had slipped past her spam filter was rather a miracle.

It didn't take a genius to figure things out. She went back through her notes, looked for the name of the reviewer. Rosemary George. She found her information, address, and phone, and placed the call.

"Hello?"

"Is Ms. George available? My name is Holly Graham. I'm with the Franklin Police in Tennessee."

"Is this about that awful woman who's gone missing?"

"Sutton Montclair? Yes, ma'am."

"I have no comment."

And the phone went dead.

Holly rolled her eyes. She didn't relish a drive to Kentucky to dig out this woman's story. She called back. The phone rang off the hook.

She called a friend she had in the tech division. "Holly Golightly, what's up?"

"Hey, Jim. If I forward you an email, can you take it apart for me? It was sent anonymously, but I want to know where it came from."

"Sure. I can trace the IP address. Shouldn't be a big deal. Send away."

"On its way. How long will it take?"

"Hang tight, I can tell you in a second." She heard typing and clicking. "It's local, a Franklin IP. Huh. That's weird."

"What?"

"Well, I've been running all the stuff from the Montclair case, right? This IP address matches their router."

"But the email, it's all sorts of gibberish. Who owns the email account?"

"You ready for this?"

"Let me guess. Ethan Montclair."

"Yep."

"But why in the world would he send me an anonymous video of his wife on some woman's doorstep?"

"No idea. But here's one more weird thing. The password Montclair gave us wasn't accurate."

"No?"

"No. It was written on a Post-it on the laptop lid—*I love Ethan Montclair.*"

"How sweet."

"Barf. Regardless, that's not the right password. I had to mess around with it, but I was able to crack it. I hooked in my UFED, knocked it out in ten seconds flat."

"'Cause you're a regular crackerjack IT dude, Jim. What the hell is a UFED?"

"Universal Forensic Extraction Device. Mine's called Sally. I can pull information from any encrypted device you give me. I don't need a password or fingerprint to get into a phone when Sally gets her way."

"Um, thank you, Sally?"

"Yes, thank you, Sally. Don't you want to know what the right password was?"

"Enlighten me."

"Ethan killed our baby."

GOOD TIMING, OFFICER

Now

A car pulled up outside. Ethan glanced out the window, saw it was Officer Graham. He also saw the bevy of news vans and microphones part before the blue-and-white car.

"Bloody hell."

Graham looked neither right nor left, ignoring the shouts and cries from the media. She came onto the porch and he sensed movement from the crowd, a surge toward the house, but she turned and said something, and the movement ceased. They stayed on alert, like hunting dogs on point, but the groundswell was sufficiently halted.

He made sure to turn his head away and stand behind the door when he opened it, just in case. Graham came inside briskly, and Ethan heard the clatter of cameras snapping.

"You're suddenly a very popular man," she said.

"Thanks to you."

A sharp look. "Hey, I come in peace. And I didn't call the media. They were already on your house when Sergeant Moreno and I left, after you reported your wife missing."

"Who told them, then?"

"I'm sorry, Mr. Montclair, but I have no idea. They do monitor our dispatch calls. Perhaps someone recognized your address and put it all together."

"Have you found something? Is that why you're here?"

"Nothing yet. I had some more questions."

"All right. Can I offer you a cup of tea?"

"Sure. Milk and sugar."

For some reason he didn't want to tell her they didn't use real milk and sugar; it seemed silly, trivial. He'd put the stevia and almond milk in the cup and let her deal with it.

He prepped the tea while she stood at the counter, eyeing the stain.

"What happened there?"

"Blueberries."

"Looks like blood to me."

The spoon clattered in the cup. "That's what happens to real marble when something acidic is left out on it overnight. We made smoothies for dessert one night. I didn't realize a few blue-berries had escaped until I found Sutton down here the next day, crying. I'd been telling her from the start the counter was going to be ruined quickly, we shouldn't get the real marble for ex-actly this reason, but she refused to listen. I was right, of course."

"Was this before or after the baby?"

"Before," he said, knowing it came out curt. "Here's your tea."

She blew on it, took a sip. To her credit, though he could tell the taste wasn't to her liking, she sipped some more, then nod-ded politely and set the cup down. "Thank you. Now, the rea-son I'm here. The protective order you submitted against the reporter who was trying to interview Sutton wasn't granted."

"I know that."

"The judge found there was no cause."

"I know that, too. Idiot. Sutton was terrified of the man, and the judge blew us off."

"I talked to the judge. He said you had no cause. That it was only a few phone calls."

"A few phone calls that made my wife sleep with the lights on. Yes, totally benign."

"What did the reporter—" She looked at her notebook. "His name is Colin Wilde, correct?"

"That's the bastard."

"According to the report, Mr. Wilde claims all he did was call and ask for comment after he'd talked with the reviewer, who goes by the anonymous moniker UMB. This UMB claimed Sutton came to her house. Wilde called you for comment. Sutton hung up on him, and you filed the order of protection. Correct?"

"It's a bit more complicated than that, but you've hit the gist."

"Were you aware that the reviewer, UMB, filed an order of protection against Sutton?"

He was silent.

"Her name is Rosemary George. She lives in a tiny house in rural Kentucky, gets by on social security for the most part. In the report, she claims Sutton came to her house, beat on her door, and when she refused to answer, lit a small fire on the front step, and ran. They have video of the incident. UMB decided not to prosecute. Your wife dodged a very serious bullet."

"I can't imagine…"

Graham put her phone on the counter. "It's queued up for you. I thought you might want to see it."

She hit Play, and he watched in lurid black and white as his wife lost her ever-loving mind on a stranger's doorstep.

When it was finished, he had no words.

Graham pocketed her phone.

"Thank you for sending this. It does help ascertain her state of mind."

"What the bloody hell are you on about? I didn't send it. I've never seen it before."

"That's odd. It came from your IP address."

"Trust me, Officer Graham. I didn't send that to you. There's been a mistake."

She gave him a completely inscrutable look, and Ethan had a moment's qualm. He shouldn't be talking to her without Robinson. He knew this. But she stepped away from it.

"I'll have my people look into that, maybe it was a mistake. Let's talk about the video. As you can see, Sutton was acting quite threatening that day. Has she ever been threatening or violent in your presence, sir?"

Ethan shook his head. He couldn't believe this. *She couldn't be that stupid.*

"Of course not. She's a mild woman, if anything, too mild. She's been trampled upon by a slew of people, and she just sits back and takes it. She cries and breaks down, sure, but she's never been violent." *Not to a stranger, that is.*

"The hospitalization. Can you give me some details?"

Ethan didn't want to remember that night, the fear lodged in his heart as his beautiful, brilliant wife threatened to jump off the third-story portico. Her hair caught in the breeze, a storm coming in from the west, the clouds roiling black, screaming, trying to get the windows open, fingers clawing at the painted-over frame. Swearing, over and over, she wasn't to blame, that she'd done nothing wrong. And why wouldn't he believe her?

"She couldn't take the pressure. She said she wanted to die, that having her career collapse so soon after the baby's death was too much for her to take. Too much for anyone to endure. I called Ivy, she came over, and together we talked Sutton off the ledge. I have a friend in town who's a psychiatrist. I called him, he agreed to have her involuntarily admitted. What's it called, Title 33 or something?"

"Yes."

He was quiet for a moment. "It absolutely tore me apart, watching them take her. She was so upset, so confused."

"Who wrote the commitment papers?"

"Dr. McBean. Gregory McBean."

"I know him. He's a good doc."

"He is. We were able to get her stabilized and out of there after a week. She seemed fine after that, quiet, subdued, embarrassed. She had to take medication. She pushed me away for a while, understandably. But that was all behind us. We've been good for weeks."

"What did you fight about?"

Ethan shifted uncomfortably. "It was stupid. Nothing."

"Clearly it was something, Mr. Montclair."

"I don't want you to think badly of Sutton. Or of me, for that matter."

"I'm just trying to gather facts. Judgment is for other people."

It was meant to be such an innocuous, comforting statement, but Ethan felt the chill spread through his body. All he could imagine was a long counter of dark brown wood and thirteen faces staring down at him.

"She asked how my book was coming. I haven't been writing, and we were sniping at each other about the bills. I told her to mind her own business, and stomped off."

Tears started to gather, damn it, there was nothing he could do. "I told her to leave me alone. It looks like she took me seriously."

The cop rubbed her neck while he pulled himself back together. Finally, she said, "Mr. Montclair, none of this is adding up for me."

"I suppose not. It isn't for me, either."

A TRAIL EMERGES

Holly forwarded the video and her write-up of her conversation with Montclair to Moreno, then headed toward Ellen Jones's home. She was trying to keep an open mind. Trying to stay focused, to be willing to see all sides of the story.

Ethan killed our baby.

The password floated into her head, and Holly reminded herself that despite all of Montclair's bravado, he was their only suspect. She knew he was lying, had to be, Jim wasn't wrong about things to do with computers. Though God, Montclair sounded so adamant. And seemed so surprised by the video. Was he simply a brilliant actor?

She didn't know anymore.

She felt like his denial was the first major inconsistency in his statements, and had made a note of it for the record. She hadn't wanted to run the risk of screwing things up with him, not while he was still being so forthcoming, so she'd pressed on in the interview. She hoped that was the right thing to do.

Holly almost felt like Sutton Montclair was speaking to her. Directing her. Giving her clue after clue, a trail of bread crumbs to follow. It seemed like she'd given each of her friends a bit of the story. She had her husband set up to take the fall.

Was this on purpose? Or was there something else going on?

Holly's baser instincts wanted to grill Ethan Montclair for hours, but that wasn't the way things worked. She needed him to cooperate for as long as he would.

No, getting combative wasn't the right approach. She would finish her interviews, then maybe she'd go talk to him again, see what she could shake loose.

Ellen Jones's home on the outskirts of downtown was as frank and straightforward as she was. A ranch with classic lines bordering on severe, the interior was fully updated, gray with white molding, populated by modern furniture and appliances that looked brand-new. The entire living room wall was built-in bookshelves, the books within shelved alphabetically, broken into fiction and nonfiction. No-nonsense, this librarian. Holly thought she might like Ellen if they'd met under different circumstances.

Jones sat primly, her legs crossed at the ankles, but there was fire in her eyes and her voice as Holly questioned her. She laid out what she knew, and let Ellen run with it. The librarian was clear, and she was emphatic.

"No, no, no. Sutton wasn't strong and self-reliant, but she wasn't a pushover, either. She was just a normal woman, an artist—a good one, too—who was put in two untenable situations in a row. I have a tendency toward believing she's simply decided to take a break, and will come back in a few days. I can't wrap my mind around Ethan actually hurting her. I've never known him to be abusive, or mean. He loves her, and she loves him. They're competitive with each other, without admitting it, absolutely. But they're partners in this marriage. Losing the baby brought them closer, even if they have been having issues. After her showdown with the reviewer, he stood by her."

"Is it possible she instigated the situation with the reviewer? Mrs. Woodson indicated it might have been a setup, a ploy to get out of a contract that went awry."

Ellen looked amused for a moment. "Knowing Sutton? She's a firecracker, Officer. She didn't like taking no for an answer, and her agent and publisher were pushing her hard to write a book she absolutely loathed."

"So she blew up her career instead of writing the book?"

"No, she wouldn't do that. Sutton wasn't an idiot. No one wants the kind of publicity she got. No one deserves it, either. I believe her when she says her accounts were hacked. She made one comment on the whole thing. The rest took on a life of its own."

"And the book she was writing? How does that work?"

"Normally she wrote her own books, but this was a one-time thing, a contract-for-hire job, finishing the final book in a popular series by an author who passed away. They paid her a wad of money to do it, too. When she started it was all fine, but before it was published, the estate dictated some changes to the story that she didn't agree with. She's a professional, though, and made the adjustments they wanted. She knew it was all part of the game."

"What was the book about?"

"The official title was *The Bedouin's Dream Bride*. She called it *Sharif and His Naughty Nightstick*. Cracked me up when she talked about it. It was terrible material, a worse story, and yes, she was appalled that she was forced to write it, but she was a professional, and she was absolutely fulfilling the contract when things blew up. The comment kerfuffle tore her apart, and it wasn't fair, it wasn't even her own story. Now, her most recent, it's a Victorian high-fantasy novel, with a Jack the Ripper–style murderer, and it is fantastic. Impeccably researched, vicious, scary, romantic. It's such a shame the contract was canceled, but I bet down the road she'll publish it herself, or someone will get excited by this situation and want it."

"But the book she was attacked about—"

"Someone took exception to the work-for-hire book—someone

always does take exception—and Sutton rightly defended herself. It spun out of control, but that wasn't her fault."

"Sutton made one comment, then ducked back into her hole, and said nothing more about it?"

"Yes. Absolutely. The second she saw where things were headed, she disengaged. Everything that happened after was on the reviewer and that jerk blogger."

"I have to show you something, Mrs. Jones." Holly grabbed her cell and opened the video.

"This is Sutton Montclair, in a stalking incident at the reviewer's house."

Ellen watched the video impassively. When it was over, she shook her head. "I hate to break it to you, but that's not Sutton."

"What do you mean?"

"I'll grant you, the hair and clothes look right, but whoever that is, it's not Sutton. A—Sutton's no dummy. She'd never stalk a reviewer. B—Sutton is much taller than this person. Thinner, too."

"The plates on the car match a rental car reservation from south Nashville in Sutton's name."

Ellen didn't blink. "Then someone's playing a very cruel joke on you, Officer. Because trust me, that is not Sutton Montclair."

I HEAR YOU'RE
MISSING A WIFE

At 6:00 p.m. Ethan's mobile rang, jarring him from his writing trance. He glanced at the caller ID, and his stomach flipped. Bloody hell. Colin Wilde, the so-called reporter who'd driven Sutton quite literally mad after Dashiell's death. How the hell had he gotten Ethan's new number? They'd changed everything, for Sutton's protection as well as to shake that stupid reviewer who made their lives such hell. Idiotic Sutton, letting her emotions get the better of her. It had landed her in the loony bin, and she'd never really forgiven him. She had no idea the trouble and cash it had cost him to get her an involuntary commitment instead of going to jail.

Ethan hadn't given Officer Graham the whole story. She didn't need to know every detail, especially when none of it would help bring Sutton back.

When Dashiell died, Wilde had pursued Sutton relentlessly, wanting to do stories, wanting to interview them, sending emails, leaving messages on their voice mail, asking if they planned to have a replacement child. The asshole had used that term exactly, *replacement child*.

When they hadn't responded, Wilde had finally disappeared. But then the online campaign against Sutton began, and Wilde resurfaced, doggedly calling nightly until Sutton finally cracked.

Ethan had to take the man seriously. He knew this as surely as he knew the sun rose in the east and set in the west. With luck, Wilde was just trying to get inside the story, to gain his precious scoop. Then again, he'd screwed them before. What would stop him from doing it again?

The stories he'd written about their family when the baby died had been, in a word, alluring. Surprising, really, because Wilde wasn't even a real reporter, not a journalist in the sense Ethan had grown up with. No, Wilde was worse than the worst hacks at the Fleet Street rags, a news blogger, as he called himself, as if he could lend importance to his own opinion by adding the word *news* in front of the ubiquitously common term *blogger*. He curried favor with his subjects by playing into the base hatred of the online mob, and set his flying monkeys on people who disagreed with him. That's how the fracas started with Sutton in the first place. Ethan had a sneaking suspicion the whole reviewer incident had been instigated by Wilde, though he couldn't prove a damn thing.

Ethan doubted Wilde made money in the endeavor. His site was littered with sponsor rolls and crowded with logos from strange companies Ethan had never heard of. Wilde was a fraud.

But.

But.

There were things about Colin Wilde he couldn't, wouldn't, ever admit. Because the things Wilde knew about them, about him, were…worrisome. He didn't want to talk to the reporter, but he was afraid not to. At least he should try to rein him in. Wilde had done so much damage already; with this chewy steak of a story, he could reignite all the fallow flames.

The ringing stopped. Ethan was filled with dread and relief. So he hadn't told Officer Graham everything. So what? What was he supposed to say, that he wanted to blame Wilde for Sutton's disappearance? That all the things that went wrong in their lives he wanted to park at Wilde's door and light on fire?

His Scotch was gone. He went to the kitchen for a drink of water. Maybe a cup of tea. They had one old-fashioned rotary-dial wall phone in the kitchen. It was a relic of Sutton's first home, something she'd clung to. Ethan found it reminded him of his childhood, as well. He stared at it, holding his tiny mobile, thinking about how truly fucked-up his life had gotten in the intervening years. The mobile began to trill again. Wilde.

Ethan swallowed, pressed the Talk button, launched the tirade.

"I told you never to call me again. Fuck you, fuck off, leave us alone, and don't you dare write anything about my wife, or I'll sue you for defamation."

There was no slamming down a phone anymore, but he'd dropped it to his waist where he could see without his reading glasses and was hitting the End button when he heard Wilde shout, "Wait. Don't hang up. I know where your wife is."

Ethan hesitated. And damn it, he knew better. *Hang up. Hang up and be done with him.*

But Colin Wilde had created this rift in Ethan's world by becoming so overly involved in his life, in his wife, and as much as it infuriated him to admit, if anyone knew what had happened to Sutton, it *could* be Wilde. He had that uncanny ability to know what they were doing, at all times. He was as much a stalker of Sutton as Sutton had been to the reviewer.

He put the phone to his ear.

"Where is she?"

A laugh, brash and mean. "Now, now, that tone won't do. Come on, Ethan. You need to ask me nicely. You know you want to."

Ethan felt the familiar rush of hate and fear. Bile rose in his stomach. Wilde's goal may have been to terrorize Sutton, but Ethan had not been left out of the charade. It had started with him. The mistakes he'd made were going to haunt him forever, and he'd come to terms with this. He'd been silent for so long, though, that Ethan actually thought they were free of Wilde, of his knowledge and accusations.

He did know that bowing down wasn't the way to make things come to a head.

"You have one minute to share everything you know, and if you don't, I'm going to call up the very nice police officer who's been hanging around and tell her to come arrest you for obstruction."

"Oh, pu–lease. You won't. You've never had the balls to do anything. That's why Sutton hated you so much."

"You don't know where she is. You're just playing with me."

"Fine. Believe that if you want. But I saw her leave your house in the middle of the night, and I saw her get into a car. I have a license plate. Call the cops, and I will deny it all. Give me $50,000 and I'll tell you the rest. There's a place, Gentry's Farm. It's…"

"I know where it is, you sick fuck."

"I figured you'd remember. You have half an hour. And leave your phone at home."

The line went dead. Empty air. Nothing.

Ethan laid his head in his hands, allowed the feeling of complete and utter hopelessness take him over, stealing through his flesh like opium. What had he done? What had he done to their lives?

This was all on him, and he knew it.

When he finished the self-flagellation, he stood, went to the safe in Sutton's office, pulled out the stack of cash they kept on hand in case of emergencies and, from under the couch cushions, an old World War I–era trench knife, the only weapon he allowed in the house, and an antique to boot. He wished he was a hunter, wished he had a gun. He wouldn't hesitate to shoot the bastard who was making his life a living hell.

He put on a pair of hiking boots, grabbed a Maglite from the shelf in the pantry. Flicked it on to make sure the batteries were strong. The beam of light shone bright as day. Of course it did. Sutton would never let the batteries die.

He glanced out the front window. The media scrum was gone for the moment, all finished with their nonexistent story and off to dreamland. The cops weren't taking him that seriously.

He put his mobile on the counter. Why have him leave the phone? That was a bizarre request.

All the while, his brain screamed, *Don't do this, call the bloody police, let them know.* And his ego said, *You can handle this. Be a man, for once. Stand up for her. Stand up for your wife. Get him in your sights and you can force him to tell you what he knows.*

He enjoyed the sense of blood rising, the anger—scratch that—the *rage* building inside him. He felt alive. He felt strong. He felt dangerous.

He was going to teach Colin Wilde a lesson. It was time.

A CORROSIVE BEAST

Blackmail.

It is such a simple, easy act. Find someone's weak spot, put them in a compromising position, get proof that can be used against them, and launch the attack.

I am an expert at this. I don't employ the tactic often, but when I do, there are serious consequences. Real people get hurt. Which is what I like the best.

People panic when you threaten all they hold dear. I have absolutely no doubt Ethan will follow suit. He will listen to my instructions to the letter. When things don't go the way he expects, he'll scurry to call the pretty little towheaded cop, and then I won't have any excuse to hold back.

The cop is catching up, I will give her that. Ethan is acting as predictably as always: panicking, freaking out, shutting down, worrying. Inebriated and sloppy. He's so banal, I simply don't know what anyone sees in him. He is almost too dull to play with. Almost.

But the cop. The cop is interesting. She's an acquired taste. Blunt. Very blunt. There's no elegance to her, no finesse. That will be learned as she grows into a real investigator. Right now she's easily led, a perfectly manipulatable puppet who can be shunted off in any direction I please. A bumper car. She's a bumper car, fumbling through all the information provided, trying to stay upright. Trying to keep her head above water.

There's an image. The sweet towheaded cop, water lapping at her sharp collarbones, the naked, pink flesh getting crepey and wrinkled from the soaking wetness. Dipped in silver wet and slippery green algae. The water rising higher and higher as the shadows deepen…

Sorry, we shouldn't go there. Not just yet.

Smash cut to Sutton Montclair.

That's better.

Here's the deal. Brass tacks. If you give a society enough information, lay down enough threads, someone will have to follow the right one. It's human nature. It's the way our minds work. In a linear fashion, point A to point B to point C. So few of us have the capability to go from A to Q to H. It takes a special person to think that way.

I'm that special person.

But you already know that.

LET'S GO FOR
A DRIVE

In the garage, the perfectly straight, organized, nary a spider or speck of dust in sight garage that attached to the back of their house through a covered walkway, Ethan stopped cold.

Her car. He'd forgotten to check her car. She'd left her keys...

A brief flash, an image formed, sending his heart to his throat, choking him with its intensity: Sutton, slumped in the front seat, engine running, a tube from the exhaust pipe into the front window. But when he got up the courage to look in her front seat, there was nothing. No one. The cupboard was bare.

Ethan drove a BMW 335i convertible, black with gray interior, latest model. He traded in his cars dutifully every two years. Sutton had a more practical forest green X5, or as she called it, the Official Williamson County Soccer Mom car. Not that they were keeping up with the Joneses. Not really. Ellen Jones drove an I3. Electric, sustainable, practical—Ellen to a T.

Ethan didn't know why he was thinking about Ellen, other than he hadn't looked in Sutton's car on day one, which struck him as a Very Stupid Move. Clearly he needed to read more mystery novels; he would know better what to do to find his wife. Amateur sleuth he was not.

Steeling himself, he unlocked the door—they always locked their cars even in the garage, a theft deterrent—and looked inside. Empty.

Oh, the relief. What would he have said if she'd been here the whole time? It would have looked bad for him, very bad.

His search of the X5 was brief. Her car was as clean and organized as she was. Nothing out of place, no stray receipts or empty peppermint wrappers or barrettes. Everything in its place. There was nothing amiss.

He glanced at his watch, cursed, and jumped into his own vehicle. When he got back, he'd look at the GPS, see where she'd been last. Maybe that would give him a clue, though she usually walked most places during the day.

He tore out of the garage. Gentry's Farm wasn't far from their house, about a ten-minute drive in bad traffic. Which was always in Franklin. It was one of the reasons they walked everywhere, the constant traffic jam of locals and tourists. Tonight was no different—the roads were busy, the lights were barely synced, and his quick ten-minute jaunt was inching into twenty before he broke free of the melee and flew west down Highway 96.

He tasted bile every time he thought about Gentry's Farm. Wilde knew exactly how to punish him.

It was their first trip out after the baby was born. They'd taken Dashiell to look at the pumpkins. Halloween was past, but there was still plenty of fall flora around, leftovers from the recent holiday haunted hayrides. Sutton couldn't resist the idea of a baby in a cornucopia, à la Anne Geddes.

He had to agree, "Dashiell in the Field" was an unexpected pleasure. They'd almost filled the memory card on the camera, they'd taken so many shots. It was how they announced the birth of their boy, a photo of him snuggled in an angelic white sleep suit, surrounded by green-and-yellow gourds and bright orange pumpkins and a small haystack Sutton had laughingly constructed, the whole tableau dotted with the red–gold maple leaves they'd found in a tidy pile nearby. Their bountiful babe. Their bounty.

Colin Wilde knew about the photos. They'd put them on their social media accounts gleefully, racking up likes and comments. Surely that's why he'd picked this place, to stick the knife in a bit farther, twist it inside Ethan's intestines, make them jump and roil.

Ethan was going to kill the bastard. He knew this as certainly as he knew the moon dictated the tides.

It was simply a question of when.

TAKE A WALK ON
THE WILDE SIDE

Ethan parked near the main entrance to Gentry's Farm. The gate was closed, but he knew that wouldn't be allowed as an excuse for missing this meeting. The darkness was severe, clouds blotting out the moon, so he switched on the Maglite and climbed over the metal railings. The farm hadn't tried very hard to keep people out, trusting the good area and their tony, well-heeled neighbors. And really, what were people going to do in a field?

His mom's face floated in front of him, and he remembered the stupid joke she'd told him when they'd sat him down to talk about the birds and the bees. *They*, because the Montclairs did everything together, including explaining how sex worked to their teenage son, who knew everything already, but humored them because this was a rite of passage and he wanted to see how they handled it.

Frankly, as it turned out. They'd spared no detail, and had done it with good humor, tag-teaming him with embarrassingly detailed descriptions. They even had a book with diagrams, so he'd be able to identify all the right parts when the time came. At the end, his mother had chucked him under the chin and said, "One last thing to remember, son. Don't ever make love near a cornfield."

Red-faced and mortified—not only had his mother used the term *making love* in a sentence, she'd talked openly about erections and vaginas and pleasuring a woman first and all sorts of other things he would just as soon forget—he'd played along.

"Why not?"

"'Cause that corn has ears!"

He'd been so caught off guard he'd started to laugh, and the three of them had howled together, then companionably gone out for curry.

He missed them. He missed Sutton. When he'd told her that story, she'd fallen over laughing, then suggested they find themselves a cornfield straightaway to test the theory.

They hadn't, though he'd wanted to, that day with the baby. With his loves, together and perfect.

He hoofed it deeper into the field. There was a track, beaten dirt, for the hayrides, he supposed. He followed it in.

Arrived deep in the field at thirty minutes past the call, on the dot.

He stopped by a hayrick. Wilde had said to wait. The money was heavy in the bag. Ethan ground his teeth and said what passed for a prayer in his nonbeliever's mind. *If he gives me Sutton, I won't kill him. I swear.*

Not right away, that is. I'll wait, then kill him when he isn't looking for me. And I'll do it slowly.

Footsteps. He ducked down instinctively, the trench knife out of his pocket, brushing his knuckles, the heavy metal blade open.

A light flashed in his eyes, momentarily blinding him.

"Whoa! What the bloody—"

"Who the hell are you and why the hell are you sneaking around here? This is private property, and you're trespassing."

Ethan stood, stowing the knife, though the blade flashed in the man's light, and he heard a little gasp. "I have a gun, you idiot—"

"Sir, I'm sorry, I'm putting it away. You scared me. I'm supposed to be meeting a friend."

"In my field? Get the hell out of here."

Ethan put both hands up. "Right. Brilliant. I'm on my way out. Sorry for the confusion."

He hurried toward the road. The old farmer stood, watching impassively, until Ethan could no longer see the lights behind him, could hear the whiz of the cars on the pavement.

He couldn't go back into the field without being shot, or at least reported. He had no way of contacting Wilde without heading back to the house. He was scared and angry and carrying fifty grand in a sack and he decided, *Fuck it, I'm going to get a drink.*

THE TIES THAT BIND

Two hours later, hopped up on excellent old-fashioneds from Grays, he found his way back to the house. His phone lay untouched on the counter: no calls, no messages, no texts. Wilde had been screwing with him. Playing the same sort of games he always had.

Ethan called the number back, but it was blocked. Of course it was.

He put the money back in the safe, went to his office, tripping a little as he walked down the hall. He was very tipsy. He felt safe again in his lair, but the feeling fled when he turned on his computer. The *New York Times* piece had run, despite Bill's assurances he'd get it quashed, and the internet was abuzz with the news about the sudden runner of Sutton Montclair.

Ten minutes of peace, and then Ethan's mobile started ringing again, nonstop, reporters from all over trying to get a quote. How did they find his number? It was unlisted, and he and Sutton had always been so careful about giving out their numbers, but someone had found it and passed it around, and they were hunting him now. Bill. He'd bet Bill gave it to them, hoping for a juicy quote and a backlist sales bump. Or Wilde, torturing him, posted it somewhere.

He didn't know which was worse.

It was all too much. He couldn't take it. He felt the familiar chest squeeze, the worry and concern turning into a monster of anxiety. The media encamped on his front lawn, the police driving by, Wilde calling and threatening to blackmail him, Sutton's friends shrinking away from him—*Dashiell's ghost, don't forget your boy*—it was too much.

He felt the desperation creeping in, the walls in his office getting close. He needed to leave. He needed to get on a fucking plane and depart for environs unknown, like Sutton, and not for the first time, the anger redirected toward her, at her selfishness. For leaving him to clean up her mess.

Maybe he needed to go for a run. Yes, that was the right thing to do. He'd wave to any reporters lurking in the shadows and run in the moonlight, the liquor sloshing in his stomach, then hole up again and ride out the storm.

If only. Ethan from another world would do that. Ethan now would sit quietly and let the panic overtake him, pour a fresh drink, and wallow while obliquely staring out the windows.

What to do about Wilde? He would call back, Ethan knew that much. He'd probably been scared off by the farmer with the gun, too. Paying him off would be a mistake, he knew that in his bones. How could Wilde really know where Sutton was? It was a ploy, he was sure of it, and Wilde would simply come back again and again and again until the well was dry.

And yet, Ethan had trotted out to the field with the money in the bag to see.

Isn't that love, wife? The risks I'm taking for you?

And then it hit him.

The missing $50,000, the money Sutton had taken.

It was the same amount Wilde asked for.

He stopped moving, sat down hard. Thought it through.

Wilde, claiming he knew where Sutton was.

Wilde, asking for money in order to share that information.

Wilde, threatening him not to go to the police.

Wilde had already hurt Sutton. It wasn't hard to imagine him doing it again.

With a sigh, Ethan went to the phone and called Officer Graham.

She answered on the first ring. "Have you heard from her, sir?"

"No, I haven't. I've been searching through our financials again, though, and I think I'm missing some money. It's well disguised, but Sutton has withdrawn $50,000 from our accounts over the past three months."

He could hear Officer Graham blow out her breath. "You're sure? We've been running your financials and nothing stood out."

He let that go for the moment. Having strangers poking around in his world made him more than uncomfortable. But he had to find Sutton. He knew now this wasn't a stunt. This was a cry for help. She'd run from Wilde. Not from him.

"I'm sure. The withdrawals are coded, and each one has a *T* in it. *T* is her tax code for *travel*."

"If your wife was trying to take money out of your accounts unnoticed, why would she bother coding them? Wouldn't that give her away?"

"Yes and no. Withdrawals without a code, though, would set off all the alarms. She's simply following her usual pattern, hoping it will cover her tracks."

"Has she not been traveling, Mr. Montclair?"

"No, she hasn't. She hasn't been on the road at all since our son died. Nor have I."

"*T* could stand for something else."

"It could. Certainly. But my wife is a meticulous person. It's almost as if she wanted me to find this and not be worried about her."

"I don't know, Mr. Montclair. Especially in light of this new information, perhaps we should just let things play out. Perhaps she *has* just removed herself from the marriage for a time."

"Or perhaps she was pressured to remove the money, in payment of some kind, and when she couldn't satisfy the demands of her kidnapper, she was killed."

"That's entirely possible."

Ethan stopped breathing for a moment; his heart thumped once, hard, then ceased to beat. It took him a minute to catch his breath. "What are you saying? Have you found something? Do you know something you're not telling me?"

"No, sir. But my job is to look at all the angles. I appreciate this information, and I'll keep in touch. As soon as I have something, I'll let you know."

And she hung up.

Ethan was suddenly relegated to the role of hysterical husband. He hadn't even had a chance to tell Graham about Wilde.

But that thought was scrambled, pushed away, making room for the more frightening train that followed.

Was he going to be charged? Was he wrong, and it was all her doing? Joel's warning paraded into his mind, Bill's cynicism joined the party. *Was* there any way Sutton could have hurt herself but made it look like he was to blame? Would she do something so awful? How was he going to cope if she were gone? Would they find a body?

"Oh, God."

He started through the house, looking out the windows, trying to ascertain if anyone was out there. Then he got a grip on himself and called Graham back.

She didn't answer. He left her a message.

"You hung up before I was able to tell you everything. I need to talk to you. Right now. I've been contacted by someone who claims to know where Sutton is. He wants money. Please ring me back."

BLACKMAIL, OR HOW DOES YOUR GARDEN GROW?

Holly had questioned Ellen Jones hard for forty minutes, but she hadn't budged. She insisted Sutton Montclair was not the person in the video.

It clouded everything Holly knew about this case, which was getting stranger by the second.

She grabbed a bag of Tots and a diet cherry limeade from Sonic and sat in the car, thinking. Ate, made some notes. The loyal friends, the missing money, the doting husband, the professional fall from grace. The note. The baby. None of it was adding up for her. It was like trying to solve a puzzle whose pieces came from different boxes.

Her cell rang, for what felt like the thousandth time today. If this was what being a detective was like…how did they ever get anything done with their phones constantly ringing? She glanced at the caller ID. It was Ethan Montclair again.

"Mr. Montclair? What can I do for you now?"

"Listen, I received a call a little while ago. I left you a message, but you didn't call me back. I'm assuming you didn't get it."

She looked at her call screen, saw the badge alert that indicated she'd received a message. "Ah. So you did. What did you want to tell me?"

"I'm being blackmailed. And I think Sutton might have been, too. I think that's why she's run away."

It took a moment, but relief swept through her. The idea of a concrete villain made everyone's lives easier. Holly made mental notes. She had to call Moreno, had to call the TBI, the FBI, get all her ducks in a row.

But first, she needed every detail Montclair could provide. "Tell me."

He did, finishing with, "Someone's spying on me. I know it."

"You sound very paranoid, sir."

"You would be, too, if you knew what I know. We have to take this seriously. I have to find her. She has to be okay."

"First, I have to tell my boss."

"No, you can't tell anyone."

"Mr. Montclair, this is nonnegotiable. We both have a lot to lose right now. I'll be right back to you. Don't move, don't talk to anyone."

She called Moreno. "You might want to meet me at the Montclairs' house. We've got a blackmail attempt ongoing."

"Who's blackmailing whom?"

"The blogger who made their lives hell has apparently called and asked for fifty grand in exchange for information about Sutton Montclair leaving the house in the wee hours. He claims he saw her get into a black car and drive off into the night, and that he knows where she is."

"Think it's legit?"

"It's been a solid forty-eight hours since she went missing. The timing stands. Then again, these are public people. It's entirely possible someone's playing a cruel joke."

"Is that what you think's happening?"

"I don't know. There is fifty grand missing from their accounts, and Ethan Montclair just tossed out the idea that Sutton was being blackmailed, too."

"He said that?"

"Not in so many words, but he intimated that perhaps she paid off whoever it was and then ran. Either this guy is playing us like a fiddle, or something shady's going on."

"I'll meet you there. Give me an hour. I'm tied up."

Ethan spilled his guts, and Holly took copious notes.

As he talked, a text message came into his phone. It said, Don't you dare mention me to the cop. I'll know if you do.

Ethan handed the phone to Graham. "It says cop. Not cops."

"Do you think that means something?"

"I do. I think it means he's watching. You're a single cop. He saw you come over."

"You may be right." She called her boss again. Ethan could hear the gruff voice of Sergeant Moreno, tried to ignore it.

"Sir, we've received another threat. I think it would be better if you stayed away. I think Wilde can see the house. He seems to be aware that I'm here. If the whole squad arrives, he'll know."

"Do we have a trace on Montclair's phone?"

"No, and we need one. Can you make that happen?"

"Yes, I'll do it. We'll also put someone on the house, discreetly. Tell him, so he doesn't need to worry. You figure out why this blogger suddenly decided to extort money from the Montclairs, and whether this is for real, or simply a diversion. We'll work from the opposite direction, try to locate Wilde." There was a note in Moreno's voice that was readily understood—*make sure Montclair isn't trying to buy time.*

Ethan didn't react visibly, though a small wave of hopelessness passed through him. They all thought he was involved. All of them.

"Roger that."

Graham hung up and faced Ethan.

"Start talking. I need to know everything you left out before."

"What makes you think I left anything out?"

The cop looked annoyed. "Mr. Montclair, please don't play games with me. I want to help you, and I want to find your wife unharmed. I have no agenda here. You called us for help. Help is what I'm offering. But you can't keep holding back on me. Tell me the truth. What's really going on here?"

"I am telling you the truth. I haven't said a single thing that's not true."

"You also aren't telling me everything, or else you wouldn't have some random blogger trying to extort money from you. Spit it out."

Ethan walked to the counter, ran his hand over the smooth surface. It had become a talisman for him now. All the fights, all the hurt feelings, over a stupid slab of stone. He was marked for life by it, and he should be. To let his marriage, his wife, slip away over such ridiculous things as ego and blame and emotionless sex branded him forever as a horrible man.

"I had an affair. Wilde found out. He's threatened to make it public knowledge before. It wasn't even a thing. I was drunk. I barely remembered it." *You sound like you're making excuses. Stop. Be a man about it.*

"Who was the affair with?"

"It was just...a woman. At a conference. We met in the bar. I was drunk. I made a mistake. It was stupid and senseless and careless of me. Sutton found out. Looking back, I wonder if Wilde tipped her off. I swore to her it was nothing, and we were finally getting things back on track."

"You never asked how she knew?"

"Of course I did. She wouldn't tell me. Wouldn't talk to me at all, actually."

"When was this affair?"

"More than a year ago. Before the baby died."

"How did the blogger find out?"

"Supposedly, someone saw us in an elevator at the hotel and blabbed to him. We were kissing. At least that's what I'm told."

"You don't remember this?"

"The evening is very, very blurry."

"Do you often drink to forgetfulness?"

"Shouldn't the question be—do I drink to forget? Because the answer to that is yes. Absolutely. As much and as often as I can. But that night...it sounds completely lame, but I really don't remember it. Last thing I remember was having a steak and a glass of wine at the bar. I woke up in her bed. I was naked, she was naked. Draw your own conclusions. Everyone else did."

"It explains why Wilde would try to blackmail you. Though if you admitted it to Sutton, the power he had over you was gone. Why try again now?"

Because I didn't tell her the whole truth. "I don't know. The last we heard from Wilde, he was claiming Sutton wrote my books."

"And you think he's trying to blackmail Sutton, too?"

"Sutton's always been blameless in all of this. It was stupid of her to engage, but Wilde is the one who dragged it on and on. Maybe he did try to take advantage, and she didn't tell me."

"Not entirely blameless. She did light a bag of dog poop on fire on the reviewer's doorstep. Thanks again for sending the video. That helped."

Ethan shook his head. "I told you before, I didn't send you anything."

"You didn't?" The cop's voice was light. "Are you entirely sure, Mr. Montclair? Because as I mentioned before, I did receive the video in an email that traces back to your IP address."

"Let me see the email."

The cop was watching him like a hawk above a field, sharp and wanting. There was more, she was holding something back.

"Let me see it again," he demanded.

"You're telling me unequivocally you didn't email me the video of your wife?"

"No, I didn't. Why would I? What would it gain?"

"You'd be helping the investigation."

"I'd be discrediting my wife, is more like it. Let me see it." Holly didn't move.

"Please, Officer Graham. May I see the video again?"

Finally, she pulled out her phone. The email address was indecipherable. She queued it up. Ethan watched. When it finished, Graham said, "One problem. Your friend Ellen thinks it's a fake."

"What do you mean?"

She queued up the video again. "Ellen felt this wasn't actually Sutton."

"That's crazy. You'd think I'd recognize my own wife."

"Watch it again."

He did. Closely. Raised his eyes to the clear hazel of the investigator's who held his life in her hands.

"Bloody hell. Ellen's right. It's not her."

WHEN ALL YOU KNOW IS FALSE

They played it back again, and again, until Ethan couldn't see any vestiges of Sutton anymore.

"It's not her. I can't believe this. I need tea," Ethan muttered, started preparing the water. "She wasn't lying. She told the truth, and I didn't believe her. I just didn't look closely enough the first time you showed me."

"Sutton denied doing this?"

"Sutton denied everything. She said she made one flip comment, and then her account was hacked. That everything that came after the first night was fake. I didn't believe her. Why would I?"

"Because she was your wife?"

"My wife whom I was having problems with. God help me, I thought she was trying to gather attention, to pay me back for the affair. Aren't I the arsehole?"

Graham pocketed her phone. She was very still. She'd stationed herself by the breakfast bar, watched him move around the kitchen. "Sir, I want to ask you something. Do you have any reason to believe your son's death was something other than SIDS?"

The lid of the teapot clattered into place. "Sorry. Clumsy. You've been talking to the weird sisters, haven't you?"

"Excuse me? Who?"

"Sutton's group of friends. They don't like me very much."

"Why not?"

"I'm a bombastic serial cheater who belittled her and held her career back. Or hadn't you heard?"

"Are you?"

"According to them. Her mother will say so, as well. What does the truth matter to a gaggle of women who don't like a husband?"

"I haven't been able to touch base with her mother."

"Lucky you. She's out of town. Canada, I think. When I told her Sutton was missing, she didn't seem at all concerned. Told me I didn't know her daughter and left for her trip."

"That seems odd."

"You don't know Siobhan Healy. She's no better than a spider—let her eggs hatch, find a wasp for them to feast on, then scurry away."

"She and Sutton aren't close?"

"Hardly. Sutton got the hell out the moment she was able to get a job and pay her own way. She hated one of the stepfathers with a passion, felt like Siobhan took his side over Sutton's. She took off when she was sixteen."

"One of the stepfathers?"

"Siobhan's on hubby number four. She never married Sutton's real father, he was a one-night stand. Sutton never knew him. She grew up hard, my wife. There was a new man every couple of years. They moved around a lot. She finally got fed up and bailed. There's something..."

"Yes?"

"Nothing, never mind."

"Everything you can tell me is helpful, Mr. Montclair."

"I can't tell you, because I don't know. Something happened when she was a kid. I have no idea what it was. Siobhan is tight-lipped, and Sutton won't even acknowledge it. She always keeps a rock-solid wall up about her childhood.

"She slipped once, when we were first dating. We were out for a night on the town, at a restaurant in downtown Nashville. A group of people came in, men and women, our age. Looked like they'd come from a big event, they were in evening attire, tuxes, and long gowns. Sutton turned white, and insisted we leave. When I asked what was wrong, she clammed up. She made it to the car before she started to cry. She wouldn't tell me why, or who had upset her, but when I asked if it was someone from her past, she said yes, but wouldn't tell me any more. I tried for a week to get her to open up, but she wouldn't. My wife is a vault when she wants to be, Officer Graham. Her mother's right. Sometimes, I wonder if I ever really knew her at all."

He poured out the tea, handed the cop a fresh cup. She declined the fake milk and sugar, took it straight.

"I'll take a look, see if there's anything she was involved in that might show up. And, Mr. Montclair, her friends aren't as unkind to you as you think they are. They are very concerned for her well-being, yes, but so far, no one's pointing any fingers. There is another odd thing that's cropped up, though. The password on her laptop."

"*I love Ethan Montclair.* Trite."

"No, that wasn't it. It was *Ethan killed our baby.*"

He set the cup carefully on the marble. "Wait. What?"

"The password you provided didn't get us into your wife's computer. We had to crack it on our own, and what we found was that accusation."

"But the notebook, I logged in myself—bollocks. I am so confused." Ethan set his head in his hands. His voice was soft. "We fought so badly when Dashiell died. We both accused the other of negligence, carelessness, of letting it happen. Accusations that would never have come up if Dashiell hadn't... Trust me, Officer Graham. I didn't kill our son, and neither did my wife. His death was a terrible, awful tragedy, and it tore us apart. But we loved him, more than we loved each other, maybe. Hurting him isn't something either of us could do."

"I believe you," Graham said. "But it seems Sutton was sending a message. Could she be trying to get you in trouble, Mr. Montclair?"

A huge sigh, relief spreading through his body. "I can't imagine why she would. She didn't hate me that much. But Wilde? Wilde is responsible. Wilde is behind this. I don't know how, and I don't know why, but I don't think my marriage was so far gone that my wife would try to set me up."

Graham nodded. "Obviously the idea of a third party makes this theory very compelling. A blackmail attempt colors the whole investigation."

"I tried to buy him off. He set up a meet and didn't show. He's playing games."

"You should have told me."

"I'm telling you now."

"When was this?"

"Earlier tonight. He was just poking me, torturing me."

"Where were you supposed to meet?"

"Right outside the city limits. He never came. Something's happened to her. I know it. No one believes me."

He sounded petulant now, and the cop eyed him like he was a weak, ridiculous child, whining because he couldn't get a piece of candy in line at the grocery. She took a deep breath, blew it out her nose.

"Mr. Montclair, I believe you. And I have to say, I am starting to agree with you. Something has happened to your wife. We need to change focus, start actively searching for her. We're currently tracing the calls to your house and cell. We'll be very discreet, but we're going to have to get someone in here to guide you in how to talk to Wilde if he calls or texts again. If he's telling the truth, and he knows where Sutton is, she could very easily be in danger."

The relief he felt was enormous. Relief, and a new fear. "I think that's rather clear-cut already, don't you?"

"I will admit something doesn't add up. An email you claim you didn't send, a password different from what you knew. A thwarted blackmail attempt. The woman in the video not being your wife. I'll take it all to my boss and lay it out for him. And if Wilde calls again, you keep him on the phone as long as you possibly can."

"Officer Graham? Is it possible for passwords to be changed remotely?"

Her brow wrinkled for a moment. "I'm not an IT expert, but I would assume if someone had managed to overtake a computer with a virus, then yes, that's entirely within the bounds of reality."

She reached out and touched him on the shoulder. Ethan wanted to weep. The touch was gentle, soft, opposite of everything he'd been getting for the past two days.

"We'll figure it out, sir. I'll be in touch."

Holly believed him. Maybe she wasn't a seasoned investigator yet, maybe she was being snookered. But damn if she didn't believe him. Now she had to find a way to investigate Wilde without him knowing Ethan had shared the blackmail demand. It was definitely time for a seasoned detective to step in. She wasn't about to blow this case, and there were suddenly more moving parts than she could handle alone. One thing she'd learned from her dad, don't be afraid to ask for help.

Holly had just gotten into her car when the phone rang. She put it on speaker as she put on her safety belt.

"Officer Graham? It's Ivy Brookes."

"Hello, Ms. Brookes. What can I do for you?"

"Could you come by the house? I have some more information I need to share."

"Okay. I'll be there in a minute. I'm close."

"Yes, you are."

The phone went dead. What was this about?

A CHANGE OF HEART

Holly was at Brookes's door five minutes later. Ivy looked pale and drawn. She didn't offer refreshments, just stood with her arms wrapped tightly around her body, clearly distressed.

"Come in."

The door shut behind her with a bang. "What's wrong, Ms. Brookes?"

"I haven't been entirely honest with you."

"I'm all ears," Holly said.

Brookes was pacing now, walking the short length of her apartment with staccato steps. "Ethan killed her. I'm sure of it."

"Why? Why the change of heart? Last time we talked, you seemed to think Sutton was the one who'd orchestrated this week's drama."

"I was trying to protect Sutton. To protect them both. They've been through so much. At first, when he told me she was gone, I really thought Sutton was just playing with him, punishing him. But now, I'm truly starting to think he hurt her, and I can't stay silent any longer."

"Go on."

"Look." A lightweight silver laptop was on the counter. Brookes turned it around to show an email account. "I just received this. It came in a few days ago. For some reason, it got caught in my spam filter."

"What is it?"

"An email from Sutton, dated Friday night. I was out of town on business. I had an away message on. I wasn't checking email. I didn't see this. If I had…"

The email was open. There was no greeting, just the stark words in black and white.

Really bad one tonight. He gets worse and worse. I think he's going to kill me one of these days. If something happens to me, make sure they know who did it.

Holly felt a punch of adrenaline. Was everything Ethan Montclair had just told her a lie? Was he that good of an actor, that he could look her in the eye and create a story? He was a professional liar, after all, paid to create stories out of nothing. Was she that big of a dupe?

"Wow. Rather damning."

Ivy nodded and closed the computer. "He was hitting her. It started soon after they moved into the house. That bloodstain on the counter? They say it was from blueberries but everyone knows the truth. He gave her a bloody nose. They were fighting over something stupid, and she mouthed off to him, and he punched her in the face. It wasn't the first time. It definitely wasn't the last."

"Did you ever see him hurt her?"

"Not directly, no. But I'd see the aftermath. The bruises. You should look at her phone. There are photos. I used to make her take a picture after every incident. I wanted her to go to the police, to file charges against him. She never would. They kept it all a secret."

"Why didn't you tell me about the abuse when I asked before?"

"Because if Sutton is alive, she will be furious with me for telling you. Like I said, it was a secret. I'm the only one who knew."

"There were calls to the police, domestic calls, when they were fighting. It wasn't that much of a secret."

"The public face of abuse is very different than the private. Look at OJ and Nicole. No one wanted to believe that their hero was an obsessed narcissist who slit her throat."

"Did Ethan know you knew?"

"I don't know." A small sob escaped Brookes's lips. "This is why I called. The email, and… I've been getting strange phone calls the past few days. Hang-ups, from a number I don't recognize. I'm worried."

"Do you have the number?"

"Yes. I'll write it down for you."

"Do you think Ethan might try and hurt you?"

"Like he did Sutton?" A little gasp, her hand over her mouth. "I mean, we don't know for sure that he has hurt her. But I can't see any other truth. Think about it. He waited for hours to tell anyone she was gone—and that's according to him. It was the weekend. She could have been gone for much longer. None of us saw her in the few days before she left. Her last email to me was on Friday. He could easily be lying about when she actually disappeared. Combined with the abuse, the fear—Sutton was constantly afraid of him—it's frightening. Alarming, really."

"I will admit, it was odd to show up to take the report and see he'd already hired a lawyer. It doesn't help his case."

Ivy blushed. "Um…that was my fault. He suggested it and I agreed it was a good idea. I was still protecting him, protecting them. At the time, I didn't think Sutton was in danger, and I didn't want him to be railroaded. Looking back, if he wasn't guilty, he would have told me I was insane and not done it."

"Can I see that number now?"

Ivy handed over her phone. Holly copied down the number.

"I'll look into this, Ms. Brookes. See if I can trace who might be calling you. Would you please forward me the email Sutton sent on Friday? That will help."

"Yes, I will."

Holly caught the barest hesitation in her statement. "Is there anything else you need to tell me?"

Brookes's eyes cast down. She planted her hands palms down on the counter, took a deep breath through her nose, let it out in a whoosh. "The baby."

"Dashiell. He died last year, of SIDS, according to the autopsy report. They found no cause to think he was hurt by the parents."

"I know what the autopsy said. But Sutton told me she thought Ethan killed the baby."

The password. *Ethan killed our baby.*

"Why? Why did she believe this?"

Brookes stared at her a moment, assessing. She chewed her lip, which oddly made her look like a little girl, then held up a finger. "I'll be right back."

She disappeared down the hallway, came back a few moments later, clutching something small in her hand. She presented it to Holly with all the grace of a cat depositing a dead mouse, practically threw it at her.

It was a bottle of liquid diphenhydramine.

"What's this?"

"Sutton found it in the baby's room. Hidden, in the closet, behind an old stack of clothes Dashiell had outgrown. They were getting ready to donate them. It's generic Benadryl."

"I'm not following, ma'am."

"They didn't test the baby for this."

"I saw the autopsy report. There was nothing that indicated anything was amiss. SIDS does happen."

"It didn't in this case. Ethan gave the baby Benadryl to quiet him. They'd had a huge fight, I already told you that. Sutton went out. Ethan couldn't get the baby to stop crying. He dosed him, and it killed him."

"The tox screen didn't show that."

"Then the tox screen wasn't done properly. I watch those shows on television. I know you can do testing after the fact. You have tissue samples on file. Have them tested again. You'll see. It was from this bottle. Sutton found it in the closet, and she gave it to me right away for protection."

"It was hidden away?"

"Yes. And trust me, this is an anomaly. They don't believe in drugs. They don't believe in anything that isn't totally pure, organic, healthy. The both of them are fitness nuts."

"Except for the alcohol."

"Everything in moderation. Sutton was never a big drinker. Ethan has food allergies. They were really clean. They'd never give the baby drugs. They barely take anything themselves."

"I have a question."

"Anything. Anything that will help find her. Anything that will stop him."

"If he's this horrible monster you portray, why stay friends with the man? You were the first one he called, right? You were there when the police arrived, giving moral support."

Brookes's eyes shone with tears. "I'm scared of what he might do if I try to pull away. I've had to keep an eye on them. I've been watching to make sure she was okay. It might not make sense to you, but I couldn't come forward then. But I have to now. I can't sit back any longer. He's evil. I know he hurt her, just like I know he hurt the baby. Ethan is a showman. He's a brilliant actor. I've always wondered…"

"What? Go on."

Brookes started fiddling with an apple, left out on the counter, a snack interrupted. She was clearly debating something. Finally, she said, "I think Ethan was trying to drive Sutton mad. I am not a computer expert, so I have no way of tracking this down and proving it, but I think Ethan might have been the one who hacked Sutton's account and was riling up the reviewer. I think he was the one who said all those horrible things.

"After Dashiell…he wanted to destroy her. He blamed her. Even if it was him who gave the drugs, he blamed her for leaving that night. For not wanting a child in the first place. For being who she was. He tried to conform her into his perfect little wife, but Sutton has a wild streak. She's always fighting herself. She hated being tied down, and the whole concept of marriage and two point four kids and a dog was the opposite of what she ever wanted. Ethan was slowly strangling her."

"Is there anyone who can corroborate this, Ms. Brookes?"

"Her mother will. They weren't close, they fought all the time, but she'll tell you. She's always known Ethan for who and what he is. A tyrant."

Brookes began to cry now, large tears gently rolling down her face. "I should have told you sooner. I was hoping she had just taken off for a few days to piss him off. But this doesn't feel right to me. After that email… God, why didn't I see it Friday, when I could have helped? I'm afraid for her, Officer Graham. Truly afraid."

Holly nodded. "This is a huge help. Thank you for your honesty, for being willing to give up your friendship with the Montclairs to do the right thing. I will follow up on all of this, I swear. I will need you to come to the station and give a full report. On the record. Are you willing to do that?"

Brookes sighed and nodded. "Yes. I'm willing to go on the record."

"Good. I'll get that scheduled as soon as possible. In the meantime, limit your contact with Mr. Montclair. Do you have any trips planned? I know you travel quite a bit."

"I'm going to stay right here until we find Sutton. Should we start organizing some sort of search?"

"I'll get back to you on that. I've gotten a lot of information in the past hour. I need to go sort through it all and get my boss moving on a few things." She pocketed her notebook. "We'll find her, Ms. Brookes. I promise."

The tears stopped. Brookes swiped a hand across her face. "I hope you do. Before it's too late."

"One last thing. Did you happen to make a call to my cell phone yesterday?"

She shook her head. "No, I didn't. Though now that I see this email from Sutton, I wish I had."

I'M COMING HOME, I'M COMING HOME

Then

"Ethan, come here!"

He hurried to the other side of the house, drawn by the urgency in her voice. She was in her office. No makeup, hair in a ponytail, spilling down her back. Feet bare, toenails polished red. She looked so young, so carefree. He couldn't help the spike of love he felt when he saw her. Sometimes he forgot how things were now. For a moment, their reality fled away and he saw her with early eyes, the ones he had before their world went to hell.

"What is it, love?"

"That asshole Wilde is after me again."

He bit back the sigh. This little drama was getting very old.

Sutton's office was so empty now. Without the baby's basket, it seemed practically frigid. They were in the first flush of winter, and the skies were gray and dreary. Looking closer, he could see Sutton was pale, black circles under her eyes. Neither of them slept well anymore. When had they slept together recently? He tried to think back to the luxurious warmth between her legs. It had been weeks.

He needed to rectify this. He needed to fix his marriage. They'd gone through hell and back, and if they had any hope of surviving, they needed to find one another again.

But all Sutton could focus on was some stupid online blogger who kept poking her crazy.

"You need to ignore him."

"I have been. You know that. But now he's attacking you."

A rush of fury. And a little voice in the back of his mind... *Hypocrite. Hypocrite. Hypocrite.* "What? Let me see."

The article was only two hundred words, very succinct. It was titled *Who's Really Writing Ethan Montclair's Books?*

"That bloody arsehole!"

"I know. We have to do something. This is defamation."

Ethan skimmed the article again, enough to take away that Wilde was intimating it was Sutton who was writing Ethan's books, from start to finish. That he had severe writer's block, or maybe he'd plagiarized the first book, stole it completely from another author who wasn't published, someone he'd come across in a writing class.

Rage filled him. His vision blackened, and it took a good five minutes before he could really hear Sutton. She was crying. That shook him from his state.

"What? What's wrong?"

"Let go of me!"

He looked down, realized he was gripping Sutton's forearm so tightly her hand was turning white. He released her as if burned.

"Oh my God, Sutton. I am so sorry."

She cradled her arm in her lap. There was going to be a bruise. It would be bad, too. Sutton was so easily damaged these days.

"You scared me. I thought you were going to hurt me. You grabbed my arm, and you wouldn't let go. It's turning black already. My God, Ethan."

He threw his arms around her. "Baby, baby, I'm sorry. I'm so sorry. I didn't mean to hurt you. I'd never hurt you on purpose."

But her eyes were wide, the pupils dilated. She was cringing in her chair, pulling away.

He tried to stay calm. He stepped back, put some space between them. "Where would he get this idea? That you're writing my books? That I plagiarized someone?"

"I have no idea. It's preposterous. I mean, all I ever do is edit you, and that lightly. Accusing me of writing them is silly. Everyone knows you write your own books. You were a writer well before you met me. I'm going to put ice on my arm."

"Let me get it for you." He rushed to the kitchen, came back to see Sutton taking a photo of the burgeoning bruise.

"What in the world are you doing?"

"I can't see it properly. It looks like two fingerprints."

"Here." He handed her the ice, took the phone from her hand. "Move your arm to the right." She did, and he snapped the picture. He handed her the phone. "See. It's not as bad as you think."

She stared at it.

"You should probably delete that. You don't want the weird sisters to see it and get the wrong idea."

"No one can tell what it is, it just looks like a smudge."

"I'm so sorry, sweetheart. Come here." This time she let him hug her. He arranged her on the small sofa, tucked the ice pack in around her arm. "Do you want some Advil?"

"No, the ice is fine."

"I'm sorry Wilde is at it again. I think we should look at hiring someone to get him to back off."

"A lawyer?"

"Yes."

"I see it takes him attacking you for you to take this seriously."

He didn't rise to the bait. "I should have been paying more attention. I've been having a lousy few weeks. The book's not working. Hell, maybe you should start writing it for me. Kidding," he said at her dark look. "Why don't I give Joel a call, see if he can give us some advice."

"I already talked to Joel, the last time Wilde acted up. He said we could sue but it's going to take a lot of time and money, and without any proof that I didn't post those notes, we're going to have a—quote unquote—*uphill battle* to get a conviction."

"But this is different, don't you think?"

"Call him, then. Let's hear what he has to say." She took the ice off her arm, started poking at the bruise.

"Stop that. You'll make it worse."

"I was just seeing how much it hurts."

"I'm sure it will hurt much less if you stop poking it."

"Call Joel."

"I am. Sutton…"

She looked at him with those blue-gray eyes, the smudges beneath hard as rain. There was no look of love or joy or acceptance in them. Of course not, he'd just hurt her, all she could be around him now was wary. They hurt each other all the time now, their words striking harder than slaps, the bruises deeper than broken blood vessels. They both knew how to use words, knew they were the greatest weapon of all.

Before he knew what he was doing, he was kneeling by her side, his head in her lap, crying. She cried with him. They ached together in their loss. The loss of Dashiell, the loss of their marriage. The loss of each other.

That they'd make love was inevitable. He was not expecting it to be quite so aggressive, quite so wild. They both went a little crazy. And when they were finished, slick and hot and sated, Sutton said, in a small, quiet voice, "I've missed you."

And Ethan's heart broke all over again.

THAT MAN IS LYING
THROUGH HIS TEETH

Now

So two people were now pointing fingers at Ethan Montclair—
Ivy Brookes and the anonymous caller. The blogger wanted
$50,000 for information, and they might now have a year-old
murder on their hands. The moment word got out, the whole
town would be turned on its collective ear. But before Holly
did anything, she had to write things down. She didn't want to
screw up. So she sat in her car and transcribed her notes, everything she'd just learned, about Wilde, about Montclair, about
the bottle of diphenhydramine, and about Ivy Brookes. When
she felt like she had things clear in her head, she called Moreno,
ran him through her day thus far. She finished with, "We need
to find this blogger, now. Jim in IT already has the files. I can
call and ask him to start a trace."

"I'm three steps ahead of you. You ain't going to believe this.
You need to come in. Right now."

Holly walked through the halls of the Franklin Police station,
her heart kettle-drumming in her chest. Moreno had comman-

deered a conference room, and that's where she headed. The stench of burnt coffee clung in the air. Wanted posters lined the walls, along with framed motivational quotes—their chief was big on supporting her troops.

Jim from IT was sitting at the table, three laptops open in front of him. His square black glasses were sliding down his nose, as usual. He gave her a big smile when she walked in, shoved the glasses up. He was cute, Jim, in a geeky kind of way.

"There's the champ. Great job, sister. You've gotten everything we need to nail this son of a bitch."

Three other detectives and Sergeant Moreno were also present. Moreno looked up from a stack of papers. "Graham, you know everyone?"

She did. Alex Young and Walt Teal were from Missing Persons, both young and agile. Carlie Cox was a homicide detective with a reputation for closing cases. They were all seasoned, experienced investigators, and Holly felt a short qualm.

"Hi there."

Moreno said, "Graham has been on this case for a couple of days now, and she's managed to extract a ton of information from both the suspect and the victim's friends. Tell them everything you just told me."

She didn't have time to be nervous, or worry about missing something. She opened her notebook and began to speak.

"We have a he said, she said. Ethan Montclair insists he had nothing to do with his wife's disappearance. He's been convinced his wife disappeared on purpose, but now he's worried someone hurt her. The wife's friends are split on whether Montclair is responsible, but one, Ivy Brookes, who appears to be the closest to them both, just broke it all open. She claims Montclair killed the baby, was abusing his wife, that there are photographs on Mrs. Montclair's phone to prove this, and she is convinced he's done something to her. Brookes also handed over a bottle of generic Benadryl she claims was used to OD the baby. Which is odd to me, because Montclair also allegedly got his wife pregnant by switching out her birth control pills. It seems strange someone who wanted a baby so much would kill it.

"Brookes also pointed out that Montclair's timeline could be completely off, that it's possible he's lying about when he saw his wife last. We'll have to figure that in to everything.

"Montclair claims he's being blackmailed by an online blogger who's been hassling the family for months. He tried to pay the ransom but the blogger never showed. Happily, there are a number of loose threads—phone calls, texts, and emails—which means Jim will be able to sort through them all. Montclair's phone is now tapped, as I understand it, so if there are any more demands from the blackmailer, we'll know right away.

"The one fact we have, there has been no word from Sutton Montclair for at least forty-eight hours. Even though the note she left is compelling, the revelations of the past two days are too important to ignore. I believe someone has hurt Sutton Montclair. I'm not entirely convinced it was her husband."

Moreno nodded to Jim. "You'll change your tune when you see what Jim's found."

Jim crooked a finger. "Come here. Check this out."

Holly obliged. The screen was filled with numbers. "I'm not the most tech savvy, you know that."

"Then I'll use small words and speak slowly."

She smacked his arm and they all laughed. "Okay. Enough foreplay. Tell me."

He clicked a button and the screen turned black, showing a dotted-white outline of the United States. There were multiple solid lines that looked like tracer fire shooting out of a small green dot in the middle of Tennessee.

Jim started tracing the lines. "The friend, Brookes, is telling the truth, or at least her suppositions are right. Looks like Ethan Montclair was trying to drive his wife batty. All of the traffic from the past couple of days, and before, is coming out of the

Montclairs' house. All the contact with the reviewer, all the contact with the blogger, all the contact with the friends, and with us, is shooting through the router in Ethan Montclair's office. The emails, the phone calls, the whole shebang."

"How is that possible?"

"A very sophisticated VPN, a virtual private network, which I was able to trace back to Ethan Montclair's world. He purchased the program over a year ago. We have the credit card statements going back three years, so we looked for anomalies and found this. Also, he bought spoofing equipment, so he could make calls to the house look like they came from outside, and burner phones. There's a rather sophisticated keystroke analysis program on Sutton Montclair's computer, too. Everything she did, every move she made, he's been tracking. All the files are on the router, in a hidden directory."

Holly couldn't help but think of Montclair's beseeching eyes when he'd asked her, *"Is it possible for passwords to be changed remotely?"*

"How hidden?"

"Took me about an hour to find it once I knew what I was looking for. The IP address on the email view wasn't a fluke. It looks like Mr. Montclair is behind this whole thing, and was betting on us not finding this hidden directory. It's a slam dunk, Graham. Dude's guilty as hell."

Moreno shut the file in front of him. "We're in a unique situation, Officer Graham. We've done this backward. Mr. Montclair gave us permission to search his files and his wife's computer, something we'd normally need a warrant to do. We've found enough to open a possible homicide investigation. We are getting a warrant right now to search the house. We're also revisiting the baby's death. Carlie's on that."

The older woman nodded. "If you can believe it, some of the tissue samples haven't been run yet. Though the case was ruled SIDS, the official COD hasn't been stated. There are still some outstanding tests. We've asked for them to be finished and sent as soon as possible." She checked her watch, a large dial with a white band. "Speaking of…I'm off to go run them down. Welcome to the team, Graham."

"Thanks. Good luck." She turned back to the rest of them. "What about the phone? Ivy Brookes told me we'd find photos of physical abuse on Sutton Montclair's phone."

Jim opened a new screen. "It's not enough for court, but there are some indications. Have a look."

She watched him open the pictures. Most were impossible to identify. They looked like blurry smudges, though one was clearly a female forearm with two distinct fingerprints denting the flesh, and another showed a bruised and swollen nose.

"If this is Mrs. Montclair's arm, that's a nasty bruise made by someone's hand. That nose looks broken. But that's all I've got on here. The rest are selfies and sunsets."

"What about the baby?"

"Nothing. Not a single shot."

"Strange."

"Not really," Moreno said. "When you lose a child, it's often difficult to have the constant reminder. Some people get their energy from looking at the old photos, setting up shrines. Some just want to forget."

"How sad," Holly said. "Well, we know she got hurt at least twice, and we've had a number of domestic calls to come out and defuse fights, though Mrs. Montclair always claimed she didn't call the police in the reports. We should look and see where the calls originated."

"Already did," Jim said. "They all came from the house, from her phone."

Moreno stuck a toothpick in his mouth. "She was probably lying to save face. That happens. I see it all the time on domestic calls. The woman's already been scared and beaten up. By admitting she called for help, she can be signing her death warrant."

The MP detectives chimed in. Walt spoke first. He had a gentle but distinct Southern accent. Holly knew he was from West Tennessee. "We're going to be doing a full-on grid search through the area. I'll be leading the exterior team, Alex will be in charge of the house itself. We'll start in the house and its proximity, then move everywhere around the neighborhood, and start working our way out. With your relationship to the suspect, you should stick with Alex. You're already somewhat familiar with the house. You can guide us there."

"Actually, I may want you here to interview Mr. Montclair," Moreno said. "Depends on how he reacts when we show up to toss the place and bring him in for questioning. You've definitely developed a rapport with him. He might just admit it all once we get him inside an interview room."

"Assuming his lawyer is going to let you talk to him," Walt said. "Joel Robinson isn't anyone's fool."

Moreno shrugged. "With any luck, Montclair is so convinced we'll never figure out he's behind this that he'll come on in like a good little boy and leave Robinson out of it."

Holly listened carefully to everything, nodding, taking notes, thinking. When they'd finished running her through the plan, she pocketed her notebook and crossed her arms on her chest.

"Sir, I appreciate that I'm new to the investigative field, but I have to say, something feels very strange about all of this. Mr. Montclair either has a split personality or he doesn't know all of this is on his computer. He'd never give us the goods to arrest him. He's too smart for that."

"You don't think he did it? We have a preponderance of evidence the man is playing a serious long con game, first with his wife, and now with us. His friends are abandoning ship. The second we name him as a suspect, they will all come forward with stories. Trust me. I've seen this before," Moreno said.

"I know you have, and trust *me*, I appreciate your experience here. But…why bring us in? To what end? If he wanted to get

rid of his wife, why didn't he just kill her and dump her somewhere far away, and not call us in?"

"Pretty boy wants to play," Jim said.

"Come on. I don't buy it. I don't disagree that everything is
pointing to a purposeful murder, and all of this looks really bad
for him. But there's something bizarre about it all. For example,
the video of Sutton Montclair at the reviewer's house. Both Ellen
Jones and Mr. Montclair agree that it isn't Sutton."

"How hard is it to hire an actress to go do something stupid
for you?" Jim said.

"Let me guess," Holly quipped. "There's a receipt for a hired
actress for the date in question?" She looked at Moreno. "Sir.
Something's weird here. This is so pat, so convenient. I don't
buy it."

"Hey, Golightly, there's nothing convenient about this. I said
I'd use small words, Graham, but trust me, this wasn't an easy
hack. Whoever did this knew exactly what they were doing,
exactly where to hide the files."

"Why keep evidence that can be used against you? Montclair
is a writer. I've talked to him at length, researched everything
I can find about him online. I won't go so far as to say I know
how he thinks, but it's clear from our conversations that he thinks
through every permutation. I can't buy the idea that he'd be so
dumb as to leave a trail of bread crumbs to his own door."

Moreno smiled. "And yet, young Graham, this is exactly what
we have. Here's the thing about criminals. They're stupid. They
think they're brilliant. They think they can get away with it.
Some of them are total sociopaths who can, but the vast majority are ego-driven little psychopaths who get their jollies trying
to out-puzzle us. The thing is, we've been trained. We know
how they think, how they pretend. In the end, a small bit of
evidence, a hair, a fingerprint, a flake of blood, is all it takes to
catch them in their lies.

"Now, it's going to take a little time to set everything in motion. You've been at it for two days nonstop. Go get a shower, get some food, get some rest. We're going to hit this hard very soon, and you won't have a chance to breathe for a while."

"But, sir—"

"No buts. You earned yourself a couple of hours off. Go. And, Graham?"

"Yes, sir?"

"We will find the truth that Mr. Montclair thinks he's hiding. Believe me."

When he put it that way, so vehemently and so plainly, she almost did. Almost.

A CRY, BUT NOT FOR HELP

Another nasty, empty morning. Ethan thought he might still be drunk. He was definitely hungover. His hands and wrists ached. He had crawled into bed somewhere around three in the morning, after writing nearly eighty pages of material. He'd never tapped in so completely. His previous one-day record was fifty pages and that had taken sixteen hours, with regular breaks, when he was young and dumb and didn't know any better.

He'd written almost a third of the story in one sitting. And it was good. Solid. Usable.

He did some light stretching, popped a few Advil and drank a liter of water, made tea, choked down some cereal, and re-opened the manuscript.

His thoughts bounced between the story and Sutton. He was consumed by images of her. The lines were becoming blurred. Whose story was he writing? His? Hers? Theirs?

Waking, sleeping, writing, he couldn't escape her. He didn't want to, reveled in the memories. When he needed a break, he looked at old photos. Then he turned back to the pages, and wrote. He didn't know what to make of this. His wife missing, his life interrupted, but his block broken.

The tone and texture of the book was changing, altered by the subliminal situation brewing in the back of Ethan's mind. He typed and thought, typed and thought.

They'd been so happy. He thought they were happy, at least. The Saturday date nights, dinners around town, expensive bottles of wine. The walks on Sunday down the Franklin streets, arm in arm, dodging baby carriages and young mothers in baseball caps, then with their own three-wheeled running carriage, the finest he could buy. The parties to which they were invited, their photos always making it into the society magazines. They were such a great couple, everyone said so. Such an adorable family.

Yet he'd screwed it up, again and again and again.

He was human. He was a man. He was even semifamous, and beloved among many.

Where were all the sycophants now?

His world had narrowed to three components: eat and drink, sleep, worry about Sutton by writing the story of a lifetime.

Eat was making itself known again. He made a late lunch with the last bits of the groceries. The tea tin was nearly empty; he scraped the last of the butter on his toast. He added the groceries needed to the iPad built into the refrigerator and clicked Order Now. The grocery delivery service would automatically bring the items requested in two hours. All hail modern technology.

As he chewed, the same refrains played, over and over. *Where did she go? Where had she gone? Why had she taken money and disappeared?*

How will it end? How will I draw the story through? Where is the next turn? Stay away from that saggy middle, it's getting marshy.

At the end of the day, he had another hundred pages. This, this was his atonement. This was his punishment. He was bound to the story, to the computer. Bound to the idea of a lost life.

And while he wrote, while he hid, while he lost himself, the police made the case against him.

THE GREEN GRASS
ACROSS THE WAY

Every case breaks. Especially when there are so many moving parts, so many edges, crevasses to climb in, dark, moist corners ripe for dissection.

The blackmail was a stroke of genius, truly it was. Everyone rushed off in the wrong direction, and here I am, left to pick up the pieces.

We're reaching the endgame. I can't imagine she won't be found soon. And when she is, Katie, bar the door.

Isn't that a stupid phrase? It's a Southern thing. It means a tempest is brewing. A storm of epic proportion is about to blow in your door. A woman will lose her temper, a man will become a raging beast.

These are the inevitabilities of life. We are afraid to die, and so we are afraid to live.

Do you think Ethan is to blame? That he put his hands around the pale stalk of her gorgeous neck and squeezed until no breath would ever be drawn again?

Do you think the cop will be smart enough to figure any of

this out? Truly, how much more does she need to put it all together?

I think it's nearly time for the show to start, don't you?

I'm not saying I'm playing the man. I'm not saying I killed
the girl. I'm just saying I think everything is going to change,
very, very soon.

A CHALLENGE
IS GIVEN

The ringing phone was Joel Robinson. Ethan had programmed specific rings into his mobile so he'd know when the calls were important and could ignore the rest. Joel was Judas Priest's "Breaking the Law," Bill was Dvořák's "New World Symphony," Officer Graham was the Darth Vader theme from *Star Wars*.

"We may have a problem," Joel said. "I need for us to have a little talk. You around?"

"I am."

There was heavy knocking on the back door. "Is that you?"

"It is. Hurry up and let me in before the vultures see me."

Ethan had almost forgotten the tribe of newspeople camped in his front yard. He was rather surprised the Franklin Police hadn't shunted them off; from what he could see, they were practically blocking traffic coming off the circle onto Third Avenue.

Ethan unbolted the back door. Joel slipped inside. He was disheveled and sweating. He'd clearly run over.

"What's going on?"

"Like I said on the phone, we have a problem. Several, actually. A witness has come forward."

Ethan felt a spike in his heart rate. He tried to keep his tone even. "They found her?"

"You should sit down."

Sit? Ethan felt like collapsing in a heap, throwing a tantrum, screaming, and beating his fists against the custom wide-planked rough-hewn white oak floors. *You're better than that. You need to stay cool.*

"Tell me," he said, steel in his voice.

"No, they haven't found her. But this witness is claiming you killed Sutton. That you were systematically abusing her. They claim you killed the baby, too. The police are reopening Dashiell's case."

There were many things he was expecting Joel to say. This was not one of them.

"Dashiell?"

"Yes. The witness claims you poisoned him with an overdose of diphenhydramine. That Sutton discovered this, and you killed her to keep her quiet. It's a very tidy story, and the police are all over it."

Ethan felt the bottom of his world falling, slowly spinning away, until he was left standing in very thin air. Wind whipped his hair, lightning flashed. The storm blew in so quickly he didn't know where it had come from. Rain began to pelt him, and he was quickly soaked to the bone.

To the bone.

To the depths of his soul.

Joel was screaming at him, pulling his arm. Ethan realized the storm was real. He was standing in the middle of the street, exposed on Third Avenue, surrounded. The newspeople were shouting at him, cameras were clicking. A sharp flash of lightning and an immediate rolling thunderclap shook the ground, and everyone gasped and scattered, seeking cover.

Joel tugged at him, finally got his feet moving, towed him

onto the porch. Shouted in his ear, "We need to go in, Ethan. It's dangerous out here."

"No." Ethan wrenched his arm away, sat hard on the porch swing, ran his fingers along the metal chain that bound it to the ceiling. Started to rock. The wind played along, helping him move. Movement was his friend. Joel stood in the front door, arm on the jamb, watching, calling, but Ethan stayed planted on the swing. Inside the news vans, he knew video was being shot, knew photos were being taken. He raised a middle finger toward them, held it long enough for everyone to get a good view.

When the storm abated, he went inside. Joel had made tea. They sat at the kitchen table, unspeaking.

Finally, Ethan said, "When will they arrest me?"

Joel shook his head. "I don't know."

Ethan wrote. He hid away from it all, the condemnation and the accusations he knew were flying, sat by himself at the long driftwood desk in the big old house on Third Avenue, with the ghosts of his wife and child, writing every word he could conjure. The story was already taking shape. He had always been able to write quickly once his idea was settled; this was no different. Thousands of words poured from his fingers. He ignored the ever-ringing doorbell. He ignored the constantly ringing phone.

He ignored the fact that no one he cared about was reaching out to help.

It had been the same when Dashiell died, come to think of it, minus the words, of course. People had kept their distance. He understood it was hard to approach them, hard to say the words. *I'm so sorry your child died.*

They'd say everything else. *I'm sorry for your loss. I'm sorry about your pain. I'm sorry, I'm sorry, I'm sorry.*

But no one could bring themselves to utter the words they really needed to hear.

He mostly didn't care. It wasn't like there was anything anyone could do. Sutton's friends had hung around the first few days, bringing casseroles, changing sheets. Ivy had made Sutton shower and dress every morning. But even Ivy had eventually been drawn away, off to a conference in Rhode Island, and then it was just the two of them, Ethan and Sutton, alone in the house with the gaping maw of death surrounding them.

Ethan didn't have many friends. Generally, he liked hanging out with Sutton. He'd been a hell-raiser in his youth, a lunatic ladies' man, an excessive drinker and partier, but once he'd married her, his wild ways had departed, and he'd become a devoted husband. And for a little while, a doting father, as well. Oh, he had a number of men around, people to have a beer with, or a pickup game at the gym, but he wasn't the type to go out with the boys, instead preferring to watch from the sidelines.

He was a classic introvert, and observation was his superpower. It's what made him such a good writer, everyone said so.

He'd gone online once, earlier, after the storm, after Joel left. His meltdown was intricately documented. He'd given them quite the show. He'd made headlines nationwide. He didn't need to read the stories. What he observed, right now: the whole world was entranced by the idea of a beautiful woman disappearing off the face of the earth. And the media bought in. They dug and pawed and scrabbled for information, sharp nails clawing for the viewer's attention, clambering over each other in an attempt to solve what had turned into a genuine, bona fide mystery.

As for the rest of them, he ignored it all. He needed to separate himself from his reality. He ignored the strings of Dvořák and the crashing of Judas Priest. Turned off the internet, unplugged the router.

He returned his fingers to his lonely keyboard. Allowed the pent-up anger and lust and love and hate to explode forth onto the page. In the back of his mind, he wallowed, thinking about all the ways he'd done her wrong.

If only he hadn't switched out her birth control pills. If only he hadn't planned to get her pregnant. If only he'd worked harder to convince her how their lives would be enhanced by a baby, if only she'd agreed to that choice. *If only, if only, if only.*

He went on like this for hours, until the pads of his fingers were bruised and aching.

The catharsis of losing wife and finding words was not lost on him. The visions of her dead would not recede, and instead made their way into his story. They dripped with sarcasm, redolent of his early work, the voice he'd long lost found again.

He finished one Scotch and poured another. Wrote and wrote and wrote. Got hammered as hell.

And still he wrote.

It wasn't until he noticed the sun had gone down and it was dark as sin that he realized his hands hurt too much to go on.

With a gentle smile, he gingerly hit Save. Stood and stretched. Played back the messages, increasingly urgent, from his agent, his lawyer, the cop.

They were looking at him now. A small flutter of something—excitement, fear? He didn't know—coursed through him. It was time.

You knew this would happen, Ethan. Why are you acting surprised? You need their help. Pick up the phone, put it back on the hook. Call Joel, have him help prepare a statement.

You fool. You actually thought you could get away with it, didn't you?

THE NEWS,
THE DAMNING NEWS

They were in front of the house, going live for the 6:00 p.m. broadcasts. Because it had been over twenty-four hours since he'd talked to anyone, friend or foe, Ethan turned on the television to catch the show.

All had been quiet. Too quiet. In between the frantic worrying, he'd written uninterrupted for almost a full day. He knew there was a search ongoing, and he wanted to be out there, truly he did, but the media wouldn't leave his front lawn, so he was stuck inside. Hoping and praying they didn't find her.

He knew the police were trying to find Colin Wilde. He knew they were looking at him, too.

He'd wanted to call Holly Graham and take her temperature, find out what the heck she was thinking, what the police were planning. It couldn't be long before they were knocking down the door with a warrant, wanting to look closer at everything.

He'd been so cooperative, though. Surely they were looking past the obvious. Surely they weren't so lazy as to simply assume he'd done it.

Then again, this much silence wasn't a good sign. He should

probably call Joel, see if he'd heard anything. The broadcast started, the spinning chyron advertising a breaking news alert.

The reporter was pretty; of course she was, they all were. Ugly doesn't sell on television.

He turned up the volume.

"I'm April O'Malley, coming to you live from Franklin, Tennessee, where we've been investigating the sudden disappearance of Sutton Montclair. The search continues, and the police seem to be spinning their wheels. We've had no confirmation that Ethan Montclair is a suspect in his wife's disappearance, but you know how these cases so often go, the spouse is the one who's ultimately responsible, and sources close to the investigation say a case is being made against Montclair as we speak. Evidence of abuse has surfaced, we've learned exclusively. Allegedly, actual photos exist."

Photos of Sutton's bruised arm and nose flashed on the screen. Where on earth had they gotten those?

Oh, her phone. The police had her phone. He fought back the urge to prank call it. *Is your refrigerator running? Better go catch it.*

No, Ethan, that wouldn't be seemly. The reporter was still talking.

"—recap what we know. Sutton Montclair, a beautiful, successful writer, disappeared sometime between Monday evening and Tuesday morning. She left behind a note asking not to be looked for, but her husband, local celebrity Ethan Montclair, called the police late in the day Tuesday, asking for their help finding his wife.

"And then…nothing. There has been no sign of her since. Her phone and credit cards have not been used, and there have been no reported sightings."

There was movement, a shadow loomed, then Ethan watched Filly walk into the screen.

"Bollocks," Ethan said.

"I'm now joined by Mrs. Phyllis Woodson, a very close friend of Mrs. Montclair. Mrs. Woodson, please tell us what you know about the investigation."

Filly practically gleamed with excitement. Her hair and makeup had been professionally done, the lights shone on her moist upper lip. Ethan looked closer. Had she done fillers, or something else equally ludicrous? Her upper lip seemed over-weight, out of proportion, the gloss slicked on thick and shiny, a pale pink that was certainly not her shade.

He heard Sutton's voice in his head, gentle and slightly amused. *"Claws, Ethan."*

I can't help it, wife. Your BFF looks like a bumblebee parked on her face and shat.

Filly's voice was slightly higher than normal. Ethan chalked it up to nerves, though she sounded so much like a horse neigh-ing he had a hard time not laughing out loud.

You're not behaving appropriately, Ethan. For fuck's sake, your wife is missing, probably dead, and you're laughing at her horsey friend on TV? You're a sick, sick man. Go wear your hair shirt. Go burn the rushes and drape yourself in sackcloth. Stop using this to your advantage.

"Fuck the fuck off, self."

From the television: "Well, we've been worried sick for days, as you can imagine. Ethan told us she was gone, but we all knew immediately something was wrong. She would never, ever just up and leave without letting at least one of us know. Now, I know that one of us—Sutton has so many lovely friends, but we're her core, her trusted advisers—"

Ethan snorted.

"—the women she told everything—" she looked into the cam-era, right at him, and enunciated the words for effect "—and I mean, *everything*. For her to leave without telling us is completely out of character. To not be in touch, to not let us know she's okay… well…"

Sniff. Tears. Blot.

The reporter was totally getting off on the performance.

"Do you know if there was any…trouble…in their marriage?" April O'Malley asked, gushing a bit.

"Well, of course there was. After losing that tiny baby, Ethan took his anger out on her. Why, there was even a bruise on her arm one night after a terrible fight they'd had. She took a picture of it, I saw it on her phone. I know the police are already looking into these things. They've been asking us all so many questions. And we're telling them everything we know, everything we can think of that will help bring Sutton home alive."

So that's what they'd been up to. The extended silence from the police. Talking to everyone. Listening to gossip. Laying out the case against him. Letting their circumstantial evidence drive them his way.

He turned off the television. There was no reason to watch anymore.

He'd already wrapped his head around the idea that the police thought he killed his wife. There was really nothing more for him to do than sit tight. They'd come round soon enough.

Might as well take advantage of the solitude.

He poured himself a Scotch, a double, and went back to the computer.

Let the words soothe his embittered soul.

NOT EVERYTHING
IS AS IT SEEMS

Assembling a murder case against a man without the benefit of a dead body is tricky at best.

They worked themselves to the bone, setting it all up. They took turns watching the house to make sure Montclair didn't run. Each report came back the same—nothing. *He had some groceries delivered. We saw him walking through the house. He peeked out the window. The television was on for a short time. No phone calls from the landline, and nothing unusual from the cell phone. The blogger never called back. If he's making preparations to run, we aren't hearing or seeing anything. He might be in there destroying everything, but it seems quiet.*

Holly had been tasked with talking to the friends some more, getting every last ounce out of them. She'd finally had a chance to sit down with Sutton's friend Rachel Temora, who was not much help, considering she was wildly ill. Newly pregnant, she had terrible morning sickness and kept having to rush off to the bathroom under the watchful eye of her sweet partner, Susannah. Finally, Holly had left them in peace. There was nothing new to be gained there.

She tracked down Sutton's mother in Canada. It was more promising, but she really hadn't learned anything Ethan Montclair hadn't already told her she'd say.

Ethan's an asshole. Sutton was tired of his antics. And my daughter loves a good drama. Look at what she writes. Are you sure she hasn't just run away? It seems more in character for her to leave than for him to murder her, the man's a gigantic pussy, but I guess you never truly know anyone. Let me know if you find her, God forbid something's actually happened. Have you ever been to Canada? It is incredible up here.

Holly had the sense Siobhan Healy would debate whether to cut short her trip if her daughter's body was discovered.

The rest of the team was doing all the hard work. There was so much paper being generated, logs and notes and files growing like mushrooms in the conference room. The whiteboard was covered in timelines and conjectures. Jim hadn't slept more than a couple of hours; he had done an outstanding job of tying together the technical forensics, from the money to the phone calls.

It was the amended autopsy report on the baby that sank them. The waiting tissue samples had been located. The backup lab had finished them, but hadn't yet sent the final report. High levels of diphenhydramine were present.

It wasn't SIDS.

The baby's death was reclassified a homicide. The only question was—accidental, or purposeful?

They kept that back from the media. It was too important a point. Moreno surmised if Montclair got wind of it, that would make him bolt. Better to spring it on him once he'd been taken into custody.

Holly filed her reports and learned everything she could. She paid attention to everything, read every page that went into the files.

The energy in the room was Red Bull on steroids. Everyone had something to contribute. Everyone added a stick to the pyre.

The evidence was damning. Not a slam dunk, not yet. But very damning.

And then they were ready. Two days of backbreaking, intensive work.

Ethan Montclair was going to go down in the morning. The paperwork was in order. The media was in a frenzy. There was still no sign of Sutton Montclair.

Finally, finally, the lights were shut down, and the doors locked. There were high fives, and backslaps. Moreno presided over them all with a benign eye, a proud papa. Instructions were given. They were going to hit him early, a predawn knock, start his day off right.

The jokes, the excitement, it all felt slightly scary to her. They were all 100 percent convinced Ethan Montclair had killed his wife. That it was only a matter of time until Sutton was found. Bodies almost always surface. It's hard to hide them properly in the spring.

She heard it over and over again. *Great job, Graham. Keep up the good work. Get some rest. Tomorrow's going to be a big day.* And from Jim, a hopeful, "Wanna get a beer?"

She'd smiled and yawned and demurred and headed home.

She had her own copy of the murder book—everyone had a copy, things were done in triplicate.

She poured a glass of wine. Heated up some dinner: a simple piccata sauce over mahi-mahi with shrimp and roasted vegetables. She was a good cook. She didn't cook for many people, she had performance anxiety about it not being perfect, but she knew what she liked, and dinner was ready quickly.

She took it and her wine into the living room. Put on a movie. Ate slowly. Watched and laughed. And when she was done, she cleaned up, took a shower, and got in bed with the murder book.

She'd practically memorized it. Memorized them. Memorized him.

She ran her fingers over a photo of Ethan Montclair. It was his author photo, printed off his website. He was impossibly hand-some, younger, not marked by the ravages of life and time. She imagined he looked about like this when he'd met Sutton Healy.

Floppy hair, penetrating light blue eyes—had they been Photoshopped? She thought back to her interviews with him—no, they were that blue, like a late-summer lake, clear and deep. He hadn't shaved, there was just a bit of scruff. His shirt was a crisp white, his jacket deep blue, offsetting his eyes. He wasn't smiling, or rather, he was, but it was a charming half grin. A smug smirk, Moreno had called it, but Holly could almost feel the amusement coming off Montclair. She could hear him in her mind: *I have to sit here and look serious now. This is my author face. Good God, take the shot already.*

Is it possible for passwords to be changed remotely?

Everything—everything—pointed directly at him. So why was she lying in bed, a hand inching down, staring at his picture like he was a model in a magazine and not her prime suspect?

Because you're an idiot, Holly Graham. Go to sleep.

She closed the book and turned out the light. But sleep was long in coming.

LIVE FROM
A CRIME SCENE

A phone, ringing. A long tunnel, harsh white light, burning her eyes.

Holly was disoriented for a moment. Where was she? What was ringing? Who was lying next to her?

Then the pieces fell: the person next to her in bed was Ethan Montclair.

She was naked. She was sore. They'd done it for hours.

And she was dreaming.

A delightful dream, indeed, a bit embarrassing, actually, considering he was a double murder suspect, but it had been a good one, the echoes lingering in her flesh, and she felt sated in a way she hadn't in months. She'd clearly been alone too long.

The dream faded. She felt a hot rush of embarrassment—yes, Montclair was handsome, but he was a killer. What was her subconscious thinking?

That he's hot as hell, clearly. And good in bed, to boot.

She came all the way awake with a jerk. Oh, no. Oh, no! She'd slept through her alarm. And the ringing was real: her cell was jangling. She squinted at the phone's screen. 5:05 a.m. She was supposed to be at the office in fifteen minutes. Crap.

The number belonged to Sergeant Moreno. This couldn't be good. Of all the days to be late. Oh, she was going to get reamed. She sat up, cleared her throat, braced for the attack.

"Graham."

"Get dressed and meet me at Gentry's Farm. We found her."

Holly stood in the middle of the fallow field on the edge of the forest in the middle of Gentry's Farm off Highway 96 where they'd discovered the body, waiting for Moreno to wave her over. She prided herself on being tough as nails when it came to death and dismemberment—she'd caught her fair share of gruesome car accidents, and people died all the time and she was almost always second or third on the scene; dead bodies were simply a way of life in law enforcement—but homicide was rare in these parts, and she hadn't ever been on the scene of an intentional murder. Not like this. In some ways, she felt like she knew Sutton Montclair. She mourned with her at the loss of her son. She felt anger for her at her treatment by the news blogger. She was maybe even a teensy bit jealous of her once-happy marriage to her excessively handsome husband.

And now she was dead, partially covered in brush, decomposing for all to witness. It bothered Holly. Tremendously. Both that the woman was dead, and that the team she'd been working with had been right about the husband.

She'd heard the rumblings when she pulled up and signed into the scene. Now she waited to see for herself whether the rumors were true. If they were, it was rather clear Sutton Montclair hadn't been the agent of her own demise.

She'd most definitely been murdered.

And everything they had pointed directly at Ethan Montclair.

The sun was coming up, peeking through the large row of oak trees to her east, casting strange, grotesque shadows across the roped-off area. People milled around; there was no urgency. The forensics team were collecting soil and insects from under and around the body—their composition would tell them how long the body had lain here, hidden practically in plain view. Chances were she'd died soon after disappearing in the wee hours of Tuesday morning, but it was possible she'd been held some-place first and then killed. From what Holly could gather from the comments floating past, there was a lot of decomposition for this early in the year. But they'd had a number of hot days in a row, and a couple of storms, so Holly wasn't too surprised. She'd spent a week studying at the Body Farm, up in Knoxville. She knew just what a muggy atmosphere could do to a body.

There were multiple jurisdictions on-site in addition to Frank-lin Police, namely two agents from the TBI and two deputies from the Williamson County Sheriff's Office. The foursome had been enjoying a pre-eighteen-holes breakfast together at Grays on Main to talk about a case and "came on by" when they heard the news. But there would be no jurisdictional fights: this case already belonged hook, line, and sinker to the Franklin Police, and the body was found well within their borders. Anyway, the body would go to the morgue in Davidson County no matter who was the lead. And she would be there, side by side with Ethan Montclair, as he identified his wife.

They hadn't told him, not yet. They wanted to be sure. Holly was going to head over with the preacher and Moreno to do the notification shortly—*and the arrest, Holly, you'll be arresting him moments after he learns the news*—and she wanted to get a good look at the body first.

Finally, after what seemed like hours, a whistle. Moreno was gesturing for her.

She picked her way into the copse carefully, eyes on the ground, making sure she didn't tread on some unseen, uncol-lected bit of evidence accidentally.

The smell hit her first. Deep, intense, rancid, and rank. Wet,

musky, rotted meat left in the sun too long. She steeled herself
for the first look.

Moreno was waiting, hands on hips. "Tell me what you see."

The first impression was unbearable. It never ended for her;
the dead and the gone were always a mimicry of themselves,
wrong, so very wrong. It took her a second to recognize death:
slitted eyes, limbs tangled, mouth drawn back in a rictus grin.
The next second registered the condition of the body. Though
decomposing, something was clearly wrong. She glanced at the
hands. Hand. Only one evident, sticking up from the muck and
mud like it was reaching to the sky from a grave. Balled into a
fist, a huge diamond winking. The rumors were right.

"She was burned."

"Correct. Why?"

"To hide evidence, maybe? She didn't do it to herself."

"No? You're sure?"

The world had reasserted itself, and Holly was able to look
closer, taking the body in sections. "There is clearly animal
damage. We'll have to wait until autopsy to see what might be
a wound versus a bite mark. Did Forensics find anything nearby,
gas cans, lighters, the like?"

The edge of Moreno's lip rose briefly. He nodded to a pretty,
dark-haired woman standing ten feet to his left.

"This is Sherrie, she's the death investigator from Forensic
Medical. Holly Graham, Franklin Homicide. Talk."

Holly kept her face straight at Moreno's introduction, simply nodded professionally, as if hearing her name and title asso-
ciated with the word *homicide* was a commonplace occurrence.
Inside, her heart raced.

Jesus, you got it. Don't blow it, sister.

"Good to meet you. We have to get her back to the shop,
give her a thorough once-over, but it certainly looks like she
was burned here. The grass and leaves are scorched around the
body." Sherrie referred to her clipboard. "To answer your ques-

tion, no, we haven't found gas cans, lighters, anything else flammable that would indicate she set herself alight. As you can see, the burns are worse on the lower extremities. Could be she was standing up when she caught flame, and then fell down. With her buried in the mud like that, anything could be hidden out of sight, but burning yourself to death without leaving some sort of evidence behind is hard to do. Whether this is our primary crime scene or just a dump site is yet to be determined. I don't see that we'll be able to pull usable prints, the hands are in bad shape, so without DNA or dentals… No sense jumping to conclusions until we have a chance to work it all out."

Holly nodded sagely. "Thanks for the rundown."

Sherrie made a note. "Cool. We'll take her shortly, Sarge."

"Do it. Make sure she's first up, okay?" Moreno wasn't asking, but Sherrie didn't look impressed.

"I'll let Dr. Fox know, sir."

She walked to the nearby gurney, started giving instructions to the morgue guys with her.

Holly blocked it out. Even the smell had lessened. She was sure this was Sutton Montclair. She wasn't recognizable facially, of course, not with the burnt skin and shortened tendons pulling her face into a bizarre death mask. Holly didn't know what Sutton's wedding set looked like, either, though based on the house, it was clear the Montclairs had money, and as such, Sutton's rings would be enormous. It was the spill of reddish-blond hair, still lovely, though matted with rain and muck and the desiccated flesh that clung to it, crawling with all sorts of bugs, that told her so. The hair was the giveaway. Plus, there were no other missing women who fit this description from the area. Hard to argue with that logic.

And then it hit her. "Her hair didn't burn."

Moreno was by her elbow again. "No, it didn't. Not all the way. Isn't that strange? You'd think it would go up like a phoenix."

"Regret, maybe? He burned her here, and changed his mind and put out the fire before it consumed her whole head?"

"Hard to control a fire like that. But that's a solid possibility. Either way, it's time to go talk to Mr. Montclair. You have your cuffs? You should make the arrest."

"Yes, sir, I do. Before we go, may I ask…how was she found?"

"Birds. A veterinarian from Animalia across the way called it in. He'd seen Sutton Montclair's face all over the news outlets, saw a huge circle of prey birds swooping around. From the number of birds and extended time frame, he knew it was something large, and phoned it in last night. It filtered down and I came out to take a look, just in case."

"You didn't call me." The words were out before she could think, but Moreno gave her that avuncular half smile.

"It was zero dark thirty and you looked like warmed-over shit when you went home last night. You needed the sleep. She wasn't going anywhere without you. And you know the first rule of homicide investigation. You can't go it alone. We're a team, and we split things up. You're here now. And now the real work is going to begin."

"Yes, sir."

She glanced to the sky. There were still some hawks hanging around, riding the thermals. Sometimes, it was as simple as looking to the sky to see where the feast was being held.

She'd been so close, this whole time.

Holly shielded her eyes against the sun and watched the ME's death investigators ready themselves to load the body onto the gurney for transport. A cry went up as they lifted the body. Sutton Montclair's beautiful, partially burned hair was still in the mud.

"Ugh," Moreno said.

"Totally."

The DI grabbed a bag and carefully lifted the remains of scalp and hair into it. Holly finally felt the gorge begin to rise. "Does that happen often?"

Moreno saved her. "Anything can happen to a body left out in the sun long enough. Come on, let's get out of here. It's going to be a long day. I'll meet you at Montclair's place. We're all set on the paper. Judge Kerr signed off on the warrants late last night."

"We should amend the physical search warrant to let us take a look around for gas cans and other flammable materials. Don't want this getting tossed on a technicality."

Moreno gave her a smile. "Yes, we should. Good call."

The van doors slammed. Holly had a momentary bit of sorrow, allowing herself to feel the loss of another human, then slapped her sunglasses down and walked to her car. Better to get it over with quickly, rip off the Band-Aid. She couldn't deny it now. Ethan Montclair was their indisputable prime suspect, and she wanted to see how he reacted to seeing the results of his elemental handiwork.

Crawling past the ever-present construction on Highway 96, wondering to herself, *Did he do it?*

For the first time, her gut told her he had.

AND NEVER THE TWAIN SHALL MEET

Ethan was watching for them. He'd woken with a terrible feeling in the pit of his stomach, almost as if he'd known today they were going to find her. When the doorbell rang, he steeled himself. Sure enough, when he opened the door, there was Officer Graham, dressed in plain clothes now, jeans and a T-shirt with a short linen motorcycle jacket over it, her gun clearly visible on her hip. There was a stranger with her, readily identifiable as a priest from his high, stiff collar.

A wave of fear and nausea went through him. She was gone. She really was gone.

"You found her?"

"May we come in, sir?"

Ethan stepped aside without a word. He saw a news van pulling onto the street. He shut the door before they had a chance to see anything. See him fall apart again. He needed to be careful. Watchful. Cautious.

Sutton.

They went to the kitchen. He sat at the table, the same spot he'd been in six days earlier when he realized she was gone. Wave after wave of emotion coursed through him. Love, fear, anger, all the horrible things they'd said to each other. Every beat of his heart brought a barrage of new, horrible words. He realized he was holding his breath.

I failed you. Oh, Sutton, I failed you.

The cop bit her lip, looked mournful. She clearly wasn't used to delivering bad news. The priest was uncomfortable, too. Ethan wanted to force their mouths open.

Finally, Officer Graham cleared her throat. "Mr. Montclair, this is Father Jameson. He—"

"I get it. He's here because you found Sutton. Tell me. I'm ready."

Officer Graham swallowed. "Sir, we have recovered a body. Unfortunately, there is no way to positively identify the remains without DNA or dental records."

Dread, deep in his gut. "Why not?"

"The body was burned."

"Burned?" Images he would never shake paraded into his mind.

"Yes, sir."

I should have called the police immediately. Insisted they look for her. I should have been out there, beating the bushes. What was I thinking? I could have saved her if I'd called. I knew the note was bogus. I knew something was really wrong.

"Who? Who did this to her?" he whispered. "Oh my God, Sutton."

And he broke apart, a million memories overwhelming him. He started to cry, heaving, jagged sobs. The idea of her body, her beautiful, lithe body, that gorgeous, smiling face, destroyed, made him want to scream. Not only murdered, but defaced with fire. It was too much.

The priest was saying things, muttering nonsense meant to calm and soothe, but Ethan couldn't understand a word. All he could hear was her name, over and over and over again, a holy wail building like a wave in his chest until he was screaming it out loud.

"Sutton. Sutton. Sutton!"

A hand on his shoulder. He vaguely heard the cop talking on the phone. Realized the look on her face had changed. The sorrow was gone, and in its place was a steely resolve.

She hung up the phone and faced him. "Sir. Mr. Montclair. I'm so sorry for your loss, but I'm going to need you to come in and have a conversation with us, on the record."

He saw her hand unconsciously inch toward her belt. Saw the silver glint of her handcuffs.

"Are you arresting me?" Ethan asked.

"We just need to have a conversation. We need to talk about all of this on the record."

Father Jameson said, "It seems to me the man needs a doctor, not a jail cell."

"Thank you for your assessment, Father. I'm following orders." And to Ethan. "I need you to come with me now, sir."

Ethan didn't care anymore. He'd known the moment they found her they'd think he killed her. It was as inevitable as the sunrise.

He shrugged. Let them think what they wanted. He knew he wasn't responsible.

Graham took him by the arm. "There are media parked outside. I don't know how to get you out of here without them seeing."

Again, he shrugged. "Whatever."

The door opened. Shutters began to click. The media rushed the porch, shouting.

Graham immediately slammed the door. "Crap. More than I expected. They've surrounded my car, too."

"I guess you'll have to interview me here."

Graham narrowed her eyes at him. "I'm calling in."

She stepped into the foyer. Talked to her boss for a few minutes, then hung up, and came back to the kitchen. "Your lawyer is on his way here. My boss is, too."

"Great. That sounds like a party I won't want to miss."

The priest put a hand on his arm. "Sarcasm isn't appropriate right now, Mr. Montclair."

"Sorry, Father. Not feeling so well at the moment." And to the cop, "I'm going to ask you again. Am I under arrest?"

"No comment. Did you kill your wife?"

He gave her a sad smile. "Of course not."

It went about how he expected. The sergeant and a few more cops arrived ten minutes post call, with Robinson hot on their heels, pushing reporters out of the way, shouting, "Ethan, don't say a fucking word," as he entered the house, which Ethan thought was rather excellent advice, considering. The media continued to mass outside, sensing something major was going down.

They all sat at the kitchen table, and talked at him. Ethan listened with half an ear. Heard words like *suspect, murder, lying, alibi, timeline, cooperation*. Robinson kept a hand on Ethan's arm to keep him from speaking and made a lot of impressive-sounding arguments, but finally, at ten after five, they said the words he'd been waiting for all afternoon, all day, all week, really.

"Ethan Montclair, you have the right to remain silent."

NOW THE WORLD KNOWS

The television was muted, but when the breaking news alert popped on the screen, the volume was turned up. A pretty reporter with a perfectly sharp blond bob, green eyes lit up like Christmas, was waiting in the shot. On cue, she began to speak.

"We have an update on the Sutton Montclair case. In a few moments we're expecting a presser from the Franklin Police Department, who will be—oh, look, here they are. On time. What a rarity. I'll turn it over to Chief Meecham, let her take it from here."

She turned toward a bank of microphones. The chief of police, a buxom blonde with strands of gray in her hair, approached the microphone. There were several people alongside, investigators on the case.

"Thank you for coming. I'm Chief Meecham, Franklin Police. We can confirm a body was found early this morning in a wooded area off Highway 96, near Gentry's Farm. Preliminary findings indicate we have found the body of Sutton Montclair. We will not be releasing any more details regarding the victim, including cause of death, or any other suppositions until after an autopsy is performed.

"Ethan Montclair, the victim's husband, has been taken into custody and is being charged with first-degree homicide. At this time there are no other suspects.

"Thanks to the tireless work of the Franklin Police Department, especially Sergeant Moreno and his team—"

The television flicked off.

A smile began.

NOW, ISN'T
THAT ODD?

Holly was unsettled. Ethan Montclair had turned into a mono-syllabic zombie the moment they'd arrested him. He'd been sitting in a holding cell for the better part of the evening, await-ing an arraignment in the morning. She stopped by to check on him a couple of times, and found him staring bleakly at the dirty floor.

She'd been given a thousand tasks in the wake of the arrest. Most involved typing up reports, which she thought might be the one thing about being a detective that bit donkey butts. Fill-ing out forms about homicide was a very dry experience any-way, and she wanted to be sure she had them right.

She hadn't gotten any sleep; her hands were shaky from down-ing cup after cup of coffee. Moreno told her the case was just be-ginning now. They all knew Montclair had murdered his wife. Now they had to prove it.

She'd asked to be at the autopsy, but Moreno had declined the request, wanting her to keep going on the paperwork instead, since there'd be too many witnesses already. She didn't bristle at the injunction; there wasn't much to be gleaned from a burned body, anyway. Plus, that smell…the reek of burned flesh still hadn't left her sinuses. She didn't know if she really wanted to stand around while the ME drove needles into the eyes to try to get a vitreous, which would probably be all they could salvage from that mess.

She checked her watch. Nearly eight. The autopsy must be finished by now. And as she thought it, the file in front of her flashed a red message indicator. A new file had been added from Forensic Medical, up in Nashville. She clicked on it, but it was empty.

Damn it.

She grabbed the phone and called the morgue. Got a receptionist, who forwarded her call to a voice mail. She left a message, hung up, scrubbed her hands through her hair, took another gulp of caffeine, and within moments, her phone lit up. It was the morgue.

"Graham."

"Fox, from Forensic Medical. You rang?"

"Hello, Dr. Fox. I got word you've finished the post on Sutton Montclair? My file updated but it's empty."

"Right. It takes a while for the details to upload sometimes. We have a lot of photos."

"Do you have a positive ID?"

"We haven't gotten DNA or dentals back yet, but we're still operating under the assumption that this is Sutton Montclair. The dentist is on a mission trip to Africa, and his office manager locked herself out of his computer using the wrong password. They'll send the radiographs as soon as they catch up with him, probably tonight. He's supposed to be out in some remote village this week, but he's been calling in every few days."

"Good grief. Can you tell me her cause of death?"

She could hear him tearing into the wrapper of something, taking a bite. After a moment, he said, "Sorry, didn't get a chance to eat breakfast. So COD, in this case, it's tricky. There's really no way to tell exactly how she was killed. Burning a body is a very effective tool for hiding a murder cause. I can rule this a homicide—there's no evidence of smoke or fire damage in her lungs, so she was dead when she was burned. There was also some whitish residue that we collected, chemically consistent with sodium bicarbonate."

"So she was burned on-site, then the killer put out the flames with a fire extinguisher? That's twisted. But it explains the hair not burning completely away."

"Maybe he's an environmentalist. Happy to burn the body, but didn't want to burn down the forest."

"Hardly. Whoever did this wanted to obscure the cause of death without drawing attention to the site."

"You're probably right." He munched some more. "That's really as far as I can go. We'll probably never know exactly what killed her."

"Okay. That official homicide ruling is what I needed. When you get the positive ID, can you let me know?"

"I will. Before you go, though, there was one really odd thing. The hair isn't real."

"Come again?"

"One of the evidence bags that came in had a reddish-blond wig in it. It's real hair, but there's a synthetic compound mixed into it."

"Why would she be wearing a wig?"

"No idea. Ask her husband, he might know. She could have had some hair loss because of a medical condition, she could be vain and want luscious locks. Either way, the scalp itself is lightly burned, and there's evidence of scraps of fabric clinging to the skull. We found some sticky residue on the top of her head. I ran it through the mass spectrometer, and it's an adhesive commonly used to help the front of the wig adhere to the forehead. Other than that, there's nothing of note on this autopsy."

"Fascinating. That's it?"

"That's it. You'll get my full written report within the week."

"Thank you, Dr. Fox. Have a good day."

She hung up, refreshed the computer screen. The report appeared. She read through it carefully, twice. Looked at the photos, enlarged several of the face and head. She couldn't tell anything.

Occam's razor. A preponderance of evidence said this was Sutton Montclair.

So why did Holly suddenly get the feeling there was something much bigger going on?

She gathered up her things and headed down to the holding cells. Gave the guard on duty a smile and a high five as she rushed by.

Montclair was sitting in the same position she'd seen when she last checked.

"Mr. Montclair?"

He didn't move.

"Ethan."

That seemed to rouse him, though he still didn't look up.

"Are you asleep?"

His head came up, and she saw a rage in his eyes that made her take a step back and reach for her Taser, which of course she didn't have on her belt since she was inside the station house. Then his eyes cleared and he smiled grimly.

"Come to mock the condemned again?"

"Not here to mock," she said lightly. "I have a question. And it's very important that you answer me truthfully. Important for me, and for you."

"Ask my lawyer."

"Listen to me. Since I'm now breaking the law by continuing to talk to you, humor me."

He shrugged. "What?"

"Did your wife wear a hairpiece or a wig? Extensions, anything like that?"

"Absolutely not."

"You're sure?"

"I sodding well am. She has the most gorgeous hair of any woman I've ever seen. Thick strawberry blond hair that is the envy of all her friends."

"But if you two had been having problems, could there be any chance she—"

"No. There is no bloody chance in hell my wife suddenly shaved her head and started wearing a wig. Now, why are you asking me this ridiculous question? Hey, Graham—"

But Holly was already out of the holding cell, running full speed toward the elevators. Back on the second floor, she hurried to the conference room. Inside, the brass were in a meeting. Moreno, the chief, a couple of other detectives.

She knocked, and opened the door. Heads turned.

"He didn't do it."

Everyone froze, then Moreno said, "For heaven's sake, Graham. Go home. Get some sleep. We're in a meeting here."

"I'm sorry to interrupt, sir. But Montclair didn't do it. I know he didn't."

Moreno narrowed his eyes at her. "Why, pray tell, would you want to rock the boat right now, Graham? You're being promoted to detective. You've done exemplary work on this case. It's a slam dunk. Even Robinson knows we've got Montclair dead to rights. He's already been talking to the DA about a plea."

"Sir, I'm willing to bet my career on this. Please."

That got his attention. He glanced at the chief, then back to Holly, a hairy brow raised. "Talk."

"The body we recovered? It isn't Sutton Montclair."

SUTTON

"Life is full of confusion. Confusion of love, passion, and romance. Confusion of family and friends. Confusion with life itself. What path we take, what turns we make. How we roll our dice."

—Matthew Underwood

MEMENTO MORI

I asked so little from this life. A husband. A family. Friends. Love, to give and receive. That's all.

And I got them. Oh, did I get them.

So when I fled my perfectly horrible life, I wanted even less.

A warm bed in a cozy garret. A garden with green ferns and white flowers. Cafés and rain, a good book, a comfortable pen to write with. Long walks, watching lovers stroll arm in arm, and painters' brushes sparkling in the dew. Solitude. I asked for solitude.

And I asked for inspiration, enough to fill four hundred pages, yes. I don't believe it is too much to ask for, is it? The desire to sit and write, to pour words onto the page, to create. It is what I do. What I did. Lusciously, deliberately. In the comforting absence of my life.

I did not expect the company of loneliness.

I did not ask to become involved.

I did not ask for the sharpness of a blade, flashing silver in the moonlight. The chaos, the cries. The sirens and rough questions and the thick wetness of blood on my palms.

Nor the stares, the stares, the stares.

ELLE EST ARRIVÉE

It was a dream Sutton Montclair had, moving to Paris.

She spent time on this dream. Invested energy. Imagined what it would be like: feeling a bit like Goldilocks as she worked her way through the possible housing list, hunting high and low for the perfect flat. The apartment on the Rue Faubourg would be much too expensive, the one near Notre-Dame too shabby.

When the dream became a plan, she did most of her research by watching reality television shows catering to international clients— *Sutton Montclair is moving 4,300 miles from Franklin, Tennessee, to Paris, France!* She narrowed down which arrondissement would be right for her. She wanted something slightly off the beaten path, residential, away from the tourist areas. She would hire the same real estate agent featured on the show to find her the perfect spot.

"A garret, that's what I'm looking for, something with Parisian charm, a good café nearby, and Metro access. Private, anonymous, French."

The *agent immoblier* would come through. She always came through. The woman had a reputation to uphold, after all.

It would take three days, but Sutton would end up in a charming furnished one bedroom in the 7th Arrondissement, on the Left Bank, with a picture-perfect view of the Eiffel Tower from the open living room. It would cost her a small fortune, but she had the advance money. After a brief negotiation, she'd secure the flat for a pirate's ransom, but she'd still have enough to live on for a year, if necessary. She was grateful her publisher hadn't asked for the money back when they canceled her contract. She was free of them, free of her old life. She could do what she wanted, write for herself. Escape. She just needed a small, brief escape from the vagaries of her life.

She would move in the same day; the tourist season was ending and the owner was tired of short-term rentals. He'd been working with a property company that catered to tourists and was desperate to leave the city and retire to Chamonix, where he planned to run a small coffee shop and ski as much as possible. The real estate agent would tell her the owner was grateful for the unexpected and quick offer to rent the apartment for a year, payment in full, up front.

Moving in wouldn't take long; she'd only have a backpack with her new laptop, new tablet, and a few worn, well-loved notebooks, a battered Hartmann carry-on bag she'd found at a local Goodwill store, along with three changes of brand-new clothes, all black, and some basic toiletries. Everything else she'd left behind.

Everything, and everyone.

And when the door closed, and she was alone, she would look around her new life. Spare. Empty. Perfect.

Safe.

What amazed her was how closely her long-held fantasy resembled her reality. Her new reality.

It didn't take as long as she expected. It always pays to do your research. She found the perfect flat in the perfect area on the most perfect street the first day. Took the keys, handed over twelve months' rent, and climbed the stairs to her new world in her gilded, ivory tower.

She'd escaped with her life. And really, that was all she could ask, wasn't it?

★ ★ ★

Sutton dragged the Louis XIV desk in front of the window, set all her writing tools on the worn wooden top. She had no internet access yet, no wireless, which wasn't an issue; she'd logged out of all of her accounts before she left, changed passwords to nonsense no one could figure out, especially her. Every single one, from Facebook to Twitter to Instagram (look, cats!) to Gmail. She'd downloaded all the files that mattered onto a thumb drive and put them on the new laptop, then reset her Dropbox account. Turned off all cloud support. It was damn hard to disappear these days, but it was doable, if you were smart. And Sutton was very, very smart.

No one had her new phone number, no friends, no business associates. Nor Ethan. Especially not Ethan.

She ignored the stab his name elicited, continued tidying her new space.

Ethan didn't know where she was. He was probably beginning to miss her now. Or not. She didn't care. She'd left a short, to-the-point note on the kitchen counter, on the richly veined Carrara marble she'd lovingly handpicked when they renovated the house. *Don't look for me*, it said. *I need some time.*

As planned, she'd walked to downtown Franklin, caught an Uber car she paid for with a Visa gift card, had him take her to the airport in Atlanta, tipped him $300 so he wouldn't say anything, dropped the disposable burner phone in the toilet and flushed it clean away, then hopped a plane and flew off to Paris, with her shiny new hair and her shiny new name and her shiny new passport.

Standing in her new living room, in her new city, her new country, her new life, the windows flung open to the cool spring afternoon, the scrolled wrought iron balconette holding her back from stepping into the sky, the birds chirping in the trees along the street in front of her, the red roofs leading to the view— the view!—of the Eiffel Tower, she took three quick breaths, pulled her newly dark hair out of its messy ponytail, and shook it down her back.

I'm free. Finally, I'm free.

She fell to her knees and began to cry.

WIFE, INTERRUPTED

Sutton woke the first morning in her new Paris flat to sunlight. It spilled through the window and edged around her bed, warming her, welcoming and friendly. She rubbed a hand across her face, wiped the grit from her eyes, and stretched. The bed wasn't overly large like the massive California king they had at home, just a standard European full, and she felt cozy and snug.

And famished, an alien sensation these past few months.

She rose, drank a glass of water, straightened the pencils on top of the desk. Pulled on a pair of tights and a tunic, slid her feet into clogs. Careful to make sure she had the key to the flat, she walked down the four flights to the street below, then up one block to the patisserie, where she bought a long, crusty baguette, then next door to the grocer, where she loaded up on fruit and vegetables, and finally, the cheese shop, where she purchased three varieties without looking at the labels. Ethan had allergies, so many of them, intolerances and sensitivities, so in order to coddle him and his bizarre issues she rarely bought food that she loved. Grabbing whatever struck her at the moment felt wildly indulgent.

She didn't know exactly when she'd stopped loving him. Wasn't completely sure she ever had.

They'd met at a book festival. Ethan was a writer, too, from London. A very celebrated novelist who had managed one brilliant book, gotten famous for it, and spent all his time now traveling the circuit, guest lecturing, and teaching the odd workshop, being paid exorbitant amounts of money to look fabulous at New York and London parties and appear frequently on Page Six with gorgeous women draped all over him like a bespoke suit.

He thought her books were trite, though he'd never said that. He'd never had to. It was in the way he smiled at her over the breakfast table, all indulgent, condescending benevolence, when she told him she was going into her office to work for the morning, and to please not interrupt unless he was bleeding or otherwise dying. She said it jokingly, but was dead serious. He had the most annoying ability to step inside her space at the most inopportune times. And lo, one hour later, just as she would be hitting her stride (the first thirty minutes being spent cruising the social networks, of course) here he would come, whistling.

"Ready for a break, darling? I thought we could have an early lunch."

"I have an article due for the *New Yorker*, would you mind giving it a polish?"

"This chapter is giving me fits, could you help?"

And she'd always acquiesce, because that's what good wives did. She fed and watered and laid herself down for sex at all hours and wrote and rewrote and polished his words till they shone, so he would stay happy, stay with her, and could continue getting the accolades that kept them in the heavily renovated Franklin Victorian McMansion they lived in, kept the adulation of the literati high.

Back in the flat, Sutton broke off a piece of the crusty bread, spread it with the soft, creamy cheese. Stared out her window at the Tour, smelled the smoke of a nearby fireplace. She was no longer a good wife. She no longer belonged to him. It was such a relief.

How had they arrived at this point, she and Ethan, as strangers again? Once, they were inseparable. They were horizontal as often as they were vertical. They had fun, laughs, joy, desires. Now, desire for Ethan was as foreign to her as this food she was buying, this city she had fled to. But that was why she came, to find a new life among the marble and grass and flowers. To escape. To start again. To start over. For herself.

Somehow, some way, she was going to eradicate the past half decade of her life.

And so she worked. And she ate again. And then she took a walk. Because that's what writers living in Paris did.

There was something so wildly freeing about being able to step out onto the sidewalks and garner no attention. She was one woman among thousands here. An anonymous creature, with no past, no worries. To anyone who noticed, she was a Parisian, through and through—the clothes she'd bought were current continental fashion and very lovely; she'd had her hair cut in the loose, natural style favored here. She bought neutral makeup, stopped coloring her nails, had them buffed till they shone. She carried a black Longchamp bag with thin brown leather handles, wore large black sunglasses, and double wrapped a well-loved Hermès scarf around her slender neck. Her French sounded native, was exceptionally fluent, with a local accent. There were so many strangers in Paris now, no one gave her a second thought. She'd overheard two women complaining that 30 percent of the people living in Paris didn't even speak French. They were becoming a city of immigrants, and the natives resented this, but if your French was excellent, all doors opened.

There was nothing—nothing—to give her away. She fit in like a grain of sand on an endless stretch of beach.

As she rambled through the fine Parisian air, she allowed herself the indulgence of a memory. She needed to wean herself off her past, slowly, carefully, so she could leave it entirely behind. But one memory wouldn't hurt.

A BIT OF BACKSTORY

Then

When she'd first met Ethan, at the requisite Friday night cocktail party for the talent, with his smooth smile and too-long, devil-may-care hair (expertly highlighted, she found out later), all she could think about was his skin. Seeing more of it. Touching it while lying next to him in the bed on a Sunday morning. Running her hands along his sides, across his broad back, and down, farther, to the silk she knew waited for her.

The desire for him, for their life to come, was sharp and immediate and she'd never felt anything like it before, with anyone. She watched his lips, full and laughing, and his teeth, shiny and slightly crooked, the front right overlapping the edge of its twin. And she just wanted to get him naked and see all of him.

It disturbed her, this reaction. Especially when she threw everything away and followed through on her urges. If only she'd resisted. Would she be here now?

He was beautiful in the way of hypermasculine men; he knew he was attractive, knew every woman in the room was imagining what it would be like to have him looking at, talking to, being with her.

Somehow, she was the one who caught his attention. She'd been drinking; these events always made her nervous and uncomfortable, so by the time she ran into him she was loose and downright flirty. There were two lines for the bar, and he was to her right. She tried not to stare, truly she did. Not only was he stunning, he was being lauded as one of the best literary minds of a generation, and the idea that she was within arm's reach of such genius made her giddy.

And there was the skin, that luscious forearm peeking out from his rolled-up sleeve.

And so she'd touched him. Stroked the fine, lightly furred skin of his arm. She didn't understand the impetus, but she'd done it. He'd smiled down at her, widely, the imperfect front teeth charming, and offered to buy her a drink.

At that point, Sutton was a foregone conclusion.

Later, they were both drunk, pleasantly so. They left the party and went to the elevator. She thought her heart would burst from her chest waiting for the doors to slide open. She knew exactly what was about to happen. The last little bit of rational thought she possessed screamed, *Don't!* But the naughty party girl in her, the one she'd so carefully excised when she'd gotten out of college, massaged her skin, slid down between her thighs, and said, *You know you want him.*

Then they were inside the elevator. The doors whisked closed. There were mirrors. They were alone.

"Here's my key," Ethan had said, rubbing up against her like an itchy cat. "Come to my room in ten minutes."

"Why can't I come now?" Too much Scotch was making her bold, so bold. "What are you going to be doing for all that time?"

"Trust me," he'd whispered in her ear, licking her earlobe, sending delicious shivers down her spine. "Ten minutes."

Trust me. Two words better off never spoken among strangers.

She'd gone to her room, brushed her teeth, her hair, put on

deodorant. Glanced in the mirror, ran a finger under her eyes so the mascara wouldn't run. Took off her panties.

The party-girl lust was making her act completely out of character, and the excitement of it was overwhelming. She couldn't wait ten minutes, stalked the hall until her watch said it had been eight, knocked lightly. He'd opened the door and swept her inside with a laugh.

"I just wanted to see how good you were at following instructions," he'd said, and kissed her, long and deep. The sex had been better than anything she'd ever experienced. He looked like he'd be amazing in bed; he lived up to his promise. Those hands. Those long, gorgeous hands.

They'd married three short months later, the flush of their love driving them to promises best not made, self-written vows about lifelong fidelity and never-ending support for one another's careers, come thick or thin.

Thin came too quickly.

Soon after their marriage, they'd been at a conference together—just once, she'd never do that again—and the moderator asked what their life was like. *Two creatives in one house. It must be amazing. You probably share an office, each tapping away.*

Ethan laughed, and there was something in that offhand gust of amused breath that made a hand go up in the crowd. A man, of course it was a man, in a voice as pompous and bombastic as Sutton had ever heard, stood and shot an arrow through her heart.

"Don't you feel, Mr. Montclair, that your books are more important than your wife's? That you, as a literary *author*, are creating significant, essential work, and your wife, the genre *writer*, is simply generating entertainment for the masses?"

Her husband, the literary star, the Author with a capital *A*, had grinned and waved his hand toward Sutton. "But she's such a pretty writer."

The whole crowd had laughed, and Ethan laughed, and Sutton had to smile along, all the while feeling small and insignificant. She knew she was less in his mind, and in the minds of many of his peers. Ethan was God's gift to literature; Sutton was a second-class citizen. Every time she thought of that moment, the words came unbidden. The words she'd heard when Ethan had dismissed her work, catering to the crowd. *You are no one. You are nothing.*

That her first award would drive a small but workable wedge between them was understandable. It was the second award, a truly prestigious one, that created the real problem. Oh, on the surface, things looked okay. Ethan claimed far and wide how very proud he was of his wonderful, talented wife. What an amazing *writer* she was. Never an author. No, never that.

All the while, at home, their happy life was withering away, those beautiful hands no longer touching her or the laptop keys or anything important. He went on long walks in the afternoons, came home smelling of bourbon and other women.

She was failing him. Failing their marriage. And then came the surprise of all surprises.

They named him Dashiell.

THE GHOST OF PAPA

Now

Paris was warm today, and Sutton was done with the indulgences. Her walk took her past the École Militaire, full of screaming, laughing children on some sort of recess break—she wondered how they ever learned anything, as they seemed to always be outside throughout the school day, shouting with glee at the singular fact of being children. Parisian mothers seemed to know something American mothers didn't, some key that Sutton had always been missing.

She did not allow their voices to remind her of Dashiell. Dashiell, like Ethan, was no longer, and she, Sutton Montclair, was a new woman without them. She had no past. She had no trials or travails. She was a mystery unto herself.

The Seine was only a seven-minute walk from her flat. She took the Left Bank by storm, arms practically swinging as she strolled along the sinuous water toward Notre-Dame, her chin up. A grain of sand she may be, but she was a Parisian grain now, and the tourists enjoying the day watched her walk by with admiration. She was their cliché—the gorgeous Parisian woman in the elegant clothes walking along the Seine. *If only*, they'd think. *If only we could be so glamorous.* There truly is nothing more beguiling than a Parisian woman.

The colors. The colors of Paris. So overwhelming. Soft pinks and vibrant yellows, inky blacks and musty greens, the creamy white marble, the sunlit golds. Sutton couldn't stop her eyes from roving, caressing each new sight, her ears attuned to every squeak of bicycle wheel, honk of horn, squawk of birds, all borne to her on whispers of the wind.

It was so much, so overwhelming, it brought tears to her eyes, so she fixed her gaze straight ahead on the gentle blue sky beyond the satiny gray bridges, looking neither right nor left until she could get her emotions under control. A breath later, or maybe it was two, the idea came to her. She rarely had to search for ideas—they had a tendency to show up unannounced, with fully formed characters, in vivid mental images, the scenes unfolding before her very eyes.

She saw a woman, with long, flowing red hair. Her clothing said eighteenth century, the skirts in layers of cream with a heavily ruched green velvet overlay, embroidered russet-and-gold leaves on the bodice. She was on a horse, approaching a large castle. There was some sort of celebration—yes, a marriage. She was arriving at the castle walls; all hail the new Queen. But it wasn't in the past, it was set in the future. A future where the world had collapsed, and a marriage between warring factions would help arrest the coming apocalypse.

Sutton smiled to herself.

It didn't matter the time period, nor the end result of the story. Was there a woman on earth who didn't want to dress in heavy silks and ride a horse sidesaddle through a portcullis while rose petals rained down on her upturned face and throngs of people cried her name with joy?

The story poured into her mind like water off a rocky ledge, unending, consistent, sparkling in the sunlight. The raining rose petals became torrents of blood and the triumphant scene turned dark, the sky melting into blackness, fires shooting into the sky, the screams of those behind the castle walls growing insistent in her ears; her Queen, her lovely Queen, lying deathly still, shrouded in a gauzy wrap.

She needed to get home right away—home, after only two days she already thought of the flat as home, how very strange—and write it all down. Her mind was sharp; the scenes would linger long enough for her to off-load them. But she never wanted to take chances. The first rule of creativity: never squander a gift from the muses.

She turned, started back. More ideas now, scenes crashing into her brain, sharp and vivid. She decided she couldn't wait the thirty minutes it would take to get back to her laptop. She stopped at the nearest café, the entrance a garden wonderland, took a table in the sunlight, signaled imperiously for a coffee, like she'd seen the other women in her neighborhood do, pulled out her Clairefontaine notebook, and began to write.

It couldn't have been five minutes before the clouds opened and rain began to fall. She scrambled inside with her coffee, laughing, shaking the raindrops from her hair.

The rest of the diners fled to the covered patio with greenhouse windows. Sutton headed into the bar.

It was then, the café garden giving way to the dim wooden interior of the restaurant, that she realized where she was. La Closerie des Lilas. One of Hemingway's haunts. She'd wandered into Montparnasse. How very apropos.

Excited now, she took a seat in the bar. She glanced around, trying not to look too much like a tourist. There was the stool with the plaque commemorating Hemingway's favorite spot, yes, but she was also surrounded by the ghosts of Montparnasse. All the great creatives of the time had come here.

The energy in the space was palpable. She'd always been sensitive to energies; usually overwhelmed in crowds, but this place, this empty, dark bar with the picture of Papa hidden on the wall above the lights that looked like antlers with red tips to the left of the bar, this place filled her with its emptiness, with its history-steeped walls. They must have left behind so much of themselves, so much of their spirits disgorged here, for her to feel their presence in an empty room. The conversations they must have had. The loving and hating and creating that took place, it had left a mark.

It was just her, and a black-haired barkeep she hadn't noticed until now, who'd stayed silent while she experienced the magic, and the sweating silver ice bucket full of open magnums of champagne.

She stayed there for hours.

The locals were in the brasserie eating mussels from the shell, so she was left alone, nodded at a few times by the maître d', who seemed to enjoy catching her eye, and once even pointed over his shoulder toward her. *Stupid Americans and their obsessions*, she thought she heard, but he was smiling, and perhaps she heard wrong, or he was talking about a family outside the walls with their bright white sneakers and expensive cameras slung around their skinny necks.

She took a sip of champagne—she had to have at least one drink with Montparnasse's ghosts—and went back to admiring the room. She liked it here. It was very quiet, the only real noises the clinking of dishes, the swish of the kitchen door, and the muted voices of the staff as they hurried from dining room to kitchen and back, their footsteps occasionally squeaking on the tiled floor. The floor itself was a masterpiece; she had to stifle the urge to lie down on it and watch the ceiling fan spin round and round in lazy circles. Incongruously, the soft French jazz on the radio ended and a favorite song came on, Jason Mraz, and a strum of ukulele got stuck in her brain. *I'm yours...*

Ethan.

Shit. Shit. *Merde*, damn, hell. It was their song. And now Ethan was here with her.

She hid a small sob in her champagne. He would have loved it here. She'd spent three hours writing in his hero's space and Ethan would be crushed if he had any idea where she was right now, what she was doing.

They were supposed to take this trip together.

They were supposed to do a lot of things together.

She realized her notebook was covered in drips from her tears. She blotted the words with a napkin, finished her champagne, and left. There were no more reasons to torture herself with ghosts from the past, recent or otherwise.

The rain had stopped. She turned left when she exited and walked toward the Jardin du Luxembourg. She wanted to take her buzz and her tears and sit in the grass and try, try to forget. Forget Ethan. Dashiell. Her life. Her past.

But how? How was she going to do this? How was she going to pull off forgetting him? Their lives for the past year had been marked by such horror and sadness, it was overwhelming in its grief. She couldn't imagine them ever being able to repair the damage. The things he'd said, the things she'd said... No, there was no going back. He'd never forgive her, and she couldn't bear the idea of forgiving him. The fire of remembrance lit her from within and she pushed her scarf from her neck impatiently, feeling like it was choking her.

Look around. Observe. Forget.

French girls read Dostoyevsky for fun in the Luxembourg Gardens, sitting on rock-hard green chairs meant to blend into the grass. Two chairs per person, one for you and one for your feet, and of course, it works well should a friend come by and want to chat. Older men set canes by their chairs, take off their shoes, and put their feet in the grass, smiles of bliss on their faces. Even the pigeons relax, cooing gently, feet folded beneath plump gray bodies in the cool, damp green.

Sutton followed suit, taking care to make the same fuss she had seen the girl next to her do—a performance, really—adjusting the chair to the exact, perfect spot. Once she was as comfortably uncomfortable as she could be, she took off her shoes and dug her toes into the grass. There was something sticky in the green growth. Disgusted, she moved the chair, the rattle of the metal legs against the stone path as jarring and grating as the tacky grass.

The girl reading Dostoyevsky was laughing quietly to herself as she marked a passage in the book. Only a student could find humor in the horrors of those pages.

The trees moved slightly in the breeze, small leaves waving. A feather floated down from the sky. A mottled white pigeon flew away over her seat, and the man to her right played an Enya CD, and the smart girl with the short hair turned a page and sighed. The French around her sat at the edge of the green expanse, staring longingly at the grass as if they wanted to frolic but were held back by an invisible barrier. The girl sighed again, and Sutton thought, *This is Paris.*

WE MEET A FRIEND

Eventually, her legs fell asleep against the hard green chair, so she rose, stretched, rewound her scarf, and headed toward her flat.

The story, her dying Queen, reasserted itself as she walked past the École Militaire Metro. She was thirsty and hungry and needed the loo, so she stopped at the café down the street from her flat. Once she'd eaten, she ordered a coffee, brought out the notebook, and began to work again, amazed at how quickly she was able to slip into the scene she'd been working on.

So lost she was in this new world that the sirens didn't penetrate her fugue until they were directly outside the bar, screaming.

Her back stiffened; she dropped the pen. Her mouth was suddenly dry, her heart pounding. The coffee at her elbow was cold, with a rime of brownish scum around the edge of the cup.

The *flics*, as she knew the Paris police were called, barreled down the street toward her, the alien sound of their sirens making chills run down her back. Her breath came short.

No, no, no, no, no.

She put her head down, let her hair hide her face. She felt the muse slinking away, drawing back into her corner, away from the biting, gnashing teeth of Sutton's memory.

The cars rushed past; the sirens bled away. The vise in her chest loosened. She took a breath, then another.

"Are you on the run?"

The voice startled her; she jumped, knocked her cup with the back of her hand. The remnants of the espresso spilled across the table, onto the open page of her notebook. Words began to swim in a lake of black and blue. She patted at them frantically, knowing it was for naught. They were lost.

The man sitting next to her had jumped to his feet to avoid the splash. *"Alors,"* he said, "you are quite jumpy. Let me guess. You murdered someone and rushed off to Paris under a false name to stay out of prison."

She forced herself not to stare. What sort of stranger says such a thing?

He wasn't French, rather, he was, but she could hear an accent underlying his words. British, maybe?

"You frightened me," she said casually in French, giving up on the notebook. There was no help for it; the words were well and truly gone. Three of the twenty handwritten pages were utterly ruined. She could only pray her imagination would keep the images on file until she could set up shop again.

She sat back in the chair. The waiter brought her a fresh cup, talking under his breath about clumsy customers. "And no, I am not a murderer. I'm on vacation. It's my first time in Europe. I've never heard those sirens in person before, only in the movies."

She was amazed at how easily the lies slid from her tongue. Then again, they weren't really lies. She was trying on another persona, that was all. She wasn't here to make friends.

"You speak excellent French for someone who has never been to Paris. And what a shame. Every woman should spend time in Paris. It is a prerequisite for a well-lived life, *mais non?*"

"I agree. That's why I took several years of French in school." She met the man's eyes at last, found him smiling quizzically at her. He was handsome—of course he was, this was Paris, after all—with dark hair cropped close to his head, an imperious, hawkish nose, blue eyes. Very blue eyes, deep, the color of dark denim. He was young, in his late twenties, dressed in jeans and a gray T-shirt. A striking man, and she looked back at her ruined notebook quickly.

He stuck out a hand. "Raffalo. Constantine Raffalo."

"Enchantée," she said, shaking his hand. It was cool and rough, and held on to hers a moment too long. She stood and threw two euros onto the table. *"Au revoir, monsieur."*

She stepped out of the tangle of chairs and small tables. The French had such an ability to sit on top of one another and never notice what the people next to them were saying or doing; their discretion amazed her. She started off down the street, in the opposite direction of her flat.

Her hands were shaking. How he'd come so close to the truth was beyond frightening. Had he known? Worse, had Ethan sent him? Even worse, could he be some sort of private investigator? How had they found her so quickly?

She forced herself not to run.

"Hey, wait up." Constantine Raffalo was suddenly striding next to her.

"I'm not interested," she said. "Please leave me alone."

"Not interested in your notebook? I know it was ruined, the pages you were working on, but the whole thing isn't a loss."

She stopped. Damn. He was grinning, charmingly so. "You ran off so fast, you left it behind."

She held out her hand and he started to pass her the notebook. When it was in both her hand and his, he said, "I have a price."

"I said—"

"Come on, I'm not hitting on you. Well, maybe I am, a bit. I'll stop. Promise. But let me buy you a coffee. I'm here on an extended vacation, and I don't know anyone. You're the first one like me I've met."

"Like you?"

"A writer. You are a writer, aren't you?"

She'd forgotten herself. She was supposed to be... Well, it didn't matter.

"I appreciate you returning the notebook, but I'm afraid I do have to go. Enjoy your vacation."

He respected the rejection this time, and she was surprised to feel the tiniest bit of disappointment. It was nice to be pursued, even if that meant absolute danger.

She felt his eyes on her back.

Murderer. It was such a horrible word. And it described her so very well.

A murderer would run, Sutton. You're acting suspicious. Now he'll remember you. Stupid, stupid, stupid.

She turned back. He was still watching her.

"One coffee, Constantine Raffalo. Then I have to go back to work."

AND SO IT BEGINS

Sutton felt the attraction begin between them almost immediately. She was no stranger to this emotion. As a girl, she'd been perpetually half in love with every boy she laid her eyes on. Tall, skinny, short, fat, straight, gay, brunette, blond—she had no type, only a need to be near them, to touch them, to talk to them. She was very tactile; it got her into trouble.

Constantine held out her chair. His hand brushed hers as she sat down, and she had to fight the urge to take it and examine it closely for signs of kindness or hatred. It was a good hand, the fingers long and elegant, like those of a pianist. She tried not to think about the length of them, the feeling they'd create inside her, how deep he could go.

She ordered a fresh espresso. He ordered a Scotch and smiled at her quite charmingly.

"It's the middle of the day," he said. "We're on vacation, you and I. Have a real drink with me. Just one."

"Champagne," she amended to the waiter, who turned away with a brusque nod. "I am not on vacation, though."

Drinking champagne with a stranger on the sidewalk of a Parisian café in broad daylight. This couldn't lead anywhere good.

Oh, but it might, Sutton. Two drinks and you might be on your back with your legs in the air, Constantine Raffalo straining above you with a look of adoration in his eyes.

The doctors had told her the preoccupation with fantasy, with imagination, with sex, was a symptom of her disease. It helped with the writing, certainly, but sometimes, she wondered if that was all she was. A disease. Her ability to create, to evoke a scene, a scent, a feeling, was all part of the disordered chaos in her brain. They'd claimed it was something to do with serotonin reuptake, and the way it didn't allow the neural pathways to connect properly, leaving her out in the cold with an overactive, obsessive imagination and a frightening sense of exhilaration, an inability to stop her mind and her thoughts from racing, to the point that she often felt the world was rushing headlong forward, the pedal all the way to the floor. Sometimes, when things were just about to turn very, very bad, she could actually feel the earth rotating on its axis beneath her feet.

Sutton knew she was only partially of this world; the day-to-day life of mankind, the commutes and the news and the seasons, time passing gently to mere mortals. When she was on the verge, she could tap into some sort of collective unconscious and see the truths of the universe.

Which, of course, to some—including her bitch of a doctor—made her textbook, bona fide, certifiably crazy.

So Sutton wrote. She felt better when she wrote. The doctor had once told her it was simply a method of controlling her psychosis, how she was able to corral the multitude of voices in her head by putting words on the page.

Sutton didn't take this dark gift for granted for a second. She knew that if she didn't have the outlet, hadn't found a way to channel her inner demons, she'd be mumbling to herself as she shuffled along the side of the road, hair in greasy hanks, clothes tattered, her feet rubbed raw from too-small shoes found at the local junk store, her life shortened by her brain turning to Swiss cheese inside her skull.

Happily, there was a pill for that. She took them religiously. She'd brought a year's supply with her. She didn't plan to stay away quite that long, only long enough to assuage some of the guilt and give her tired mind some room to relax. Time to get Ethan fully out of her system.

Goodbye, Ethan.

She had no doubt that if she hadn't been cursed with all the extra mental goodness, the words would be gone, too. Would she be happier without them? Would she be normal? Would she have had a cadre of girlfriends and they'd have wine and cheese parties and girls' weekends and send their men off to play golf and talk about periods and breastfeeding and the latest innovations in diapers and swill champagne by the bucket at book club meetings?

Would she want that from her life? She thought not. She thought—and it was one of those wonderful lightning flashes of epiphany, the kind that leave you slightly breathless and perfectly content—that no, she wouldn't like a normal life at all, thank you very much.

Besides, how do you trade a gift—Sutton always felt her writing ability was a gift, dark as its biological genesis may be, no doubts there—for sanity and normality? How? Wasn't it a slap in God's face? He'd made her in his image. Did that mean God was suffering from some sort of mental disorder, as well?

Feeling mildly sacrilegious and quite pleased with *that* thought progression, which had taken less than ten seconds, exactly enough to take a single sip of her champagne and cross her legs, she gave Constantine Raffalo a genuine smile. He was pleasant to look at; his teeth were white and straight when he smiled. She often wondered if she could judge a person solely by their teeth. An inversely proportional ten to one scale. The straighter and whiter (a ten) they were, the lower on the scale of trustworthiness they went. Straight, white teeth meant money spent to make them that way. Money meant coming from a world she hadn't been familiar with.

Her own teeth suffered from an odd dentition, the canines eagerly pushing forward so her front four teeth lay back, flat against her lips. It would only have taken a retainer to fix, but there was no money in her childhood household for such luxuries. Ethan's crooked front tooth...

The voice that lived in her head and called so many of the shots in her life said, *Stop it. Engage. You're drifting again.*

"Where are you from?" she asked.

A plain Midwestern voice, now unaccented, spoke. "Ohio, originally."

"Really? I thought you were British, or Parisian. Your French is quite cosmopolitan. And Raffalo..."

"I went to school here for a while. I've lived all over. My dad's military, and of Greek descent. He was the one who saddled me with Constantine. No American kid should have more than two syllables in their name. It's an open invitation to be a target."

She could hear the various influences in his speech pattern. It was almost disconcerting. One minute American, then words laced with French, and some with straight-up British.

And military orthodontia. Her estimation of him rose a notch. Not a trust fund baby, then.

"Tell me your name," he said, leaning forward slightly at the tiny table.

"Justine Holliday," Sutton replied without missing a beat.

HELLO, MY NAME IS...

Justine Holliday.

It was the identity she'd set up for herself before fleeing.

Sutton had spent a great deal of time thinking about her escape. She'd had the week in the hospital—against her will, the idiots, she was quite fine, only looking at the bottle's directions, it was a fluke the bottle had opened and the pills had gotten into her mouth, she'd only wanted a moment of bliss—to decide what she wanted to do with her life. Life after incarceration. A moment in her life marked forever. Before incarceration, and after incarceration. BI life was odd and unexplainable, with careers and husbands and babies. The pressures of being happy, happy, happy, oh, we're so very happy, can't you tell?

AI life was more manageable. It was just her. Abandoned, castoff, alone but not adrift, no, never adrift. She could be whomever she needed. Whomever her mind dictated at that moment.

Justine Holliday was a combination of two names picked out of a board of directors' listing on a pamphlet for the Christian organization that sponsored a halfway house where the doctors had wanted her to stay for a few days once she'd been discharged. Like being saved on her way out the door was going to change how her broken, adrenaline-flooded mind worked. Please.

Justine Holliday. That's who she'd become. Her progenitor was brilliant at creating characters, remember. She tried on the persona, felt it mold to her body like cashmere.

Justine Holliday was young and single, in Paris to follow the dream. She was a fan of Ernest Hemingway and Gertrude Stein. She knew her way around the City of Light. She was writing a memoir—can you imagine that? Trying to, at least. She had money, some from her family, some that she'd saved, a minuscule amount from an advance against the sale of the book, and had taken a flat in the 7th Arrondissement, which was more affordable than some of Hemingway's old stomping grounds, but still expensive enough for an expat to be safe and anonymous.

Justine Holliday was from Hollywood, Florida (how silly of my parents—we were known as the Hollidays from Hollywood). She'd grown up in a normal, middle-class house with a screened-in back porch with a pool, the only way to keep their two small dogs safe from alligators. They'd had a normal, middle-class, know-everyone-in-your-town upbringing. Her mother made cookies for the school bake sale. Her father coached the Little League teams. Her older brother was a high school football star who worked at a car dealership now, was married to his prom queen date, a girl he'd known since they were thirteen, and had a baby on the way.

Justine Holliday was blissfully, completely, emptily normal. She had her whole life stretched out in front of her. She was in Paris to write, had a handsome young man named Constantine Raffalo buying her champagne, and was currently experiencing a decidedly non–Justine Holliday emotion, a small tingle squeaking up her spine that said, "Go to bed with him. It will be fun."

Perhaps the enjoyment of sex with relative strangers should be part of Justine Holliday's life. Yes, an enjoyment, but plain-Jane vanilla missionary sex was Justine's thing, with maybe a hint of tie her up and ride 'em cowgirl, if she knew you very, very well and had been charmingly overserved.

Yes. There. That worked.

Justine was simple and carefree and looking for a good time, and shook her black hair off her face.

Justine wasn't a murderer.

"Tell me about growing up all over the world," Justine said to Constantine, leaning forward just a bit. "It sounds terribly exciting."

"You have the terrible part right." Constantine laughed. "Every time I had to pack up my model airplanes and stuffed bears into this old green duffel of my dad's, I thought, 'This is the last time.' Of course it wasn't. We never stopped moving."

"And your mother? Did she enjoy moving house and having new adventures?"

His face changed slightly, becoming at once harder and more vulnerable. "She died when I was eight. We were in Düsseldorf. She caught pneumonia and was gone within the week. She never had time to say goodbye. One day she was fine, a little glassy-eyed and coughing. We were playing Hearts—the card game, you know it? We'd played at least fifty rounds, all afternoon, and she hadn't cooked dinner, and my dad was so mad when he got home to a cold stove. They had a fight, she went to her room pleading a headache. Dad and I cleaned up the cards, ate toast and beans, which was fine by me, I loved toast and beans. I knocked on her door and shouted good-night, not knowing she was so sick. They told us later that by then, when I knocked, she was already too far gone to save. She never woke the next morning, and died a week later." He shook his head, gave her a rueful smile. "I've never told anyone that before. I don't know what's gotten into me."

"The Scotch, probably, or the pollen from the cherry blossoms."

Justine was witty! Imagine that.

"I think it's you," he said, those electric eyes on her mouth. "I think Justine Holliday is making me senseless."

"Pas possible, mon enfant." God, why had she called him that? A pet name, already? They hadn't even known each other for twenty minutes. *Don't be an idiot, Justine.* She sipped her champagne casually. "We're simply ships passing in the night."

An offer, passed on. She noticed Constantine relax a bit, saw right into his thoughts in the uncanny way she had. (Justine isn't like that, Sutton warned herself.)

He'd been trying very hard to make this a romantic moment, something to remember, perhaps a wonderful anecdote to trot out at parties and tell their grandchildren. *"Your grandmother fell in love with me over champagne at a tiny table in a seedy café in Paris, children. Watch, and learn."* He was a man on the make, a man looking for love in the most romantic city in the world. He'd found a willing target and was going to work hard to sweep her off her feet.

He probably had genital warts. Or herpes.

His smile was more relaxed now, too, and his eyes had gone from predatory to warm, inviting, comfortable. She could sink right in, like walking through waves into a deep, blue ocean.

"So tell me about you, Justine."

"About me?" She touched his bare forearm with a curious finger and the voice in her head said, *Watch out for sharks.*

A BABY IS BORN

Then

Dashiell Ethan Montclair came two weeks early, practically in the parking lot of the post office where Sutton had just dropped their check in the mail. Thank goodness Ethan saw her double over as she exited the building with their PO box mail in her hand. He managed to get her to the hospital with fifteen minutes to spare.

Dashiell was always in a hurry.

Ethan complained the name sounded like a hero from one of Sutton's novels. She explained, in unending detail, why she'd chosen the name. After Hammett, of course. A crime writer. A man's writer. A man's man, Hammett. *For heaven's sake, Ethan, you call yourself a writer?*

After the nearly inauspicious beginnings to the child's life, Ethan caved. Whatever Sutton wanted, Sutton got. That was their deal.

Dashiell was an adorable baby. All fat cheeks and pink lips and deep blue-gray eyes, just like his mother. He was a watcher, quiet and calm, easily amused, with a gurgling, contagious laugh, always willing to go down for a nap so Sutton or Ethan could work. Sutton kept him in a basket on the floor next to her desk, like a cat, or a dog. She'd tap the edge with her foot, set it to rocking, and Dashiell would lie content and sated in his nest.

Ethan adjusted to their new life faster than Sutton. She was—admittedly—a selfish woman. She liked their old life. Parties at night, late-sleeping mornings, sex anytime they wanted, travel galore. Liked not having to answer to anyone, not having a boss, nor having a get up and leave the house and sit in traffic and make jokes at the watercooler about last night's *Dancing with the Stars* job.

They had freedom still, yes, and now they had a child, which made Ethan happier than anything before.

But after the "Summer of Acclaim," as Ethan called it in his most condescending voice, things were a bit rocky.

Rocky. What a silly term to describe a marriage on the rocks. *Tumultuous* was a better description. Stormy. Torturous. Of or relating to Tantos, the pits of hell.

I got that bruise when I walked into the refrigerator.

Of course you're sorry and it will never happen again.

Yes, I still love you.

That phone call? Just some fan, wanting to meet for coffee. They're so very aggressive these days.

They built a house, a life, on lies.

There were good moments. Great moments. Calm moments.

Croissants with butter in bed, flakes getting on the sheets.

Walks along the river, with blossoms from the trees raining down in the breeze.

The trip to New York, that night at the Waldorf Astoria, after too many bottles of wine at dinner with Ethan's agent and editor. They'd had *fun*, damn it all. They pretended it was their first time, reenacted the events of their first fateful meeting. He left her in the hall waiting to come into the room, without her panties, for ten minutes.

That trip.

Sutton knew better than to get pregnant to save their marriage. That's something desperate women did, and she wasn't a desperate woman. She had a *rocky* marriage, but they were trying to smooth the jagged edges. They'd turned the page in New York, she was sure of it.

Turned a page, yes. Then they'd driven the car right off a cliff, holding hands and crying hallelujah.

Dashiell truly was a surprise, an accident. *No, not an accident, Sutton, a blessing. He was a blessing, then and now.* An angel. A cherubic little angel, a gift from God.

The Lord giveth. He giveth more than we can handle, sometimes.

Her doctor told her there was a reason the birth control pill had a 3 percent failure rate, even for women who took them religiously. Which she had. She'd even set an alarm on her phone and carried them in her purse. She was never a moment behind schedule. She ran her birth control like she ran her life, seamlessly, organized, structured.

She didn't like to think of her baby as a statistic.

But the cracks were forming before the pregnancy. The mangled car was at the bottom of the cliff, still smoking.

Dashiell, while adorable, was a thorn in her already *rocky* marriage. A baby meant scheduling—for the sex, for the trips, for their (her) work, for their life. They were no longer carefree, untethered. There was a constant flow of things that needed to be handled, from diapers to feedings to naps to babysitting. To nannies. Many, many nannies.

It was her Goldilocks nature again. This one was too strict, this one too loose. This one she walked in on getting high in the laundry room. Sutton blamed herself for that one; the girl's name was Moonshadow, for heaven's sake.

Finally, finally, they settled on a genuinely lovely young woman named Jan, Just Jan, as Sutton liked to think of her. She was plain, with pale blue eyes and white-blond hair done in two braids that swung on either side of her neck like a butter-churning dairy maid. She had a degree in elementary education, but hadn't liked teaching. She was better off one-on-one. Sutton thought she probably had a touch of Asperger's—her social cues were severely lacking—but she was devoted to Dashiell, and he to her.

With Just Jan on board, things returned to a more normal routine. The sex got better, and more frequent. They took a few trips, all together: Just Jan down at the pool with Dashiell under an umbrella, covered head to toe in light layers and a tiny floppy hat; Sutton and Ethan on the balcony, eating grapes and drinking champagne. It almost felt familiar. It almost felt right.

So right, Ethan started a new book. He started many new books, and generally grew tetchy and bored after a few weeks. This time, though, he'd stuck to it, and there were pages, actual pages, on the floor of his office, waiting patiently in their manuscript box for their brethren to arrive.

Ethan was a madman when he wrote, comically Einstein-esque in his eccentricity. He worked for hours, paying no attention to the normal order of things; sunrises and sunsets and bedtimes of others were irrelevant. His hair stood on end; he forgot to shower. He needed odd foods at odd hours. Eggplant parmesan at ten in the morning. Pecan-maple pancakes and crispy bacon at four in the afternoon. Always from scratch and with high-end organics, nothing premade, store-bought, or delivery would do.

Sutton cooked whatever he wanted, because that's what good wives did. She cooked and cleaned and mothered him, and sometimes she even had time to mother her child, as well.

She began to wonder if she was in an abusive relationship. What would she say to a therapist? *He pays for everything, hired me a perfectly wonderful nanny. But now he won't let me do my work, and he makes me cook for him. All the time.*

She couldn't tell the truth, obviously. That would never do.

She decided, pound for pound, her life was simply comical. Her career could wait. Once he finished the book, she'd be able to return to her schedule. What was a few months, after all? She did so love to cook.

And then he'd gotten stuck. Ethan always got stuck. But this time, it was deeper into the meat of the novel, the important part, where the main character reveals himself to the reader for the very first time, and is judged. A seminal moment. In her brand of novels, it was called a plot point, but in his, it was *seminal*. Even their language had to be separate, different, his more important, always, always.

As sudden as an unexpected storm and an ear-shattering clap of thunder, his flow ended. No more fingers clattering on the keyboard at all hours, no more random food requests. He slunk around the house, hollow-eyed and pale-cheeked, pulling books off the shelves in the library, leaving them scattered on the chairs by the window that overlooked the front porch.

She offered to help. She'd helped him before. *Tell me what the issue is. Let me see if I can come up with something.*

She couldn't leave the house for a week, even had to avoid Just Jan. Her swollen, bruised nose took forever to heal. There was so much blood, so many apologies. The fallout haunted them forever. It seemed fitting that she would ruin the marble she so loved with her own blood.

It had been a stupid mistake to offer like that. Everyone makes them. She hadn't thought. And she'd paid the price.

The story should have ended right there. With the black eye and the broken nose and the baby screaming from his withy basket because Just Jan had the day off.

But that was where the story really began.

CAFÉ AU LAIT IN BED

Now

Sutton opened her eyes. The view was startling—to the left, the man beside her, and to her right, the Tour framed like a picture postcard in the window.

You wanted a new life. You've got it. You've started it. With a mother-fucking bang, no less, sister.

Her fall from grace hadn't taken long. Sutton—Justine—was simultaneously furious with herself and wallowing in the glory of sex with a new person, in a strange bed, in a strange but all too familiar city.

Constantine felt her stir and put a hand possessively on her hip. She stopped moving and he fell back asleep.

She shut her eyes, too, blocking out the world, and thought about Ethan.

It was wrong to. She knew that. Thinking about a man while in bed with another wasn't a good, healthy way to live. It seemed she'd done it once too often lately, too.

They'd been happy in the beginning. She remembered telling her mother how very happy they were.

"We are happy. So very happy. Happy, happy, happy.

"We're perfect for one another. Both writers, both creatives.

We are on the same schedule—we both like to write first thing in the morning, like to stay up late, watching movies and TV shows. We both like action movies, and despise horror films. We don't read the same authors, so we're able to expose each other to new ideas.

"Money? Well, not to brag, but he has plenty, but you know, Mother, so do I. Maybe not quite as much as he—okay, Mother, if I tell you a secret, will you swear not to say anything? I actually made more than he did on my last contract. It's just the nature of commercial fiction versus literary. We genre writers are always seen as being so vulgar because we actually make money at our art. But don't tell a soul I told you that. You promise?

"Yes, he loves me, Mother. He really does.

"Yes, he knows.

"Yes, I told him.

"Oh, for God's sake. I need to go."

Her mother. Was it ever possible to have a normal, loving conversation? Always dredging up the guts of the past. Threatening and cajoling.

Once, as a teenager, so fed up with her life and needing a little sympathy, Sutton concocted a fantasy for her friends. She confided that the woman she called Mother, Siobhan Healy, wasn't her real mother. Sutton had no idea who her real mother was. She had a name, of course, off the birth certificate, but that woman had left Sutton behind on the steps of a fire station in Indiana and hadn't ever come back. Finally, when she was old enough, Sutton had done the research and learned who her biological mother was. She'd tracked her down, saw the woman's shiny new life, with her shiny husband and three shiny children in a shiny house with two shiny cars and a shiny fucking dog, and had known she'd never fit in there. So she'd gone home, back to her decidedly nonshiny trailer with Maude, her foster mother—she hadn't yet changed her name to Siobhan—who was between husbands and needed a little extra cash, and so gamed the system to allow her to foster. Maude, pedestrian old Maude, who smoked Pall Mall cigarettes and drank rotgut vodka out of Coke cans because she thought that vodka didn't make your breath smell like alcohol and her boss at the Kroger didn't know she was showing up shit-faced.

It had been fun while it lasted, pretending not to belong to her reality, but word got back to Maude, who set the friends and parents straight, then grounded Sutton for lying.

Still, Maude was a poor substitute for a real, loving, kind, gentle, guiding mother. The woman thought of when she thought of mothers, and had an urge to have a conversation with a maternal figure, was her aunt Josephine—a cousin to Maude once removed by marriage—who'd swooped in to rescue Sutton after Maude was sent to court-ordered rehab for a DUI. Josephine had raised her for a while, made sure she was fed and clothed and had a roof over her head, until Maude got out of rehab and went to AA and found God and straightened out and changed her name to Siobhan and found a boyfriend named Joe, who had a nice two-story split-level near Nashville, and moved them in with him before he could change his mind, lickety-split.

No more Aunt Josephine. No more loving, motherly conversations.

Instead...Joe. Joe the Schmo.

Her mother didn't know what Joe was saying to Sutton behind her back, or didn't care.

Oh, stop already. Enough of that train of thought. You're supposed to be thinking about Ethan, not Joe the dickhead Schmo and the consequences of your mother's inability to see him for what he was.

Ethan was good in bed. Electrifyingly good. He knew exactly what turned her on, which buttons to push, and didn't ever miss a chance to take her screaming over the edge into oblivion.

Constantine hadn't been awful. He'd actually been pretty good. A little wider than Ethan in terms of penis girth (she was a bit sore), and she'd been exactly right about those long fingers and what they could do and how they would feel.

The thing was, as much as she hated to admit it, no one else would ever be quite good enough for her. Ethan was mind-blowingly spectacular in the bedroom. There was some truth to the old adage, it's not the size of the ship, it's the motion in the ocean. Ethan may not have had the biggest dick on the planet, but man, oh, man, did he know how to use it.

The first year they were together, Sutton made a small dot in her journal every time they had sex. They were so far above average it wasn't even funny; she stopped keeping track.

The second year, she started tracking again, and noticed it had dropped off. The third year, well, that was the year of the first incident, the house, and that little cunt, so it shouldn't have counted at all.

Because inevitably, Ethan's eye began to wander. He was beautiful, with a great accent, a sharp wit, and a brilliant mind, and he was being pushed up against pretty young things at the conferences and book signings and private teaching gigs, and he was a man, after all. A man like any other, designed to go forth and propagate his seed in every available fertile vagina.

Did he have any other children?

The thought brought her up short. Nausea spiked. She'd never thought to ask, or to accuse. Except for the one time, he always denied cheating on her, but she knew he lied. It was nice of him, in a way, to try to protect her feelings by not openly admitting the humiliation. She expected the worst of it happened while she was in the hospital (that damnable place) when they wouldn't let him in to see her for a week. She'd been in bad shape and had made it very clear she didn't want him to see her this way, and the staff listened. When she got home there was a pair of skimpy undies under the bed. Red. Thong. Barely anything but string and a scrap of lace. The kind an expensive whore would wear, or perhaps a graduate student in English wanting to impress her favorite writer by showing him how very inventive and free she was.

Truly, Sutton had never expected to be able to keep him all to herself forever. But to fuck another woman in their bed, a bed they'd shared while busily making their child, when she was incapacitated? That was beyond heartless. Couldn't he have just taken his whores to a hotel? Did he have to shove it in Sutton's face? All because he hadn't wanted the house?

Stop it, right now. It's over. The past. It doesn't matter. It doesn't.

Sutton—Justine—got out of the bed, made a cup of tea. Glanced over her shoulder at the handsome man sleeping face-down, the sheet pulled loosely over his firm, round buttocks, which had a dent in either side, strong muscles pulling taut against his very young, smooth skin.

She filled the kettle quietly. Ethan was behind her now. She had to keep looking forward. She didn't want to dwell in the past. She didn't want to be that woman, the one who couldn't let go, who grew bitter and miserable. It was time to move on, and they both knew it. Time to set him free, to set herself free.

She'd taken several baby steps over the past few weeks, and leaving for another continent had been a line in the sand, of course, but the first giant leap had taken place only an hour before, when she'd allowed another man to put himself inside her. She stared at this stranger in her bed, remembering how his fingers had dipped in and out of her like he was playing piano, how his mouth had roved across her breasts, how she'd traitorously reveled in the largeness of him as he thrusted into her. She'd been pummeled instead of gently, expertly seduced. She'd rather enjoyed it.

Constantine must have sensed her watching him, or the sound of the kettle on full boil roused him. He rolled over, the sheet whispering away to the side. He was lazily unconcerned with his naked-ness. Sutton—Justine—pulled her robe a bit closer. He stretched, giving her a full view of his stiff and ready penis, and held out a hand. "Justine. Take off your clothes and come back to bed."

One breath. Another. His lazy smile. Abandoning the tea, she untied the silken string holding the two triangles of fabric closed, and, leaving her robe on the back of her desk chair to drift and flutter in the soft Parisian breeze like the petals on the cherry branch in the window, she did.

AN AFFAIR TO REMEMBER

Constantine was insatiable. They had sex twice more, and now Sutton—Justine—really was sore. The sun was setting when he started in for a fourth round, and she put him off. He didn't like that, teased her a bit about being a delicate flower, literally swept her off her feet and threw her back onto the four-poster and then had her squirming under him, first in aggravation, then in delicious, illogical enjoyment of being dominated by this man she barely knew.

Anything not to think. Anything not to feel. She'd gambled and lost, knowing deep down it was going to happen, knowing she didn't deserve anything good in her life. But this felt good, and though she knew from long experience she'd feel empty later, for the moment, she let herself ride the waves of pleasure being with a new man gave her.

Finally, he gathered up his clothes, casually wiped himself with the edge of the sheet and dropped the condom in the toilet, and claimed he needed to head out. She promised to meet him the next day. The sky was deeply pink and gray when he left.

Sutton—Justine—showered, changed the sheets, ate some

cheese. She was suddenly possessed by a single thought. *You idiot girl, you should have taken him to a hotel. Now he knows where you live. How could you be so stupid?*

It was the champagne. She wasn't a good drinker; the meds made it even worse. One was always her limit in social settings. They'd ended up splitting a whole bottle of champagne, followed it with some crisp, cold Sancerre and a couple of croque monsieurs, and when she'd felt the warmth of his lips on her neck, delicately asking without saying a word, she'd thrown caution to the wind, as she did, and suggested she take him home.

It had been her idea. Make no mistake. Though she'd been loose with alcohol, she'd wanted Constantine badly, wanted to feel those fingers trailing along her thighs, wanted the oblivion she knew she'd find with him.

Inside her flat, the door barely closed, when he'd kissed her on the lips, gently at first, then insistent, something inside her cracked open. She could barely see straight with the thought of it, the desire, the wanting.

It wasn't the first time she'd bedded a stranger. Ethan was simply the one she'd married.

Constantine had been a lovely diversion, but she had work to do. The night was young and fresh, early moonlight spilling in the window, the clock pushing ten, and she was desperate to get some words down from her earlier thoughts.

Hair wet and draped into a loose bun, she sat at the desk and opened her computer. For the briefest of moments, she laid her fingers on the keys and wanted, so badly, to open her internet browser and type in her name. See what the world was saying about her. But she knew that was how she'd be found. One of the books she'd read had been very specific. It was by a skip tracer, a man who hunted down people who disappeared to avoid jail, or paying large sums in divorce settlements. People who faked their own death.

The first rule: don't Google yourself.

She slapped the laptop closed. Sipped some water. She had a dreadful headache from the champagne, and the sex. An orgasm hangover.

She'd followed all the steps, all the rules, for disappearing. For the few weeks leading up to her departure, she'd carefully plotted out her path without a qualm. She needed the freedom of starting over. She needed the anonymity being in this city could bring her. She couldn't be Sutton Montclair anymore.

But just in case someone really came looking for her, like a detective, or private investigator, she'd followed the course of action she'd found in a book. It was a trick recommended for battered wives who need to leave their husbands. She'd left behind a single Post-it note with a single phone number in her Day Runner. The phone number rang directly to the Metro Nashville Sex Crimes desk.

If—if—a professional investigator came searching for her, they'd get that number and realize she was running away from an abusive relationship. They'd back off. They'd leave her be. She'd be free.

When she'd left the number, she'd felt badly about it, for a fraction of a second. The police might think there was foul play, a woman disappearing from her life in such a manner. They might look at Ethan. They might make his life hell. But he'd made her life hell, so tit for tat seemed fair enough.

The thought of his name, his face, so familiar to her, caused the strange feeling of love commingled with guilt and hate to rise up in her. She must stop thinking about the past. She needed something to help her focus on the future.

Constantine? Perhaps, though she hardly wanted more than a roll in the hay from the man. He'd be gone soon enough, and she could continue moving on with her life. Justine Holliday was writing a book in Paris, and it was going to be a smash hit.

She opened the laptop again, the scene from the café replaying in her mind. Glanced at the Tour as it began its hourly sparkling in the night. She felt the new world opening, sucking her in. Saw the roses flung from the parapets, felt the horse's strong muscles bunching beneath her thighs, smelled the sweat of her guards, and she was gone.

PAST LIVES REVEALED

Then

Sutton was on a roll. The words were flying out of the tips of her fingers, the thoughts coming faster than she could capture them. She realized she was panting from the mental exertion. She pushed on, didn't want to catch her breath, wanted this astounding flow to continue.

The flags were flying and the battle raged, swords flashing as they cut through the air, blood spraying from the blades. Ellaclaire ripped the bottom of her dress and sprinted for her life across the field, knowing if she could just make the Grove, she would be safe in the embrace of the wood nymphs, her family. An antelope, flushed from the field, kept pace with her, its liquid brown eyes urging her to move faster, quicker, to follow the path it was creating for her through the long grass. The pounding hooves of a horse grew louder and louder, the beast bearing down until she could feel his breath hot and rank upon her face as she turned to measure the distance until she was captured, watched the shining blade swinging toward her head, and...

"Sutton? Knock, knock."
The door to her office opened. She tried to ignore it.

She stumbled, and the blade swung above her, missing her tender white neck by a fraction. The knight leaped from his steed...

She heard laughter. The knight would not be laughing in this moment. The knight wanted her dead. Fuck you, knight.

"I brought you a cup of tea. From the sounds of it, you were going wild. I thought you might be thirsty."

Husband. Not a knight.

Fuck you, husband?

Her fingers ceased moving. She sniffed, smelled the strong, comforting scent of Earl Grey. Decidedly not the primordial ooze of the forgotten forest she was writing about, bathed in blood and fear.

The scene was fleeing, running from her imagination like her characters had fled across the battlefield. She shut her eyes in a vain attempt to capture it, but elusive as a whisper, it was gone. No more forest. No more knight on the verge of murder. No more Princess Ellaclaire. She was squarely back in her office in her staid house on her boring street. Damn it.

Sutton opened her eyes to see her handsome husband looking at her fondly, a cup of tea and a plate of biscuits in hand. "Cuppa and a snack, darling. Thought you could use a break. You've been at it for hours."

She glanced at the clock on her computer screen. Forty minutes. She'd only gotten in forty minutes. The word counter flashed at her, a measly thousand words. Her heart sank. Her deadline was next week and she still had the whole final act of the book to write.

Ethan was not able to pick up social cues. It was something she'd found charming when she first met him, and now...well, now she wanted to kill him. Literally break the plate in his hand across the edge of her desk and shove a shard of sharpened Limoges china deep into his neck.

He didn't seem to notice her tight grimace, her darting eyes.

He set the cup and plate on the desk and started in massaging her shoulders. "What are you doing in here, pounding away? Getting close to finishing?"

Dear God, the man was settling in to have a whole conversation.

Her therapist whispered harshly inside her brain, *Sutton Montclair. Stop that. He's lonely. Dashiell is gone. He needs the connection between you. Reestablish a connection with your husband, Sutton. You need it as much as he does. You need each other. That's how you will survive this.*

And now it's your turn to fuck off, Doc. The only way I'm going to survive this is by meeting my deadline and making sure there's a paycheck to feed this man in back of me.

She dredged up a smile. "Just reworking the beginning a bit. It was too slow. You know how it is."

He didn't. He never had to rework his beginnings. Of course, he hadn't been working at all lately, which was the reason he was in here, pestering her. She forced herself not to glance at the clock. Every interruption cost her at least twenty minutes, and she only had four hours blocked off today; she had her quarterly lunch with her mother at one o'clock. She would cancel. Save herself the aggravation. Mail the envelope instead. Gain another couple of hours. Screw Siobhan.

"Have your tea before it gets cold," Ethan chided.

She took an obedient sip. It was delicious, of course. The man was British, it was in his blood. He had two talents—he was brilliant in bed and brilliant at making tea. She had herself a catch, everything she'd ever wanted, and all she could think was, *Please go. Please go. Please go. Just leave me alone...*

Connect, damn you.

Her smile was a bit wider now, comforting, knowing. She turned in her chair, put her hand on his. "Ethan. Darling. Are you going to get back to work on the book soon?"

His face closed. His arms crossed. A complete body language

shift. His lower lip practically jutted out. He was pouting. Ethan could pout with the best of them.

"Don't start in on me, Sutton. I was only trying to be nice."

"I know you were, and I don't mean to nag, but you know Bill has been waiting for you to send that first one hundred pages. He called again last night. I don't know how much longer you'll be able to put him off, darling. The publishers want their book, and if you're not going to deliver, you need to let them know."

"Bloody hell, Sutton. I am trying to be caring and show you how much I love you, and all you can do is throw this in my face? The chapters will happen when I'm damn good and ready for them to, and not a minute before." He stood and stormed out of her office. After a moment's hesitation, she used her foot to shut the door behind him.

You are a devious bitch, Sutton Montclair.

She reread the paragraph she'd been into before he interrupted her. An antelope? Where the hell had that come from? It was crap. Stupid, ridiculous crap. She cut it, took a sip of the delicious tea. Felt the anger start.

It was their ongoing battle. Ethan had an unerring ability to interrupt her just as she was at the most crucial moments in her work. She understood exactly what was going on. It was his own resistance to writing his new book. She'd always been understanding and forgiving, even going so far as to follow him back to his own office off the cavernous kitchen and help him get started. He liked for her to start his sentences. It helped him work.

After Dashiell died, none of that mattered. She didn't want to help him anymore. The bastard had tricked her into getting pregnant, and instead of hating the situation, she'd fallen head over heels with the small, bald, smelly, diaper-clad result of his deviousness, and karma had ripped the child away from them both, as they so justly deserved.

The thought of Dashiell sent a stake through her, and she shut the laptop. There would be no more work today.

Connect with Ethan, Sutton. Save your marriage. Do something. You can't continue to live like this.

The voice in her head had been worse, lately. Whispering, sometimes, things she couldn't quite catch, couldn't exactly understand. She needed to up her meds, she knew she did, but she also needed the lack of control that the hypomania brought to her work. If she upped her meds now, she might shut that edge down, and she just needed to get the damn thing done and then she could anesthetize the voice until she needed it again.

It was exhausting, the delicate knife blade of her life. Too many pills and the voices disappeared, too few and she couldn't make heads or tails of things.

It would be so much easier to simply be dead. If she were dead, she wouldn't have to finish the book. They would write nice things about her in the trades—*Writer Gone Too Soon: The Inevitable Madness of an Artistic Life.* There would be stories polished and reprinted about suicide and its impact on writers. Fifty or so writers would try to capitalize on her tragic death to talk about their own battles with depression, and *oh, yes, please buy my book.*

No. She wouldn't give them the satisfaction.

She felt light, suddenly. A beam of happiness drove through her. She always had this moment, with every book, when she felt that it would be easier to die than finish. It meant she was going to have the breakthrough that catapulted her to the end.

Sutton wasn't entirely insane. She knew herself very, very well.

Smiling, she took the empty cup and saucer to the kitchen. Now she was in the mood to connect, in more ways than one. And Ethan never said no to a good lay.

In the kitchen, Ethan was sitting at the table, a book in front of him. A rush of emotion filled her. It was his battered copy of Stephen King's *On Writing,* the one book he turned to in times of need. Signed by the author, no less. Of course it was.

He was struggling. That's why the pages weren't done. Ethan was struggling, and Sutton was doing everything she could to make his suffering worse. She blamed him. She blamed him for everything. She was a horrible person. Horrid. Evil to her very soul. Only an evil woman would let her husband suffer when she could alleviate the pain and despair with a touch.

Why are you still blaming him, Sutton? It was an accident. Worse, it was completely, utterly random.

But was it? Had he killed the baby to punish her?

Had she killed the baby to punish him? She'd been so drunk. The last thing she remembered was holding Dashiell, crying into his onesie, the soft fleece blanket wrapped around her shoulder, sheltering him. Had she smothered him unknowingly, then set him back in his crib facedown?

She dumped the teacup in the sink with a clatter and walked out of the room without saying a word, ignoring Ethan's eyes boring into her back.

He had no idea how bad this was. Losing Dashiell was something unrecoverable; not knowing exactly how he'd died was life threatening.

She was broken inside, broken in three parts now. She'd been whole once. Then she'd been torn in two, and she'd barely recovered. And now she'd been torn again, and there was no way to repair the rent. There was simply no way to go on like this. One minute upset, the next happy. Swinging from the branches of her once-perfect life, to and fro, completely unable to control her emotions.

No, she couldn't continue living this way at all.

She stalked back to her office. Pulled up her Facebook page. Sometimes, when she got herself distracted, a few minutes reading nice things people said to her about her work could get her back on track.

The comment was on the top of her page.

I can't believe I wasted my money on this trash. Sutton Montclair should be shot. Don't get me near a gun, ha ha.

Shocked, she read the message over and over again. It had fifty likes, though the vast majority of the comments expressed absolute outrage.

She looked at the username, didn't recognize it. Clicked on to the page. It was anonymous—no profile picture, no photos or albums, no status updates, only one like to its credit, Sutton's fan page. Without a second thought, she deleted the comment and blocked the user. She had absolutely no problem with people not liking her work—she had expressed that on many a panel and blog—but there was something ominous about the comment that made her uneasy.

She shouldn't have done it. She should have told someone, made a note of the username and the comment itself. Hitting the delete button was a very big mistake. When the police tried to track who she claimed was the real stalker, that was the only clue to their true identity. She couldn't defend herself.

But that morning, so long ago, after drinking her delicious tea and having mixed feelings toward her slightly estranged husband, Sutton had no idea where it was all going to go.

MURDER, SHE WROTE

Now

That night, the evening of the afternoon Sutton took a stranger home to her bed, there was a murder.

A double murder.

On the steps of Sacré-Coeur.

A young American couple was stabbed to death. They were visiting from Wauwatosa, Wisconsin, both blond as sin and blockily built. College students on a year abroad, they were studying at Oxford, in England, but had come to Paris for a mini break. They were boyfriend and girlfriend.

What no one knew was that in the moments before they died, they'd become more. He had just proposed. He—Rick—had given her—Lily—a ring that he'd brought from home, one he'd bought with tips from his job at Jack Rack's Pizza, where he'd worked every summer and three school nights a week to save up enough to study abroad for a year, and when he met the new girl in town, Lily—Lily, what a lovely, old-fashioned name—he fell madly in love, and knew he wanted her to be his wife. So he asked her to the movies, added two extra shifts a week, and after two rough years without much sleep, used that money to buy a small blood diamond—the best he could afford; beggars couldn't be choosy about buying cheap blood diamonds versus the much more expensive conflict-free, ethically mined ones— and had been planning this special moment for two months.

Can you see it? He, homegrown Midwestern goodness, on his knees, pledging his eternal troth. She, a hand clapped over her mouth, face suffused with a pleasant blush, happily having the moment she'd long dreamed of, tearily shouting, "Yes, yes, yes!" Him, sliding the small blood diamond onto her finger, and leaning in to kiss her. Their future, set. A perfect moment, years in the making, but as the tableau unfolds, the camera pans back, and a shadow grows. There is a glint of a blade in the moonlight. You almost want to scream at them to watch out, to run, don't you?

The killer stabbed the boy once in the kidney, forcing him to stumble forward in shock. The killer then ripped the knife across the neck of the girl, and pulled the ring from her finger as she fell. He waited for them to stop struggling, dispassionately.

Careful not to step in the blood, he swiped the top and edge of the ring box in the deepest spot of wet burgundy, wrapped it in plastic, and stashed it in his pocket, then arranged the students on the steps so Lily was on top, facedown, with her arms around her lover, her fiancée, and the moment that should have been the happiest for them both mingled with their spilled blood on the bone-white marble steps and they died that way, together.

It was quick, don't worry. They didn't suffer. They were too shocked by the blitzkrieg, and then too empty of blood to really know what had just happened. And if you think about it, it wasn't a terrible way to go. At least they had happiness in the end, and each other.

There were no witnesses, rather miraculous, really, when you consider how many people were in the vicinity when it happened. But, conveniently for the killer, the young lovers had wanted a private moment, and so had stepped away from the main thoroughfare, where the view wasn't quite as good but there was no one else around.

A man walking his dog found them, piled on top of each other. He thought for a moment they were making love, and smiled to himself at the folly of youth, then his flashlight showed the pool of blood, and he knew something was very, very wrong. While the man called emergency, his dog stepped delicately along the edges, sniffing, leaving tiny red paw prints around the scene.

When the Parisian police arrived, they were suitably frantic. A contaminated crime scene, for one, and clearly the arrangement of some deranged killer. But worse, the identification in purse and pocket.

American tourists being murdered is very bad for business.

Very bad indeed.

THOSE SACRED HEARTS

Paris held many secrets. Sutton wanted to discover them all. She rose early, brushed her hair into a thick ponytail, put on a pair of dark New Balance sneakers, threw her laptop in her bag. Today was for exploring. She needed a change of scenery.

She didn't know where she was headed, just grabbed the first train at the Metro and rode for fifteen minutes. She'd gone north, across the Seine. She didn't recognize many of the stops, but one name pulled at her consciousness. Montmartre. Constantine had told her the light from Sacré-Coeur was some of the most amazing in all of Paris. He'd suggested they meet there for lunch today. Perfect. She'd visit the cathedral, see the sights, settle in to write at a café nearby (there was always a café nearby, this was Paris), then, if she so desired, would walk down the hill and meet him for lunch.

She gathered her bag and stood. When the train stopped, she waited for the doors to open. Nothing happened. A teenager knocked her in the shoulder as he reached for a small metal latch and opened the door. Oh. *Tourist move there, Justine.*

She climbed the stairs to the surface, a periwinkle emerging from the sand. She'd never need to exercise at this rate. Paris was nothing if not filled with stairs. The street appeared before her. It had a different feel than her neighborhood, immediately more cramped and artsy. She thought of Constantine then, the thick arms that had held her—well, no, not really held, more pinned her down. He'd been rough, and she'd enjoyed it, though now, looking back, she felt like things weren't as blissful as she'd made them out to be. Revisionist history, tainted by alcohol. Her specialty.

Instinct told her meeting him, continuing this dalliance, was a bad idea. She knew better. She knew she should be more careful. She'd just been feeling so reckless, and the alcohol had gone to her head. She still felt ill. Regret and a two-day hangover, the breakfast of champion writers everywhere. Great.

So why was she even considering meeting him? She should blow him off, let him disappear into the fabric of the city, like she was trying to do. Connections were the last things she wanted.

He wouldn't like it. She could tell he'd been very interested in her. A strong miasma of desire and dread filled her. *You are a stupid fool, Justine. To risk all you've overcome to please yet another man.* She wanted to see him badly; she didn't ever want to see him again.

She took the funicular to the top, surprised to find it empty. The path was also quiet in the early morning. She walked in silence for a few moments, her sole companion a small black cat with white socks who mewed happily in a friendly French manner when she stopped to scratch his ears.

Constantine was right. As she emerged from the winding, leafy path from the funicular and made her way to the church grounds, the city unfolded before her. Rooftops and cathedrals, the lone skyscraper in Montparnasse straight ahead, the aggressive, thrusting buildings of La Défense to her right. Greens and golds and white, painfully beautiful to behold. It was as if she were the only person standing on the top of the world. The white marble of the cathedral so perfectly lit in the sun, the brightness nearly burned her eyes.

She shut them, took a breath. This was something she'd wanted for so long, and here she was, feeling more alone than she'd ever been.

Ethan.

The name came like a whisper on the breeze.

What was he doing? Did he miss her? Was he so thrilled to have her out of his house, his life, that he was planning a huge party?

She shouldn't have done it this way. But she knew if she'd told him she wanted out, really out, divorce and separate lives out, he would talk her down from the ledge and she'd be stuck. He was so good with his words when he wanted to be. A clean break, disappearing from her life, it was the only way. She wasn't strong enough to do it otherwise. She was so broken lately. The past year had been hell incarnate.

People arrived, flowing around her. The spell quickly broke in the face of their intrusion. So many languages. So many colors. She wanted to be alone again. She walked to the western edge of the courtyard. There she saw two *flics*, and it seemed like they were guarding something. She walked closer, but one held up a hand and barked, *"Arrête."* Stop.

She froze. She could see now there were many people beyond the perimeter. He approached, speaking rapid French. "What are you doing here? You need to leave, right away. This area is closed."

She smiled and nodded. "I'm so sorry. Is it construction?"

"No. Move along, now."

He went back to his partner and took up his station again, hands on hips, legs spread, frowning at her. With a last glance at the knot of people down the hill, she walked back the way she'd come, through the leafy green canopy to a small square. There was no way to be alone now, which was a shame. She'd felt something deep connecting her to the city atop the hill. Something strong and good. A beginning, maybe. Or an end.

Winding down the hill, past the artists who'd been painting the sunrise over the city, she took a seat at the first café she saw, asked for coffee and a croissant, opened her laptop. As she was putting in her earbuds, two women took the table next to her. She couldn't help but tune in when she heard the tone of their voices, so unlike the usual happy babble of the Parisian café. This was filled with dread and wonder and excitement.

"Did you hear? About the murder? A young American couple. Pierre said their bodies are still up there."

"I heard they were gutted."

"I heard she was beheaded."

"These terrorists are ruining our city."

"Pierre spoke to the *flics*. It was not terror. They were targeted. It was cold-blooded murder. In our backyard, no less."

Sutton felt a small frisson. It was rude, frowned upon, to eavesdrop, but Sutton couldn't help herself. She needed to know more.

"*Excusez-moi. Le meurtre des Américains, c'était où?*" Where?

The women turned. They were so classically French, at once painfully plain and yet ethereally beautiful, one brunette, one blonde, both perfect, elegant, lines on their foreheads, no makeup outside of a swipe of red lipstick, their hair in identical styles, shoulder-length, straight, flipped up on the ends.

In English, the brunette replied, gesturing over Sutton's shoulder, "Sacré-Coeur. You're American?"

"I am."

"You should go home, and you need to be careful. If there are murderers about, Paris is dangerous for a young woman such as yourself."

Their breakfast interrupted, the two women stood and left.

Normally Sutton would be hurt by the brusque exchange, but she ignored their slight. The two *flics*, on the back side of Sacré-

Coeur. Had they been guarding the bodies of the two young Americans who'd been murdered?

She tied in to the café's Wi-Fi, pulled up the website of French24, the English language website and news station she'd been watching online for the few weeks prior to leaving. The murder was the lede, the details thin.

She read rapidly. The Americans were young but unidentified, only named as exchange students. The cause of death was not listed.

She gulped down her coffee, wrapped the croissant in the paper napkin, packed away her laptop. There was no peace in the day for her anymore.

She starting winding her way down the hill. Half a block later she came across a flower stand. So many gorgeous blooms, all the colors of the rainbow. Those children—it was hard to think of anyone in school still as an adult—dead by a stranger's hand in the most beautiful city in the world. It broke her heart.

She plucked a bunch from the water, paid for it, then trudged back up the hill. She didn't know why she felt the need to mark their deaths—these two were nothing to her—and yet she was compelled. Maybe the fact that they were Americans, maybe that she'd come close again to death and the flowers were a sort of protection against it following her home. She didn't know, and she didn't care.

She walked directly to the white steps of the cathedral, set the flowers there, whispered a short prayer, and hurried away.

AN APPOINTMENT MISSED, A DISASTER AVOIDED

Back in the 7th, the murders were the talk of the whole neighborhood. Amazing how quickly news spread, amazing how many strangers were fascinated with the story. Sutton walked to the café on the corner, her place, as she'd come to think of it over the past few days. She set up shop with her laptop and delayed breakfast, but everyone was buzzing, and she finally closed the lid of the computer and listened to the chatter.

How odd, Sutton thought. The rumors all agreed on one thing. The victims had not been robbed. The girl's purse was there, zipped, intact; the boy's wallet and phone and money clip were still in his pockets. They both wore watches. Passports left behind, too.

It felt weird to everyone.

"If it wasn't random…" they whispered.

Americans being targeted in Paris was cause for alarm for everyone, especially expats on the run from their lives, who couldn't completely pass as Parisians. And to think, she'd been right there, had practically walked into the crime scene. The thought chilled to the bone.

She wondered briefly about Constantine, whether he'd be disappointed when she didn't show for their lunch date. She'd decided on the Metro home, it was for the best that she didn't see him again. He'd filled his purpose, helped her make the break with her past. That's what she needed. A break from her past.

There was nothing more to learn this morning. She slipped in her earbuds and started to write.

A tap on her shoulder yanked her back. She pulled out the left earbud, only half processing who'd interrupted her. Startled at the familiar voice.

"Hello there."

Constantine.

"Oh. Hi."

"You don't look happy to see me," Constantine said, leaning in to kiss her on the forehead. She forced herself not to draw away, though she wanted to. "I thought we were meeting for lunch. You weren't there." His hand lingered on her shoulder, squeezing gently, possessive and familiar.

She rolled her neck to knock his hand away unobtrusively, feigned looking at her watch. "Oh, my goodness. I lost track of time." All the while thinking, *You tracked me down? Uh-oh.*

It was nearly three in the afternoon. She was cramped from crouching over the computer on the tiny table, but she had ten new pages on the book. She was just about to cut out for the afternoon, drop off the laptop, and go for a walk.

Sitting, he leaned close and whispered, "Why don't we go back to your place? I've been dying to see you."

She could smell him, a combination of man and subtle cologne and sex. *He smells of sex.* Who had he been with? Was it just left over from her? She tried not to notice he was still handsome, still had that animal magnetism. Tried not to listen when a nasty little voice inside her said, *Why not?*

Don't be an idiot. Don't be an idiot.

"I can't, Constantine. I'm afraid I must work." She heard the ice in her tone. The old Sutton was back, empty, devoid. No more mistakes, no more dalliances. It was how she'd been talking to Ethan for the past month, since she found the allergy medicine in the closet and started planning her escape. Cold and remote.

That tone cut like a knife. She'd honed it well. There was hurt on Constantine's face, and she felt terrible. Why must women worry about hurting feelings?

Don't give in, don't be stupid. Stay emotionless.

"Did I do something wrong?" he asked, sitting back in the chair.

"No. Not at all. I had fun. It was fun. But I came here to be alone. I wasn't planning to get involved with anyone."

He ran a finger along her arm, like she had to him when they first met. She swallowed. What could it hurt, once more?

"It's all good fun. No involvement necessary. I'm not asking for anything."

"I know you're not. I acted impetuously. But it can't happen again."

Constantine's eyes walked over her body, and she could swear she saw the barest predatory gleam in them when he licked his lips and shrugged, then stood. His voice was no longer warm and cajoling. It was cold, the perfect match to hers, but there was genuine hurt and confusion, and she felt the pull, the need, the desire to be loved and to love, to connect.

"Suit yourself. It was nice knowing you, Justine Holliday."

He started to walk away and she felt the shroud lift. What a dumb mistake she'd made, allowing her baser instincts to take over. *Maybe when you're settled here, maybe when you've made up your mind that this is permanent, then you can think about moving on for real.*

She saw him disappear around the corner and squared her shoulders.

Stick to the plan. Stick to the plan.

And then she was up, on her feet, tossing bills on the table, running after him.

SECRETS AND MONSTERS

Then

They had to do something with the nursery.

Sutton couldn't stand the idea of it sitting there like a shrine, and yet she couldn't bring herself to dismantle it. It smelled good, and it smelled wrong. Baby powder and emptiness, the lavender-scented blankets still stacked up high on the table by the crib, vestiges of Just Jan and her tidy, almost architectural folding abilities. Sutton asked her once if she was into origami, and Just Jan had laughed and said no, she was just careful with her things, and her thick braids swung forward, two perfect, fat, winding snakes, and Sutton didn't believe her.

OCD, maybe.

Was that safe for Dashiell, being around someone who was so precise?

And her inner voice reminded her she liked Jan, and Jan was good for Dashiell, good for her and for Ethan as well, and to stop being a jerk.

A week after Dashiell had died, Just Jan had offered to pack the nursery for her. Just Jan had thusly been sent packing herself, divested of her keys, the alarm codes changed, and a fat sever-ance check in her back pocket. (Ethan's doing. Sutton had tried to scratch her eyes out.)

There was no reason for Just Jan to exist for them anymore, anyway.

But now, Sutton was stuck, poor Sutton, all alone, in the door-way to her dead son's room, having to make a decision. Close it down or keep it open?

Ethan, not surprisingly, had abdicated. He wouldn't get near the nursery. He'd go down the back stairs to avoid having to step past the door, as if some unseen monster was going to reach out and grab him.

Sutton supposed there was a monster lurking inside their dead son's nursery, jaws gaping, saliva dripping off sharp fangs. She wanted it to take her, to rip out her throat, leaving her unable to breathe on the floor, drowning in her own blood, and so she stepped inside, ready and willing.

Nothing happened. Just sadness, and emptiness. She didn't die.

Isn't that the problem with loss? You don't get to go with death when it comes for your loves.

Suddenly industrious, she began putting things away, blan-kets into drawers, tiny blue onesies onto miniature hangers in the closet. They kept the diapers on the top shelf. With some-thing so quickly used, so easily disposed of, she had never both-ered unpacking them into the cute diaper box she'd received at her shower.

She reached for the cardboard. At the very least, she could do-nate the diapers to the shelter. Diapers weren't part of her son's life. They were generic, expendable, anonymous. She couldn't get emotional about a fold of fake cotton meant for shit and piss.

She was tall, able to reach all but the last box. She grabbed the three-step stool from behind the closet door. Pulled the last one from the dark recess. Her knuckles brushed something hard. It fell over with a quiet clatter.

She dropped the diapers on the floor and climbed up one more step, so she could see. There was a bottle on its side, small, brown, a pink label. She picked it up and examined it. *Children's Allergy Relief.* The bottle was nearly full, but not new. It had been opened.

Sutton's heart began to race. She had not bought this medicine. So why was it here, in Dashiell's closet, hidden deep in the closet, behind the diapers?

She clutched the bottle to her chest and snuck to her office. Ethan was around; she'd heard him banging on something earlier. He couldn't see this. She needed to know. She needed to know, now.

The words on her computer screen, fractured because she was reading so fast. Not for use under 12 months. Excessive sedation. Overdose. Warning. Never give infants sedatives...

And because she had to torture herself, she typed in the words: *infant overdose Benadryl symptoms.* The results were immediate and overwhelming.

Death of Infant Attributed to Sedative Overdose
Babysitter Charged in Dosing Incident
A Mother's Warning after Babysitter Murders Infant with Sedative

She clicked on the last story, scrambling now, heart in her throat. Read the piece. Saw the words that changed everything.

The babysitter claimed she put the infant down for a nap, and when she went to check on him, saw he was not breathing and called 9-1-1. The initial findings pointed to a SIDS death, but subsequent toxicology reports showed high levels of diphenhydramine in the infant's blood. The babysitter was subsequently arrested on the charge of first-degree homicide.

In her deposition, she admitted to giving the child the drug when he wouldn't stop crying.

There was more, but that was all Sutton needed to see. The knowledge poured over her like freezing water. Her teeth began to chatter. She grabbed her arms to keep the shaking under control. She knew what had happened. Finally, she knew. She'd been right all along. The nagging suspicion that ate at her day and night and ruined her marriage, her life. The words that had been whispering through her brain for almost a year.

Ethan killed the baby.

Sutton didn't know what to do. Should she go to the police, tell them her husband was a monster, that he'd killed their child? That he'd been abusing her? She had proof: she had the pictures of the bruises on her arm, the shots of her broken nose. All those times the police had come during their fights... She hadn't called them, it was the neighbors who heard the yelling and tried to protect her from afar, something she'd always been livid about, but now, knowing she was living with a murderer, she was utterly grateful for their interference. What might have happened if they hadn't called?

Ivy had warned her Ethan was volatile. That she should always have a plan, just in case. And now she understood why.

Ivy. Of course. She'd go to Ivy. She'd know what to do.

"I have something to tell you."

Ivy poured the wine into Sutton's glass, ruby liquid purling against the edges. Set the bottle on the table. Picked up her own glass and made a small salute. "Ching-ching. What is it?"

"It's about Ethan."

Ivy's glass stopped moving, the wine tipped precariously. Then she took a long swallow. "What about Ethan?"

Sutton reached into her purse and pulled out the bottle of diphenhydramine.

"I found this. In Dashiell's room."

Ivy took it, turned it over, read the back. "Okay. What is it? You know I'm not the mother here."

"It's generic Benadryl. For allergy attacks."

"Oh. Isn't he a little young for this? I mean, far be it from me to talk about motherhood, but it clearly says on the label not to give it to children under a year old without a doctor's supervision."

The words spilled out of Sutton's mouth in a torrent. "I didn't buy it. I'd never give him something like this. I've never given him anything the doctor didn't approve first, and those were just his vaccines. He'd never gotten sick, there is no reason for something like this to be in the closet. It was hidden. And after I found it...I did research. This drug can cause an overdose that would mimic SIDS. There are cases online where babysitters have used it to dose children and they've died. I think..."

"Wait. Hold on. Take a breath, Sutton. You're going a mile a minute. You can't think Jan would have—"

But she couldn't stop, the words were there, on her tongue, glowing and pink, the moment they came out, the world was going to change.

"Not Jan. I think Ethan killed the baby."

Ivy sat back in the chair, wineglass forgotten. "Sutton..."

"Hear me out."

"No, wait—"

"I know what you're going to say. 'There's no way. Ethan adored Dashiell. He'd never hurt him.' But he has a dark side, Ivy. He's not the man you think he is. I love him, he's my husband, for better or for worse, but there's a darkness inside him, sometimes he just turns off, goes blank, and the next thing I know, we're not speaking to each other for days."

Ivy sighed heavily. "I know. I know how hard it is. I know how bad it's been between you. But this...to murder his own son. That's beyond the pale."

"Is it?" Sutton was furious now. She stood and paced Ivy's small living room. "Is it so hard to believe? He's punishing me. He's always been jealous of Dashiell. God, he wanted that baby so badly, and when I gave him a child, instead of appreciating me for it, he was consumed with the idea that I loved Dashiell more than him. He never forgave me."

Or was it the other way around? Had she not loved the baby enough to keep him safe? To see the predator lurking under their roof? The unspoken words imprinted in her brain almost as if someone was whispering them to her in the night.

He's going to hurt you, he killed the baby.
He's going to hurt you, he killed the baby.

She was rocking, panic rising, and Ivy's arms were around her, she was crooning in her ear. She had no idea of time or space, just the overwhelming rush of blood roaring through her ears and her heart thumping so hard in her chest she couldn't breathe.

Finally, she heard soothing words. "Shhhh, it's okay."

Sutton slowly came back to herself, calmed, her heart rate dropping, the tears drying.

"I'm so sorry," she muttered, and Ivy released her.

"That was a bad one."

"It was. I apologize. I've not been myself lately. I feel so on edge, all the time."

"The medicine the doctor gave you, does it help?"

Sutton reached for her wine, took a huge gulp, a few more deep breaths. "Honestly? No. I feel like I'm buzzing all the time, like all my nerve endings are on fire. The only thing it's been good for is the writing. The rest of it, I'm not sleeping, and I'm horribly jumpy. I have an appointment this week to go on something different."

Ivy tucked her hair behind her ears. "Maybe it's not the medicine. Maybe it's your intuition warning you something's wrong. Like you're in fight or flight, can never relax?"

Sutton stared at her friend. "That's a very astute observation.

It's exactly how I feel, like I'm in danger. Like I constantly have to look over my shoulder. I didn't used to be this way."

"Tell me the truth. Do you think you're unsafe with Ethan?"

"I don't know. Before this afternoon I'd say no, of course I'm safe. Yes, we fight, but I've never felt like he was going to purposely hurt me."

"But he's hit you in anger before."

"He's hit me by accident before. He's never done it on purpose. There's a huge difference."

"That's what all abused women say. What they tell themselves."

"Seriously. I'm not deluding myself."

"He's abusing you, Sutton. He's been abusing you since well before the baby died. I mean, come on, he switched out your birth control pills so you'd get pregnant. That's practically rape."

"You've told me that before. You're a feminist, I get it. He apologized. Profusely."

"For God's sake, Sutton. Can't you see what's right in front of you? The man's been verbally and physically abusing you. You find a random bottle of allergy medicine and decide immediately that he hurt your child. Your reaction should tell you something, even if your head can't grasp the truth."

"But, what if I'm wrong? What if I accuse him, and I'm wrong? He'd never forgive me."

"Think about it this way. Say he did kill Dashiell. How long will it be until he tries to kill you? He's already hurt you. It's not out of the realm of possibility. You know this."

"I don't know. I don't know."

"I'll tell you this. We've all been worried sick about you. *I've* been worried sick about you."

He's going to hurt you, he killed the baby.

He's going to hurt you, he killed the baby.

Sutton sat back, looked at Ivy with fresh eyes. "I didn't know that. Why didn't you say something?"

"What do you say to your best friend when she's clearly not herself? You needed to come to this conclusion for yourself, not hear it from me, or the girls. You would never have listened if we came to you with this. You'd shut us out of your life, and I for one didn't want that to happen. I wanted you to see the problem for yourself."

Ivy was right. Sutton would have gotten her back up and told them all to go to hell. She'd defend Ethan to the death, even if she was furious with him.

She deflated. The pain and worry overwhelmed her, and she slumped into the chair. "What do I do?"

Ivy didn't hesitate. "That's easy. You leave."

"He won't let me go. He won't let me walk away. Divorce is not in the cards."

"Then you'll have to figure out another way."

AMERICAN WOMAN

Now

Sutton was a liberated woman. Smart, sexy, confident. Systematically broken down by the events of the past year, yes, but she was all these things, and more.

But the second she ran off after Constantine, her narrative switched. She became the same weak, mewling cunt her mother had turned into when she'd run off after the dogs she called "husband material."

Sutton didn't know why she did it. Revenge on Ethan wasn't enough to debase herself like this. To bed someone she knew she didn't truly want. It took her back to a time she'd rather forget, a time when she was indiscriminate, looking for attention and popularity any way she could find it. It had gotten her in a huge mess then and she had the same sneaking instinct that her actions of the past few days were going to have the same effect.

She was losing her nerve.

After everything she'd done to assure herself a clean getaway, a fresh life, a break from the world that intimidated and threatened her, lying under Constantine's straining body all she could think of was going home. Slinking back to Nashville with her tail between her legs.

It wasn't worth it, this. There was no medicine in the world, psychotropic, alcoholic, or sexual, that would fill the empty, gnawing hole in her.

She wanted her baby back. She wanted her husband back. She wanted her career back. She wanted her life back.

She wanted. God, she wanted. She'd spent her whole fucking life wanting. As a child, wanting to create. As a teen, wanting to fit in. As an adult, wanting to land the perfect man. And she'd finally achieved all the things she wanted, and she'd thrown them away. It had taken this empty affair to show her the way.

An hour later, feeling sore between the legs and sick to her stomach with self-hate, she had just enough respect left for herself to tell Constantine to leave.

Good night and goodbye.

He'd looked at her sideways, as if to argue, but kissed her chastely on the forehead and left, whistling, as she shut the door on him. He didn't seem to have picked up on her isolationist thought process during their sex. Certainly hadn't worried about pleasuring her. He was in it for himself, something she'd already known, but had to prove to herself yet again.

She cleaned up, made some peppermint tea to settle her stomach, decided to check and see if there was anything new on the murders of the poor kids at Sacré-Coeur.

Their deaths were the fulcrum. There was something so wrong about it. She felt violated, though she hadn't had anything to do with them. Her adventure—and let's face it, that's what this had turned into, a vacation from her life, not a fresh start—was over when she heard they'd been killed. She couldn't escape reality anywhere. People were always vicious, wherever they were.

The television was inside a cabinet. She hadn't planned to watch it, ever, just in case, but now she grabbed the dusty remote and brought it to life. It was already tuned to France24; not surprising, since this flat had been a popular spot for American tourists prior to Sutton claiming it.

There was nothing new on the story, except the families had been notified, so they were now releasing the names of the victims. Rick Lewis and Lily Connolly. Wauwatosa, Wisconsin. High school sweethearts. Exchange students in England. Their families didn't know they were in Paris. The girl's mother was suspicious; the boy's father posited they were probably getting engaged, because his son had told him he wanted to do something grand, sweeping, romantic. He wanted it to be memorable. They led quiet lives, in a quiet town, with a quiet future ahead, raising a quiet little family to live another quiet life. The exchange year abroad was the most outrageous thing they would ever do; they both knew this. Rick's father, standing stooped and defeated behind a bank of microphones, said he was certain his son was giving his lifelong love a proposal she'd never forget.

Sutton snapped off the television, rushed to the bathroom. Was peppermint sick, kneeling on the hard black-and-white octagonal tiles. When she was finished, she wiped her mouth. Their deaths were horrible. Their deaths were meaningless. Their deaths inspired an idea.

That's what made her ill, the horror of seeing the terrible story, the loss, the forever torment of absence that would exist for those left behind, and her awful writer brain immediately saw a path to a story that would capitalize on their suffering.

And so, she wrote. As the fine strands of sunlight danced around her head, she typed and plotted, she created. Creation was life to Sutton. Without the outlet, she would surely go mad. Perhaps that was the point of all art, truly, to eliminate the need for madness. And the poor souls who couldn't surrender themselves to creation ended up ratty and homeless with tinfoil hats and lives lost to the wandering streets.

It was a romantic thought, that the work was divine and she

was simply its channel. But she believed, as all great artists do, and gave herself up to the process.

Before Ethan, she'd had a method. A plan. A schedule.

After Ethan, she was happy to put those things on hold, to walk a different path. A path that led her into the darkness of death and loss, all over again.

That's why her writing desires had changed. She was changed. She was forever changed.

With a simple prayer of forgiveness to the families, she created a new world around their worst nightmare.

THE HEADLINES
ARE GRABBING

Here's irony for you.

Sutton, in the grips of a sudden creative urge, flipped off the television before the story of the lovers' murders finished playing, and so missed what would have been a very important moment in her life.

The story France24 followed with, rare for a European television station, was about the sudden disappearance of an American woman. A writer. Normally this foreign news wouldn't be worthy of coverage, but the woman was the wife of a celebrated and much-loved author who was very, very popular in France. Not only did his book sell well in French-speaking territories, but he'd once written the scripts for a hugely popular television show that was still in syndication.

She missed the headline: Author's Wife Missing.

She missed the delicious broadcast innuendo that followed: author is suspect in wife's disappearance.

She missed the fabulously replayable footage of her gorgeous husband standing in the middle of the street in front of their house, pale and wild, screaming at the reporters while rain hammered him and made his thick hair plaster to his head.

She missed the still shot of him flipping the bird as he entered the house.

She missed the subsequent footage of a towheaded blonde cop entering her sanctum.

She missed the interviews given by her best friends, the people she hadn't trusted with the truth of what was happening in her world.

She missed it all.

If she hadn't missed it, what would have happened differently? Would she have realized she was truly loved? That she'd caused worry and concern throughout a community, and now, the world? Would she have packed her things and gotten on a plane immediately?

If only she had. If only she had.

RISE AND SHINE

Sutton woke hard, alone, unsure for a moment where she was. Her back hurt, and her mouth was dry. The sun was shining outside, puffy white clouds meandering through the bluest sky she'd ever seen. She raised her head, the room coming into view. The picture window in front of her showed the black metal lines of the Tour, which centered her.

Paris. She was in Paris. She was Justine Holliday, from Hollywood, Florida. She was writing a memoir. She'd met a handsome young man and had a fun few days of pleasure. Just what the doctor ordered.

So why didn't she feel all romantic and gooey inside?

Probably because she'd stumbled on a nasty crime scene and all the magic of Paris was lost to her now.

She peeled herself up off the desk. She'd fallen asleep with her head on the keyboard. She was stiff and sore and headachy. Her stomach was still queasy. She must be coming down with something. She probably picked it up on the plane. Great.

She drank a glass of water, stretched a little. A croissant wouldn't go amiss. She knew she had to be careful with the carbs; she'd turn into a house if she didn't watch her diet, but right now, with an upset stomach and a stiff neck, the prospect of warm, flaky dough drenched in butter and jam sounded heavenly.

She dressed quickly, grabbed her bag, put on a pair of dark sunglasses. She took the stairs down, for the exercise. Outside, the air was crisp as if it had rained overnight and washed away the stickiness of the pollen, but the streets weren't wet, and the air was still suffused with floating yellow fairies.

It was a beautiful morning.

The café on the corner had a small set of tables in front of their windows with a red-and-white-striped awning overhead. It was so French. So perfect.

She was being ridiculous. She needed to stick with the program. She'd planned this for weeks and now she was here and she needed to stop being a wishy-washy child and roll with the decisions she'd made. This was what she wanted. Paris. Freedom.

Yes.

Suddenly ravenous and filled with love for her new life, she purchased two croissants with strawberry jam and sat at the table, drinking cool water from a small glass. The waiter brought her a steaming hot café au lait. She opened her notebook and wrote a few lines. Really, wasn't this exactly what she was hoping for? She wanted to smell the Parisian air, feel the cobblestones under her feet. Finishing her breakfast, she made a few more notes, paid the check, and decided to walk before working more.

Her choice of neighborhood had been inspired. She was so close to the Seine. She already had her bearings, could sense the river to her left, how the sky lightened between the buildings. Ten minutes later she found herself by the gray ribbon of water. She strolled along the quay toward Les Invalides. There were houseboats lashed to the banks below the *ponts*—why hadn't she thought of that? Living on the water, able to lift anchor and float away if necessary, the constant glow of the sun on the small rippling waves, would be the perfect life for a woman trying to remain unseen.

But it might be hard to work on the laptop, she did get a bit seasick. At the thought, a small qualm went through her. She chased it away with a nice, deep lungful of heady river air.

A *bateau-mouche* full of tourists cruised below her. They waved madly and shouted when they realized they'd caught her attention. Students, by the looks of them, young, carefree, so open and ready. Did they have any idea what waited for them in the world? The sorrow and pain and misery? Were they simply lost in their own narcissistic little lives?

When she was their age, she was heavy with… But no, she didn't want to think about that today. Today was for reveling in her new life. Today was for Justine Holliday.

She waved back, and they cheered.

Oh, the possibilities. Oh, the places you will go.

The Seine is a dynamic beast, ever changing as the day goes by, and she witnessed its many variations with pleasure. She walked miles, up the left bank, past the Pont Neuf, down to Notre-Dame. Pont des Arts's charm was no longer—the new Plexiglas barrier was disheartening; she'd so been looking forward to seeing all the locks attached to the wires, half a century of lovers' declarations. She crossed the Seine on the Pont de Bercy, moved back up the right bank until she found an open bench beneath a willow, and watched. Lovers, tourists, businessmen, artists. The banks of the Seine drew them all, like moths to a flame.

She preferred the right bank; the wide paths were lined with willows and lindens and horse chestnuts, their leaves green and yellow, begging to shelter.

The gray stone and stormy water and the green trees with their brown bark, peeling in places, waving to and fro in the gentle Parisian spring breeze, allowing bits of sunshine to peek through, made for a lovely afternoon. Sutton wrote in her notebook, napped a bit, allowed herself to unplug. Dropped petals from a lily she found into the water, let their passage sweep away her shame. Let the guilt and horror she'd been living with go.

Lighter of spirit, she walked slowly up the river toward her new home. It all felt so right. So good.

Back in her neighborhood, she grabbed fresh crusty bread and fragrant onion soup from the café on the corner. The sun was setting as she mounted the steps to her flat. She unlocked the door, went inside. The rooms were filled with pink light. She admired the view one last time, ate her soup, dipping the bread into the broth, had a small glass of wine, and went to her desk to start transcribing her notes. She pulled out her chair.

The metallic clunk startled her. She leaped backward. The knife just missed her foot.

"What in the hell?"

She bent down and picked it up. It was a hunting knife, large, with a clean edge on one side and a serrated edge on the other. The handle was dark bone, with a metal rivet at the base, where it met the tang of metal. It smelled off. Like bleach, but less strong.

There was tape on both ends, the sharp and the dull. She set it down, got on her hands and knees, wedged her head under the drawer, and looked under the desk. There were trailing edges of masking tape, the two sides ripped apart. She fit the knife into position, saw it matched the edges. The knife would fit perfectly in the space.

Which meant the knife had been taped under her desk. What in the world? Jesus, had someone broken into the flat and taped it under her desk?

She crawled out from under and stared at the knife. The handle had something on it, flecks of... God, was that blood?

Something like panic began to crawl up her spine.

This was not her knife.

So whose knife was it?

WHEN THINGS GO SIDEWAYS

Heavy pounding started on her door, and Sutton dropped the knife to the desk. It clattered against the edge, then fell onto the floor.

Urgent calling in French now, the pounding getting louder and more frantic.

She dropped her purse on top of the knife and went to answer the door. Took three deep breaths before she opened it, wiped her hands on her pants. Turned the knob.

"Oui?"

Two men stood before her wearing police uniforms. The *flics* stared at her aggressively. The one who'd been pounding dropped a hand to his waist and said, in English, "Mademoiselle, we respond to your call of distress. How can we be of service?"

"I didn't... I don't... *Je ne comprends pas.*"

He looked confused. "You are not being attacked, then?"

"No. I'm alone. I didn't call you." *Yes, I'm alone, just me and my hunting knife covered in blood.*

He didn't buy it. "If you do not mind, we shall look through your apartment, to be sure you are not telling us mistruths under duress."

She found his broken, formal English charming, but there was no way she was going to let them in.

"I am fine, as you can see. No duress, no calls. I fear you have received my address by mistake. Which means there is someone out there who *is* in trouble and needs you. Thank you, gentlemen."

The second *flic* looked at his notebook. "You are Justine Holliday? You have rented this flat from Monsieur Gallupe, for the term of one year?"

They knew too much. The panic was returning. Sutton—*Justine*—didn't handle interrogation well. *Get rid of them.* She had to get rid of them, now.

"As I have said, I am fine. Thank you for your concern."

The haughty tone seemed to work this time. They both nodded and allowed her to close the door. She heard their steps retreating toward the elevator, heard the slam of the metal interior door and the grinding of the gears lowering the car, and breathed a huge sigh of relief.

Something was wrong. Terribly, terribly wrong.

First the knife, then the police?

Sutton hurried to the desk, moved her purse. The knife, its wicked edge gleaming in the sun, made her horribly uncomfortable. She had no idea who'd put it there, if someone was trying to send her a message, nor what that message might be. But part of this escapade in Paris was staying off the radar. And instead of staying off the radar, she'd already talked to two different sets of police.

She looked out the window toward the street. The police were no longer in sight.

Could the two incidents be related? Or was someone playing a game with her? Or worse, was she losing it? Had the stress and fear and chaos finally taken its toll?

Possible. All too possible.

Colin Wilde's name floated through her mind.

Sutton, don't be ridiculous. No one knows where you are, especially him.

No one knew she was gone but Ethan, and with how things were going between them, she figured he would be happier to see her gone than to have her around.

But a huge, wicked knife, with blood on it, smelling of bleach, in her flat? And police coming to her door for a distress call she hadn't made?

It was beyond weird, and the strange familiarity of the police showing up when she hadn't called them creeped her out.

Think, Sutton. Think.

Constantine had been in the flat, obviously, but she'd been with him every moment. There was no way he could have distracted her enough that she wouldn't notice him climbing under her desk to tape a knife there.

Could he?

No. No, it wasn't possible. The previous owner had been very, very anxious to get out of town. In his rush, he must have forgotten the weapon was stashed under the desk. Or maybe a renter had put it there and forgotten it.

She'd probably knocked it loose with her knee in her sleep the previous night, and when she pulled out the chair, it had torn loose from its moorings and fallen to the floor.

She laughed aloud, relief flooding her body. Two unrelated incidents, surely.

You should write more mystery novels, Sutton. Justine. Maybe Justine wasn't working on a memoir after all, but a thriller.

She found the masking tape in the kitchen drawer. The torn edges matched the pieces of tape under the desk that had held up the knife for God knew how long. Proof, then, that the knife was here well before she'd arrived. Guns were not common among the Parisians; this knife was an excellent deterrent, especially for someone who rented his home out to strangers for part of the year.

It had been left behind. Yes, she was sure of it.

Keep lying to yourself, Sutton. You're so good at it.

Ignoring the voice, she debated what to do. Tape the knife back into position under the desk? Stow it in a closet?

No, she couldn't stand knowing it was here. She didn't want it around. No matter how benign, it was very large, and she had no idea how to use a knife in self-defense, so it could easily be used against her. She needed it far away, right now.

She should just throw it away. Put it in the trash inside a bag and let it be taken to the refuse facility. But what if someone was hurt? What if the knife cut the plastic and fell on a child, cutting them badly?

No, that wouldn't do at all.

Instead, she wrapped it in napkins and stashed it in her purse. Locked the door to the flat and started off, toward the river.

The Seine, the beautiful Seine, such a short walk from the apartment, was shining silver in the moonlight, waves splashing against the quay from the passage of a small boat.

She hurried. She was tired and ready to go to bed; the sudden rush of adrenaline through her system at finding the knife and the *flics* coming to the door had left her drained.

There were people around, she needed to be careful. Then again, there were always people around. She'd chosen Paris for the romance, the idea of writing a book in the City of Light, and the ability to hide in plain sight in the throngs of people. Now she wished she'd chosen something remote, someplace she could disappear and no one would see her or recognize her from day to day. What had she been thinking, coming here?

Under the unflinching metal gaze of the Tour, she walked onto the Pont d'Iéna, went to the middle of the bridge. Feigned nonchalance, leaned against the rails. When she felt no one was looking, she slid the knife from her purse.

A hard hand grabbed hers.

"Mademoiselle Holliday."

She started and looked up to see the twin forms of the *flics* who'd been at her door earlier, one on either side.

"What are you doing, mademoiselle?" But the man had already wrenched the knife from her grasp. "Who belongs to this knife? It is yours, yes?"

"I… No… Please."

The younger of the two, the one who'd knocked on her door, shook his head. She didn't know if it was with pity or disgust. "You must come with us. A crime has been committed, and you must answer questions."

"What crime? I haven't done anything. Where are you taking me?"

"You will come now for questioning."

They were already marching her toward their car, one on each arm. She thought to struggle, or to scream, but she was so shocked, so frightened, she was frozen in silence. Without another sound, she let them move her off the bridge and into their car and take her away.

AN ARREST IS MADE

Sutton hated the police. She hated the smell of the stations—
even here, in Paris, it was just the same as that hateful place she'd
been forced into overnight as a teenager. She was trying hard
not to panic. Though she'd done nothing wrong, she wasn't
stupid. Being apprehended standing on a bridge about to throw
a large, bloody hunting knife into the water below didn't look
good at all.

They took her to the police station on Rue Fabert next to
Les Invalides. When she finally got her wits about her, Sutton—
Justine—kept up a steady patter of protests and demands to see
a lawyer, though they ignored her. They put her in a room,
brought her a bottle of water, and shut the door.

She had no idea how the French legal system worked. She
didn't know if she could be charged without evidence, whether
she was allowed a phone call, or a lawyer. She was breathing
hard and trying to keep it together, but it was difficult. She was
supposed to be off the radar, living quietly in Paris, and not even
a week in, she was in a police station.

She prayed her identity would hold up. She hadn't brought
her passport, it was at the flat, but she assumed they would go
there and look through her things and find it.

You're Justine Holliday from Hollywood, Florida. Just remember that.

But as the minutes ticked past, the panic rose.

They were doing it on purpose, of course. Knowing she was scared and alone, leaving her thinking and sweating in a metal box in the middle of the night, with ultrabright fluorescent lights overhead, would rattle anyone. They had no idea the fear she had of being a rat in a cage, of being falsely accused. She'd been there before. She hadn't liked the outcome.

Breathe, Justine. Be calm. They won't make you wait forever. They have to tell you why they've brought you in. Wait and see what they're up to first.

She was right. She sat for two hours before a female officer came into the room, with the young *flic* behind her. She spoke excellent, though heavily accented, English.

"Bonsoir, mademoiselle. I am Inspector Amelie Badeau. I apologize for the delay in coming to visit with you. I am afraid I was home, getting some rest. It has been a very difficult twenty-four hours for us."

"Well, I'm sorry for you, but I'd like to know why I'm here. No one has bothered to tell me." She looked pointedly at the young *flic*, who stared back impassively.

"*Non?*" Badeau glanced over her shoulder at her young colleague. "I am sorry about this confusion. If I have been told correctly, you were found on the Pont d'Iéna with a knife, about to throw it into the Seine. A knife that we believe was used in a double murder last evening. While I was being summoned, our laboratory ran an analysis on the knife and found it had blood on it. Further analysis showed two blood types, both of which match the blood types of the victims at Sacré-Coeur last evening. We will have to wait a few days for the DNA testing to be complete, but it seems to me you were caught disposing of a murder weapon."

This isn't happening. This isn't happening. This isn't happening.

"I have no idea what you're talking about. I don't know about any murder."

But of course she did. It had been all the talk, all day, while she was enjoying herself strolling through Paris. All the disparate threads of conversation she'd overheard throughout the day ran through her head:

Two Americans died on the hill, did you hear...

This makes us look so bad, and after all the negative press this year...

They nearly cut the girl's head clean off...

They were posed, as if they were having sex...

Can you believe these stupid tourists...?

At the base of the church steps, such sacrilege...

I am scared, I hope they find who did this...

"You have not heard? It is such a shame. Two young lives cut short. With your knife, mademoiselle."

"I didn't do this. I found the knife..."

"*Oui? D'accord*, that may be. We have all night for you to tell me about the knife. But why don't we get comfortable and discuss what brought you to Paris? I understand you have recently arrived and rented a flat. You applied for a work visa. You plan to stay for a year?"

Sutton wasn't about to be swayed from the topic at hand. "I didn't have anything to do with the two murders. Those children, Lily and Rick, I don't know who killed them. And I want a lawyer."

The woman smiled kindly. "I didn't tell you the victims' names. So you are aware of the case, are you not, mademoiselle?"

Sutton shut her eyes briefly. *Stop being stupid.*

Badeau continued in that friendly, concerned tone. "You are not in America, Mademoiselle Holliday. You don't have the same rights as you might be afforded at home." She settled back more comfortably into the chair as if getting ready for a nice, long chat. "Now, tell me, what brought you to Paris?"

Sutton closed her mouth, her lips seamed together as if sewed shut, and shook her head. She wasn't going to say another word. This was bad, very bad, and she couldn't take the chance of screwing herself more. She knew she'd get a lawyer eventually, but shit, what was she going to do, call the embassy and ask for help? She had a fake passport, a fake identity. She was here under very false pretenses, and that was illegal. She couldn't imagine the embassy staff was predisposed to helping foreign nationals who flouted the law.

She shook her head at the woman, who smiled as if she understood completely.

Badeau signaled her compatriot to leave, then, when the door shut, leaned close, and said, "You might as well start talking. We know what you've done. And we know who you are. We have video of you on the grounds of Sacré-Coeur, trying to admire your handiwork, and again, later, laying flowers to make it seem you were simply there as another grieving tourist. The murder weapon was found in your flat. We are searching it thoroughly as we speak for more evidence. It does not take a genius to pull the threads together. Now," she said, smiling kindly, "it is time for you to tell me the truth about your involvement in the murders."

Sutton fought back tears. Oh, God. She was well and truly screwed.

"I want a lawyer."

"Pfft." Badeau gave a Gallic shrug. "If you are not willing to talk to me about the murder, would you perhaps like to talk about the real reason you're in Paris?"

"Lawyer."

Badeau shook her head and sighed heavily. "You will do well to cooperate with me, Mademoiselle. I want only to get to the truth, to understand what is actually happening."

Silence from Sutton. She was a sphinx. She would not break.

"Suit yourself. I was going to wait to talk to you about this. You're possibly the most famous missing person on the planet right now. A missing person, and the number one suspect in a gruesome double murder. Yes, we know who you are, Sutton Montclair, from Franklin, Tennessee."

SOMETIMES, YOU GET EXACTLY WHAT YOU WANT

In a darkened apartment, barren of anything but an old, dusty couch, a cobweb across a cracked window, and a state-of-the-art laptop computer, a phone rang.

When answered, a voice said, "It's done. She's been arrested."

"Has she been charged?"

"I don't know. But she's been in there for five hours now. They caught her red-handed trying to toss the murder weapon. She doesn't have a chance in hell of getting out of this. She's not that good a liar. And they know exactly who she is. I left nothing to the imagination."

"Good. Make sure she's charged, then come home." A pause. "I miss you."

"I know you do. I'll see you soon enough."

"Have you enjoyed yourself?"

A throaty, satisfied laugh. "You have no idea."

EVERYONE

"The world breaks everyone, and afterward, some are strong at the broken places."

—Ernest Hemingway

LIAR, LIAR, PANTS ON FIRE

Hey. It's me. Miss me? Yeah, I didn't think so.

Have you figured it out yet?

They're lying.

But I know the real truth.

Which means you're going to have to listen to me.

Ha ha. Joke's on you.

You realize they get paid to lie, don't you? It's what they do for a living, so of course they lie to each other, and of course they've lied to you. I mean, come on, they can't even agree on where they met, or how the evening went down. It was Chicago, if you're wondering. Not London or New York. They were at a conference in Chicago, and the only thing they both agree on is they got bone drunk and screwed all night. Have they told you about their significant others at the time? The ones they dumped? No?

Well, let me tell you. When Sutton and Ethan met? Sutton was practically engaged to a man named Tobias Winters. Good guy, Toby. A little older than her, gray hair, gray goatee, plenty of cash to keep her feet warm by the fire. Madly in love with her, too. He'd do anything she asked.

And Ethan was living with a woman. Nel, her name was Nel. She used to do his hair. She was a doormat, absolutely worshipped the ground he walked on. Now, I understand his scenario a bit more than Sutton's. I mean, who wants to be with someone like that? It has to be boring—vanilla pudding, vanilla ice cream, vanilla milk shake—all day, every day. You can't really blame him for looking for something more, he's a man, and Sutton is a temptress witch, and it's easy to understand how she could pull him away from his life, his work, his world, without a second thought to the people she'd hurt if she did. She's a home wrecker. Always has been. This isn't the first family she's broken up.

Ethan didn't stand a chance against Sutton, and neither did that vanilla milk shake of a woman he was with. When Sutton burst onto the scene, Ethan forgot all about poor old Nel. Dumped her on the side of the road, put her clothes on the street at the end of the driveway. She came home, three days after his trip to Chicago, and found everything she owned on the street and the locks changed.

Come to think of it, Nel could have done it. Or Toby. He is perfectly capable of murder. I hear the breakup there didn't go as smoothly. Toby threatened to kill Sutton. They shouted and screamed late into the night. The police were called. There will be records on file should you care to check.

Until now, have you even stopped for a single moment to consider the people they hurt? Thought about the betrayal and pain they'd felt? Who's to say Nel and Toby didn't meet for a drink one night and concoct a plan to take Ethan and Sutton down?

Would you blame him? Would you blame her?

I wouldn't.

I understand the desire to see them both rotting in the ground perfectly.

Now, I have to get ready for my date. I bought new lingerie for the occasion. Red. I do like red.

I miss good old Ethan. He was fun.

And he's going to enjoy tonight, whether he wants to or not.

I am going to enjoy it even more. Because everything I have worked for is happening.

Stupid Sutton. She has no idea what I'm capable of.

And neither does he.

AIN'T NO REST FOR THE WICKED

Franklin, Tennessee

Ethan's patience was running out. Not only had he sat in this infernal cell all night, counting the bloody tiles (four thousand four hundred and seven tiles on the floor and wall; he managed to count them twice), the towheaded cop had rushed in, asked him strange questions, and rushed away before explaining what the bloody hell she was talking about. And he'd been left alone again.

Graham was clearly mad. Sutton didn't own a wig. Did she? Did he know his wife at all anymore?

Oh, what did it matter? She was dead. He was in jail. He shifted uncomfortably on the hard pallet. In jail, about to be arraigned, paraded in front of the courts and television cameras.

Bill would be thrilled. There would be a massive bump in backlist sales. Offers would come from every house to write the true story of his marriage's demise. He could hear the rejoinders now: Why did you do it, Mr. Montclair? Why did you kill your wife?

Would they let him do pressers from the penitentiary?

He'd been on this thought train for about an hour when the

door opened and Joel Robinson walked through, eyes shining in excitement.

"We need to talk," he said.

"I only want to hear that you can get me out of here, right now."

"Actually, I think I can."

Ethan stood up. "What's happened?"

"You might want to sit back down."

"Joel. Please."

"They aren't 100 percent sure the body they recovered is Sutton."

Ethan sat, hard. "What? How? Her rings…"

"That blonde cop, Graham? She's saved your ass. She's insisting you're innocent and the body isn't Sutton's. Apparently, there was an inconsistency at autopsy. We're still waiting on dental and DNA, dental will be in anytime, but she's already pushing for you to be released."

"God bless her. Now, tell me everything."

Robinson adjusted his pants. "You sure? If it turns out she's wrong…"

Ethan only paused for a moment. "I'm sure."

"Okay. I have two shots they let me take from the crime scene photos. The body was burned, right?"

He grimaced. "So I heard."

"They have Sutton's wedding set, recovered from the victim's left hand. Here's a picture. These are her rings, yes?"

He turned his phone to face Ethan. It was a close-up shot. All he could see was the shine of platinum and diamond against a sort of ashy black background. He swallowed hard and nodded. "Yes, those are her rings, without a doubt. The wedding band was new when we married, we picked it out at Tiffany, but the stone is my grandmother's. I've been seeing it all my life."

"All right. Here's the other."

Robinson swiped to the left, and Ethan saw a mass of red hair on the ground.

"From what I've been told, when they took the body, the scalp fell off. They bagged it and took it into evidence. Only it wasn't a scalp. Once the ME started messing with it, he realized it's a wig. The scalp of the victim was burned, and the real hair, if any, was seared away. This is definitely a wig."

Ethan got a glance of strawberry and dirt, then the phone lit up, obscuring the picture. Robinson answered, smiled grimly, and pocketed the phone.

"It's not her. Dental doesn't match. They're coming to let you go."

Ethan was too shocked to fully comprehend what was happening. "But...her rings... Who is it? Who's dead in the field?"

"Who, and who killed her, I dunno the answers to either. Truth be told, right now, I don't care. All I know is whoever it is, it's not your wife. And that's very good news indeed for you, my friend. Without a body, everything they have is sketchy and circumstantial. You're not in the clear by a long shot, you're still their number one suspect, but now they have nothing definitive to hold you on."

"What do they have? How in the world could there be evidence when I didn't commit a crime?"

"Guy who runs the farm out there? He saw you walking in the field Thursday night. That's pretty damning evidence for the cops, you being at the scene of the crime, after dark, with a witness to place you there."

"But I went there to pay off Wilde."

"So you say. The cops see *suspect* and *dead body* within five hundred feet of one another, and they draw their own conclusions. Anyway, there's all kinds of computer stuff pointing your way, stuff I barely understand, and the search of your house turned up gas cans and rags in the garage, but that's something I can easily explain away. Every responsible car owner has a spare gas can lying around. There's something else happening, too. It's to do with your son's case."

The thorn that had been pulled from his heart when he realized Sutton could still be alive smashed back into place. "What is it?"

"That's what I need to find out. I was hopeful that there'd be a discovery after the arraignment this morning, but since you aren't going to court, I'm not going to find out right now. My main objective is to get you home. We'll go from there. They'll be down here shortly. Ethan." Robinson shook his finger. "Do not, I repeat, do not say anything, just gather up your things and leave. I'll be waiting outside to drive you home."

Ethan nodded. As Robinson was walking out, he said, "Joel?"

"Yeah?"

"I didn't hurt her."

Robinson nodded. "I know."

Half an hour later, Officer Graham came through the door. She looked like she'd been up all night. Her hair was standing on end, she had circles under her eyes, but when she approached, her smile was genuine.

"Time to go home, Mr. Montclair."

He stood, hands in his pockets, feeling the tug of his loose waistband sliding onto his hips. They'd taken his belt and shoes when he entered the jail.

"I know you've heard that the body we found is not Mrs. Montclair. I was also told you've positively identified the rings the body was wearing as your wife's wedding set."

He followed her out the door, not speaking, as Robinson had instructed. Graham walked him to the counter where they'd done his intake processing. He wondered if he could ask to see his mug shot.

"We're not finished, not by a long shot, but for now, Mr. Montclair, you're free to go. Shirley here will get your things back to you. Your lawyer is waiting outside. There's a boatload of media, too, but I figured you might want to walk out smiling for once. If you're able."

He gave Graham half a smile, accepted his wallet, shoes, and belt from the gray-haired battle-ax behind the counter. Fitted the worn leather through the hoops, slid his feet into his loafers. Stayed silent as the grave.

Graham walked him to the jail door. She pushed it open. A shaft of sunlight and fresh air encompassed him, and he took his first full breath in days.

Against the advice of his attorney, he softly said to the cop, "Thank you for believing me."

Graham shrugged. "I wouldn't say I believe you, sir. If you killed Mrs. Montclair, I will find out. And then I'll nail you to the wall."

ADMIT IT

Paris, France

Sutton didn't panic, not right away. She just couldn't believe how quickly it had all fallen apart. She hadn't even been in Paris a full week, and here she was, at a police station, a murder suspect.

So they knew who she was. That was problematic, but explainable. She prepped the conversation in her mind, for when she was forced to speak the words aloud.

My husband was abusing me.

I ran away.

The new identity is for my safety so he can't find me. I'll be in danger if he does.

She listened to Inspector Badeau with half an ear. Deciding she'd wait for a lawyer to be present was self-preservation at its best, but Sutton's grudging silence hadn't stopped the woman from talking and talking and talking.

It wasn't until Badeau said the name Ethan that Sutton tuned back in. My God, had she nodded off?

"Pardon?"

"Madame Montclair, are you listening to me at all?"

"It's very late. I'm very tired. What were you saying?"

"Your husband was arrested earlier today."

She couldn't help herself. "Arrested? For what?"

"Murdering you."

Sutton's brows creased. What in the world? This was a trick, a trick to get her to talk. She said as much, then asked again for a lawyer.

When Badeau frowned, a small crease appeared on her forehead. Sutton had gotten used to this.

"Madame Montclair. Allow me a moment to speak frankly. I will admit, now that we have become aware of this information, something feels...off about this situation. According to the American police, your body was found, murdered and burned in a field outside the town in which you live. I was told the body was wearing your wedding rings. Your husband was arrested for murdering you.

"And yet, here you sit, very much alive, a murder suspect in your own right. There are two bodies here in the morgue, brutally murdered at Sacré-Coeur. We have video of you at the crime scene. We have the murder weapon that you were trying to dispose of. And there is this."

She pushed a small gray-and-black box in a plastic bag toward Sutton.

"This was found in your apartment."

It looked like a ring box. As she watched, Badeau unsealed the evidence bag, creaked open the box. Flakes of black fell onto the table. Inside was a small diamond engagement ring.

"The blood on this ring box also matches that on the knife. There is no more logical conclusion other than to assume it must have been taken from the Sacré-Coeur crime scene."

"I've never seen that before in my life."

Badeau's brow furrowed. "I thought you would claim as much." She leaned forward, almost as if she was going to touch Sutton's hand. "Madame, you are in very serious trouble. I implore you, explain yourself."

Sutton shook her head.

Badeau sat for a moment, unmoving, unspeaking, then shrugged. "My superior is at this moment making a call to the police in your town to tell them we have you in our custody. And that we will be charging you with double homicide. It would not surprise me at all if a third charge will not be pending."

"A third?" Sutton blurted out.

"*Mais oui*, madame. It seems quite logical to me that you attempted to obscure your flight from the United States by murdering someone, putting your rings on the poor soul's finger, and fleeing here to Paris. Your murderous rage took you to Sacré-Coeur, where you killed the two innocent students, hid the murder weapon, then casually returned to the scene of the crime to lay flowers in an effort to make yourself look sympathetic. You are quite the dangerous creature."

Sutton felt the blood draining from her head as the woman spoke, each word a nail to her heart. This was not what was supposed to happen. This was not how she meant for anything to go. A sick and deep nausea gripped her. She knew she was going to be ill. Sutton clapped a hand over her mouth.

"Please, the trash can."

Badeau shoved it toward her with her foot.

But she didn't get sick, just sat miserably, sweating, the gorge rising. She hadn't eaten, there was nothing to throw up. Her stomach churned. What had happened? What was going on? A dead body, wearing her rings? She'd left them behind in Franklin, with...

Everything, crashing into place. The past month: the plans made, the precautions taken, the confidences given. The "plan" was for Sutton to get away from it all, to start a new life. To excise Ethan without the messiness of a separation and divorce. To get away from the man she was afraid of, the man she feared killed their child. Self-preservation, yes, but something more, something else. Punishment. For both of them. For what had happened, and what was to come.

Paris was the obvious choice. The place they'd talked about. The dream location. If you're going to escape your life, you might as well do it right.

And now there were bodies, one wearing her rings, two more practically lying at her feet, and a horrible realization started deep within her.

Ethan, arrested.

Sutton, arrested.

Only one person knew what she'd planned. Had helped. Had encouraged. A shoulder to cry on, a compatriot in the plot. And now...

She had to get out of here. She had to get home. She had to fix this. Dear God, what had she done?

"Are you going to be unwell?" Badeau asked.

Sutton coiled her hair in her hand, lifting its mass off her neck, passing her hand quickly behind to fan herself. "Yes, I'm going to be unwell. How would you feel if someone accused you of murdering three people when you did no such thing?"

Badeau smiled, briefly. "It is warm in here. Would you like a drink of water?"

"Yes, I would."

The door opened and a bottle of Evian was handed in. Sutton opened it and drank. She felt better. It was hot in the stifling little room. She hadn't had any sleep, or food, and she was tired of being harassed. It wasn't smart, speaking without counsel; she could hear Joel Robinson's voice in her head, warning her off. Actually, it was terribly reckless, but she was sick and scared, and being pushed was never something she could handle. And truth be told, Sutton's specialty was recklessness.

There were more people listening to the interview; the water had been forthcoming almost immediately. She needed to be careful, but she needed to talk, to clear herself, to get home to Ethan. She needed him. He needed her. They were going to have to face this threat together.

"I didn't kill anyone," Sutton said.

"Are you willing to make a statement, for the record, then?"

"Yes. On one condition. When I finish, I want to call my husband."

"We cannot guarantee anything, madame. But I agree to pass on a message to your husband should you answer our questions adequately."

Sutton took a deep drink of the water. And then she told them. She told them everything.

ONCE A JUVIE, ALWAYS A JUVIE

Holly didn't think she'd ever seen anything so insane as the media frenzy when Ethan Montclair walked out of jail and the chief had to eat crow for arresting him before they'd formally ID'd the body found at the farm off Highway 96. Which the ME hadn't been able to do yet. There were no other officially missing women in the area, so unless a family member came forward or the dental database got a hit—which she doubted they would, because the victim clearly hadn't been being treated by a dentist recently, so current radiographs were a long shot—they had a Jane Doe on their hands.

An anonymous victim. Lost. No way to determine age, ethnicity, or identity, thanks to the very well-placed fire. A stranger, wearing Sutton Montclair's wedding set.

Rings on her fingers, bells on her toes. Holly couldn't get the refrain out of her head.

Once the crow had been eaten, the friends lined up for more interviews, both with the Franklin Police and the media, now begging Sutton to come forward, to show herself, to stop the charade. Ethan Montclair drank himself into oblivion while Joel Robinson gave proxy interviews begging Sutton to come home.

Holly ignored it all. She shut the doors to the conference war room and went back to work.

Because now, they were acting under the assumption that Sutton Montclair was a murderer.

It was quite clear from all the interviews that she'd been parceling out information to her friends. Phyllis, the comforting knowledge she was the only confessor. Ellen, the honor of intelligence and professional intimacy. Ivy, taken advantage of the most, given the Benadryl bottle to make it look like her husband had killed their child. Holly imagined Sutton to be a disturbed woman, volatile and unpredictable. A woman with problems, who was lashing out at everyone and everything around her. *A woman who lost her child, Holly. That alone would drive anyone insane.*

Lost? Or was Sutton Montclair responsible for her baby's death?

It was an easy hypothesis. Kill the baby, lose her mind, fake her own death, set up her husband. Perhaps it should be the realm of fiction, but it wasn't outside the bounds of reality. People had done worse for less.

Holly needed to speak again to the friends, especially to Ivy. The one who'd so adamantly insisted Ethan Montclair had hurt his wife and possibly killed his child. To whom pictures had been shown, murder weapons given. It seemed to Holly that Sutton Montclair was a master manipulator. She'd killed her child, done a mighty fine job of trying to set up her husband for murder, all under the guise of *poor little me, I'm an abused wife*. She'd deceived everyone around her, including the women who thought she was their friend. She needed to run this past them, and see who thought Sutton Montclair capable of this level of deception.

Holly hated her. Which was ridiculous. She was mad at a woman she'd never met, because she'd managed to turn everyone's world upside down, and two people were dead because of it.

The whole team had been digging, and Holly had been digging, too. Deep. She'd talked to Siobhan Healy in Canada again, who'd called Holly back at the station when she heard that her daughter's body had been found. The conversation that ensued was one Holly wouldn't ever forget. Mrs. Healy had expressed disbelief, as was to be expected. And then she'd said, "Well, since she's dead, I guess you can unseal the juvenile records now, can't you?"

Holly had nearly dropped the phone.

"What does she have juvenile records for, ma'am?"

"You'll see. This truly is a shame. I never did believe Ethan had the balls to murder her. Do I need to come home? No, of course I don't. We should be able to finish our vacation before the funeral." And she'd hung up. The woman was cold as ice. But of course she was. Her daughter had to learn it somewhere.

Was the mother involved? She'd skedaddled out of town quickly, but if there was one thing all the people in Sutton's life agreed on, it was her prickly relationship with her mother.

Holly tapped her fingers along the base of her laptop. She was three cups of coffee in and needed a bathroom break badly, but those juvie records were calling her.

She typed in *Sutton Healy*, came up with nothing. Tried *Siobhan Healy*, nothing. It was half an hour later, deep in the system, she found a name change petition. Maude Wilson. Mother of Elizabeth Sutton Wilson. Maude's new name was Siobhan.

Now who was being devious? Looked like Sutton came by it naturally.

She plugged in *Wilson, Elizabeth S.* There was an immediate hit. She opened the file, and started to read. An hour later, she emerged from the computer, rinsed her coffee cup, used the bathroom, and perched on the edge of her desk to think.

Sutton Montclair wasn't who she said she was.

And Holly wasn't surprised at all.

HAZE ON THE SEINE

Sutton talked for two hours. She explained everything that had led up to her fleeing from Tennessee in the first hour, and in the second, everything that had happened since she'd arrived in Paris. Badeau and the unseen others listened without interruption until she brought up Constantine.

"Constantine Raffalo. Did you ever see an identification for him? A passport, a license of some sort?"

"No. But you say you have me on video at Sacré-Coeur? I was supposed to meet him there. That's why I went, to see the sunrise, work, and meet him for lunch. He encouraged me to go. Perhaps he will be on the video. And if there are cameras at my café on the corner, he was certainly there a few times. He is involved in this. I don't know how, but he is. He must be. If I were a paranoid woman, I would say he is Colin Wilde, and he's set me up. But that would be quite a leap."

"He was in your apartment alone? He had access? Did you give him a key?"

"No, I didn't give him a key, but that means nothing. He could have made a copy. He could have picked the lock. He could have watched to see when I left the flat for a walk or for food. He could very easily have gotten in when I was gone, any number of times. I've spent more time walking the streets than

I have at home." Sutton shrugged. "It's Paris. Why stay inside if you don't need to?"

"It is very convenient, this phantom man who you barely know."

"But it's the truth, Inspector. I'm not proud of my behavior, but it's all true."

Badeau stared at her a moment, then stood. "I will be back. Can I bring you coffee?"

"Do you have any tea?"

Badeau nodded and slipped out the door.

She believes me, Sutton thought, practically collapsing against the chair. *Thank God, she believes me.*

Twenty minutes later, Badeau returned. She had a mug of tea in one hand and a slip of paper in the other. She set both down on the table in front of Sutton.

The tea was milky, sweet, and hot. Sutton felt tears rise when she took a sip. Just like Ethan made for her, though this wasn't as strong. Still, it was warm and sugary and comforting as a hug. She took another sip, then looked at the paper.

It was a grainy still photograph of Constantine.

"That's him. That's Constantine."

"You are certain?"

"I am. Where was this taken?"

"Sacré-Coeur. You were correct. He was there the morning after the murder, as well. I would be interested in speaking with him. Do you have any way to contact him?"

"I don't. I broke it off this morning. Yesterday morning?"

"You have been here for nearly twenty-four hours."

No wonder she felt so awful. No sleep, no food, only the tea. "Then yesterday. I told him I came to Paris to be alone, that I didn't want to see him anymore."

"Was he upset by this? Angered? Threatening?"

"No. More…disappointed, but not hurt, or rejected. He

seemed cold but not angry. He left without fuss. Can you find him?"

"Not without considerable help."

"Why is that?"

She slapped down another photo, this one much clearer. Shot from above. Constantine, but not Constantine. The man in this picture had surfer blond hair and a grim smile on his face. His tall body was clothed in khakis and a blue button-down. He was midstride, carrying a black leather duffel bag.

"The man who told you he was called Constantine Raffalo took a flight from de Gaulle last night. Paris to JFK. We have made calls to the FBI to warn them. Hopefully, they can arrest him quickly. When they do, they will arrange for us to have a discussion with him."

"I don't understand. He bleached his hair and caught a flight to JFK?"

"He changed his name, as well. Or lied to you. The passport he flew under names him as Trent Duggan. American citizen, thirty-five years old, birthplace, Orlando, Florida. The passport's issuing office is also in Florida. The problem is, the name, address, social security number, and passport number do not match anyone from the state of Florida. I will need to see the passport itself to make the determination, but, like yours, I believe his papers are false. Your issuing office is the same as his."

Sutton tried to wrap her head around it. "But he said he was a military brat. That he grew up all over the world."

"More lies, it would seem." Badeau sat down. She seemed tired. Sutton supposed she must be; she'd been here the whole time.

"If am I to believe you, madame, that you are here because you are in trouble, this is the narrative you expect me to put forth to my superiors. You arrived, you found a flat, you explored the city, started writing your book, then went to bed with a man who gave you a false name, a false background, and, apparently from the photographs, a false look, as well. You are utterly innocent of any wrongdoing. Everything that has happened since your arrival is some sort of coincidence, which, as a police officer, I am reluctant to believe in. Yes?"

Sutton nodded. "It's the truth. I didn't hurt anyone. I swear it."

"And yet we have two murdered students at Sacré-Coeur, a female victim in Tennessee, and you've admitted to traveling under false papers, which, as I'm sure you know, is a very serious crime, especially in light of our current security situation. You are a contradiction in terms, as they say."

"I didn't do any of it, except for getting the fake passport. I swear."

Badeau nodded. Was the woman softening? Sutton felt a glimmer of hope.

"Tell me again how you came by the false papers?"

"My friend got them for me. She said she knew a man who could help me disappear. He does work with women's shelters, getting abused women new identities so they can flee their situations and still be able to get a job. He creates a whole backstory, gives them a new passport, new license, new everything. It's like witness protection, only run by real people, not by the government."

"I will need this man's name."

"I don't know it. My friend handled everything. Inspector Badeau, please. I know you don't believe me, and we can hash through the details as long as you want, but I have to make a call. I need to warn my husband. If my friend is behind this, if she's trying to hurt me instead of help me, I have to talk to him. I have to make sure he's watching out. If he gets hurt because of my stupidity, I'll never forgive myself."

"I must alert the police in your home state about this situation. Once we have discussed things, you may make a phone call."

"Are you arresting me? Formally?"

"Not yet."

"Can I leave?"

"Most certainly not. As I said, there are many unanswered questions. You have broken a number of laws, and you must answer for those crimes. To start, I will need the name of your friend, the one who got you the papers."

Sutton nodded. She hoped like hell she was wrong, but there was only one person who knew where she was. "Her name is Ivy Brookes."

Badeau took down the name as if Sutton hadn't just betrayed the past few months of her life by uttering those innocuous words. She stood. "I will have food brought to you. I will be back soon, madame."

Sutton put her head in her hands on the table.

Oh, Ethan. What have I done?

THROUGH A GLASS, DARKLY

Ethan walked through the door to a stranger's house. The home, their beautiful Victorian home that they'd rebuilt from the inside out, still stood grandly, but he no longer recognized it. Too much had happened. Too many hurts and lies and painful nights brewed together under the roof. Too many ghosts. Far too many ghosts.

He was exhausted. First his wife was missing, then dead, then missing again. Someone, a stranger still, had been murdered, wearing Sutton's precious rings. The idea that Sutton would go to such lengths to escape him broke him in places he hadn't previously known existed. To kill another soul, to murder someone to make them look like her, that took a mind so devious, so black and twisted, that he could hardly believe his wife was capable of such a thing. And now Robinson had said they were reopening Dashiell's case. Why? Why would they do that?

Unless there was new evidence. Unless Sutton had killed Dashiell.

He sank to his knees in the foyer, finally allowing the reality of his situation to seep in.

How was he supposed to recover from this? His beloved wife, turned grim reaper? And was this the first time?

It was terrible of him, but he'd always wondered if she'd done it. Accidentally, of course. Not on purpose. She'd been drunk, she'd been last in the nursery. But the autopsy had been so clear, everyone so adamant. *It was a tragic event, but you're not to blame. You're blameless.*

They were never blameless. Not him, and not Sutton.

And now, with the police looking closer at Dashiell's death, what horrible truths were they going to find?

A knock on the door. His entire body tensed. Friend, or foe?

He clambered to his feet, went to the window, glanced out. The media hadn't gotten themselves set up on his doorstep yet; they were still all at the jail, interrogating the chief.

He opened the door. Ivy stood on the porch. She had a bottle of wine in one hand and a yellow bowl covered in plastic wrap in the other, something like a smile on her face.

"Food and drink. I figured you could use it."

"Thank you. Come on in."

She set the bowl on the counter. "Pasta salad. Fresh. And a nice Nebbiolo. You like the Langhe, don't you?"

"How do you remember these things, Ivy? Do you secretly write them all down in a notebook when we're not looking?"

"That's exactly what I do." She laughed, getting out two glasses for the wine. She set them on the table. "I'm so glad they let you go. I'm so glad she's still out there somewhere. It gives me hope that this horrible week might end well. And since you're free and clear, I thought we should celebrate."

Ethan watched her move around the house, so practiced, so casual, as if it were her own. Something niggled at him. He didn't feel like celebrating, and what an odd choice of words. How could he celebrate? A woman was dead. Sutton was still missing.

"I appreciate the thought, Ivy, but I'm really not hungry. I was planning to have an early night. I didn't get any sleep at the jail."

She ignored him, started opening the wine. She was wearing a red dress, and he could see the outline of lace beneath it, cupping the roundness of her ass. He felt the usual shameful stirring, the odd combination of loathing and longing he felt every time she was around.

She began to pour, the ruby liquid splashing recklessly against the glass. A few drops landed on the counter. She ignored it, handed him a glass, raised hers in a salute. Took a sip.

"Did you ever tell her about us, Ethan? I mean, she knew about the affair, that awful blogger made sure that happened. But did you ever tell Sutton that it was me you slept with that night?"

He nearly spit out the wine. They didn't discuss this. It was an agreement. That night had never happened. He couldn't remember it, didn't want to remember it.

"Of course I didn't. She was hurt enough as it was. And like I told you, no offense, but I was so drunk that I don't remember that night at all. Just waking up. I got most of the story from that arsehole blogger."

Her face had whitened, her mouth a thin line. "You don't remember anything? It was good. It was fantastic, actually. I've always wanted to do it again." She set her glass down, inched closer to him. She started to slide her dress up her thighs. "What do you say, Ethan. Shall we give it another go? This time, I swear you'll remember everything."

"Ivy. I don't think now is the time."

"I think now is the perfect time, Ethan. You know you want to. I see how you look at me. I see the way your eyes follow me when I cross the room. What's it been like, all this time, with Sutton cold as a fish, knowing that I have been ready and waiting for you?"

"I don't want this, Ivy."

"You've always wanted this, Ethan. Sutton, gone, and me, ready and willing for anything, in your bed. That's what you told me that night. You don't remember, so you claim, but I see it in your eyes. I see how much you want me. Now she's gone, and we don't have to hide it anymore."

Closer now. He could smell her perfume, see the lace thong. Her dress had a deep V-neck; she was wearing a matching set. Just like what he'd woken up to that horrible morning. Him: naked and suffering from the most epic hangover he'd ever had. Her: bedecked in red lace, hot as a lit stick of dynamite and ready for another go.

He'd turned her down. He'd been so sick with himself that he'd cheated on Sutton that the idea of doing it again was repugnant. He felt the same sense of loathing right now. He didn't want Ivy. He never had. There was something about her, yes. She was beautiful and smart, but he'd never wanted her like he wanted Sutton.

Ivy grabbed his hand and made a credible attempt to put it down her panties.

"Ivy, stop. She's your best friend. What are you doing?"

"Anything you want," she purred.

A lesser man would already have his dick out. Ethan wasn't even aroused.

Their eyes locked. Ethan looked away first. He pulled his hand free. "I don't want this."

The house phone began to ring.

"Yes, you do. You know you do."

He didn't give a shit who was on the phone, he needed this situation to end, right now.

He whirled away, grabbed the handset and barked, "Hullo," into the mouthpiece.

"Ethan? Oh, thank God you're okay."

His heart stopped. It literally stopped, and he couldn't catch his breath.

"Sutton? Oh my God, Sutton, is that really you? Where are you?"

"Ethan, you have to listen to me. You're in—"

He turned, smiling now, to tell Ivy, but the front door was open.

No one was there.

The room was empty.

"Ivy?" he called.

"Behind you," she answered. He saw the flat edge of a board a second before it hit him square in the face, and went down, hard, the phone spinning away, Sutton calling, "Ethan? Ethan?"

POISON IVY

So now you know.

My name is Ivy. Like the poison.

I told you at the beginning you weren't going to like me very much. You really don't like me right now, do you? Am I a horrible person? A loathsome creature? You bet. I'm evil to the core.

And I warned you. I warned you, and you didn't listen. I know what you're thinking. Why? Why would I try to hurt the two people who've shown me nothing but love and friendship since I came into their lives?

I don't think I'm quite ready to share the whole truth with you. Sorry. But I will tell you this. They aren't the people you think they are.

Do you think I don't care about how Ethan feels? Do you think I don't care how Sutton's going to feel when she finds out the whole truth? Well, I do care. I care so much it hurts my very soul.

I'm doing this to make them hurt the way I do. I'm doing this so they understand exactly who and what they're dealing with. They have no idea what it has cost me, finding her, tracking them, devising this plan. It's been years in the making.

Sutton thinks she can run away from the truth, can hide from me. She is wrong. She is so very, very wrong.

So, now that we've been properly introduced, I present: my goals.

I want to see Elizabeth Sutton Wilson Healy Montclair exposed for the fraud she really is. For the predator that she is. I could see it from the first moment I laid eyes on her. She has a coldness in her soul. You know how you can tell? Take a picture of her. In person, she's this absolute glamour-puss with all that red hair and lissome figure. But try to capture her on film, and you can see who she really is. The lens is an inanimate object. It can't be bewitched, can't be fooled. No glamour can be put upon it. It shows the truth. And the truth is, her soul is empty. Black and rotted and bottomless. She is ugly, she is loathsome.

She is not a good person, and nothing will make me happier than taking her down.

And neither is Ethan. He is a cheat and a liar, the worst sort of man. Wait until you find out what he did. Then you'll see. You'll see exactly what kind of a man he is. You won't blame me in the least.

They deserve each other. So I will make sure they get everything they deserve.

Everything.

I want them to bleed. And they will. Trust me. Ethan already is. I think I've broken his nose.

Oops.

So much fun to be had here. But first, I need to deal with something. Join me, will you?

ABOUT...FACE

Holly's desk phone rang, something that only happened if someone was calling in-house from another phone in the station, or the receptionist. Fifty-fifty shot. She much preferred in-house calls than the *blind squirrel finds nuts* ones she got from outside. Still, she had to answer. It was policy. She grabbed the receiver and kept typing with one hand.

"Graham."

It was the receptionist. "I have a call for you. Paris police."

"Paris?"

"That's what she says. The accent is a bit of a giveaway, too. She certainly sounds the part."

"Okay. Put her through."

A click, then the static of an open line. "Graham here."

"Bonsoir, madame. My name is Amelie Badeau. I am an inspector with the Paris Metropolitan Police. I have a woman in my custody by the name of Sutton Montclair."

Holly stopped typing. "You're kidding me."

"I am not. We have her in custody on a double murder charge. She insists on her innocence. But I need more information. Do you have a moment to talk?"

"Boy, do I ever," Holly said, whipping out her notebook. "Please, tell me everything."

"Are you familiar at all with the name Ivy Brookes?"

"I am. Brookes is one of Sutton Montclair's best friends. She's been incredibly helpful to the investigation into Montclair's disappearance."

"If what I am being told is true, you should pick up Mademoiselle Brookes as quickly as possible. She could be a very dangerous person."

Holly listened in utter disbelief as Badeau talked. After fifteen minutes, the woman said, "I will send you all the supporting documentation I have. We are, as you can imagine, very anxious to speak with Mademoiselle Brookes, and Monsieur Duggan is currently being searched for by your FBI. I am hopeful they will find him quickly."

"I need a number where I can reach you immediately, at all times."

Badeau rattled off a string of numbers. Holly gave her own mobile number, and the direct number to Homicide, too, just in case. She hurriedly thanked the inspector, hung up, and rushed into the conference room. It had been disassembled, the murder investigation had moved to the squad room, but Jim was still in there with his computers.

"Where's Moreno?"

Jim pushed his glasses up his nose. "Home. Getting some sleep. I don't think I've seen him shut his eyes all week. What's wrong? You look like your hair's about to burst into flame."

"It is. I need you to do your magic for me."

"Lay it on me, sister."

"A few days ago, Ethan Montclair asked me if passwords could be changed remotely."

"I remember. Of course they can."

"Could someone from outside be watching their cyber tracks?"

"With all the malware the Montclairs have on their computers, the Russians could be spying on them. But, Holly, it's been pretty clear all along Montclair was the one spying on his wife."

"What if it wasn't him? Is it possible to mimic the IP address so it looks like it came from his computer?"

"Again, sure. But you don't think Montclair is innocent of all this now, do you?"

"I don't know what to think. But tell me this. If someone wanted to really screw with a person, make it look like they've been harassing someone, it's doable, right?"

Jim started to look excited, all notes of exhaustion gone from his voice. "Are you saying there's a third party involved?"

"Exactly what I'm saying."

"Montclair's been claiming this Colin Wilde person has been harassing him and his wife for months now."

"And everything we have says Colin Wilde is a sock puppet created by Montclair to terrorize his wife, to cut her down, ruin her career. That Montclair himself was responsible for all of it. But what if we're wrong? What if Colin Wilde is real?"

"I'll bite. Who is he?"

"If Sutton Montclair is to be believed, he's probably a man named Trent Duggan. And he's working with Ivy Brookes."

"Whoa, whoa, whoa. Come again? Where are you getting all of this? Brookes is your most reliable witness."

"She has been, yes. But Sutton Montclair is sitting in a Paris jail cell, and claims Brookes helped her plan a getaway, and she left her rings in her possession. If that's true, then Ivy Brookes is our murderer."

"You found Sutton Montclair?"

"Sure did. Just got a call from the French police. They've got her for murder. A double murder, actually. She's denying it, of course, and the Paris inspector on the case seems to feel Sutton is innocent. And I'll tell you, Jim, Montclair never felt right to me for all of this. It didn't jibe. Why systematically try to ruin your wife? Why not just divorce, or leave? He may not be Captain America, but he doesn't strike me as the malicious type."

"You've always been starry-eyed for him."

"I'm going to ignore that statement, and when it turns out I'm right, you can apologize over a steak dinner."

Jim's eyes lit up. "Deal. So what do you want me to do?"

"If Brookes is behind this, there will be a trace, right? There's no way to do it completely clean."

"Yes, that's true. And there is a phantom IP address that came through with all the others, one from here in Franklin that I haven't been able to track down. It went through about fifty routers, bounced all over the world. It doesn't seem to be registered anywhere, though. It's a loose thread."

"You find it for me, Jim. Stop looking inside, and look at it from the outside. As if someone is purposefully misleading us. Knowing it could be coming from outside after all, and not from the Montclairs, you trace it down, and make sure it's airtight."

"I don't know, Holly. All the fingers point to Montclair."

"I know they do. All of them. How often do you see a case that lines up so perfectly? How often have you ever seen a case that was so clear? Everything points at him. Everything is so neatly assembled that perhaps, perhaps, someone wanted it to look like that. And if this someone has connections to people who can forge documents, and helped Sutton Montclair get out of town… Trust me here, Jim. My gut is screaming at me. Reset your thinking on all of this, and find me some proof so I can have a nice, long chat with Ivy Brookes."

"You really believe it's a setup?"

"And a good one. We totally fell for it. We got all excited and arrested him, and it turned out the chick in the field wasn't his wife and we have no actual proof of wrongdoing on his part. And his wife's arrested in Paris for a murder, too? I don't buy it. I think they're being targeted. I may be wrong, but that's where the steak comes in."

"You better call Moreno."

"I'm doing it right now. Right after I call Ethan. Because if we're right, he could be in danger. We already have one dead body on our hands."

"This is nuts, you know that."

"I do." She dialed Montclair's mobile number. After six rings, it went to voice mail. She tried the house. There was no answer there, either. Her screaming gut started to hurt.

"I'm going to take a run by. I'll call Moreno from the car."

"Holly?"

She stopped in the door frame, hand on the knob. "Yeah?"

"Be careful. I'm looking forward to that dinner."

She grinned at him. "Me, too."

Holly was on her way to Montclair's when the call came. She didn't recognize the number on her screen but answered, anyway. A polite male voice, accented, said, "Is this Detective Graham?"

"It is. Who are you?"

"Would it be possible for me not to leave a name? I saw the drawing. I have a tip about the body in the field."

She pulled to the side of the road, the car's tires slipping in the scree as she skidded to a stop. She grabbed her notebook, put it on her knee.

"Go ahead."

"I think her name might be Marita Gonzales. She has been missing for a week now."

"How do you know this woman?"

"We've been cleaning houses together. There was an ad, in the paper, for a cleaning lady. She answered it. It was a full weekend job. She was supposed to do it last week. She did not come to our work last Monday and I have been very worried. She is a responsible woman."

"Where does she live? Family, friends?"

A pause. "She lives with a few families in a house off Nolensville Road."

The dime dropped for Holly. "Ah. Is she here illegally? It's okay, I have no interest in jacking up her or her family. All I'm concerned with is identifying the victim we found and finding who might have hurt her."

"The ad was in the paper," he repeated. "Marita Gonzales." And he hung up.

She called Jim as she pulled back onto the road, told him the story. "Can you find this ad, and call Forensic Medical and tell them we have a possible ID to work with?"

"I can. Also..." Silence for a moment, then the booming voice of Moreno.

"Graham. You're turning into quite the detective. Update me."

She did, and he said, "We'll track down the name and the ad. Good work. I have information for you, too. The FBI caught the accomplice. They sweated him, finally offered him a deal. According to him, Brookes put him up to it all. We got a new address, too, think it might be where she's staged this whole mess from. Jim matched it to the phantom IP. I'm sending people there now. Good thinking there, Graham."

"Thanks. She's slippery. We're going to need all the help we can get to take her down."

"Call in from Montclair's, let us know if he's okay. I'm sending a couple people to meet you there. No going it alone, not with a crazy woman on the loose."

"Yes, sir. I'll call in. Thank you for watching my back."

"When a case breaks, it breaks wide open. Good job, Graham. Good job."

LEAN ON ME

His name was Henry Tomkins. In school, his friends called him Hank.

Hank led an ordinary life in an ordinary town in the middle of nowhere, Ohio. He was, in turns, an unremarkable student, a slightly better athlete, and a champion drinker. He also liked acting. His parents, sensing the wild streak in their son and hoping it might be the trick to keeping their only child out of jail, encouraged this interest. They attended all the plays, from first grade's Thanksgiving festivus to the pinnacle, *Hamlet*, Hank's senior year.

That's where it all went off the rails. Hank lost the lead role to a quiet African American kid named Barent Goodson. For years after the indignity, the Tomkinses would say the school simply wanted to lay claim to having a black Hamlet, their bitterness disregarding the fact that Barent Goodson was one hell of an actor, who went on to appear alongside Denzel Washington in a cop movie, and subsequently became a star in his own right.

When Hank was shunted aside for his more talented classmate, (even though he took the role of Claudius, and played it well), the situation hit him hard. He'd worked his whole short acting

career to be Hamlet, knew all the soliloquies by heart. He identified with the young prince of Denmark, probably more than
anyone around him knew. And where a disappointment of this
magnitude would normally send a young man of relative means
to the next step regardless, like moving to New York and waiting tables and trying for an off-Broadway play, or maybe even
a trip to California to take some acting classes and try writing a
screenplay or two, Hank Tomkins was made of lesser grit, and
was destroyed. Flattened.

This damage was irreversible.

The drinking, a pastime moderated by the acting, grew to
epic proportions. DUIs followed, and a stint in jail. Drugs were
next, and another stint in jail, this time for dealing marijuana.

The downfall was fast and complete. Disappointed Hank
catapulted himself to the dark side, and didn't look back.

It was a deficit in his character, absolutely, that made him so
unable to handle even the simplest of bad situations, but a person's true character is rarely revealed until they are staring into
the face of adversity. Hank's test came early, when he wasn't
emotionally mature enough to handle it after being coddled by
parents and friends his whole existence, but it would have shown
up sooner or later.

He was handsome, Hank, and a partier, and always had a little
cash on hand, which meant he attracted women who thought to
enjoy his attentions. He took great advantage of said attentions,
but then he met a girl who started to straighten him out, and
things began to look up. Neighbors whispered Hank Tomkins
had outgrown his childhood disappointment and was going to
be a responsible young adult. But then the idiot cheated with
Alicia Barstow, his high school crush. And of course, Alicia
got pregnant and told his girlfriend, and the whole world collapsed down around him again. Wash, rinse, repeat—only he
was caught dealing meth this time.

A sympathetic judge took pity on Hank and threw him into

rehab. Which turned into a life-changing experience for our young man.

Sober for the first time in years, he acquired the tools and learned the trades a man needs to succeed in life. Like how to commit fraud, check kiting, identity theft, and where to find the shadow men who did all sorts of things behind the scenes for criminals who had needs, desires, and money.

This wasn't the education the judge wanted him to receive, but Hank happened to be there at the same time as a kid named Jake, who was one of the most successful con artists Ohio had seen in recent years. So good he'd conned a judge into sending him to rehab instead of jail after his last infraction.

Jake and Hank were inseparable. Jake taught Hank all he knew. Turned out Hank, with all his intelligence, had an aptitude for the long con. He was a very good actor, after all. Brilliant with accents, mimicry. He kept them all in stitches doing impressions during group therapy.

And then there was Ivy.

She arrived on a Wednesday at two in the afternoon. Ivy was hot in the damaged way of all lost young women. Doe eyes, scraggly blond hair with dark roots, waif thin. She wouldn't talk to anyone, or meet anyone's eyes. She shuffled around the edges, watching without looking. There were rumors, always rumors. Suicide attempt, probation violation, assault while under the influence. None of it mattered; all of it was true.

She was a swan among ducklings. She was a queen. She ruled them all, one bashful Mona Lisa smile at a time.

Hank, understandably, fell hard. She became a project. To win a smile, that's all he wanted.

He'd always been the friendly sort.

It only took him a few days to make the connection. He told her of his life. His passion for acting. The disappointments he faced. The changes he was going to make.

When she shared her story, Hank was lost. And forever marked by the lonely waif.

When he got out of rehab, he waited for her.

When she got out, three months later, she was changed. There was a hardness in her, a coldness. Armor had been developed. Protections put in place. Gone was the lost girl. In her place was a woman.

A woman with ideas. A woman with a plan.

And Hank, lovesick Hank, bought in.

Five years later, when the police picked him up on the Jersey Turnpike, Trent Duggan's passport in hand, he denied knowing anyone named Ivy Brookes. Denied being in Paris. Denied killing Rick and Lily. Denied ever having met or slept with a woman named Sutton Montclair.

He stuck to the script, like he'd been told.

It didn't matter. There was DNA evidence at Sacré-Coeur, his hair on young Lily's body. The FBI had him dead to rights for a double murder, and this time, he was going away for good. His only chance, they told him, was to make a deal.

They pressed him hard. And in the end, he caved. The story he told them was beyond anything they could have imagined.

THE TRINITY

Ethan came awake with a groan. His head was splitting. The situation rushed his memory. *Ivy.* One second he'd been standing, in horror, realizing the woman he'd called friend was betraying him, and the next, it was night, he was on the floor, and he knew for a fact if someone were to observe him at this moment, they'd see small bluebirds circling his head, tweeting and chirping.

Ivy had gotten him good.

Ivy, you betrayed us.

His nose was broken; he could feel the blood running down his chin, thick and warm. He shuffled himself to his elbows, sat up. Ran a hand below his nose, tried to swallow, coughed up blood onto his shirt.

Realized someone was banging on the door, calling his name. It sounded like Officer Graham.

Good. He needed to report the bitch.

He rose to his feet unsteadily, used the edge of the couch for support. Somehow made it to the door. Threw the dead bolt, and pulled it open.

Holly Graham stood on his porch. She was on the phone, and held up a finger so as not to be interrupted.

Ethan started to laugh. All hail modern technology.

"Yes, yes, it's fine. I've got him, he's alive." And to Ethan, "Who did that to you?"

"Ivy," he said, and Graham nodded curtly.

"It's just like we thought. Send an ambulance, he's hurt. We'll get him patched up. He's lucky to be alive. I'll check in shortly. Right. Thanks, Jim."

She put the phone in her pocket and gave Ethan a long look.

"I'm glad you're okay," she said finally.

"I don't need an ambulance. But I do need to sit down. Want to come in and tell me what the bloody hell is happening? My head's about to explode."

"Brookes isn't here?"

"Not that I'm aware of. I've only just woken up, you see. I had a run-in with a board or a bat of some kind, been out for a while."

A police cruiser pulled up in front of the house with two officers in it.

"Stay right here. Don't move," she said, then walked back out the kissing gate. All three got in the car. They conferred for a moment, then doors were flung open and people scattered. One started around back, the other took up position on the front porch. Graham hurried Ethan back inside.

"What the hell is going on?" And then it came back to him, the phone call. "Sutton—"

"Mr. Montclair, I have a lot of information to share and not a lot of time to do it. Come and sit down. I'll get you some ice."

Ethan didn't demur. He felt like he'd pulled five Gs straight into a wall, a crash test dummy whiplashed into being. He sat heavily at the kitchen table and accepted a Ziploc bag of ice and a kitchen towel from Graham. He applied these to his face.

"Talk. Please," he said.

"Sutton is alive."

"I know. She called me. I heard her voice, thought I might have been dreaming. And then it all went to pot."

"Your wife is in Paris. Currently in police custody but they're willing to discuss extradition."

"Paris? Custody? What did she do?"

"The Paris police thought she killed two people, and arrested her. Sort of like we thought you killed Sutton."

Ethan tried to wrap his head around these alien words. *Sutton. Paris. Murder.* It was too much. His head throbbed.

"Terribly sorry, but can you get me some Advil? Cabinet by the fridge."

She retrieved the bottle, handed him two pills. He swallowed them dry, then said, "We've been set up, haven't we?"

Graham set the bottle on the table, put her hands on her hips. "I think so, Mr. Montclair. Some of it has been proven, some is conjecture. But it looks like your good friend Ivy Brookes is out to get you."

"She certainly knocked me out. Sutton called and Ivy attacked me. Which makes no sense, as she was in the process of trying to seduce me. I think. I'm a little fuzzy."

"Well, here's what we know—"

He jerked upright, then grabbed his head with a muffled curse. "The front door...it was bolted. I threw the bolt to let you in. She must still be in the house somewhere."

Graham shook her head. "No one's here. She has keys to the house. She has access to everything of yours. She probably locked the door behind her to slow us down, or mislead us. But we're on to her now. We'll find her, quickly. There's a BOLO for her car, and her description has been sent to all the law enforcement in the region, plus transit. She won't elude us for long."

Ethan sat back, dumbfounded. "Tell me everything."

"We don't know everything." Graham sat now, opposite him,

the ever-present notebook out. He thought she'd make a good writer, the way she diligently recorded everything.

"Right now, a man named Hank Tomkins is in custody in New Jersey, and he claims he's been working with Brookes for the better part of a year trying to make your lives—you and Mrs. Montclair—a living hell."

"Let me guess. He has something to do with Colin Wilde?"

"Colin Wilde is Hank Tomkins, on orders from Brookes. Apparently she's the one who's been driving the online train against Sutton. She's very good. She fooled me entirely. She's been working both of you, hard. Trying to turn you against one another. Even Dashiell, your child—"

Ethan shut his eyes at the familiar spike of Dashiell's name. This time, the spike was poisoned. "Did Ivy hurt our son?"

"There were traces of diphenhydramine in his tissue samples. It takes forever for those tests to be run, they've only just come back. When we revisited the case, the lab pushed them to the front of the queue. I'm so sorry."

"He was murdered."

"Without a confession, it can still be ruled accidental, but I'll tell you this, Brookes handed over a bottle of medicine she claims Sutton brought to her and accused you of killing your son. She laid the blame at your feet like a cat with a dead snake, eyes brimming with tears the whole time. Meanwhile, she was filling Sutton's mind with the idea that you killed Dashiell and were planning to kill her, too. That's why Sutton ran. Brookes helped her plan the whole thing, even procured false documents for her. She convinced Sutton you were a monster."

"And the woman in the field? Are we to assume Ivy actually murdered this person and made it look like Sutton to help along this charade?"

"We may have a tentative ID. We'll need dental or DNA to be sure. She looks like an innocent bystander, lured into Brookes's web for the sole purpose of filling the temporary role of your dead wife."

"Dear God. But surely, if Ivy is this smart, she'd have to know you'd figure out it wasn't Sutton posthaste."

"I think she was planning a grand escape once your lives were ruined. You say she was trying to seduce you? Perhaps she wanted you to run away with her. Either way, Sutton was lucky. If they hadn't caught Tomkins—"

"Who is this Tomkins bloke, and how does Sutton know him?"

"I don't know all the details," she said, but he could tell she was lying, and a small burn began in the pit of his stomach. "She met him in Paris, and he insinuated himself into her world very quickly. He murdered two students at Sacré-Coeur and framed Sutton for it. She can give you all the details."

"I suppose I deserve that. Tit for tat."

"Sir?"

"'Insinuated himself' is code for fucked my wife. And I suppose I do deserve payback from her. For the affair I had. The alleged affair. The woman at the hotel at the conference? It was Ivy."

"It was?"

"I woke up in her bed at the hotel. She was wearing expensive lingerie, lounging in the bed, so thrilled when I woke. She kissed me, and took a picture of us together in the bed. A selfie. I was too much in shock to think straight. I had a wicked hangover, my head was fit to burst, and I didn't remember anything past the drink at the bar the night before. Running into her felt odd at the time, but I'd had a few pops, and was surrounded by strangers and sycophants. I was relieved when she sidled up to me, all surprised, *what a coincidence, we're at the same hotel*, and we chatted for a few. I hit the loo, came back, and that's the last I recall until I woke up and she showed me the pictures."

"Sounds to me like she may have dropped a little something in your drink, something to make you compliant."

Ethan set the ice pack on the table. "You're being kind. I don't remember, but even if she slipped me the Mickey, it's no excuse. Sutton and I were having trouble. Ivy had been hanging around a lot. I was happy to see her, I remember that. Happy to have a friendly face. She may have tricked me, might even have drugged me, but I'll bet I went willingly. I am such a complete arse."

"That's your conscience speaking, not mine."

"She's had that hanging over me for over a year. Every time I saw her, I was filled with shame and revulsion. And Sutton, I couldn't tell her the truth. I admitted screwing around, but I swore it was a nobody. That's what Wilde had on me. He was threatening to tell Sutton the woman was Ivy, not some inconsequential barmaid."

"It's solid blackmail material, for sure."

"It would have killed her. She would have left me without a backward glance. Everything I've done has been to prevent that from happening. I love my wife, Officer Graham."

"I don't doubt that for a moment, Mr. Montclair."

"Where is Ivy now? What's her next play?"

"I have no idea. Like I said, we're looking for her. And we're going to have protection here around the clock until we find her. I get the sense she's not done yet."

"Why? Why would she do this? Why would she target us like this? Is she barking mad, or is she wanting something? Money, fame? What is she after? What does she possibly stand to gain by hurting us like this? To ruin our lives, to take our child from us? What sort of madwoman does such a thing? I don't understand."

Graham played with the edge of a place mat. Ethan caught the gesture. She knew something. There was more. He steeled himself.

"What is it? I can tell you're holding something back."

Graham looked up, and he saw true pity in her gaze.

"There is one last thing. I need to talk to you about what happened to your wife when she was a teenager."

LEAVIN', ON A
JET PLANE

Paris, France

Things quieted down. Ethan, left alone to write and come to terms with the lies his wife had told him, was under constant watch by the Franklin Police in case Brookes tried to hurt him again. And as a reward for her hard work, Moreno sent Holly Graham to Paris to bring Sutton Montclair home.

The agreements made between the two governments on the charges to be filed against Sutton Montclair and Hank Tomkins were drawn up and executed in near record time, considering. The French had been quite cooperative in the terms of Sutton's extradition agreement, most likely because the FBI was going to let them have a crack at Hank Tomkins sooner rather than later, an action met with resounding approval by the Parisian police. Such a high-profile murder case solved so quickly made everyone feel better.

Graham arrived at the station on Rue Fabert in the morning, looking sharp considering the red-eye flight she'd just been on. She met with Amelie Badeau for fifteen minutes, signed a great deal of paperwork, and was then escorted to meet Sutton Montclair, who was alone in an interview room.

Sutton brightened when she heard Graham's soft Southern accent. Relief coursed through her. Whatever her punishment was to be, at least she'd be doing it on home soil.

The cop was pretty in a Tennessee back-roads way: pert nose, white-blond hair, narrow hips, a black-and-gold badge attached to the belt of her gray slacks, a gun strapped to the other side. Young. Excited. Tired.

Badeau and Graham escorted Sutton back to her flat in the 7th, where she packed her small new life into her small new used suitcase and ruefully accepted the fact that she was never going to be allowed back into France again.

Despite this, she counted herself lucky.

Badeau drove them to the airport herself. Along the way, Badeau and Graham shared what they felt was appropriate for Sutton to know about the case, Badeau reciting the facts animatedly in her staccato accent; Graham supplementing with her side of the story. Sutton couldn't help herself; she really wanted to make both of them characters in her next book. Assuming she'd ever sell one again.

Sutton learned Ivy Brookes had gone to ground. No one knew where she was. After her incident with Ethan, who was sporting a wicked black eye and a broken nose, she'd departed the house on Third Avenue and disappeared.

Constantine's real name was Hank, and the only thing he'd allowed Sutton to see that was real were the bones under his skin. The entire conceit of the man she knew as Constantine Raffalo was a carefully manufactured persona designed specifically to attract Sutton, a bee to honey, from his worldly accent to their intimate conversations. Sutton had always been easily seduced; with three years of friendship confessions to Ivy, Hank was playing with a full deck of information on how to work Sutton to the core.

Sutton was embarrassed. She'd been had by a brilliant con, yes, but she'd been searching for something to break her from her life and had seized upon the first available dick to do so. It was beneath her. The indignity of it rankled.

When she mentioned it, Badeau told her not to worry. Lesser women had been felled by lesser men. Sutton got the sense Badeau may have known whence she spoke, and left it alone.

The deal negotiated meant Badeau saw them onto the plane and then waved them away. Graham wasn't much of a talker, so once they were buckled in their uncomfortable, last row window/aisle seats, Sutton accepted the headset from the flight attendant and plugged in, pretending to watch a movie, and instead stared out the window at the darkening sky, trying to come to grips with her new normal, where she was escorted onto flights by police officers, and probably faced severe punishment at home.

After takeoff, once the meager meal had been served, it was clear to both women that neither was truly resting, and so they began to talk. Cautiously at first, but Sutton soon realized the blonde cop knew more about her than any woman she'd ever met, and so she let down her guard completely, and told her the whole story, start to finish.

SHINE A BRIGHT LIGHT
IN THE CORNERS

Then

Sutton at thirteen: a stunner in the making. Long colt legs, flowing strawberry hair that grazed budding breasts, eyes the color of summer skies. She became a woman overnight, it seemed, one day a gawky, bespectacled geek who got along with everyone; the next, in contacts and a new outfit, a glorious creature who struck awe in the eyes of everyone around her.

This sudden transition made her a very unpopular girl. It seems contradictory: teenage beauty should be the golden ticket to love and popularity, but on Sutton it worked the opposite way. She kept a few friends, though even they wandered away soon after, not wanting to be in her shadow.

There was Joe, too. Joe was Siobhan's third husband. He was a metalworker of some sort, held down a good, steady second-shift job at the plant in Smyrna. They met at a bar on the outskirts of town. He drove her home and never left.

Sutton knew the timing of her losses had more to do with Joe's arrival in their lives than with her budding beauty. He wasn't bad at first. Brought Sutton candy, treated her mother well. Was entranced by their hard–luck backstory, humored Maude's name change to the more glamorous Siobhan. He liked the idea of glamour, Joe did.

After a couple of months he asked Siobhan to marry him, and she saw a good paycheck and a warm body for cold nights, so the ring went on her finger, and then he started turning…skeevy.

He hung around Sutton's room too much for her liking. She yearned for real privacy, but they were living in Joe's house, and it was the first time in a long time that she had a room with an actual door instead of a curtain drape, so she couldn't complain too much. Joe would stop by when he got home from work. *Knock, knock.* He wanted to hear about school. He wanted to hear about her friends. He suggested they have a sleepover party. He even provided the booze.

Seven hungover twelve- and thirteen-year-olds draped around the kitchen table made the parents quite angry, and of course, Sutton took the fall, almost willingly. After all, she now had a cool stepdad. She had a room with a door. She didn't want to jeopardize things. Didn't want to rock the boat. The newly bribed sleepover friends peeled away, one by one, until Sutton was left alone in the microcosm with Siobhan and Joe.

Soon after the disastrous sleepover, Joe came home from second shift, *knock, knock,* sat next to her on the bed with the pink princess comforter, put his hand on her knee, and explained the birds and the bees to her.

Sutton, aghast, complained to Siobhan, and a huge fight ensued.

Joe, though, was nonplussed. "Look at her. She's beautiful. There's gonna be boys hanging around her like wasps to sugar water, and she needs to know how to protect herself. She needs to know what to expect. That's all I was trying to do, explain the ways of the world."

Still, it felt wrong to everyone, and the household was filled with tension. Siobhan, instead of getting them out of there, was jealous, unhappy that her catch was eyeing her kid.

Sutton was forever aware of how Joe looked at her, his eyes sliding over her nubile form like he was taking stock. Sutton decided a room of her own wasn't worth what was surely about to come, and began acting out. It was logical to her. If she became a bad kid, he'd get mad and ask them to leave.

She started hanging out with a crowd of tattered boys who kept rolling papers in the glove box and fifths of Jack under the front seat, and the fights started almost immediately. She was grounded. She snuck out. Her phone privileges were taken away. They forced her to ride the bus, but she cut school anyway.

Her actions worked wonders. As her home life (happily) deteriorated, her street cred rose. She was willing to do most anything she thought would piss Joe off, and soon she had herself a *you can call me your boyfriend, if you want.*

His name was Hayden. He was seventeen. She thought she might even love him.

She'd had her eye on him from the start of her rebellion, certain he could help her on her path to fury. Hayden did his own tattoos, and they weren't bad, considering. Secondhand Doc Martens, too-long black hair falling in his eyes, teeth as askew as scattered dominoes. A fog of cigarette smoke clung to him, and sometimes patchouli, just so everyone could know what he was really doing when he cut class.

He had a beat-up Jeep Wrangler and a certain way of talking about Kerouac and Proust that made her crazy with longing. She rode in his Jeep without a seat belt, drinking beer out of brown paper bags and smoking cigarettes. They made out in the cramped back seat, squirming around, taking things almost too far.

She didn't want to live a biscuit-colored life. She wanted excitement and joy, pain and exhilaration. She wanted it all.

So when Hayden suggested she come to a party at his friend's house, she jumped at the chance. Accepted the upperclassman-only party invitation with sheer delight and excitement coursing through her teenage veins. She knew exactly what was going to happen. She'd been planning this for a while. Finally, they would have the proper privacy to do all the things she'd been dying to try.

God bless that little idiot.

She was thirteen, angry at her parents, trying hard to be popular by taking risks—no, not taking, throwing herself against them like waves against a rock—seeing a boy who cared nothing for her and knew exactly how to take advantage of her. What happened next was almost inevitable.

When Sutton missed her period, she didn't think anything of it.

The second month without one she blamed on jogging, which she'd taken up with a vengeance in lieu of throwing herself at bad choices. She might even go out for track. Wouldn't that be fun?

The third month, when she was feeling sick and sore, she bought a test. Two pink lines. Her first thought: *I'm going to die.* The second: *They're going to kill me.*

Once she couldn't deny it anymore, she did her best not to panic. She knew exactly what had happened that night, even though she couldn't remember it all in detail. She'd gone in wanting to be the cool party girl, and wow, had she ever gotten her wish. And now she was going to pay the price.

But she was going to handle things herself. She knew what she needed to do. Get rid of it, and fast. There was no way in hell she was going to face any of the boys who'd been there that night, especially Hayden, that prick, and tell them she was in trouble. Hell, no.

But Joe Schmo kept a purple Crown Royal bag full of cash in a barrel in the garage. She'd seen him sneaking bills into and from it plenty of times. He'd catch her eventually, notice the missing money—$300 was a lot, even to a man who had a good job—and she'd be punished, badly, but at least she'd be in the clear. Her life wouldn't be ruined. No more than it already was, of course.

The day she threw up for the first time, she skipped seventh period, the first time she'd cut since the party, and snuck out to the parking deck where the kids assembled to smoke or make out or catch a quick high. The sun was blasting, the day so hot and humid that she felt like she was going to melt into the pavement and die.

She'd been feeling like she might die a lot, lately. She was such an idiot. What a huge, stupid mistake.

She borrowed a cell phone from a guy who was in her chemistry class. She'd looked the number up last night, memorized it. Dialed while she walked to a shady corner of the deck. The Planned Parenthood office answered on the first ring. She made an appointment for the next day. Deleted the call from the cell and gave it back. Took a nice, long toke from a joint passing through the crowd, which made her feel better than she had in a couple of months, then hurried to the house to get the money.

No cars in the drive. Siobhan wasn't home, which meant Joe was off somewhere with her. Sutton's ploy had worked well. He had become so disgusted and fed up with Sutton's bad behavior he'd left her alone, and Siobhan got all his attention, which her mother didn't like but put up with because free rent was worth a black eye here and there, wasn't it?

So when Joe came home early, alone, and caught Sutton opening the lid of the barrel, a fight ensued.

He'd threatened to call the police. She'd told him to fuck off. He'd slapped her, hard enough to send her head backward into the wall.

Something inside her had snapped, a taut line breaking, and she attacked. The lid of the barrel was heavy in her hands, and she slammed it into Joe's head with all the force she could muster.

He went down, and that was it. Legs, nails, teeth, everything she had that could hurt, she used. And like all bullies, Joe the Schmo proved to be weak. Her fury and frustration and fear overwhelmed him, and she beat him until he was crawling on the floor, trailing blood, moaning for her to stop.

She finally did. Her hands were bruised; one finger was definitely broken. She had skin and hair under her nails. Joe was in bad shape; she could hardly believe the damage she wrought.

She went for the Crown Royal bag. She'd need all the money now, some for the abortion and the rest to get out of town. She took the wad without counting, threw a few things in a ragged backpack, and ran.

She slept in a field on the outskirts of town. She was hungry and thirsty and cold and desperate. The police caught up with her the next morning, trying to keep her appointment at Planned Parenthood.

They arrested her for assault. The irony—and yes, she knew the meaning of the word by now—was not lost on her.

Elizabeth Sutton Wilson gave birth to the baby in juvenile hall, three months before she was released.

All she knew was its sex. It was a girl.

HOME IS WHERE THEY HAVE TO TAKE YOU IN

Now

Graham was a good listener. She didn't judge, she didn't interrupt.

When Sutton finished, exhausted and sad from revisiting her darkest time, the seat belt sign was on. They were descending into Atlanta.

"Ivy knew all of this, of course. She knew exactly how to manipulate me. God, I am so stupid."

Graham's voice was gentle, forgiving.

"She's a very disturbed woman, but that isn't your fault. Now, buckle up. You'll be home soon enough."

The second flight—Atlanta to Nashville—was short. They were in the very last row again, which meant the seats wouldn't recline and Sutton's legs were cramped. The television screen wasn't working. Graham had shut her eyes on takeoff and was clearly sleeping. So Sutton sat with the ignominy of her actions and tried, *tried* to find some sort of peace with the situation.

The whys were unfathomable. Did they matter? Sutton decided that yes, they did, very much. Looking back, she could see every step of Ivy's scheme. Every conversation, guided. Every confession, coerced. Every bit of advice, calculated.

If Sutton really thought about it, the entire friendship must have been a setup.

But why?

She forced the why away again. Crazy people existed in the world. There was no real way to understand or comprehend Ivy's actions unless they caught her, sat her down, and listened intently to her rationale.

Maybe they'd gotten lucky and Ivy (loathsome bitch) had run away and Sutton wouldn't ever see her again. My God, Ivy had murdered someone to try to make it look like Ethan had killed his wife. What sickness, what sociopathy, had driven that?

Sutton stowed away the hate. There would be time for that later.

Ethan.

She hadn't dared even think about him for the past few hours. One oh so brief conversation, in which she'd warned him and he'd gone suddenly dark, but in that moment, she'd heard such relief in his voice when he said her name. It filled her with incredible joy. She wanted to talk to him again. Actually talk. Not accuse, not aggrieve, but see each other, be present, touch hands. Like her therapist had wanted. She'd always insisted they needed each other. Sutton realized now they truly did.

Maybe, now knowing they had been cruelly manipulated by an outside force, she and Ethan could find their way back to each other.

Dashiell.

He came to her as gently as a whisper, smelling softly of baby and love. The searing pain she felt when she thought of his small, sturdy body fled in the face of such adoration. There was still fury there, and anger, yes, but also a deepening of emotion, and a final sense of peace. She had failed her child. She had allowed a viper into his swaddling nest. But the viper had slithered in through a window left ajar. It had not come from within.

To be able to blame herself for negligence, but not murder, was the forgiveness her soul had craved. To blame an outsider, instead of her baby's father, was the balm on the burn.

A wave of nausea coursed through her stomach, but this she welcomed with a caress along her stomach.

Sutton thought she had fled her perfectly horrible life. But in truth, the life she craved grew within her. And that was all the forgiveness she would ever need.

Ethan met her at the airport gate. How his presence there had been arranged for, she didn't know, and didn't care. The moment she saw him, broken and bruised and uncertain, his eyes searching every face until he saw hers and smiled, she rocketed out of the gangway and flung herself into his arms.

TRUTH WILL OUT

There were words, and hugs, but Sutton was so tired and relieved she hardly understood them, just clung to Ethan's hand as they made their way out to the parking lot where the unmarked car awaited them. As they got into the car, Sutton saw Ethan and the cop share a look, an almost marital glance of understanding. She felt a second of jealousy, but pushed it away when Ethan plopped into the back seat next to her with a grin, grasped her hand, and passionately kissed her lips. She saw the cop look at them with something akin to satisfaction on her face, and felt only gratitude.

Ethan was a handsome man, and he'd clearly been through something with this cop, but Sutton was not going to allow her petty emotions to get in the way of a true and full reconciliation with her husband. Never again would she doubt him. Never.

Goodness, she was feeling emphatic.

The drive to Franklin was slow, traffic south on I-65 heavy, and Ethan and the cop filled her in on everything they knew. It was the safest conversational topic. Sutton had things to say, confessions to make, and she sensed Ethan did as well, but those revelations would have to wait. They needed to be made in private, with care and understanding.

But as the car wound its way south, the words from their

mouths were still difficult. Ethan held tightly to her hand the whole time, and she allowed their words to wash over her.

"We've positively identified the woman who was supposed to be you. An immigrant who answered an ad in the paper."

"When she hit me, I had a second to look in her eyes, and they were blank, empty."

"She used a wig and your rings to make it look like you."

"They reopened Dashiell's case. He was most likely murdered, but he wouldn't have felt a thing, just went to sleep and didn't wake up."

"It seems she put software on the computers that allowed her to see every keystroke, so she had passwords, access to your accounts, everything. She and her friend were the ones behind the internet incident, and she was the one who went to the reviewer's house dressed as you, facial recognition positively ID'd her."

"I think she stole $50,000 from our accounts, just because she could."

"The French aren't pursuing charges against you, but you're going to need to make a full statement so my boss can decide whether to press charges. No, I don't know if he will. It all depends on what happens when we find her."

"Filly and Ellen and Rachel were senseless with worry. They thought I did it, though. Not sure we can have them over for dinner again."

"Yes, the man's real name is Hank Tomkins, and we're waiting to see what sort of deal they gave him, but he'll do extensive jail time for the murders."

"I'm so glad you're okay."

"No, we don't know where she is."

"Officer Graham made detective. She was just given her badge. She was the only one who believed in me."

"Thank you. I'm sorry it happened this way, but I'm glad I caught the case."

Ah, there was the connection. She saw it now, gleaming like

a silver thread between them. Not sexual. Gratitude. Ethan had been a suspect, but Graham had held back her judgment, sensing something wasn't right about the case. Her instincts had been handsomely rewarded, and Sutton's husband was a free man because of it.

Then, finally, "We think we might know why she's done it, but I'm going to let you two discuss it. Here we are."

The house on Third Avenue appeared. The cocoon of safety in the car vanished. There were two more police cars sitting outside the house, and a man on her porch wearing a uniform.

Ivy was still out there. They weren't going to be safe until she was in handcuffs.

Detective Graham spoke into her walkie-talkie, then said, "Okay, we're clear. Let's get you inside. I still wish you'd let me get you a hotel room somewhere."

"We've been through this," Ethan said. "We're no safer there than we are here. Come on, sweetheart."

He shielded her body and hurried her inside. Graham searched the house—overkill, surely, if there were guards—but Sutton didn't care. She only wanted to be safe, and then, to be alone. Graham talked to the man on the front porch, then gave Ethan and Sutton a small salute. "I'll see you in a couple of hours."

Sutton was surprised she was being given this much latitude but didn't complain. When the door closed, she went to Ethan, put her arms around him. The hug was long and meaningful, the kiss sweet and soft.

And then she said, "We need to talk."

He cradled her chin in his hand, his smile gentle and forgiving. "We do. Darling, why didn't you tell me you had a baby?"

YOU SHOULD
HAVE KNOWN

Holly was running late. She'd promised to be at the table by eight sharp; her father was a tyrant for punctuality. Thankfully the Montclairs' house was just around the corner from the restaurant. She felt good. This case wasn't over, not by a long shot, but the two of them were reunited, and safe, for now.

There were no parking spots on Main Street. She drove around the corner, found an empty space three blocks away on Bridge Street. If she hurried, she'd only be five minutes late, would only receive a heavy-lidded glance and purse of the lips before an enfolding bear hug.

She hated to be late for her father.

She locked the car, the familiar squawking beep ringing out. She turned her mind to the menu. She was famished; she'd shoved down a bag of cookies from the vending machine at the airport, riding through the afternoon on a wave of crumbly sugar and coffee.

She ran through the conversation. Moreno was tough; a great cop. She'd already learned so much, knew she had much, much more to go. But she'd done it. She'd made it.

She fingered the shield on her hip, a small smile on her face. This was going to be an excellent dinner. She could already see the pride in her father's eyes when she brought it out to show him. *So yes, he's pushing me hard, but, Daddy, they made me detective!*

Detective Graham.

The dinner would turn into a celebration immediately. They would drink champagne. She loved champagne, the tickle of it going down her throat, the warm surge from her stomach.

All thanks to Ethan Montclair. And her gut. Wow, Sutton Montclair in person was amazing. A Botticelli angel, carved of ivory. Holly could only imagine what the real hair color would make her look like. They were a pair, the two of them. Unforgettable.

The case that leapfrogged her career into action. She should buy them some wine or something.

A shadow formed behind her.

She caught it out of the corner of her eye, a flash reflection in the window of the building she was walking past.

The hair stood up on the back of her neck.

She turned just in time to deflect the first thrust of the knife. It caught her in the shoulder. She gasped and got her hands up, but her attacker was fast, and had the advantage of surprise.

The blade stabbed again, and this time, Holly felt the flesh of her stomach part. The knife was large, it went deep. There wasn't pain, just shock and confusion and a sudden concern for her parents. They'd be waiting at the restaurant, worrying about her tardiness.

A searing fire began. Holly fell to her knees, hands cradling the handle of the blade jutting absurdly from her stomach. She heard the words, whispered, maybe she dreamed them, she didn't know, it all hurt, so much pain, she'd never felt anything so horrible, she felt invaded, could feel every inch of the metal inside her. She tried to pull the knife away, felt the warm gush of blood, and realized she was dying.

"You should have left it alone."

And there was nothing more.

ADMISSIONS
OF GUILT

Yes, I did it. Of course I did it. I've done all of it. Did you really have any doubts?

And before you turn away in disgust, you need to understand something.

The cop needed to be taught a lesson, just like Sutton and Ethan needed to be taught a lesson.

She'd been warned and wouldn't leave it alone.

They didn't understand the gift they had in their cherubic little boy. Sutton didn't, for sure, though Ethan might have. But if they weren't so wrapped up in their own drama, this wouldn't have happened. If they'd been paying attention at all, this wouldn't have happened.

They will be so surprised when they figure out it wasn't negligence on their parts. That I did this to them. That I knew deep in my soul what had to happen.

The boy didn't feel a thing. I swear that. I am not that much of a monster. I have no desire to cause an innocent pain. No, the pain had to be delivered properly, to the sinners, the parents. It could not be mitigated.

Would you feel better if I told you it was an accident? Enough people die by accident that it's entirely possible. I know we want to turn aside, look away, find all the ways this couldn't have been a purposeful act. But let me let you in on a little secret.

It's always intentional.

Somewhere, deep inside, there is a kernel of hate that each and every one of us must push away. Push down. Pretend it doesn't exist. We're all such good people.

Until we're not.

Until something pushes us over the edge.

And then we act out. Whether it's taking a life, hurting a loved one, breaking a law, we all do it. No one is perfect. No one is blameless.

I tried to tell Ethan once, to admit what happened, to make him understand it all, but he wouldn't listen to me. He laughed it off, told me I was drunk and full of it, and to get off his damn lawn.

He actually said that. "Ivy, get off my damn lawn," in that posh British accent that makes most women cream their jeans, but sounds like nails on a chalkboard to me now.

I am definitely not blameless. If only he'd listened to me, I could have saved him a lot of heartache.

Oh, and I'm back on their lawn now.

Literally.

Are you ready?

Here we go.

BE SHRIVEN

"You have to be kidding me. There's no way."

Ethan handed Sutton a cup of tea. She wrinkled her nose and put the mug on the coffee table. Her taste for the tea was altered, her mouth felt tinny and metallic. Her office felt too small for the both of them, but she wanted to be in there, with her books, her things, Dashiell's small basket hidden in the closet. The world she'd abandoned, gathered around her like a cloak. She might not ever leave again.

"Graham thinks it's the most likely scenario. Ivy is your daughter."

"But she's not the right age. She doesn't look anything like me."

"She's younger than you think. Graham found a birth certificate at her house. She was born January 16, 1992. She's only just turned twenty-five, though she's been posing as someone much older. She was adopted out of the judicial system just after birth. The biological mother's name isn't readable on the certificate, but Graham was able to trace the date, time, and hospital to your record. It all fits, Sutton."

The day was right. Dear God, the day was right.

"You went to jail...?" he prompted.

"For assaulting my stepfather."

"He was the father? Oh, Sutton."

"No, he wasn't. I tried to pass him off as the father, tried to convince the police he'd been screwing with me, so they wouldn't charge me. But it wasn't true, and they didn't buy it, anyway. I don't know who the father is. I was semi-dating an older boy, and he invited me to a party. I knew I was going to sleep with him, I so desperately wanted to grow up, to be liked, to be the cool girl. He had a slightly different plan for the night. He and his friends got me drunk and high, and he and I had sex, but then a few of his friends came in the room. I don't remember all of it. I don't want to remember all of it. I felt like such an idiot afterward, *that* I do remember. Taught me quite the lesson. I straightened up after that, started getting myself together, but then found out I was pregnant."

She looked at him then, tears in her eyes. "You understand now, don't you, why I didn't ever want to have a child? I was thirteen. All I wanted was to have an abortion and forget the whole thing. I was taking the money for my appointment when my stepfather caught me, and we had a huge fight. It got physical. I was just so angry at him.

"I was arrested for theft and assault. Joe and Siobhan wouldn't sign the papers to let me have an abortion, so I was forced to have the baby. I hated it. I hated every second of being pregnant, of the situation, of being in juvie. It was humiliating, and frightening, and I just wanted to have that one piece of myself be sacred again."

"And I took it from you."

She squeezed his hand tighter. "Yes, you did. And for a long time, I hated you for it. But I swear to you, I loved Dashiell with every fiber of my being. When I thought you'd hurt him...it unhinged me. And now, to think that it was Ivy all along, that she could be mine from so long ago..."

"It's insane. And if it's true, then she's insane."

"There has to be something more. To tear apart our lives in

retribution because I had to give her up? It's not like I had a choice. I was thirteen and in juvie. They didn't exactly give me options. And my mother…"

"What about her?"

"She threatened to tell you. Threatened to ruin everything. To tell you that I'm a criminal, that I was in jail. That's why I pay her an allowance. So she stays quiet and lets me have my life with you."

Ethan closed his eyes for a moment. "I'm so sorry you didn't feel like you could trust me with your story, Sutton. I will never forgive myself. And we will never, ever allow Siobhan in our home again."

"Thank you. I hate her. Hate the twisted, awful world she's forced me to live in. I feel like such a fool. My mother, Ivy… I've let them both manipulate me."

"Never again. I swear. And, Sutton, listen to me. Being manipulated by Ivy doesn't make you bad or weak. She's a sociopath, a very troubled woman. Graham's still piecing together the whole picture, but everything the bloke Tomkins is saying has checked out. And according to him, Ivy has been in and out of hospitals and rehabs. Severe borderline personality disorder, supposedly. Like—"

"It's okay. I know what you were going to say. Like me. Like the character in your book. A situation you misinterpreted. Those doctors, they were wrong. I just have a run-of-the-mill anxiety disorder, which, under the circumstances, no one could blame me for. I've done the research. I don't have any of the issues they claimed I did. All the meds… I don't need them."

"So you're totally sane, and I've been writing," he blurted out. He looked so ashamed she actually laughed.

"That's good, Ethan. I'm very happy to hear it."

"It's been pouring out of me. I don't know what the hell happened, but when you left, I was so worried and so torn, and the dam broke."

"Maybe you had a feeling about Ivy from the get-go, and she's the one who inspired you. Maybe you've been writing about her, and not me, all this time."

"Maybe. Sutton, there's more."

She breathed a small sigh. "I think I knew all along. Or at least suspected she was the one you slept with."

He was dumbfounded. "How?"

"I've seen the way she looks at you. After you admitted your indiscretion, and we'd gotten things back on track, she started coming around more. You got tense every time she showed up, and she always had this private little smile for you."

His mouth was open, his eyes shocked and wide. "If you knew it, why didn't you say anything when I told you? And more, how could you stay friends with her?"

"Oh, Ethan. I didn't *want* to see it, didn't want to believe you'd do that, or she would. And deep down, I knew whatever it was didn't continue. Things were so messed up between us after Dashiell… I didn't want it to be true, so I convinced myself that it wasn't. I didn't want to have everything in my life go to hell all at once."

"I never wanted her, Sutton. I've never wanted anyone but you since the moment I saw you. I don't even remember that night. Graham thinks Ivy drugged me. That it was all a setup for 'Colin Wilde' to use against me."

"I think that's very possible, considering. Looking back, Ivy always made little comments about you, asked inappropriate questions about us. How you made love, how we talked in bed. At the time it was just stupid girl talk after too much wine, but now I see it for what it was. She was wringing me for information, squeezing out every last drop. She loved you. She always has. I was in the way, and she couldn't just kill me. So she set everything up, slept with you, thinking you'd continue the affair. When you didn't, and confessed, it infuriated her. So she killed our baby to pay us back."

"But she knew you were her mother the whole time. That is truly sick."

"I'm no psychologist, but if I had to guess, I'd venture to say she wanted to take away everything that mattered to me. You. Dashiell. Our marriage. And punish us both in the process."

"She bloody well nearly succeeded."

Sutton went silent for a moment. "Ethan... There's more. In Paris. I—"

He held up a hand. "Tomkins—he called himself Constantine, right?—told Graham all about it, and she gave me the basics. I forgive you. My God, if you can forgive me Ivy, and Dashiell, it's the least I can do."

"You are forgiven," she said. "For everything, and I hope you'll forgive me, too, and we can let them go. They deserve each other. But I have something much more important to tell you. In Paris...I found out that I'm pregnant."

Ethan reared back as if she'd slapped him. "By that douche you slept with? Hell of a way to begin forgiving—"

She laid her hand on his. "Ethan, no. Oh my God, no. I was pregnant before I left. I swear. I thought I'd lost it. I took a test three weeks ago, and it was positive, but right after, I started to bleed. I assumed I was miscarrying. Maybe I was, or maybe it was a fluke. I took it as a sign. It seemed fitting. I was so afraid you'd hurt Dashiell, and if I were pregnant again, then we would both be in danger. I prayed not to be, and then I started to bleed, and I thought, for once, God's answered my prayers."

"I would never hurt Dashiell. Or you."

"I know that now. I started feeling ill the first day I arrived in Paris. I figured I'd gotten into something on the plane. I didn't think. No, that's not true. I wanted to run away and pretend my life hadn't turned out how it did."

"When did you know for sure?" he whispered.

"Inspector Badeau noticed how sick I was during the interrogation and thought something was up. She brought me a test, and I took it." She pulled it from her purse and handed it to him. The two lines stared up at him like slitted eyes.

She rubbed her stomach ruefully, one hand still tangled with his. "I am pregnant, and the baby is yours. Only yours. I screwed up royally in Paris, by leaving, by running away from all of this. And I know you won't be able to forgive me for my stupidity in thinking that I'd be better off away from you. Now that we know Ivy was trying to ruin our lives… Well, it's too much to ask you to open yourself to me again. But if you're willing to make a go of this, of us, I am, too. And if not, I will understand."

"And the baby?"

She smiled. "I will see him or her as a blessing, now and forevermore, no matter what happens."

"So you're keeping it?"

She nodded, a faraway look in her eyes. "Yes. I am. We've lost too much already, don't you think?"

Ethan stood and walked out of the room.

Sutton sighed, sipped her tea. She couldn't say she blamed him. It was a lot to dump on a man. *I thought you killed our child, I thought you'd kill me, too, so I ran away and screwed another guy, and oh, by the way, now I'm back and knocked up, and aren't you thrilled, it's yours!*

A minute later, she heard him coming back. She set down the tea and moved forward in her chair, leaning toward the doorway. When he appeared, her breath left her.

He held the pregnancy test she'd taken before she left in his hand.

Ivy was with him. And she had a gun to his head, and a crazy smile on her face.

"Hello, Mom. Did you miss me?"

THE RECKONING

Ivy tugged roughly at Ethan's arm, pulling him into the room. His face was ashen. He was trying to tell Sutton something using only his eyes, but she couldn't understand. She was too focused on Ivy, and the snub-nosed revolver, and the blood on her hand, casually trailing down her arm, disappearing into her sleeve. Where was the blood from?

"So, Mom, I must say, I'm impressed. You have it all figured out, haven't you? You've written my villain's speech and now we get to end things. Is that what you think?"

"The police—"

"Are otherwise occupied."

Sutton heard the sirens now, insistent and frantic.

"What did you do? Oh, Ivy, what have you done?"

"I did what I had to. She should have left well enough alone. Now…" She shoved Ethan and he stumbled toward Sutton. "Sit. Both of you. We're going to have a little chat."

Ethan put his arm around Sutton, his grasp warm and sure. She felt his strength, felt him reassuring her. "Why are you doing this?" Sutton asked. "Why?"

Ivy's voice was calm and eerie, disassociated and furious, all at once. How had they missed this, the rocket fire burning in this woman's soul, as they talked and played with her day in and day out?

"You have no idea what it was like for me, growing up without you. I want you to know. I want you to understand."

"You told me you had a great childhood. You said—"

"In my mind, maybe. It was hell. I was alone. Abandoned. Stuck in that jack hole of a place they have the audacity to call an orphanage, because the foster care people didn't want me in the system."

"Why not? What was wrong with you?" Ethan asked.

"Nothing was wrong with me," she answered, voice rising, edging closer, her eyes narrowed. "Nothing has ever been wrong with me. I was made this way. Made by you, *Mom*."

Her voice rang through the room now, bouncing off the books.

"I didn't make you, Ivy. I took you in when you showed up in town, friendless, alone. You came in from the rain, sat dripping at my table in Starbucks, looking for all the world like a drowned kitten, knowing I would take pity on you and take you in. I introduced you to my friends, to my family. I allowed you in my world. I shared my life with you, willingly, happily. And how do you repay me? By drugging my husband, murdering my child, kidnapping a stranger and burning her to death, and trying to destroy my life? You're sick. Sick and twisted and your soul is black."

"I didn't burn her to death. I strangled her first. She was expendable, a means to an end. But yes, you're right. My soul is black. It's the same color as my mother's."

"You're insane."

Ivy laughed. "That I've known for a long time. Other people saw it immediately, and cast me aside. Not you. I find it amusing that you of all people never, ever guessed. You are so stupid. So vacuous. You're incapable. You're empty. You and your silly, embarrassingly bad little books. Even Ethan thinks your 'work' is shit."

"Not true," Ethan said, but Sutton talked over him.

"At least I'm earning an honest wage. What do you actually do, Ivy? You're certainly not a stockbroker, like you claim. All those business trips, all the stories you told about things you did on the road, the places you saw, the people you met. All lies, aren't they?"

Ivy went to the window, looked out. "Oh, I'm so much better than a broker. You think the hack I did on your world was something? You should be proud, Mom. You gave birth to a certifiable genius. I've forgotten more about computers than you will ever know. More than Jobs and Gates combined. I can make them do whatever I want. Attack. Siphon. Inform. All without a trace."

"You left traces here," Ethan said. "You changed the password on Sutton's computer between the time you got into it for me and when I handed it over to the police. *Ethan killed our baby* was a bit over the top, don't you think?"

"I think it was highly appropriate, and I left the trace because I wanted you to know. Did you think I was going to let you walk away unscathed from all of this, either of you? Things have gone perfectly. Exactly how I planned, from start to now. The big finish."

"Oh?" Sutton said, an eyebrow cocked. "So perfectly the police know who and what you are? They're going to hunt you down like a dog."

Ivy laughed again. Sutton realized she was enjoying this.

"Did you know, Mom, I was almost adopted once? It was a foster family, and I'd been so good. It happened when I was nine. I was theirs for less than three months before they sent me back. They didn't like me. They thought I had an edge. That's what they told the orphanage. I had an 'edge.'"

"I can imagine," Ethan said, sotto voce, but Ivy was lost in memory, and ignored or didn't hear him. She was stroking her cheek with the edge of the revolver, gently caressing herself with the metal.

"They had a dog. Oh, don't get all weepy, I didn't hurt the dog. They were assholes. I put steak bones in their bed one night so the dog would attack them. How's that for an edge?"

"You are utterly and completely mad," Sutton said.

Ivy grinned, a perfectly sweet smile Sutton had seen on her face hundreds of times before. "Oh, yes, I am, thanks to you. You abandoned me. You didn't want me. What sort of woman doesn't want her child? Oh, that's right. You. You've never wanted a child. Not then, not with Dashiell, and not now."

"I was thirteen, Ivy. I was in jail. What did you expect, that the moment I got out I'd go searching for you and we'd live happily ever after?"

"Sutton," Ethan cautioned, but Sutton wasn't going to sit back and be cowed.

"Ethan, let's be real. Ivy's holding a gun. She's already killed two people herself and had two more murdered in her name. We aren't going to talk her out of killing us. Bullets in our heads are a foregone conclusion."

Ivy laughed. "You're right. You're both so dead. No one's coming to save you. There's been a sighting, you see, down in Murfreesboro. The ones who aren't tied up with the little situation on the square are already on their way south. By the time they realize they're mistaken and get back up here, you'll be dead, and I'll be gone."

"Planned it all out, did you?" Ethan asked.

"I've been planning this for years, you swine. You're terrible in bed, by the way. Limp dick. Couldn't get it up. Sloppy kisser, too. I don't know how she stands it."

And to Sutton, in a completely new tone, curious, watchful. "I thought you'd at least recognize me when I found you."

"You look nothing like me."

"Oh, but I do. If you cross me with your sweet punk rocker, Hayden Stone, add in some red hair, and give me blue eyes, I am a dead ringer. Can't you see me? Or are you being dense, *Elizabeth?*"

Sutton flinched at the use of her given name. She flashed back to the stringy black hair and sophomoric homemade tattoos of Hayden Stone. She could barely pull his face into her memory, her hazy memory, so conveniently erased after all these years removed from the situation she placed herself in. At least she knew, now, who'd gotten her pregnant that night. Bile rose in her throat.

"He was a sick fuck. Taking advantage of me like that. If he is your father, I see you get your psychopathy naturally."

"He told me you wanted it. He told me you asked for it. Yes, that's right, Mom. I talked to dear old Dad. He remembers you fondly. Remembered, I should say. He's gone now, too. Don't think I did it for your honor. He was a waste of space, like you are."

Sutton shook her head, her newly dark hair raining around her face like a shroud. "What a disappointment you are, Ivy. After all this time, instead of simply telling me who you are like a normal person, you had to make this into an event to make yourself feel more special."

Sutton stood up. The gun wavered briefly.

"Sit down."

Sutton took a step, then another. "I could have been a mother to you. I was a friend, but clearly that wasn't enough. Nothing will ever be enough for you, will it? No one will ever be enough."

The flash of anger in Ivy's eyes was black and absolute. "When you're dead, and I've taken everything, then it will be enough." She leaned against the doorjamb, braced the gun with her left hand cupping her right, a small smile playing on her face.

"Do you know how easy it was? To slip the syringe in his little mouth and push? He went away almost immediately."

Sutton stopped moving. "No, Ivy. Don't. Stop. Stop!"

"No pain, no struggle."

"I'm warning you—"

Ethan was on his feet now, too, stepping to Sutton's right side so they formed a wall. His fury was barely contained; Sutton could feel it coming off him in waves.

Ivy didn't notice, or didn't care, so lost she was pulling them into hell with her.

"I saw you find him, did you know? I was in the closet, waiting. I wanted to see your reaction. When I came in the house you were drunk, snoring. Ethan was in his room, out cold. I watched you both. And then I watched him. I very nearly changed my mind. Dashiell was innocent. I nearly went back to my house, got my gun, and came to shoot you both instead.

"But I knew that would be much too easy on you. You needed to hurt. You needed to bleed. Now, you're going to."

And she fired.

DEATH, AND REBIRTH

In the moments after, three things happen at once.

Ivy pulls the trigger again.

Ethan dives to the right.

Sutton rushes forward, something like a growl emitting from her throat, toward the woman who is her child, a glint of silver in her hand as the trench knife that Ethan keeps hidden in the couch cushions slashes down toward Ivy's throat.

It is like Sutton has become someone else. A switch has been flipped. She's felt it flip once before, when she was thirteen and locked in heated battle with her stepfather.

She feels it again now.

It is rage, pure and incandescent, the power and fury of the angels in the palm of her hand. It courses through her, blinds her, eliminates judgment and worry, makes her a machine.

There is a flash of silver in the moonlight.

The knife is hot in her hands.

The blood is thick on her palms.

Ethan is by her side, holding Ivy down.

Sutton drops the knife and sinks to her knees.

The growing wail of the siren accompanies her heartbeat.

Her husband kneels beside her and holds her to his chest.

"It's over, Sutton," he says, again and again through his tears. "It's over. It's over. It's over."

And when she comes back to herself, oh so many minutes later, the blank eyes of the woman who tried to take away her life stare up at her. Cold, empty eyes. The monster that claimed to be hers, staring, staring, staring.

JUST WHEN YOU THINK IT'S OVER

Six months later

"I hate you."

Sutton said the words simply. A recitation of fact.

Ethan laughed. "You don't. You love me. You love us."

"That doesn't mean I don't hate you."

It had become something of a joke between them. The more she said she hated him, the more it meant she loved him. Most of the time.

Her aunt Josephine had once told her that making love is the most honest thing you can do with another person. So if you're not ready to lay bare your soul to a boy, she'd said, you should probably wait.

Sutton wished she had waited. She wished she'd done so many things differently. Especially facing the demons when they'd come for her, instead of running away. There was a life to be led now, one fraught with terror. She caressed her stomach, the life within her. Yes, she was scared. So very scared. But there was hope again. A chance for them to start anew.

Therapy had helped with the guilt. With the pain. The knowledge her own child had created an untenable world for her, had manipulated her, had murdered her son, and tried to kill her and Ethan as well, was hard to fathom. Surreal, at times.

That Sutton had killed her daughter in turn was difficult to live with. It would never get better. She would always carry the blame, the sense that if only she'd acted differently in her teens, Ivy wouldn't have turned into a monster.

The therapist made her understand that it wasn't her fault. That Ivy's actions were her own.

Joel Robinson had defended her in court, and she was finishing her probation next week. She'd gotten off lightly, and she knew it. The government had good cause to throw her in jail, but Robinson was as good as they came, and the plea deal was very satisfying to all parties involved.

Through it all, Ethan had been a rock.

They weren't fixed, the two of them, but there was hope. They'd been changed by the horror of all they lost, and what it had cost them. Changed by purposefully forgiving themselves. Changed by visiting the grave of the woman who'd wreaked terror in their lives. Changed by retreating to their art and each other, the only things they ever truly needed. Changed by finding truth in their love.

Things were almost too perfect. Sutton decided not to think about it. If she didn't, perhaps things would stay this way forever.

However you looked at it, they were healing, cleanly. Together.

In the afternoons, they sat on the porch, in the swing. Touching, always touching. The air was cool now. Forgotten leaves littered the lawn, a final spray of gold and rust. Today, Sutton's head was in Ethan's lap. His right hand rested on her burgeoning belly; his left held a book he'd been asked to endorse. It was quiet. Calm. Normal. The breeze and the book's pages whispered together.

They were quiet again for a moment. Sutton stared at the ceiling of the porch. "We need to repaint those boards before the baby comes. In a couple of weeks, we're going to be up all night and day and—"

Ethan leaned down and kissed her. Ran his hand along her palm. Kissed the scar, white now, thick and twisted and shiny, from where the knife had slipped that horrible night. She'd been marked, in so many ways.

"The ceiling will wait. I'll need something to do to get me out of tour."

"You can't get out of tour, and you know it. The book is too important. It's too good. It's going to change lives, Ethan."

"It's changed ours, and that's all that matters to me."

They'd talked about it before, his book, the one that would change lives. She truly thought it could. It was searing, honest, real. The reviews were already insanely good. There was talk of Pulitzers and National Book Awards.

To his credit, Ethan had done his best to ignore them. Oh, a spark of pride popped up now and again, but Sutton knew—hoped—it was more a function of profound relief that he'd managed to write another book, and that she had loved every word.

Ethan set aside the novel he was reading. "How is your book coming? You haven't said much about it this week."

She sighed, a happy sound. "I finished the last scene this morning. I think I can move to the epilogue now."

Ethan's smile was huge. "Honey, that's great. Why didn't you tell me?"

"Because Holly called and I got sidetracked. I've only remembered now. Pregnancy brain."

"What did our favorite detective want?"

"She's going to stop by tonight. Said she has a surprise."

"I hope it involves wine."

"I hope it involves food."

Holly Graham, their new best friend. She'd nearly died for them, had spent two weeks in a coma, her frightened parents hovering over her like birds on the nest. When she'd woken up, all of Middle Tennessee had cheered. It took her a solid month in the hospital, multiple surgeries, and setbacks, but when she was cleared to leave, she insisted on doing it under the cover of darkness, ostensibly so no one could see her limp. Sutton and Ethan knew the truth. She didn't want to be lauded as a hero. She loved her job, and was grateful she'd be able to return to it.

It didn't matter. Word leaked. She'd walked out of the hospital, hand on her cane, to a massive crowd of well-wishers and media. When she waved to the cameras, the crowd shouted in happiness.

The story, as was to be expected, was everywhere, even now, six months hence. Sutton and Ethan had been approached countless times about interviews, television, movies. Holly had been accosted by directors. They were all fielding offers to write a book. Holly refused outright. Sutton didn't think they should, either, and Ethan agreed. But Bill and Jess were pushing, hard.

Ivy was gone. Her accomplice was in jail. Their lives were their own again.

The baby rolled lazily under his father's hand, then kicked his mother in the kidney for good measure.

"Oof," Sutton said, enjoying every minute. "He's going to be a football player."

"Cricket. The boy will play cricket."

Holly Graham's unmarked car pulled up in front of them.

"Holly's here," Ethan said.

"Oh, Lord, help me up. I look like a whale lying here."

"You look beautiful." But he helped her, laughing, a hand at her back. She was ungainly; she was adorable.

Holly gave them both careful hugs. "Should we go inside? I have some news."

"Uh-oh. I've heard that tone from teachers about to slap my hand with a ruler," Ethan joked. But Sutton said, "Yes, let's go in. It's too cool now, anyway."

In the kitchen, Sutton ran her hand along the marble counter. She sat on a breakfast stool, pressed her aching back into the tall seat. Ethan sat next to her. Holly stood.

"This will be difficult to hear."

"Go on," Sutton said, feigning nonchalance. She knew the words were coming. She could feel them in the air.

"Ivy was wrong."

Ethan was pacing by the window, a caged tiger, fury emanating off him like a storm.

Sutton hadn't moved from her spot.

Holly was still talking, explaining, soothing.

"We're absolutely sure. We found her notebooks, her computer records. All her research, all the painstaking details she'd sifted through, all the assumptions she'd made, all of them were wrong. The only fact she got right was that she was the daughter of a woman who had her while in juvenile detention."

"But not me," Sutton whispered.

"No. Not you. Not even the same facility. When all the juvenile facilities went online, as mandated by the State of Tennessee, the records were accidentally merged together. On paper, Elizabeth Sutton Wilson was named as the mother of a little girl the nurses called Ivy."

"So who is she really? Who was her mother?" Ethan demanded.

"Legally, I can't share that information, but she's gone. She died from a heroin overdose the month after she got out of juvie."

"But my daughter? Do you know—"

"Wait," Ethan said, striding toward Holly so quickly she almost flinched. Almost. "Before you answer, Holly... Sutton, you need to think this through. There's no going back."

Sutton nodded. "I know."

Holly tapped her notebook. "I have as much or as little information as you want, Sutton. The adoption was closed, but under the circumstances..."

"Give me a moment. I need some water."

Ethan hurried to the refrigerator, pulled out an ice-cold bottle. Poured her a glass and handed it to her, watching her carefully.

Sutton drank, willing her heart to slow. She set the glass on the counter. "I don't want to know who she is. I don't want to know where she is. I just want to be sure she's okay, that's all. That she has had a good life. That she's not a freak like Ivy. That I didn't create a monster. That's all I want to know."

Ethan blew out a huge sigh, sounding strangely relieved.

"I understand completely," Holly said. "I can assure you that she is a happy, well-adjusted young woman."

"Then that's all I need. She deserves a chance at a happy, settled life. It's why I gave her up in the first place. I don't want to ruin her life. I especially don't want our notoriety to influence her. We have too much baggage now."

"Stay for dinner," Sutton said, starting to get up, but Holly waved her off.

"I promised Jim I'd come over after I talked to you. He's going to open some wine, make us steaks. Besides, you need time. If you change your mind—"

"I won't. Get rid of the notes, Holly."

"I will. I'll see myself out. Y'all have a good night, okay?"

Ethan followed Holly to the door, anyway. He retrieved the book he'd left on the porch, then turned the dead bolt and came back to the kitchen. He rubbed Sutton's shoulder, and she leaned into his warmth.

"Are you okay?"

"I'm all right. I'm relieved, actually."

"All that pain, all that fear and loathing, all for nothing."

"Ivy wouldn't have said it was nothing. Ivy would have seen the abandonment regardless. She would have found a way to ruin someone else's life, instead of ours."

"We're not ruined, Sutton."

The baby kicked in agreement, and she smiled. "You're right. That's the wrong word to use. I'm sorry."

"Do you need some time to think about all this?"

She paused a moment. "Maybe thinking isn't what I need right now. Why don't I go do something mindless instead? I need to answer some email, anyway. That's perfect."

He searched her eyes, but seemed satisfied she was telling the truth. "Okay. Off with you. I'll get things started."

Twenty minutes later, Ethan opened her office door and stuck his head in. Grinned at his beautiful wife on the couch, legs up, laptop opened. She closed the lid.

"Dinner's ready?" she asked.

"In five. I made carbonara. I figured you needed something warm."

"Sounds perfect. I'll be there in a second. Almost done here."

Sutton waits for the snick of the door, then opens her laptop to the blue-and-white banners of the social media giant that destroyed the world's anonymity.

The photograph is thumbnail-size, but a quick click opens it to fill the screen.

A young woman, standing on a beach, silhouetted by the sun.

Her legs are long, still coltish, her hair a soft shade of strawberry. Her nose seems carved from ivory; she has the profile of a Botticelli angel.

She is unaware of the camera, a hand shading eyes Sutton knows are blue.

She seems so hopeful, Sutton thinks, smiling at the photo. Hopeful, as if a new world awaits her.

It does. Oh, it does.

Sutton traces the outline of the young woman's jaw, her fingers barely touching the screen. This girl, this goddess, hers as surely as if she reached out into the heavens and stamped her from a cloud.

No one needs to know. This is her secret. And she'll take it to the grave.

"Hello, Josie."

★ ★ ★ ★ ★

AUTHOR NOTE

Paris, France
May 2014

An author sits at a café in Montparnasse, drinking champagne, thinking about murder.

Over the course of the week, in cafés and restaurants, from the hills of Sacré-Coeur to the bowels of the Metro, from Versailles to the swanky streets off L'Arc de Triomphe, after miles upon miles of walks along the Seine, to the shadow of the sparkling Tour Eiffel, a book is born. A story of betrayal and danger. A story of need and desire. A story born in a homely black notebook, the kind Hemingway used, because the writer is a romantic who likes the old ways when it comes to storytelling.

I went to Paris looking for inspiration, but didn't know I'd return with a real story. I had page after page of notes on the idea of a woman obsessed by a stranger's murder at Sacré-Coeur, and how her life derails when she can't leave it alone. The idea grew from day to day. It was an in-between story, the one I couldn't let go, even though I had other book responsibilities. I worked on it every free moment, then dedicated last summer to it, until the idea became a story, and the story became a novel.

Which, for the first fifteen months of its life was called, aptly, if not uncreatively, *The Paris Novel*. Eventually, it became more vicious, more visceral, more real: *Lie to Me*. A much more evocative title, don't you think? It's certainly more fitting to the story.

I went back to Paris again last year so I could capture the magic I'd felt when I started the book. Large swaths of the story were written in Hemingway's old haunts. There is an energy to these dark bars and sunny cafés; the spirits of the literary masters linger on for those who wish to honor them. I have no doubt my words were influenced by their presence.

Lie to Me was a huge challenge for me, the biggest one thus far in my career. I stretched my wings in completely new ways. My book journal is full of reversals and new ideas, many of which were abandoned as the story grew. I have several notebooks full of notes and plans and snippets of dialogue. It's very fun to read these nascent thoughts; the enthusiasm is clear. Even now, several months removed from finishing, it bleeds through the page.

I am so excited to share Ethan and Sutton's story with you. I had a specific goal in mind with this story—stretch myself beyond my limits. My daily to-do list had a permanently starred entry: *Be willing to take one more step with LTM*. I have, and I'm thrilled to take you along with me.

J.T. Ellison
Nashville
November 2016

ACKNOWLEDGMENTS

I owe debts of gratitude to so many people who believed in, cheered for, and otherwise stood by my side while I wrote this novel.

First, the incredible folks at MIRA Books, who saw the potential in me years ago and have stood by my side waiting for this book to come along, thank you, from the bottom of my heart. I couldn't do it without you. Most especially, I need to thank my brilliant editor, Nicole Brebner, who helped me see the forest for the trees and made this book sing. The rest of the family deserves more accolades than I can possibly give: Craig Swinwood, Loriana Sacilotto, Brent Lewis, Merjane Schoueri, Margaret Marbury, Amy Jones, Randy Chan, Heather Foy, Stefanie Buszynski, Emer Flounders, Shara Alexander, Linette Kim, Margot Mallinson, Catherine Makk, Miranda Indrigo, Malle Valik, Susan Swinwood, Monika Rola, Olivia Gissing, Larissa Walker, and last but never least, Sean Kapitain—who designed this gorgeous cover. Thank you, from the bottom of my heart, for everything.

My loving tribe of friends and fellow writers, without whom I would be lost: Laura Benedict, Ariel Lawhon, Paige Crutcher,

Jeff Abbott, Helen Ellis, Allison Brennan, Catherine Coulter—you keep me motivated and sane and full of memes and philosophical conversations and queso, and walk me away from the many cliffs that arise when a book is being birthed. I love you all!

For those who help with more than only words: Sherrie Saint, Joan Huston, Andy Levy, Lyzz Pickle, Sara Weiss, Anna Benjamin, Brandee Crisp—you are all incredible!

The fine town of Franklin, Tennessee, one of America's absolute treasures, was the backdrop for this tale. Many an evening was spent in Grays on Main, people watching and writing. Thanks for the delicious old-fashioneds! Many pages were also drafted in the Coffee House at Second and Bridge, which sustained me with gluten-free crepes and endless cups of Earl Grey. Thanks to them, and to my YA tribe in Franklin, too.

For the librarians and booksellers who share my work with their people—a heaping helping of blessings on you all. Also, so many thanks to my incredible Facebook and Twitter friends, who are my daily dose of inspiration, and are always there when the going gets tough.

My agent, Scott Miller, without whom *none* of this would happen—thank you for always believing in me, and the exclamation points when you read this proposal, and your faith in this book. I am forever grateful for your steady guidance.

My fabulously kind family, who truly get me. I am extremely grateful for their support—this means you, Mom, Daddy, Jeffrey, Jay, Lisa, Jason, Kendall, and Dillon. You're the most wonderful blood.

My right hand, Amy Kerr—aka #TheKerr—to whom the book is dedicated, who read this proposal and was so excited and enthusiastic about it that I was finally compelled to turn it in (I wasn't going to, you know...). Thank heavens for you, babycat.

And for the man who took me to Paris as a surprise for my birthday and started this whole thing, who promptly took me back to Paris for our anniversary so I could write some more, who sat quietly by while I lost my ever-loving mind with excitement writing in the bar of La Closerie des Lilas, the man who supports and loves me in ways I probably don't deserve, thank you. Randy, darling, you are the heart and soul of everything I do, and I love you more than you can possibly know.